Di Morrissey lived in Guyana in the 1970s and climbed the awesome Kaieteur Falls, the world's longest single fall of water. At the top of the falls lives the world's rarest frog, which has become the symbol for this novel. Di revisited Guyana in 1995 to research *When the Singing Stops*.

Australia's most popular woman novelist, Di Morrissey is well known as a TV presenter on the original 'Good Morning Australia'. She has also been a journalist, screenwriter and advertising copywriter. Her five previous novels are all bestsellers. Di now lives and writes in Byron Bay, NSW, in between travelling to research her books.

DI MORRISSEY

WHEN THE SINGING STOPS

PAN
Pan Macmillan Australia

This is a work of fiction. While certain actual historic events and names are used, this novel does not reflect current events or people in Guyana.

First published 1996 in Macmillan by Pan Macmillan Australia Pty Limited
First published 1997 in Pan by Pan Macmillan Australia Pty Limited
St Martins Tower, 31 Market Street, Sydney

National Library of Australia
cataloguing-in-publication data:

Morrissey, Di
When the singing stops.
ISBN 0 330 35985 1
I. Title.
A823.3

Printed in Australia by McPherson's Printing Group

ACKNOWLEDGEMENTS

As always, to that special man who has loved me
through every book

For my children, Gabrielle and Nick, in the hope that they too will
return to Guyana and find its beauty unchanged

For Jim Revitt for his invaluable input with loving thoughts as he
sets out on a new phase in his life

My wonderful mother and all my family, including
Uncle Ron Revitt for his great drawings

In Guyana, so many dear friends whose hospitality, generosity and
knowledge has been invaluable. Especially, Gabriel and Phillip de
Freitas who first took me to the interior to climb Kaieteur in 1978

Ted Johnston for his proofreading

To all my supportive and helpful friends at Pan Macmillan in
Australia and the UK

Carolyn Beaumont for her input and editing skills

And for those who gave me an insight
into their specific fields of interest:
Professor Michael J. Tyler, Dept of Zoology, University of
Adelaide, South Australia
Brian Maher, Sydney, Australia
Tony Grey, Polartechnics, Sydney
Dr James Armstrong, Director of Science and Information, Dept of
Conservation and Land Management, Perth, Western Australia
Brian Sykes, Georgetown, Guyana

If the frogs stop singing, the planet will die . . .

GUYANA

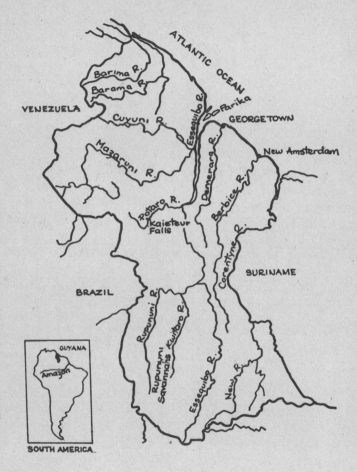

PROLOGUE

Guyana, South America, 1979

The cameraman peered through the oval window at the sheets of drifting mist below the Islander aircraft. Between the clouds was a daunting vista of compact jungle that seemed to be endless, smothering mountains and valleys in every direction. Conversation in the small aircraft had stilled within half an hour of take-off. It was too much effort above the noise of the groaning twin engines and the four passengers were left with their thoughts. 'Broccoli,' thought Venti at last. The cameraman had been struggling for ten minutes to find a word to describe the jungle canopy spreading as far as he could see. 'Yeah, that's it, as tightly packed as a head of fresh broccoli. If we go down we won't be found for a hundred years.'

Similar thoughts flashed through the minds of two of the others, but not Sir Gavin Rutherford, BSc, University of Bristol, academic turned television celebrity. He leaned back, smoothed his silver moustache and closed his eyes, relaxed and confident. Edwina, the producer, distracted herself by flipping through a tattered magazine. In the two years she'd been travelling with the *Planet Earth* team she'd been through some hair-raising journeys to reach locations from the Mojave Desert to the Galapagos Islands, from the Indian subcontinent to the Surrey countryside. And now Guyana.

What had started as an educational series about the animal kingdom and plant life of the Earth, narrated by the esteemed Sir Gavin, had caught everyone at the BBC by surprise when it turned into a ratings sleeper. Sir Gavin's enthusiasm and knowledge, with a dash of debonair charm, had propelled him more and more from doing voice-overs with an opening and closing stand-up to camera, to becoming a full-on integrated explorer in almost every scene.

Viewers saw him tiptoeing behind elephants, hanging from a hide in a tree to observe a lion kill, bobbing in a rubber duckie close to a birthing whale, lifting up a log to expose a brilliant snake or peering from under his trademark canvas hat to watch a Venus flytrap close on an insect. And all the while his breathless whisper of facts, in suppressed excitement at what he was seeing, infected and captivated viewers who shared his adventures in the safety of their living rooms.

The soundman known as Rabbit, short for the velveteen rabbit or less kindly, cloth ears, because he only paid attention when listening through his padded ear cans, tried to stretch his legs and wondered if the pilot had dropped any of their luggage on top of his sound gun. He hadn't liked the way their gear had been banged into the rear of the aircraft. The casual weighing of passengers and freight had been sloppy and he hoped they navigated and landed with more sense than the pre-flight manoeuvres indicated. He didn't even want to think about aircraft maintenance.

This seemed a bit of an over-the-top expedition for just two brief on-camera segments. Sir Gavin paddling a dugout canoe through a floating raft of Victoria Regina waterlilies, conveniently filmed in the Georgetown Botanic Gardens, and now this bloody trek to some waterfall to find a frog. The frog better not be too near the falls or Sir Gavin's piece to camera would be drowned out.

Next to him, the cameraman continued to gaze down at the jungle where now a wide fat river snaked in twisted brown coils. The splashes of white in patches of the river he recognised as the surge of rapids. Here and there were signs that small-time goldminers had dredged great bites from the river banks, adding to the pale muddy silt that flowed along with the coffee-hued water. Sometimes the virgin green was slashed by small logging operations, tracks from vehicles, a few blue plastic tarpaulins over a camp site and great bald orange patches sprinkled with matchstick-sized logs. But they were all puny impressions against the vastness of the jungle.

Despite Venti's cynicism and jaded attitude, his visual eye was still fresh and he was mentally framing shots as great green walls rose towards them, the canopy sprinkled now and then with a burst of pink and orange flowers. They were getting close, but the wet cloud cover was a worry. They hadn't planned on camping up here to wait for clear skies. The plane was only waiting an hour for them, then returning to Georgetown. Light looked to be a problem too. Water, glare, humidity and clouds. 'Great. Just great,' he groaned to himself. How the hell did they ever find these falls in the first place, what sort of nutters went charging into places like that down there?

He looked across at Sir Gavin, who was making snuffling sounds in his sleep. Nutters like him. Poor old boy, always felt he'd been born a hundred years too late. This belated blooming of adventure had salved a lifetime's frustrations and earned him a knighthood to boot.

Edwina suddenly let out a small exclamation as she looked out of her side of the aircraft and signalled frantically to Venti.

'Christ! Look! The falls!'

The pilot banked and swung up the gorge, through mist swirling like smoke surging up from the rocky base of the escarpment. The plane headed straight towards the majestic curtain of water from the broad Potaro River that thundered over the lip of the gorge. Boiling creamy foam powered down and down over Guyana's magnificent Kaieteur Falls, two hundred and twenty-six metres to the base from the tannin-coloured Potaro.

There was a collective gasp at the beauty and power of this spectacle rising out of nowhere as the little aircraft flew up and over the drop and was once again in cloud. Venti cursed not having the camera with him. The plan was to shoot the falls as they left. Mistake, he thought gloomily. It was not one of the Australian-born cameraman's better days. Too much rum the night before.

They descended within minutes, crunching down on a bare red clay runway cut between tufts of wet grass.

The location for the first piece to camera was at a lookout with the drop of the falls in the distance. Sir Gavin earnestly and admiringly paid homage to the *'brave and tenacious plant soldiers who fought their way up this barren sandstone escarpment to cling in a hairline crevice, establish a base camp and germinate, nourished by spray from the falls and humus forming around their roots'.*

Here they would cut in close-up shots of frail lichens, mosses, orchids and ferns clinging to the sides of the waterfall.

'Left undisturbed for centuries, living in this mini eco climate, plants we consider rare and precious have flourished into benevolent monsters.'

At this point the crouching Sir Gavin straightened up so that the falls were visible over his shoulder and told Edwina to make a note 'to get a shot of that giant bromeliad back along the track there'. Turning to the pilot, who was acting as guide, Sir Gavin barked, 'Right, Mr McPhee, on to the falls'.

Venti and Rabbit brought up the rear of the group, panting and sweating in the steamy humidity under the weight of their gear. They stopped as the pilot pointed out that caution was needed on the slippery, dribbling rocks covered in lichen that skirted the falls. They couldn't see the falls but they could hear the roar of the water close by, and the mist of spray was refreshing as they picked their way through breaks in the foliage.

Venti rested his tripod on the ground and drank the tepid water from the recycled rum bottle passed around by the pilot, Gibson McPhee.

Suddenly they burst out of the thicket and walked straight onto rocks at the top of the extraordinary falls. 'Breathtaking, huh?' called Edwina to Venti, who was bracing the tripod and figuring out how to keep the mist off his Arriflex lens.

He paused and raised an eyebrow. 'Be all right after a bit of rain.'

Edwina laughed. She liked Venti's sense of humour, very Australian, she thought.

The pilot watched with some amusement as Sir Gavin inched his way to the edge of the falls where the river slid over the abyss.

Rabbit clipped a small microphone onto Sir Gavin's shirt and went back to take a sound level, observing to Venti, 'Can you imagine if this were America? They'd have wire fences, hot dog stands, souvenir stalls, key rings, teaspoons, the lot'.

Venti smiled. 'It'll be some time before this spot is chocka with honeymooners like Niagara. It's five times the height of Niagara, you know.'

'I wonder if the tourists even know about this place.'

'Come back in twenty years time, in the 1990s, and see if it's been overrun.'

Edwina interrupted. 'Please chaps, we haven't time for little touristy chats. We have to move along. Mr McPhee is anxious about the clouds if you want shots flying out.' She cupped her hands and shouted, 'One take please, Sir Gavin'.

'Go and fix his hair, or tell him to put his hat on, Edwina,' said Venti peering through the lens.

'I'm not going any closer to the edge than this. You know I've got this thing about heights and cliffs. Anyway he doesn't care what he looks like on camera, you know that.'

Damp patches on his shirt, silver hair flying away, wet shiny face, she knew it wouldn't bother Sir Gavin. He felt it all added to his authenticity. Off camera, however, he was fastidious about how he looked.

'Action!'

Sir Gavin swept an arm from the falls behind him to

gesture towards a patch of small glossy green bromeliads clinging to the edge of the rock.

'*In order to discover the rare treasures of our world, one has to travel to places like this . . . the top of Kaieteur Falls in Guyana to find this . . . the world's rarest frog,* Colostethus beebei. *The golden frog. They live here and only here, in these bromeliads constantly wet from the spray from these mighty falls . . .*'

'Cut,' called Edwina. 'Sir Gavin! How are we going to cut in a shot of a gold frog? Wherever are we going to find one? We haven't much time.'

Sir Gavin beamed. 'Come and see for yourself!'

The crew gathered around, peering into the spread of waxy wet leaves. There, blinking out at them, was a tiny frog.

'God, it's beautiful. It looks like it's solid gold. With diamonds for eyes!' gasped Edwina.

'Beats the green frog that used to be in the drainpipe at Mum's,' conceded Venti.

The pilot chuckled. 'It's a perfect living symbol of this part of the world. This place is supposed to be riddled with gold and diamonds.'

Venti angled the camera into the heart of the plant and felt that special thrill when he saw through the lens a perfect shot. The small flat frog, the length of Edwina's thumb, crouched motionless, its skin glittering as if gold-plated.

'Not even Tiffany's could better Mother Nature here, eh?' grinned Sir Gavin with great satisfaction. He always liked a win for nature.

Several times as the taxi headed back to the Pessaro Hotel from Ogle airport, Sir Gavin yawned. The beam-

7

ing adventurer was replaced by a tired and slightly bored aristocrat. 'Edwina, be a dear and get the hotel manager fellow to rustle up some decent wine for dinner. Tell him to put the hard word on the British High Commissioner if necessary. I couldn't face another of those dreadful rum punches.'

'A country with no wine and no potatoes,' mused Venti.

'But gold frogs and diamonds,' smiled Edwina.

Sir Gavin had lost interest in nature. 'A full-bodied claret would be excellent. Help the appalling food go down.'

ONE

Sydney, Australia, March 1996

It was one of those seductive Sydney autumn days. The excessive heat of summer had given way to weather that was easy to wear, like comfortable shoes. It was a fine clear day with a slight nor'easter that moved the yachts on the sparkling harbour along at a leisurely but determined pace. The roof of the Opera House dazzled high gloss white and in the streets people stopped hurrying and paused to savour the moment before burying themselves inside city skyscrapers.

Matthew Wright stopped and lifted his head to the clear, blue sky. The day matched his mood—effervescent—while the soaring building he was about to enter reflected his career. Matthew was a young man on the rise. At twenty-nine he'd already reached a level of success as marketing director for a leading Australian mining management and consultancy company, which gave him his confidence and assurance. His ready smile, quick laughter and good looks made him attractive to women. His grasp of the changing events in his business world, his adaptability and creative thinking had him marked by senior executives as an employee to watch. No matter where he travelled in the world, he was recognised as a particular breed of Australian man—open, honest face, suntanned complexion—though his sister nagged him about protecting his skin from dangerous UV rays. He had hazel eyes, light brown hair, was slim and fit from early years of competitive swimming and surf lifesaving. These days, he mostly swam to keep in shape. He smoothed his tie and unnecessarily adjusted his suit coat, then stepped with a bounce in his stride towards the revolving doors of the skyscraper near Circular Quay that housed the Sydney offices of AusGeo Mining Consultants.

He stepped out of the elevator on the 36th floor and returned the smile the girl on reception threw him as she fussed with a tall vase of gladioli. Behind her hung a large Aboriginal painting by Josephine Nugurri, an elderly woman artist in Utopia. The company had done a lot of work in the Northern Territory. The artwork from the famous desert school of artists had become a much talked about feature of the reception area.

Matthew tapped the desk as he passed. 'The shrine to the grande dames of the tribe, eh? Nugurri and Dame Edna Everage. Glad to see gladdies are back in vogue as symbols of elegance.' He smiled to himself thinking of the 'Mrs Average' creation of Aussie humorist Barry Humphries, whose middle-aged matron had become synonymous with the gladioli she flung at audiences during her stage monologues. He continued down a corridor where framed colour photographs of bauxite, coal, iron ore and gold mines hung beside shots of smelters and other mineral processing plants. AusGeo had no financial stake in any of the sites in the photographs. They were instead an impressive testimonial to the company's record of winning consultancy contracts and trouble-shooting all over the world.

During the boom years of the eighties AusGeo had grown from a small business, working mainly in Australia, to an internationally respected corporation that specialised in turning around mining companies that were experiencing major difficulties because of predatory investors, unstable governments or plain inefficiency.

Inside his office, furnished in AusGeo's signature rolled stainless steel and black leather appointments, Matthew swung his briefcase onto his desk and rifled through the papers and messages neatly stacked there by his personal assistant, noting a phone call from his sister, Madison. He stood with his back to the sparkling harbour hundreds of metres below the floor-to-ceiling windows, reading through the day's engagements. Then leaving his jacket on, because he was due at an executive meeting in fifteen minutes, he dialled his sister at the five-star hotel where she worked. When he finally got through to the receptionist in the promotions department, he was told his sister's line was engaged. He made a mental note to phone her later.

The boardroom had panoramic views of Sydney harbour. The six men sat around the long oval table cut from Australian red cedar. A glass of water, a bone china coffee cup, a notepad and sharpened pencil were set by every place. Dainty dishes of Smarties lined the centre of the table. They were a little eccentricity of the chief executive officer, these bowls of confectionery.

As the men settled into conversation, the CEO's personal assistant carried in a silver tray set with coffee pot, cream jar and sugar bowl. She placed it gently on the table and withdrew, shutting the door quietly. Stewart Johns, the chief executive officer, made his entrance, walking briskly. 'Morning team,' he said cheerfully. 'Top day for sailing.' The CEO always had a better idea for spending the day other than conferencing. It was his idea of an executive joke. He opened a folder, put on his glasses and looking around the table began speaking, permitting himself a small smile.

'Well, there's good news and there's bad news. The good news: we are invited by the International Funding Organisation to submit a proposal to rehabilitate a struggling bauxite mine in South America. The mine is run by the government, which wants to privatise it. We have to make a detailed study of its prospects for public tender. We'll need a team on the ground to make the final evaluation and deliver our presentation. I've made a brief trip out there and I've brought back financial and production data for analysis. I consider this mine is worth our time.'

He paused and looked around the table. Kevin Blanchard, head of the engineering division, took up the obvious cue, 'What's the bad news?'

Stewart Johns grinned. 'The mine is in Guyana.'

Kevin shrugged. 'So? Sounds all right to me.'

'Yeah, but your last assignment was Somalia,' joked Matthew, to smiles around the table.

The senior staff of AusGeo were familiar with mines all over the world and it was well known that Guyana had been one of the world's top producers of high quality bauxite, in demand for the manufacture of aluminium.

'Rather backward country, isn't it?' said Matthew.

'Yes, a basket case. A true-blue banana republic. It's on the coast of South America, next to Venezuela and Brazil. It was British Guiana, and a Dutch colony before that. The French had it for a bit. There was a big sugar industry that's been stuffed up, and it was the site of the Jonestown suicides.'

Kevin Blanchard jumped in. 'That's right, the People's Temple episode, late seventies, wasn't it? The Reverend Jim Jones had that big commune and they shot the US politician and everyone drank Koolaid laced with poison.'

'Unfortunate way to put a country on the map. What's the place like now?' Matthew asked as Stewart Johns sat back watching the reaction around the table.

'Hasn't changed a lot from my superficial recce. The mine has gone down the tube following twenty years of political interference and mismanagement since it was nationalised. The whole economy has been in a mess for years. The government tried to flog the mine off to various aluminium companies but anyone who took a serious look at it turned and ran. The whole joint has been let go too far. That applies to several other mines in Guyana as well. The plant and equipment are hopeless, there are no resources to fix or replace anything, morale and work effort are at rock bottom. Production, delivery and technical capacity have deteriorated to such a degree the market share has been lost. So it's an almighty albatross.'

'Is there any hope at all?' Kevin wondered aloud.

'Well, since the end of the socialist regime in the mid-eighties, Guyana has been trying to join the capitalist world of free enterprise,' Johns explained. 'Now the new government has come up with this deal to work with the

13

International Funding Organisation and it's hiring a management contractor to get the mine into shape to make it a more attractive proposition to sell.'

'Is that going to be possible?' asked Matthew. 'You paint a grim picture.'

'That's what you and Kevin will have to find out. If we take the job, we'll be relying on the rest of you to analyse the data we send back each day,' Johns said. The men around the table nodded. This was the sort of work they were best at and they liked the challenge.

'How much time have we got to get the proposal in?' asked Kevin.

'No time. The sooner we tender, the sooner we win because I've heard the other tenderers aren't overly enthusiastic. I've already discussed the idea with the relevant government minister and he sees us as highly commendable. The fact we are acting positively about the concept gave me the impression they were leaning towards us. I've had a full brief prepared to give you background on the country and the project.'

Stewart Johns indicated a pile of spiral-bound documents to be passed around the table. 'It spells out the aims and the challenges facing us. Any suggestions—and I expect them in written submissions—will be most welcome. We'll meet again on Monday. Enjoy your weekend reading.'

It was the CEO's usual Friday act, thought Matthew, as he flicked through the briefing paper. No nonsense, straight to the point, an expectation that everyone would abandon their weekend plans in order to meet a deadline.

By late Saturday morning Matthew had digested the material. Then he made a fleeting visit to the Manly library only to be told there were no recent books about Guyana in Australia. He bought the Saturday *Sydney Morning Herald* and the *Australian* and drove around the headland to Le Kiosk at Shelly Beach where his sister was joining him for lunch.

Over a cappuccino he browsed through the papers, occasionally distracted by the scenery and activity about him. A small coach of Japanese tourists arrived. They trooped to the water's edge and, with sun-drenched Manly Beach as the background, embarked on a splurge of photographs. To their surprise, a couple of scuba divers suddenly surfaced and waded onto the sand after taking off their flippers. They carried spear guns and several large blackfish. It was a photographic opportunity that not one of the tourists missed. Matthew chuckled to himself. It seemed so ordinary to him, so commonplace. He took it all for granted, as no doubt did the scatter of families on the sand and around the barbecues in the park. The lucky country, he thought, and this was the perfect image of it.

A group of well-heeled and voguish young urban professionals arrived and noisily arranged the merging of some nearby tables for lunch. Matthew looked at his watch. Madi was late again.

He was into the *Australian* business section when a shadow fell across the page. 'Ho, Matt. How's the stock market? AusGeo's shares holding good? Big gold, oil and diamond strikes this week?'

He looked up at his sister, Madison. They exchanged grins and he thought, as he always did, what a great looking girl she was. They'd become very close in the past few years.

'Hi Madi. Can't give you any scoops, that's insider trading.'

He kissed her on the cheek and she returned the compliment. 'Good to see you, bro.' She smiled and realised how glad she was to see her big brother.

Matthew studied her while she settled herself, taking off her sunglasses and putting her bag on the spare chair. 'So . . . How're you doing?'

She wrinkled her nose, twisting the thick blonde braid that fell over one shoulder. Her large hazel eyes flecked with gold specks clouded over.

'So-so I guess. I'm feeling fidgety, restless. The divorce becomes final in three months. Then I'll be on my own. Psychologically, anyway. I feel I should mark the occasion when it rolls around. Then again, I mightn't even notice the day. Perhaps we could go out to lunch with a couple of your hunky mates?'

Matthew grinned at his sister who at twenty-seven still looked like a schoolgirl. She was average height and build and deceptively slim for he knew she was very strong. She could lift almost anything he could. They'd moved her furniture into the new flat and he'd been amazed at her strength. But now she seemed somehow smaller and frailer. She looked pale too.

Even though she was two years younger than him, he'd felt she'd been through more than he'd had to deal with.

'Madi, you were "on your own" for six years. Ever since you rushed into that mad marriage. All I can say is thank heavens there are no kids. Geoffrey was a wimp, a procrastinator and no good for you. Let's not go through all that again. You know I never cared for him. I was glad I was overseas so much of the time. You're well out of it. Why don't you change jobs, ask for a transfer? Move to an interstate hotel in the group? Better yet, go overseas. Be good for you.'

The waitress appeared with glasses of water and menus. Madison ordered a cafe latte and picked up the menu, then restlessly put it down and reached for the glass of water.

'I'm having warm octopus salad. I recommend it. With garlic bread,' said Matthew.

'Sounds fine.'

Matthew had the feeling he could have suggested stewed cardboard and she'd have agreed. He gave her an encouraging smile. 'What's really bothering you?'

'I'm not sure. Well, I guess I do know . . . Geoff, of course. I'm glad it's over but you feel like your skin has been gone over with sandpaper. You feel very exposed and vulnerable. Things creep up on you, you wonder why you didn't read the signs better. I thought we really had it together and I didn't see what happened, what he did to me . . .' her voice trembled, '. . . what I did to myself.'

'Madi, you didn't *do* anything. Maybe you were too nice, too soft. I never understood how you let him walk all over you. Those little zingers he slung at you, so often I wanted to thump him. You were always so apologetic, it made me ill.'

He leaned forward and spoke seriously, 'Where's my sister? Where's the person I've always looked up to, who has looked out for me all our lives and I thought nothing could shake her. Where's the fun, gutsy, spunky girl who I thought was going to take on the world?'

Madison's lip trembled and her eyes filled. 'I don't know, Matt. I wish I did. I've just lost it. My confidence, my self-esteem, he trampled on me . . . He told me so often I was worthless, I'd never be anything . . .'

'He was just trying to make himself feel good and powerful and boost himself by putting you down. Madi, you've held a good job, a responsible job . . . for years.'

They paused while the waitress placed Madi's coffee in front of her and Matthew gave their lunch order.

'You're right,' Madison admitted. 'My job at the hotel has been my lifeline. Marketing and promotion can be hard work. But I'd have gone crazy without that.'

Like her brother she'd been an achiever. Graduating from Sydney University with a BA in business administration and marketing, she'd gone into the hospitality industry, getting in on the ground floor of a new international hotel and quickly showed a natural flair for promotion. She had fresh, attention-grabbing ideas and her job description had become more elastic as her opinion was sought on various aspects of promoting the hotel and its services as well as its corporate image.

She was a respected executive and dressed accordingly in subtle suits—some with short skirts, others with well-cut pants. Today she was a complete contrast in a short white cotton skirt and blue and white striped tank top.

Matthew put his hand on hers. 'The hotel must value you and it's part of an international group. Go to the manager and tell him you want a transfer for personal reasons. Do they know about the divorce?'

She shook her head. 'No. I never let it interfere with my work. I mean it wasn't like he was bashing me. I felt it was sort of admitting I'd failed and would diminish me in their eyes.'

'Oh Madi, I wish you'd shared more of this at the time. I don't think I really knew how hard it was for you. He bashed you up pretty well emotionally.'

'Well, it's over now. And you've been, are being, such a help.' Her face brightened and she gave a stronger smile.

'So, are you going to do what I suggest?'

'I'll think about it. It seems a big step. To be truthful I think I'd like a holiday . . . away from multi-star hotels. That's my work.'

'Want to hear my big news?' He sipped his coffee.

'A new girl?'

'Nope. I'm going overseas again.'

'Oh, Matt!' She couldn't hide her disappointment. She'd come to rely on Matthew for brotherly support as well as his company. 'I'm shattered. When? Where?'

'Guyana.' He laughed at her puzzled expression. 'Sit back and I'll fill you in on the place. I've become an expert—since yesterday. Boy, it's some story!'

'Start with where it is.'

'South America, but the people are more Caribbean/ West Indian. There's a lot of African influence from the slaves who were brought in for the sugar plantations. The country was held by the Dutch, the British, the French, reclaimed by Britain to become British Guiana and is now Guyana. It became an independent republic in 1966. The capital is Georgetown with roughly eight hundred thousand people, but there are six races and they all drink rum.'

'From the sugar . . . what else does the place have?'

'Not much by the sound of things. It has a spectacular jungle interior but it's never been developed. The joint was stuck at an amber light for thirty years under Forbes Burnham the socialist prime minister, later president. He formed his own party and courted western governments who were afraid the place was turning communist and would become a Cuban satellite. So he got the usual

American backing, promptly rigged elections, became a dictator and ran the country downhill into debt and disrepute. He died in 1985—and boy, is that a saga in itself. The place still hasn't recovered under the new democratic government, despite its good intentions. Corruption is ingrained and there's no money to aid recovery. It's going to be a slow process.'

'What's the saga about the poor old dictator dying?'

'The report we were given reads like a part farce, part thriller.'

'Tell me.'

'Forbes Burnham went into hospital in Georgetown to have an operation on his throat because he'd had problems and had to speak at a huge rally celebrating the freeing of the African slaves—he was African. So he flew in specialist doctors from Cuba, refusing to trust the local doctors. Apparently he thought himself invincible so he rejected the normal pre-op tests and sailed into the hospital the morning of the operation. The Cuban doctors had no idea he'd had a heart attack in 1977, and right after the operation his heart stopped. What happened after that has become part of Guyanese legend . . . to the effect that they rushed to the cupboard to get a resuscitation machine. It was locked. No one knew who had a key, so they broke into it only to find the equipment had been stolen. Burnham died of cardiac failure, a victim of the sort of bureaucratic breakdown he'd let flourish. The doctors were rushed straight out of the country to avoid an investigation. And in the official announcement of the death, all celebrations and parties were banned.'

'You mean people were pleased?'

'Seems it was more like relief, they were fed up. Apparently, when the news was broadcast over the public address system of a shopping mall in Miami, all the Guyanese migrants there started dancing and cheering. Anyway, Burnham was buried with pomp and ceremony. Then his followers decided the body should be exhumed and embalmed and placed in a mausoleum in the Botanic Gardens like Lenin in Russia, so that future generations could see him laid out to rest.' Matthew paused as the waitress arrived with their meal.

'At first they planned to parade the body in an open gun carriage through the city—this place is just above the equator remember. And at the morgue, they'd had an electricity breakdown. Anyway the funeral procession got under way in the cool of the afternoon and was attended by huge crowds. Then the body was rushed back to the mortuary where the refrigeration was now functioning again.'

Matthew glanced at Madi who held a mouthful of food on her fork in mid-air, a look of disbelief and amusement on her face. 'Go on.'

'It then took ten days just to get the body out of Guyana, to be flown to Russia for the embalming. It was a bureaucratic nightmare. It went via Cuba, where apparently the coffin was handled by Havana officials who had no respect for the occupant's former role of office. So the departed PM turns up in Moscow three weeks after his demise. Meanwhile there was a flurry to build the grand mausoleum in the Botanic Gardens at a cost to the country of two million dollars. However, the budget didn't cover air-conditioning or a back-up generator to cool the temperature in the chamber for a body on display. Other factors like security and maintenance of the electrical equipment were also overlooked. Meanwhile Burnham's party was splitting into an ideology faction on one side and a pragmatic faction with a sense of new order on the other. So at the end of 1986, more than twelve months after his death, Forbes Burnham's remains were buried in a modest ceremony, at the site of The Seven Ponds in the Botanic Gardens and there he apparently—and finally—rests.'

Madi shook her head, rather bemused as she fussed with her salad. 'Why on earth would your company want to go there?'

'It's an initiative of the International Funding Organisation. There's an IFO official—incidentally, he's an Australian—already there. Apparently he's decided this bauxite mine, called Guyminco, is worth rehabilitating. Now he's taking tenders from consultants and that's where we come in. Stewart Johns our CEO thinks it's just what we need to keep us out of trouble.'

'And you're looking forward to this assignment?'

'Yeah, you know me, I love to travel. Unlike most people, I get to spend extended time in a country, tap into the people and the place. Apparently that's what hooked Johns. He went there for a quiet recce before deciding whether we should tender. He told me after the briefing that the place has a magic about it. Especially the people. Despite the problems he thinks we'll enjoy it. A stimulating challenge as he put it. He also told me to be sure and tick the NO box on the visa form that asks, Do you intend to preach?'

'Whatever for?'

'Remember the terrible incident of the Reverend Jim Jones from San Francisco and his 900 followers who ended up committing mass suicide after the murder of a US congressman?'

Madison raised her eyebrows. 'Oh, right. Preachers not welcome, huh?'

'Not really. They never did figure out what sort of a

deal he did with Burnham to set up Jonestown. No inquiry was ever held and no one knows what happened to all the money and valuables supposedly kept at the People's Temple.'

'I wonder what's left now?'

'Since 1978 . . . not much, I guess. Anyway the place was in the middle of nowhere, near the Venezuelan border, so Johns says.'

'Well, it sounds extraordinary. How rough are the living conditions?'

'Hard to say, I'll be out at the mine site a lot of the time, that's some way out of the city. Though I'll have a base in the town. I'll need to liaise with government officials and the like. Probably share a house with Kevin Blanchard, our engineer. Johns will stay at the mine. Georgetown's not too safe, certainly not a tourist destination like most of the Caribbean. And there's Brazil and the great Amazon River at the back door. You know who did go there?'

Madison shook her head.

'Sir Walter Raleigh. He went there looking for the fabled lost city of gold, El Dorado.'

'You're joking!'

'I'm going to find his book and read it. He wrote about his expedition, how he was lured there by a story about a "golden man".'

'Who was he?'

'Some ancient king whose wife and daughter drowned themselves in a lake because he mistreated them. To appease the gods and bring them back, the king painted himself with gold dust and threw gold into the middle of the lake. This became part of the legend of El Dorado, the Golden City. Raleigh didn't find the lake or the gold but he wrote glowingly of what is now Guyana. Who knows . . . it's kind of fun to think there could still be a lost city of gold somewhere in the rainforest.'

'I can just see you doing a little gold prospecting on weekends. Sounds like our own Lasseter's Reef . . . truth or myth, it's still a good story,' laughed Madison, her troubles now forgotten as Matthew enthused about his new challenge.

'Well, we know there's gold there. And diamonds. Probably all sorts of minerals. But being mostly rainforest jungle, it's hard to get at.'

'Why not leave it there?'

'The country is poor, if it has rich resources they should be utilised . . . in a responsible manner, of course,' he hastened to add, aware of his sister's sympathy for 'green' politics. 'Let's not get into a philosophical environmental debate.'

'I know the mining industry is your life but I always thought you had a sensitive side and didn't approve of what some companies got up to.'

'*Some* companies, sis. Times are a'changing,' he sang lightly with a smile. 'Most miners are learning how to be good corporate citizens and do the right thing by the environment.' He threw his hands up defensively. 'I know . . . you think too much of it is sheer window dressing, that in the end the almighty dollar rules supreme. And please, don't raise the Ok Tedi argument again . . . not this time, it's too nice a day.'

'Well, it seems to me that this Guyana isn't that different from Papua New Guinea,' responded Madison, who had been appalled at the headline-making stories of pollution of the Fly River by discharges from BHP's Ok Tedi gold and copper mine in the remote highlands.

'Anyway, you work for the tourism industry. Slapping up resorts, hotels and golf courses in sensitive wilderness areas isn't very environmentally correct either,' shot back her brother.

'Okay.' Madison waved her hands in the air. 'Let's call a truce and not spoil a good lunch.'

'Right. Now how about *this* for a really great idea? You've always loved travel. Why not get away from all the hassles of the divorce and pop over to Guyana for a holiday with me . . . a sort of cleansing rite to start your new life?' He leaned back and folded his arms, delighted with the idea.

She gave him the dismissive look which, ever since childhood, she had used to greet ideas he thought brilliant and she thought appalling. 'I'm not that desperate, bro.'

TWO

Matthew was going through a mild form of culture shock after only a few days in Guyana. He felt his mind pausing, then snapping and freezing an image that brought home to him, as it always did, the fact he was in a strange country, a new continent, an alien city. Georgetown was as different from Sydney as anyone could conceive. He kept seeking parallels and familiarities, but found only comparisons and contrasts.

It was Saturday morning and he caught what was possibly the only elevator in Georgetown to the sixth and top floor of the Pessaro Hotel. He stepped out onto the terrace that ringed the tower of the city's 'best' hotel, a landmark that had been updated and homogenised to universal mediocre tropical hotel standard: white cane furniture, glaring bird-print upholstery, mass-produced paintings of more native birds, stands of glossed greenery and staff in uniforms featuring bits of gold braid and badges. White shirts and smiles, and an accent that his ear was still tuning to a comprehensible wavelength.

A sluggish wind assaulted him with hot equatorial breath that suffocated rather than resuscitated. He walked to the iron railing and gazed across the ocean. He recalled suddenly the Saturday lunch with Madison at Shelly Beach just a few weeks ago. No blue Pacific here. None of those dazzling Australian colours. Only the slow slurp of the cafe au lait sea slapping at the seawall, a flimsy-looking structure that held the Atlantic Ocean back from slipping over the cityscape, an ocean stretching east to the slate horizon where heavy rain clouds hung sodden, over-burdened, bladderful. He felt he could almost see the air he dragged into his lungs as he took a deep breath.

To the west the city sprawled in the distance. Immediately across from the hotel was the affluent area of the city, dominated by the cream fortress of the US embassy. It covered a block where previously three gracious colonial homes had stood. In the 1980s after the hostage crisis in the Middle East, Washington had issued an edict to fortify all US embassies behind walls that could withstand the impact of a truck loaded with dynamite driven into them at fifty miles an hour. Also for security reasons, the ambassador now lived in a fortified contemporary 'palace' in another part of Georgetown.

The solid structure of the embassy contrasted with the rest of the city which, for all its history, looked terribly temporary to Matthew. Nothing much had risen to great height and most of the low concrete and wooden buildings were of nondescript design. The city was heavy with trees that thrived in the wet and humid conditions and

27

Matthew speculated that if all the people quit the city it would not take very long at all for nature to turn it back into a swampy jungle.

It was the cricket pitch that stopped Matthew in his slow stroll around the hotel's parapet. The green sward with clubhouse was at last something he could relate to. He found it surprisingly like the oval at Manly and smiled in recognition of at least one thing he shared with this strange and distinctly odd-looking city. Cricket was one of his passions and, until this assignment, the only time he had been conscious of Guyana was when one of its cricketers turned up to play Australia in a West Indies' team. And that was another odd thing about this place. This wasn't the West Indies, it was South America. Yet everyone he had spoken to so far had that lilting West Indian English, almost a calypso way of talking, that said loud and clear this was a Caribbean country.

A breeze swept up a mixture of sound and scents from the street. The traffic was frenetic and very dependent on excessive use of horns. The pedestrians were an artist's palette of colour, in skin as well as dress, and a hint of many accents drifted up between lulls in the traffic. And the scents—spices, curries, salt air, tropical fruit, the lushness of flowers, and a slightly rancid smell of something wet and rotting.

There was a Saturday morning vigour about the street below and Matthew suddenly felt so remote, so alone, looking down from his modest tower and he had an urge to get down there among the action. He looked at his watch. It was almost time to meet the local representative from the Guyminco bauxite mine. He walked to the lift with a feeling of relief, pleased to escape the heat and attack on his senses.

*

Vivian Prashad, born and educated in Georgetown, had been with Guyminco for eight years. His parents had come from Bombay, originally to work on a sugar plantation and had gradually improved their circumstances. As assistant operations manager of Guyminco, Vivian Prashad was ambitious and a hard worker. He had additional responsibility for introducing the expatriate executives to the city and to the operations of the mine. He opened the rear car door for Matthew then slid in beside the African driver. 'I take you on a little tour, Mr Wright, then we inspect the house we have rented in Georgetown for you and Mr Kevin Blanchard. Mr Johns will be living at MacGregor.'

'That's the mine township?'

'Yes. It was nothing until a Scottish chappie took a canoe up the river in 1910. He found high grade bauxite. He made a very good deal with an American venture company. They bought up a lot of land and started digging in 1916.' Prashad shook his head. 'They were the good old days, now not so good. Things are very bad for the families of the workers. People are worried if the mine goes down, the town will die.'

'Well, we're here to see things get better,' said Matthew making an effort to put some authority into his voice. 'We've had tougher projects than this one.'

'Oh, that is very good news. Very good news indeed,' enthused Prashad, swinging around in his seat and smiling broadly at Matthew.

'How big is the mine town?'

'Seventy thousand people. A very big place. But it is a nice place. I like living in MacGregor.'

'How long does it take to get there?'

'Under two hours. For years the road was terrible. Now it is excellent. The best in the country.'

That wouldn't be hard, thought Matthew as the car shuddered over another batch of potholes.

They turned into the central part of the city. Now the streets widened into broad avenues, and he could more fully appreciate the influences that had shaped the city named Longchamps by the French, Stabroek by the Dutch and Georgetown by the English.

'This is Main Street. Many important buildings here. Lot of people hanging about here. Dangerous for choke and robs. Robbers hang out near Guyana Stores, the bank, the Tower Hotel. You mind your watch, wallet. Tell your lady not to wear jewellery,' advised Prashad with a lifted eyebrow and half smile.

They drove parallel to large open drains with grass verges which to Matthew's surprise seemed relatively clean despite the rubbish and litter scattered everywhere. 'Were they built as drains or stormwater overflows?' he asked Prashad.

'The French began some town planning but it was the Dutch who really created the city with the streets in a rectangular grid pattern on old plantation land. Georgetown is below sea level so they built the seawall along the coast. Then they extended the plantation drainage system, putting in sluices, kokers and dams to control the tides, rivers and stormwater. Oh yes, very clever people, the Dutch. The sugar industry used the canals to move the cane. Here in town we use the stormwater to flush the canals.'

'Thanks for the briefing,' said Matthew.

'You are very welcome. Guyana is an interesting country to study. So many European influences from the colonists. Add in the African slave people, we East Indians, the Portuguese, the Chinese and the Amerindians who are the indigenous people, and you see we are quite a mix. I'll show you some old houses that have multicultured architecture.'

'Now that's something I recognise—multiculturalism.'

Matthew stared at the chaotic throngs of people on bicycles, on foot and in ancient battered and much-repaired cars. Occasionally an expensive German or American automobile, the occupants screened by tinted glass, pushed its way through the crowd. Once Main Street had had pretensions to a boulevard, with a green dividing strip planted with flowering saman trees dropping red and gold blossoms. But the chaos in the streets detracted from the graceful design planned by the original city fathers.

'There you are, some of the original planters-style houses,' said Prashad. 'They were built up off the ground because of flooding and to make a place for animals. Now that bottom area is generally laundry and servants' quarters.'

'I like the verandahs and the woodwork,' said Matthew.

'The verandah is an important fixture. Very necessary in our heat to catch the north-easterly breezes,' enthused Prashad.

Like grand ladies fallen on hard times, the houses retained an air of grace and splendid occasion despite the present ignominy of genteel poverty.

'Now that place looks good, what's that?' Matthew pointed to a large double-storeyed building with spacious verandahs, manicured lawns and flowering trees hanging over a high concrete fence.

'Ah, that is the Georgetown Club. Very posh, very hard to get into. Number one club. Always has been. Of course in the early days only the British went there.'

'And now . . . what's it take to get in?'

'The committee decides . . . money, standing, position. But it's good. All sorts of people belong. More mixed. You tell Mr Johns to get AusGeo people in.'

Matthew smiled, knowing Stewart Johns would never make it a priority. 'Where else is there to go?'

Prashad chuckled. 'Oh, many places now. People like the Palm Court, number one restaurant on Friday nights. And over there is the Park Hotel . . . good value. Three course meal and drink less than one thousand dollars.'

'Ten dollars Australian, that's value all right. Hey, I like the look of it.' The Park retained a colonial air without being grandiose, with a wide upper verandah, colonnades and comfortable cane furniture.

'We Guyanese like a good time. Tonight, you will see a typical Guyana party, eh?'

The AusGeo team had been invited to a reception at the residence of the Guyminco general manager, Lennie Krupuk and his wife Roxy. Matthew hadn't been anticipating a raging great time. These sorts of receptions tended to follow a formula. The reception line of officials in descending order of importance, their wives stuffed into overdone dresses, hair lacquered into obedience by an afternoon salon visit, catered finger food and a mixture of government people, businessmen, social-scene setters and economic officers from various embassies.

The US Stars and Stripes caught his eye as the car cruised past a low simple box-like building.

'That was the old US embassy, before they built the Hotel Hope.'

'Hotel Hope? You mean that cream Fort Knox?'

'Yes. Everyone goes there hoping. Queues start first thing every morning, everybody hope for a US visa.' Prashad shook his head. 'It's no good. All the people want is to make enough money to go to Miami, New

York, Canada, London. No one wants to stay here and work and fix up this country. We need good people here.'

'And you Mr Prashad, do you want to get a US visa too?'

He shrugged. 'If I had money, maybe. To give my children an American education. Everyone in Guyana has a relative outside, eh?' He nudged the black African driver who grinned.

'Dat for sure.'

Matthew had the distinct feeling the driver had put in time in the queue at the Hotel Hope.

'So what goes on in the old embassy?'

Prashad gave him a broad smile. 'Information people. Spooks, you know. That's what they call the spies.'

Matthew laughed. 'No secrets in this town, I see.'

'No secrets and plenty of rumours and gossip. Sometimes true, sometimes not . . . but always worth repeating,' chuckled Prashad without malice.

The car glided past the impressive High Court with its red roof faded to rusty orange. Like the other elaborate wooden structures in the city, peeling paint and shabbiness dimmed its unique attractiveness. Queen Victoria gazed blankly above the seething throngs outside the court's wrought iron fence. 'The Queen has lost a hand,' noted Matthew.

'Lucky she didn't lose her head. She had been lying for years in the grass, in the back of the Botanic Gardens after being knocked down. The new regime brought her back to court. It is the Victoria High Court after all,' explained Prashad.

At the northern end of the broad Avenue of the Republic they swung around the pride of the city, St George's Cathedral, a wooden Gothic fantasy which had survived fires that destroyed many of the city's important buildings since its construction in 1892. 'The tallest wooden building in the world,' declared Prashad, and Matthew smiled.

They skirted the seedy Stabroek Markets which sheltered beneath a bright red roof and fancy wood trim. The open ground in front of the markets was a teeming bazaar of vehicles, bicycles, pedestrians, peddlers and smaller stalls that couldn't afford to shelter in the great shadowy confines of the marketplace.

'Is it this busy every day?' asked Matthew who suddenly wanted to stop and dive into the market.

'Yes, every day is like this. But there are a lot of teefs here. You send your maid to do the shopping.'

'Teefs? You mean thieves,' asked Matthew.

The driver and Prashad exchanged grins. 'Local expression. Doesn't sound so bad when we say "teefs",' explained Prashad.

Ten minutes later, they swung into a fenced, overgrown grassy square. Goats grazed mid-field and a pack of small dogs patrolled the road. There were no footpaths or shoulders, and some residents had put duckboards across the mucky grass outside their gates.

The modern cement houses had upper storeys and verandahs featuring breeze blocks and glass louvres, with the metal box backsides of air-conditioners jutting from bedroom walls. Most had fancy wrought-iron gates, all were securely fenced and one or two were being remodelled into grandiose nouveau riche monstrosities. Matthew wondered what business these neighbours were engaged in that appeared to be so financially successful. Undoubtedly he would discover in time.

'This is the house you and Mr Kevin Blanchard will occupy,' said Prashad as they drew up outside a comparatively modest bungalow. 'Four bedrooms, two bathrooms, big living and entertaining area, small balcony, big garden,' he recited as they dragged open the unlocked gate.

At the scrape of metal on the concrete drive, a sleepy figure appeared. A solid dark-skinned man with a shock of wavy white hair and dressed in a singlet and voluminous old khaki shorts hurried forward in bare feet. Prashad ignored him, went to the house and unlocked the front door. A flight of polished wood stairs led to the main area and Matthew followed Prashad up. The open plan was light and airy leading to the front balcony. A second small deck ran along the rear off the bedrooms and was screened by metal grillework. Through this could be seen a large garden filled with banana and fruit trees, tropical shrubs and flowers. A thatched gazebo leaned in one corner facing a small pond smothered in waterlilies. Several hammocks were strung along the verandah.

Prashad continued. 'There is a maid, Hyacinth, who we recommend you hire. She lives downstairs. She will cook, wash, clean for you. You need to hire a guard and a gardener.'

'Who's the old bloke downstairs?'

'He was here when I brought Mr Blanchard out yesterday while you were in the ministry office. I'm not sure who he is. We just leased this place.'

'I'll just take a turn around the garden,' said Matthew.

Although Prashad and the other mine staff had not been informed yet, AusGeo had been granted the mine contract almost as soon as the Australians arrived in the country. Matthew couldn't wait to tell Kevin how it had come about. In the meantime this house, which had been leased with an option to extend, would be more than suitable for a long stay.

He didn't bother checking the domestic rooms, that was the maid's domain. He would divide his time between Georgetown and the mine. Kevin would be doing the same, though they would possibly be on different schedules. Matthew paused and looked at the little gazebo. Yes, he could see himself sitting out here with a sunset rum. He turned back as the old man emerged again from under the house which sheltered the maid's room and laundry. He was now wearing a shirt and he gave Matthew a smile. 'Are you living or working here?' asked Matthew.

The man straightened and announced, 'I be Singh. I come with de house.'

'Is that so. I'm Matthew Wright.' Matthew shook his outstretched hand. 'I'll be moving in here tomorrow. What are your duties, Singh?'

'I be de guard and I do garden, boss.'

'Very well, Singh. If you say so.'

'You be British, Mr Wright?'

'No. Australian.'

'Ah. Australian. Very good. Top welcome to Guyana, Mr Wright.'

Singh held the gate open as they drove away. 'We can do better, I'm sure. There is a security service we can hire,' began Prashad.

'Singh comes with the house,' said Matthew emphatically. For some reason he'd taken an instant liking to the old Indian. 'He'll be fine.'

As dusk fell over Georgetown, Matthew and Kevin sat on the verandah of the Pessaro Hotel, enjoying a beer as they talked over the events of the past twenty-four hours. While Kevin had visited the bauxite mine, Matthew and Stewart Johns had met the IFO's representative Connor Bain and a group of government officials for discussions about Guyminco's future.

Bain had made it clear the IFO, which was funding the contract to clean up and sell the mine, wanted the AusGeo team. And Johns was satisfied that, with IFO backing, they could do the job. Finally one of the public servants, to keep face, told them the government had already decided not to accept the only other potential tenderer for the contract.

'At least,' Matthew told Kevin, 'it saves wasting time on presentations. Now we can get the real job done.'

Ordering a second round, they decided Bain, who'd told them he was originally from Western Australia, was a good bloke, the kind they could share a few beers with on this mutual assignment.

After dark they got into a taxi outside the Pessaro and gave the driver directions to the Guyminco general manager's residence. The genial executive, concerned about his future at the mine, had suggested he host this reception to give the AusGeo team a chance to meet senior and middle management of the mine in a more relaxed atmosphere.

'I thought our house seemed pretty good,' said Matthew in the taxi. 'By the way, did you meet the old Indian fellow staying there? I told him he could stay on as guard and gardener.'

'No, didn't see him, I just rushed in and rushed out. I'm not going to be spending much time there. I met the maid, Hyacinth. She's a card.'

The taxi pulled up in a street lined with cars. Flame torches flared by the gates of a large white colonial house

37

and music from a steel band rolled over the garden wall almost drowning conversation.

'God, is every band in the country here?'

The driver pointed to a truck with neon-hued painted designs and the logo of *The Silvertails*. 'Good band,' he shouted. 'Best party band, won prizes in Trinidad last year.' Matthew paid him and nodded. He didn't want to shout an answer.

The twelve-man band was in the garden where more flame torches on poles gave a flickering light. The players were dressed in bright green satin shirts with glittering sequinned silver birds on them. Matthew and Kevin stood and watched the swaying, gyrating, grinning men belting the different sized silver drums with tennis balls on short sticks.

'They're cut down and bashed out forty-gallon drums,' declared Kevin, 'a big band sound to be sure . . . amazing.'

A guard pointed them to a flight of stairs up into the house as the band segued into the calypso beat of *Spanish Eyes*.

The two men beamed with pleasant surprise as they stepped into the main room. No formalities here. A waiter immediately offered them rum punch, and their hostess dressed in a long sarong hurried forward, her arms outstretched.

'Dear boys, welcome! I'm Roxy Krupuk and you must be Kevin and Matthew . . . which is which?'

They introduced themselves, grinning at the effervescent dark-skinned Guyanese woman with the killer smile and short bobbed hair. She was in her early fifties, curvaceous rather than plump, personality bubbling from every pore. Stepping between the two men she linked arms with each. 'Now let's find some pretty girls to talk to, eh?'

Matthew and Kevin exchanged an amused grin above her head, this was not the normal boss's wife. On most foreign assignments they found their hostesses keen to protect their young women friends from men like them who only stayed in one place for a short time, although they'd never had much trouble breaking down the barriers. In Roxy they immediately sensed a warm-hearted, fun-loving, candid helpmate.

Though they were on time it seemed to the two Australians that the party was well under way. Everyone was talking animatedly, laughing and dancing. Most people wore bright colours and favoured a more flashy style of dress. The dancing to the loud, insistent reggae beat was uninhibited, bodies swayed and gyrated provocatively, damp with exertion and heat from the crush of people. Over the heads of those dancing they spotted the figure of Connor Bain, grinning and lifting his glass in a welcoming salute.

In minutes they were deposited amongst a group of young Guyanese women of different ethnic backgrounds, all attractive, bubbly and easy to talk to. They soon learnt this was to be no ordinary cocktail party.

An attractive Indian girl in a brilliant turquoise sari, her hair tied back in a knot at the nape of the neck with a gold clasp, introduced herself. 'I'm Sharee Gopal. I hope you're ready for this adventure Roxy has planned.'

'I thought it was just drinks. This is a full-on rage,' said Kevin.

'No. It's dinner . . . if you figure it out!' she laughed.

'What exactly does that mean?

'It's like a scavenger hunt . . . a mystery tour . . . a

progressive dinner, of sorts,' added Viti Leung, who was a sweet Chinese girl in a red silk cocktail dress, her long black hair cut in a straight fringe over her almond-shaped eyes.

They found out the details as they took their second drinks. Roxy began circulating with two hats, one filled with the names of the men, the other with the women. 'Draw a partner,' she chortled, and winked as she offered the hats to Matt and Kevin and the two girls last.

There was another round of drinks as everyone matched the number beside their names to meet their partner.

Kevin grinned as he found himself teamed with Viti, and Matthew shook his arm in the air in a cheerful salute as he found his name paired with Sharee.

Roxy stood on a chair and shushed the crowd of eighty people. 'Right. You get your first clue now and when you've followed that, you'll get coded directions to help you find the next clue. Along the way there will be refreshments until you arrive at our secret location for the main course. Good luck!'

'What a crazy idea . . . I like it,' said Kevin as dozens of couples, some strangers like he and Viti, started huddling and whispering and running for cars. 'It's a scavenger hunt too, you know. You have to collect items along the way,' called Roxy to the two Australians as they moved with their partners towards the door.

'Hey, Matthew, do you want to go in my car or yours?' Sharee asked.

Matthew shrugged his shoulders. 'I came in a taxi.'

'Then it's mine. I have a driver, so we will be able to concentrate on decoding the directions.'

'Good idea. You realise I'm a complete novice in this town.'

'It's a small town,' she smiled softly. 'And this is a good way to get to know it.'

Matthew's discovery tour led him to some strange places that night.

They found the first stop easily. The bar of the Pessaro Hotel was where they had to buy the next clue, with the bartender saying he was to charge them a piece of their clothing. Matthew pulled off his belt and Sharee looked down at her sari, shrugged, and handed over her sandals, to the amusement of the other patrons. 'I'm assuming this will all turn up at the end of the night,' said Matthew. 'Fancy a quick drink while we're here?' As they sipped their beers, two other party guests rushed in, handed over a tie and a hair scarf and scurried off calling, 'Don't miss dinner!'

The clues were far from easy. '*It's almost rubber*' said the clue they'd bought at the bar. 'Rubber. Something to do with rubber,' mused Matthew. 'You don't suppose it's to do with spare tyres?'

Sharee giggled. 'There's a tyre place a few blocks from here. Let's drive past and see if there's a light on.'

The Mighty Bird Tyre Shop, where piles of old tyres were stacked and chained together, was in darkness. As they stopped outside, another couple were reading a piece of paper by their car's interior light. Matthew tapped on the passenger's window, startling them. 'Do we make a foray into the yard or not?'

'We were thinking the same thing. The place is locked up. I'm sure we're not supposed to break in. Something made of rubber, maybe we should find a dictionary.'

'My aunty lives down the block,' his companion said. 'Let's go and borrow hers. Good luck!' They sped away.

Sharee got into the back seat with Matthew and said to the bemused driver, 'So, Benji, what do you think of when I say rubber?'

'Tree.'

'That's it!' Sharee flashed a delighted grin. 'A rubber tree . . . there's a very famous one in the Botanic Gardens. Of course. Well done, Benji. Let's go.'

They scrambled through the dark gardens, Matthew thinking the whole exercise rather fun until he took a spill, tripping over something large and solid. A cow staggered to its feet as surprised as Matthew. 'Good grief, Sharee wait. There's a cow here. And more of them there . . . what on earth are they doing here?'

Sharee who had been hurrying ahead despite the constraints of her sari, came back to Matthew. 'These belong to the old prime minister's wife. Mrs Burnham has a small dairy herd she grazes here.'

'In the Botanic Gardens!' Matthew wondered if the night's surprises would ever end.

'They're fenced off from the rare plants. Though they often get out. She once had the fence electrified but it's illegal so now they keep breaking through. If you go to visit her you can have fresh cow's milk in your tea.'

'I'll look forward to that,' muttered Matthew rubbing his sore elbow.

They found the tree and plucked one of the huge thick glossy leaves to add to their scavenger collection, then walked around its giant base probing the roots. 'Where do you suppose our next clue might be? Ouch!' Matthew banged his head against a solid basket hanging from a branch.

'In there I'd say,' said Sharee, grinning at him as he rubbed his forehead.

'Where next?'
'To light the way or sink and swim.'

They stood at the base of a small red and white striped lighthouse at the tip of the seawall and rapped on the locked wooden door. Their answer was a basket lowered on a rope. In it was a small bottle of rum, two chocolate bars, a bag of mixed peanuts and a white envelope.

Sharee began eating one of the chocolate bars. 'Do you think this is dessert and we missed dinner?'

Matthew took a swig of the rum and read the note in the envelope.

'Her name is Candy Delight, knock and ask for Joe where the camel stops at night.'

'What's that mean?'

Sharee looked puzzled. 'Let's ask Benji.'

They handed over the chocolate and nuts and the driver chewed slowly. 'Only one place with a camel in dis town. Be de Camel Pit.'

'Ooh,' Sharee's hand flew to her mouth. 'It's a rum shop but really a brothel. It's always being written up in the newspaper because of fights and things. I'm not going in there.'

'I'll go. Let's check it out, Benji.'

It was a narrow street, crammed with wooden buildings that were strung with coloured lights. Amplified calypso was blaring and a lot of people were strolling or talking in groups along the roadside. There was no missing the painted billboard of a camel with a scantily clad voluptuous black woman straddled between its humps. A tough-looking African man wearing an abundance of gold jewellery lounged at the narrow doorway. Matthew stared at the building with some apprehension.

'Dat be de place, eh boss,' said Benji. Then when Matthew didn't make a move from the car, added, 'You want me check 'im?'

'I'll come with you,' Matthew eased out of the car.

'What we lookin' for, boss?'

'Joe . . . I think.'

'Hey man. You be Joe, eh?' asked Benji.

The beefy gold man flexed his muscles. 'Yeah. Who's goin' up?'

Matthew glanced behind him to where a rickety staircase led above the boisterous rum shop and bar.

'Up?' he asked.

'Yeah. T'Candy. She be waitin' for yo.' He grinned and gave a mock bow. 'Let de white man pass, bro,' he said to an unseen figure in the shadows.

Matthew went up the stairs to a landing and dark hallway where several doors were closed save for one which stood partly open, a red light glowing inside. 'Candy?' he called.

'In here, handsome . . . I hope you're handsome!' The woman gave a throaty chuckle.

Matthew stepped inside the door and, for a minute, thought he'd walked on to a bad movie set. Except it was too tacky. Red velvet thrown over a chair and bed, cushions with tarnished gold tassels, a red fringed lampshade, the bulb covered with red cellophane paper casting a sickly pink glow over the bed and its occupant. She sat centre stage, centre bed, hand on rolls of hip, one fat leg crooked, the other stretched along the bed bulging over red fishnet stockings—holed—a garter straining against black thighs that emerged from a short satin skirt. Breasts cascaded from black lace. Oiled hair, thunderous lipstick, some glittery cheap jewellery, and a smile that told him she was enjoying every minute.

44

'You're Candy?'

'Candy Deee . . . light.' She laughed again. 'You want somethin' from me, right man?'

'I guess so,' Matthew grinned. 'Whose move next?'

'Honey, I ain't movin', dat's for sure. Come closer . . .'

He hesitated. Candy leant provocatively towards him revealing a slip of paper jammed between the bellows of her breasts. 'Come and get it, fella.'

Matthew reached out but couldn't extract the paper without inserting his hands between hot slippery flesh. 'That's the biggest thrill yo gonna get tonight, honey,' she laughed.

Matthew glanced at the paper, relieved to see it had an address on it. No more searching. He was getting hungry. 'The night's still young, Candy.'

'Then maybeceee we see yo later. Bring yo money with you!' She laughed again, rolls of flesh rippling. 'Man, this is the quickest and easiest gig I ever get.'

Matthew escaped, wondering if he should have tipped her, but realised he had no Guyanese cash on him.

Sharee looked wide-eyed as he related the episode. 'What if one of the girls goes up there?'

'Candy won't bite . . . Unless you pay her, I guess.' He found himself laughing Candy's laugh and handed the address to Benji.

The dinner party, this time at the large sprawling home of Guyminco's finance controller, was in full swing. More than half the guests had so far found their destination and were relating tales of escapades and misdirections. The band had moved here too and so had Roxy, who was overseeing the food spread on buffet tables in the floodlit garden. A dance floor had been set up and a bar serving cocktails was surrounded by revellers. Lennie Krupuk, looking very unlike a general manager, in a wildly patterned calypso-inspired shirt, came towards them. 'So you got here . . . didn't get side-tracked by Candy, eh?'

'No, the riddle of the rubber had us stumped for a bit,' Matthew said.

'I made one blue,' said Kevin, coming up with Viti to join them. 'I told the lighthouse bloke to send the key down, which he did, in the basket. So I opened the door, went all the way up the stairs and asked him for the next clue . . . once I got my breath back. And he points down the bottom to Viti and says, "I sent it down to her in the basket"!'

They sat down to a feast of spicy food, a lot of starchy vegetables, fruit and rum-soaked puddings. The drinks kept coming and the band played faster. Sharee and Viti became lost in the swaying crowd while a string of girls kept showing Matthew and Kevin how to dance calypso style, pushing their hips to feel the rhythm, flirting and laughing. They pocketed a lot of telephone numbers as the night wore on, sometimes jotting them down while still gyrating to the hypnotic rhythm. The evening became a noisy blur as the excess of rum took hold of everyone's senses.

Matthew and Kevin were driven back to the Pessaro by a taxi very late, or very early if you looked at the soft light rising above the horizon.

In his bedroom, a euphoric Matthew stripped off his clothes with fumbling fingers, staggering slightly while trying to stop the room from spinning. As he collapsed on the bed his last thoughts were, these Guyanese sure know how to party, and I'm going to have a terrible hangover. He fell instantly asleep.

THREE

The luxury motor launch *Roxanne* nosed away from the wooden jetty in Georgetown and out into the Demerara River. In contrast to the darkness of their jungle surroundings, the cruiser flashed like a jewelled pin on a plain dress—plush fittings including crystal glass, flamboyant animal skin print upholstery, accommodation for six and state-of-the-art radar and navigation equipment. The six men on board in casual shirts and dark glasses, wore an assortment of hats—Panama, baseball, Aussie Akubra and a Guyanese straw confection that drew some critical fashion comments. Matthew was hatless and quickly moved into the shade of the cockpit. 'Think I'll be investing in one of those Stabroek market hats like Kevin. Might look ridiculous but that sun is hot.'

The boat had been bought for Guyminco by Lennie Krupuk, who hailed the tall African skipper at the wheel. 'Hey Skip, you have a hat tucked away there for our friend?'

'No, really. It's all right,' protested Matthew as Lennie, who lacked the genuine warmth of his wife Roxy, took the wheel. He was a light-skinned man of East Indian and Portuguese mix, loud, bombastic and relentlessly cheerful. 'Nah, I know we got some there. Even blacks burn you know,' he roared as the silent skipper lifted a seat cover and pulled out a canvas hat, handing it to Matthew.

'You look like you're going fly-fishing,' said Kevin with a grin. Kevin had olive skin tanned from years of surfing and the sun had bleached streaks into his brown hair. 'This sun's twice as hot as Sydney's, mate,' he said.

The skipper's offsider handed around iced beers and rum punches. Stewart Johns' mouth tightened and he pointedly asked for something soft. 'We have work to do even if it is orientation,' he said a little firmly, to remind everyone there was a reason for this day out.

Lennie was unfazed. 'This is all part of getting to know the Guyanese way of doing things . . . where possible enjoy life!'

Johns turned away for a quiet aside to Matthew and Kevin. 'A nice idea to get to MacGregor by river but I guarantee we'll lose most of the day the way this guy operates.'

'He's been minding the shop and I'd say that was all,' said Kevin with a raised eyebrow. 'Isn't he due to leave when the new deal starts?'

'I hope so,' said Johns quietly.

'The execs out here certainly know how to have a good time,' said Matthew. He absently rubbed the side of his aching forehead. 'Lennie and Roxy's party was quite something.'

Johns grinned. 'Glad you enjoyed it, you'll be lucky to have a weekend off from now on.'

Matthew let the observation pass. He'd had a great night and looked forward to more of the delights that the social round in Georgetown had to offer in what appeared to be attractive abundance, although he resolved to avoid hangovers as severe as the one that was making this trip quite hellish.

The motor launch rode smoothly up the broad Demerara and the men relaxed and fell silent as they swept around the curves of the river that looked as dark brown as the sugar that bore its name. The water was clear, not soupy despite its rich colour which resulted from the dyes of vegetation, roots and minerals washed in from the surrounding jungle.

Lilies, palms and a tangle of creeper-laden evergreens lined the banks screening what lay beyond.

'What do you think is in there?' mused Matthew.

'More of the same, I suppose,' replied Kevin. 'Perhaps villages, camps—not much.'

'I'd like to explore this place. Go up the rivers. There is a huge water run-off from the high rainfall in the ranges. A massive complex of waterways apparently.'

'They don't call it Land of Many Waters for nothing, I guess. I can see you in a pith helmet and breeches paddling up the Amazon,' laughed Kevin.

They passed an aluminium fishing boat laden with crates of beer and supplies, the people on board giving a hearty wave and thumbs up as the *Roxanne* overtook their chugging outboard. Closer to the shore a wooden dugout canoe with an Amerindian family aboard lazily made its way down river, the father steadying it as the wash from the two boats chopped up the water. Two small children, perched between piles of vegetables, looked at the large boat but didn't return Lennie's big wave.

It was a pleasant trip and Lennie, ever the genial host, talked of how glad he was he'd invested in this 'company craft' and used it to get from Georgetown to his 'week-ender' up the Essequibo River. 'Of course, the company owns the place, unbelievable fishing. Hunting too if you want. Swimming, rafting, hangin' out on the old deck with a rum . . . great place . . . I feel like Hemingway when I go there.'

Matthew and Kevin exchanged a glance but said nothing. Neither looked at the boss. There was clearly going to be a cultural problem with their CEO. He was never one for mixing pleasure and business.

Soon the thick vegetation thinned, and finally they saw the roofs of MacGregor township glinting in the sunlight. Rising above the town were chimney stacks from the calcining kilns where the bauxite crystals were washed and heated to reduce them to white aluminium oxide powder, alumina, that looked like castor sugar.

Johns immediately noted only two of the stacks were in use. A bad sign. 'Production must be on the low side today.'

'Not so much dust about the place, eh?' said Lennie. 'Don't worry, the senior people and expats live up wind.' He laughed. 'There's the stelling, right in front of the company houses and our clubhouse. Give the girls a blast, skipper. Tell 'em to start getting lunch ready, eh?'

The skipper obliged and sounded a long blast on the launch's siren. Johns glanced at his watch. 'I'd like to show Matthew around the plant first. Give us some ideas to discuss over lunch.' Stewart Johns was determined to keep to business.

Matthew was entranced with the beauty of the scene. There was a row of large wooden houses, all painted white and separated by spacious gardens that rolled down to the water and a small jetty—or stelling to use the favoured Dutch word.

'How many expat families are left up here?' asked Matthew.

'The engineer Robbo, that's Andy Robinson, along with the operations manager and their wives. The government brought them in to help run the mine.'

'How do the women find it out here?' asked Johns.

'They like it well enough . . . no choice really, eh?' Lennie laughed heartily, then added, 'Nah, they don't mind it. Go to Georgetown every so often with a driver, servants, nice lifestyle, they find plenty to gossip about'.

Matthew was trying to visualise Stewart Johns' elegant wife, a Sydney North Shore type, in this place. That led him to think of his sister, Madi. She'd love this strange multicultural country, he reflected. She'd really get a buzz from this incredible scenery and the parties too. He decided to write to her that night.

At the wharf there were brief introductions to other company employees and some confusion as transport arrangements were sorted out. They then headed to the mine itself, twenty kilometres away. Here the bauxite ore was blasted out of two deep open cut pits and loaded by a dragline onto old 35-ton haul trucks.

The Australians were glad to see the focal point of their assignment from the various lookouts which gave an overview of the mining operation. But they were each becoming uncomfortable in the oppressive humidity and glaring sun, and Lennie's commentary was more in the jovial tourist style than an informative recitation of facts that would really interest the newcomers.

'And now we have the big bang of welcome,' he announced and waved his hat in the direction of what appeared to be no one in particular. Within seconds one of the mining ledges erupted in a long cloud of ore and dust, and a great rumbling roar of exploding dynamite rolled over them.

'How about that?' shouted Lennie, waving his hat in apparent acknowledgement to the unseen miner controlling the blast. 'As good a bang for the buck as you'll get anywhere,' he shouted and slapped his thigh in obvious enjoyment at the whole thing.

Kevin, always the engineer, whispered to Matthew, 'Probably used far more explosive than was needed. And it didn't move that much ore. The drilling of the blast line probably wasn't right.'

When they reached the plant service area, a smiling Vivian Prashad greeted them. 'I am Prashad. Assistant operations manager. Engineer. University of Georgetown,' he announced to Stewart Johns before Matthew or Kevin had time for a more formal introduction. 'So nice to meet new engineer friends. It is very good that you are helping us achieve world-standard work practices at our mine.' He shook hands with them all, bobbing his head and smiling broadly to show perfect white teeth.

The Indian conducted them around with a more focused commentary than Lennie's and the team left it to Johns to ask the hard questions while they made occasional notes.

To each of them the first problem was obvious. The equipment looked dangerously shoddy. Proudly Prashad pointed out the skilful and inventive ways staff were making repairs to the crumbling equipment.

'Very admirable,' murmured Johns. 'Normally the procedure would be to replace, not repair, such parts.'

Vivian Prashad shrugged a little defensively. 'Oh yes, quite so Mr Johns, quite so. But when there is no money for parts, we use whatever resources we have—and that usually comes down to the men's skills.' He smiled widely. 'You will find that we are very good at making do, as you say in Australia. Yes, making do is important in everything in Guyana.'

Lennie interjected. 'Did you know that, some years back, to keep the locomotives running here, the railways supervisor had the men taught to rewind traction motors. One mechanic left Guyana and migrated to the USA and got a job with Amtrak. There he found they threw away failed traction motors. He showed the foreman how to rewind one and the Amtrak company saved heaps of money. When the foreman asked where he learned to do that, Amtrak sent an executive to Guyana and recruited everyone who could do the job.'

Lennie roared in delight. 'Clever workers, aren't they? Be careful though, they can be a bit too resourceful . . . like burning out cable so they can rip out the copper and sell it.'

They moved into the administrative section, to a room where an accountant was using a calculator and writing entries in a big ledger. Two female clerks were at work at old manual typewriters. In a larger office next door, eight staff sat behind gleaming computers.

The CEO, who had clearly not been in this area before, stared in amazement. 'What the heck is this?'

'My initiative. Putting everything into the system. Hasn't all been programmed, of course, but they're working on it.' Lennie beamed around at the row of computers.

'Why? And why do you still have people writing stuff in ledgers and typing things on 1950's Remingtons?' asked Johns softly.

Lennie was defensive. 'Hey . . . this is Guyana. The power fails regularly, the computers go down, bingo, we lose the lot. And besides, these guys are still mastering the system. But hey, you're getting there, right?' he demanded of the harried and silent employees attached to each machine. They all smiled and nodded emphatically. Kevin itched to sit with any of them and just see how far down the track they really were in understanding the equipment in front of them.

Matthew made another bet with himself. 'My money's on the Remington.'

They were given a quick tour in a company bus that spluttered around the township, but Stewart Johns, his brow furrowed and deep in thought, scarcely seemed to notice the surroundings.

Matthew nudged Kevin as they passed over a bridge with a bold notice forbidding animals to cross 'unless they are working'. Several goats and a cow stood in the centre of the bridge in a confrontation with shouting horn-blowing drivers. The engine of the bus died and the driver jumped out to fiddle under the bonnet at the same time kicking a goat that ambled over in curiosity. Matthew leaned across the aisle to his boss. 'Do you get the impression that they've got a couple of problems?'

The CEO grinned and rolled his eyes in affirmation then mimicked Vivian Prashad. 'Oh yes, but do not worry, Mr Matthew. We are very good at making do.'

Matthew chuckled then became serious. 'Did you see the state of some of the vehicles around the plant? They had to be so cannibalised, I reckon the only original part left on any of them was the number plate.'

They were driven to the Guyminco management housing compound which included a beautiful old guesthouse called Wanika House where they would stay overnight. Wanika House was decorated in what Kevin described as 'Guyana Grand'. It had guest accommodation for visiting dignitaries, social rooms and entertainment facilities. A few staff members were eating in the main dining room but a private dining room had been set for luncheon for 'General Manager Mr Krupuk and Party', according to the inscription on the small stand by the elaborate double wooden doors.

Before lunch Matthew and Kevin were shown upstairs to their rooms, which were tropical colonial-style suites reminiscent of the days of Somerset Maugham. Large rooms with high ceilings swamped the very basic furniture. The floors were polished wood, and the sluggish ceiling fans and louvred window shutters made an attempt to cool the temperature. A wide upper verandah, enclosed by glass louvres, was set with loung-ing furniture and an intricately-woven Amerindian tibisiri mat.

Matthew looked out to the river, just fifty metres away. Huge mango and palm trees dotted the lawn that ran to the glassy water. The water level had dropped, leaving muddy exposed banks. A voice behind him fol-lowed his train of thought.

'Big rains and high tides, de river flow all over de grass, round de house . . .'

Matthew turned and smiled at the plump black African woman in a starched white uniform holding a large silver teapot. 'Thank you for the explanation. You one of the locals?'

'Yeah, I bin born here. My daddy work on the river boats. Dem were days, eh. Good days.'

'And now?'

'Bad days at the mine some years ago. Every place in Guyana, eh? Now tings still not good. Very quiet. Maybe they close down, yeah? Oh my, de parties dey used t'give here. Oh my.' She chuckled.

'My name's Matthew Wright. I'll be staying up here off and on I expect.'

'I be Shanti. You tell me any ting you want, I get for yo.'

Matthew gave her a smile. 'Many thanks.' He glanced across the river. 'What's out there, past the town? Can one go walking or exploring in the bush?'

She pursed her lips. 'Now why you wanta go and do dat for, eh? You stick to the river. More nice. More safe. Over dere be jumbis. Big moon coming tonight, not safe for walking.'

'Well, I wasn't thinking of going walking in the bush this evening actually . . .'

Shanti peered through the louvres. 'This bad time of year, rains, big moon and dis night de jumbi walks. You keep dem windows shut in yo room. Put on de air-conditioning.'

'Oh no, the fans are fine. I like the fresh air. Now Shanti, what are jumbis?'

'Dem be bad spirits . . . like ghosts. Come in many types. No good to meet a jumbi.' She shivered at the thought. 'I got to take dis silver down for lunch.' She turned back to him at the stairs. 'Yo take care tonight.'

Matthew raised the subject of jumbis towards the end of the meal and Lennie threw back his head. 'They're a

56

superstitious bunch. Man, oh man, can they bring up a story to get 'em out of doing something. But you hear some weird stories about spirits, their sort of African voodoo, I guess. But they certainly seem to believe it.'

That night the Australians met Stewart Johns at his house to discuss their takeover of the mine. 'It's a damn shame, good people, a good resource, a good opportunity. But it's one helluva mess, right?' The CEO lapsed into one of his famous conference silences. It was a signal for the others to volunteer statements.

'From a technical standpoint we can do it, but the cost will be horrendous,' Kevin said bluntly.

'And can we sell it to cover the cost?' added Matthew.

Johns didn't answer right away but after a thoughtful pause said, 'I believe so. AusGeo has never been known to walk away from a challenge, but obviously it would put the company in jeopardy if we took on too many lost causes like this. However, I think we can make Guyminco a reasonably viable proposition for privatisation in twelve months. We can begin by instilling a climate of confidence that's sadly lacking at the moment.' He leaned forward, elbows on the table. 'Despite the government raping the whole operation financially, the current staff have done well given the lack of cash, spare parts, management back-up and overall support. But it can't continue. They are facing six minutes to shut down,' he concluded.

'I suppose they all know that,' said Kevin.

'This is their future. The investment climate in Guyana is healthier now than it has been for a long time. If the people of this country want to get on their feet, then getting this plant running to full capacity and making a profit will be a signal to the government, the people and the rest of the world that there's a new season starting here.'

He looked at Matthew and Kevin, and the men nodded. If the CEO said it could be done, they'd do it, despite their reservations. That's why they had stuck with AusGeo even when other opportunities presented themselves. Johns was an inspirational leader. They loved working for him because it often meant achieving the impossible.

'Right then. We'll put our thoughts and solutions into a detailed plan of action over the next few weeks. You each know the area you're to focus on. Get to it, men. I'll hold the usual daily whinge session at 4.30 Monday to Saturday. Sunday, you're free.'

Kevin and Matthew strolled across the lawns in bright moonlight back to Wanika House. 'I don't envy you drumming up a marketing campaign,' said Kevin.

'Got to have a much stronger product to sell first. They've lost a lot of ground, market wise, I agree.'

They went quietly upstairs, had a nightcap together on the verandah and went into their rooms. Matthew noticed the bed was turned down, the windows shut tightly, the air-conditioner blasting cold air into the room. He turned it off, opened the louvres, switched off the light and, ignoring the mosquito net, fell into bed. He hadn't noticed that the mosquitoes were bad and anyway he felt claustrophobic under a thick net.

He awoke during the night to a pleasant breeze on his face. But he felt uncomfortable. He stirred and rolled on his side and immediately recoiled and leapt up at the knowledge some creature was on him. Matthew bashed and slapped at his head. Flapping and scratching had suddenly brought him wide awake and he beat something off his neck and reached for the light. The sight of blood on the pillow and more running down the white

T-shirt he was wearing, shocked him. He'd felt nothing. A spider, a snake, what . . . he went cold as he looked on the floor beside the bed where a small stunned bat lay, one of its wings beating feebly. For a moment it looked soft and innocuous until he saw the sharp nose, the long teeth, and he shuddered at the realisation it was a vampire bat. He put his hand to his neck and felt the blood trickling in a steady stream. God, how much blood had he lost, he wondered. He felt weak, was it from loss of blood or the horror of how he'd lost it?

Still holding his fingers pressed against the puncture wound, he went out onto the enclosed verandah, but knew waking Kevin wouldn't help him. He headed downstairs and went through the lounge and dining room and into the large kitchen. In the moonlight he could see bulky appliances, a refrigerator, a long table and free-standing work bench. He opened the fridge and groped for the tall jug of boiled water, opening cupboards to find a glass. He gulped down the water, refilling the tumbler several times and then pulled open two folding doors that revealed the pantry. Maybe there was a Red Cross kit in here, though what the hell did one put on a vampire bite?

He was fumbling in the dimness, moving large cans about when the kitchen light snapped on and Shanti, in a faded floral wrapper, stood in the doorway, staring at him in surprise.

'Yo still hungry, Mr Matthew?'

Then as she saw the blood over him, she gasped. 'Oh my, oh my Lordy. What happen to yo?'

Matthew slumped into one of the chairs around the table. 'Bat bit me. A blood sucker . . . vampire thing. Do they have diseases?'

'Dey no good, no good. You bleed em out long time,

Mr Matthew. Maybe is good we go to obeah man. Take on yo clothes and we go dere, right now. He fix you up good.'

'Now? Is he a doctor? Is it far? How do we get there?'

'Yo quit yo talking and get you ready. Yes, we go dere, right now.' Shanti bustled, almost talking to herself as she hurried back to her room to dress.

Matthew felt his neck. It was still sticky and oozing blood. He was too tired to argue. He trudged upstairs, pulled on his jeans and a cotton shirt, throwing the blood-stained T-shirt on the bed.

They walked swiftly through the grounds and along the drive to the dirt road that led into the township. 'It not be far,' said Shanti.

'Who is it again we're seeing?' asked Matthew, suddenly aware of how crazy the situation seemed. Why was he following the solid shape of the housekeeper through bright moonlight at some ungodly hour? He'd gone to bed close to midnight, it must be about 2 am, thought Matthew. He'd left his watch by the washbasin in his bathroom.

Shanti turned into a lane beside darkened wooden shacks, partly screened by banana trees and straggly palms. 'We see Pundit Silk, he good Indian obeah man.'

'What's an obeah man?' It seemed to Matthew he had heard stories about them at the Krupuks' party, but now couldn't recall what exactly.

'He be spirit doctor. Take out bad blood and spells from the beast dat bite you.'

Matthew stopped suddenly. 'Wait a minute, you mean he's like a witchdoctor? Not a doctor-doctor?'

'He be doctor.' Shanti took his arm and urged him

forward. 'You no fret yoself now. You must do dis or you get sick. Maybe die.'

'From what exactly? Rabies?'

Shanti looked at him in exasperation, pointing to his bleeding neck. 'You have bad spirit put in you, maybe someone put spell on you. Maybe mean for someone else. But you got it, boy. You fix 'im up, Pundit fix you up. True, true.'

'Isn't there a western, a European doctor in the town?' asked Matthew miserably, as he continued to follow Shanti.

She stopped outside a simple wooden cottage. 'You wait, I tell Silk we is here.'

Matthew watched her go to the house and open the door. There was a murmur of voices and a dim light flowered inside. Shanti appeared in the front yard. 'Come, Mister Matthew. Silk be here. He fix you. He say he knowed dere would be someone here tonight.'

'Is that so.' Matthew felt defeated and figured he'd go along with this unless it got really weird. He walked into the house.

He couldn't see much because it was dark, then Shanti took his arm and they went into a room where a lantern burned. A tall thin man, who looked to be in his sixties, stood before them. He was clean shaven though his hair was long and he wore what at first seemed to be pyjamas but Matthew then realised was a long, loose, collarless shirt over baggy cotton pants. He had an imposing air, he held himself very straight and he gestured to Matthew to be seated as though receiving guests in a well-to-do establishment. His poise and confidence inspired a sense of trust and Matthew sat on the stool he indicated. 'I am Silk. Pundit Silk. So, you have been attacked. This is not good. But have no fear, Silk will attend to you.'

He leaned forward and began examining Matthew, probing the glands in his neck, peering at the small wound. He was as professional as a western medical practitioner. He directed Shanti to light candles while he reached for a bowl partly filled with water. With a clean square of cloth, he began to cleanse the wound. Matthew started to relax slightly.

'Is it infected? What do these creatures carry? I guess I shouldn't have opened the windows.'

Silk raised a hand to still Matthew's talk. 'They be after you. Now, first we stop the blood.'

In the additional light from the candles lit by Shanti, Matthew saw an array of small jars and pots and dried grasses. Silk began painting a variety of creams and oils across the puncture marks on Matthew's neck. The smells were strange and Matthew closed his eyes asking, 'What's that, what's that one?'

In a slightly singsong voice, Silk reeled them off. 'White lavender oil, dragon's blood, indigo blue, bergamot, oil of seven planets. Now you hold these musk leaves while I say the prayers.'

'Oh, here it comes,' thought Matthew. But he sat still because after an initial flush of heat, his neck felt looser, the swelling and tightness seemed to have lessened. He supposed this was some sort of herbal remedy. But within minutes he felt sleepy, and he struggled to open his eyes. He was aware Silk was saying something about the Book of Moses, psalm 29, casting out evil spirits and then he heard no more.

Kevin arose early after a restless night. He was not normally a dawn riser, but he padded out onto the verandah and, noticing Matthew's door open, stuck his head inside.

'Matthew?'

Seeing the room empty he was about to turn away but something caught his eye. He went to the bed and picked up the bloodied T-shirt. 'Matthew . . .?' He slammed into the bathroom, finding it empty but noting the blood in the sink and a bloodied towel. 'Jesus, what's happened . . .' he ran from the room.

In a few minutes a wide-eyed houseman and one of the maids stood gazing about Matthew's room. 'We no hear nothin', chief.'

'I'd better call Stewart Johns . . .'

The houseman stooped by the bed. 'Oh ma Lordy, dis be de devil. He bin bit.'

'What?' Kevin spun around as the African man pointed at the floor. He hurried to his side. 'What, what are you saying?'

'Dere, chief. De devil bat.'

'My God, is it a vampire bat?'

Matthew opened his eyes to discover he was lying on a small bed and the daylight was bright outside. He sat bolt upright, his hand going to his neck. There was a neat white cotton square taped in place. He suddenly felt stronger and ravenously hungry.

As soon as his feet hit the floor a smiling Shanti appeared in the room. 'You all better now, me tinks, eh?'

'God, what time is it? What happened?'

'Silk said spirits suck away yo blood, put in bad tings. Silk take dem out. He put in good tings. He wash you with dead water and use de medicine and say de prayers. Now you good Guyanese, go to obeah man, eh?'

'I guess so. I feel better, that's for sure. What's dead water, Shanti?'

She busied herself and didn't look at him but answered matter of factly. 'Water dey wash dead people with.'

A shiver of revulsion went through Matthew and his stomach turned over but he refused to dwell on this. 'I'd better get back to Wanika House before anyone panics.'

'I got to do de breakfast, come, we go. You say farewell to Silk 'nother time. He busy.'

'Don't I have to pay him something?'

'Yeah, Mister Matthew. Just little bit. You got American dollar?'

'No. Now only Guyanese money.'

Shanti laughed. 'Lotta Guyanese money no buy too much, eh? You give him ten dollars. Silk say you easy one.'

Matthew reached into the hip pocket of his jeans to pull out his wallet and discovered a small pouch tucked in beside it. He turned over the little leather bag. 'What's this?' He lifted it up to open it. 'God, it smells awful.'

'Dat be yo talisman. Obeah man say you keep it by you. Keep you safe.'

'No more bat bites, eh?' Matthew was slightly bemused at the neatly stitched waterproof pouch. He opened it to find a scrap of paper with Hindi characters written on it and a sliver of strong-smelling gum resin.

'Asafoetida . . . smell bad but keep evil spirits away,' explained Shanti.

'And possibly friends too.' Matthew grinned and slid the little bag back in his pocket, pulled out ten dollars and left it on the table by a candle and fresh flower.

They strolled back along the little road now active with early morning traffic. Matthew pondered at the difference between walking this unknown path at night, fearful and faint, and now in sunlight, feeling extraordinarily well and cheerful.

They walked down the drive and Matthew delighted in the scarlet flowers on a tree, the grand white Wanika House, the greenness of the lawns and the vista of the river behind. Life felt good. He liked this place, this country. He was overwhelmed with a sense of well-being and he decided he would persuade Madison to come out here and join him.

'What's for breakfast, Shanti? I'm starving.'

At that moment a shout rang out. 'There he is! Christ, Matthew, what happened to you?' Kevin came sprinting towards him. Several other men appeared around the guesthouse and at windows that faced the front drive.

'Oh God, you're all looking for me. Sorry.'

'At first we thought you'd been murdered. Then we saw the bat and thought you might be bleeding to death or fallen in the river. The groundsman started telling us these bloody horror stories.'

Johns joined them. 'You gave us a bit of a fright, Matthew. You look all right. Where did you go? I tried to find the local doctor in case you'd tried to get medical attention.'

'Is there a regular doctor here?'

'Not full-time.'

'Shanti took me to the obeah man. Pundit Silk. I guess I'd lost more blood than I thought. I passed out, I think. But I'm fine now.'

'Are you sure?' Johns glanced at Shanti going into the kitchen entrance of the house. 'These magic men can be a bit . . . dubious.'

'What did he do to you? Smells a bit off.' Kevin peered at Matthew's neck dressing.

Matthew was reluctant to pass on too much of what happened. It now seemed like a strange dream. He pulled the cotton bandage to one side showing the bites on his

65

neck, now just slightly red. 'It was hard to stop the bleeding. They must use something to help the blood coagulate. I'll make sure I shut the windows tonight.'

'They're not common. It was a million to one chance. Don't let it put you off the place,' said Johns.

'Funny thing is, it hasn't. In fact, I feel like I'm on some sort of high. Thrilled to be here, can't wait to get involved in the rich tapestry of Guyana . . .'

They all laughed and headed towards the dining room.

'That toast and bacon smells good,' declared Kevin.

'I'll just have a quick shower and be right with you,' said Matthew.

Standing under the hot water was a relief, despite the erratic pressure. Matthew wanted to wash away the dead water and whatever else was on his skin. But his sense of euphoria didn't fade and he couldn't shake the idea that Guyana was going to be a very significant experience in his life.

FOUR

It was a fat envelope and Madison studied the large bright Guyanese stamps. One was a purple orchid—*Cattleya violacea, Queen of the orchids* was printed in small letters. The other stamp was a strange bird—*Opisthocomus hoatzin (Canje Pheasant) National Bird of Guyana*—which looked like a prehistoric winged reptile. The small coloured squares gave her a feeling of anticipation and excitement. Savouring the delight to come, she slid the unopened envelope into her handbag. Her brother's letter would be a treat to have with a cappuccino.

She felt utterly wicked as she browsed through dress shops debating whether to buy a new suit for work. Yet here she was for the first time she could remember, taking a 'sickie', a day off work for no good reason. Well, she did have a reason, even if it was vague and would not please her boss or the doctor. She was unsettled. It wasn't tiredness or depression or a feeling of not coping. It was an uncomfortable sense that life had no essence to it. No real meaning. She was going through the motions.

As if reflecting her apathy, none of the clothes pleased her though there were some attractive executive outfits amongst them. They looked good on her but she couldn't work up enough enthusiasm to buy one, to the barely disguised frustration of the salesperson. Then her eye was caught by a display in a resort wear shop. A plaster mannequin, high cheekbones, impossibly thin lanky body, stood poised in khaki shorts, a linen shirt and cotton vest buried under flaps and pockets, leopard print belt and cotton socks rolled over canvas boots. From under a stiff pith helmet her sightless eyes stared through the plate glass, across busy Military Road on Sydney's North Shore, to some far off jungle horizon.

Madison paused, strangely held by the slightly absurd display, then she turned away and headed for the nearest coffee bar conscious of an urgent need to read her brother's letter.

She had to smother her laughter at the description of the party and was horrified by Matthew's account of the vampire incident. She read slowly, savouring each anecdote and his assessment of the country.

'. . . *There are massive problems here, not just in our area but within the country as a whole. The bureaucratic frustrations are endless and some basic consumer goods are unavailable. But the people are incredibly warm and hospitable and the mix of races and cultures is colourful. What intrigues me most is the vast interior. I've seen only a little of it but it's very beautiful. It's a pity it's not more* accessible. Before I leave I will definitely take a few trips. The Kaieteur Falls—five times the drop of Niagara mind you—is an absolute must.

Madi, I do wish so much you were here to share some of this. I've been in some exotic places in the world as you know, but this place has something special. It's so different in every way imaginable. It casts a spell. It would be good for you and it's about as far away as you can get from Sydney! I repeat—make a move, sis! Mum and Dad are still fit and they've settled into their new business on the Gold Coast. They're doing well without us.

I know your skills and talents, and you could climb further up the corporate ladder at your hotel but you need to get into the international field. Get out and play in the big league, give London or Europe a shot. I know you can make it, give yourself the chance to prove yourself to yourself, Madi. Nuff said, I won't nag you again. But I'll be disappointed if you chicken out. You were always the one who dared me to do things. But at least consider coming here to visit me. Hang the cost, you wanted a break and there are NO swish joints and not a gold chain, white shoe, designer swimsuit or sunglasses in sight. Hey, I take back the gold chain bit, I was thinking of those dreadful Queensland resort developers. Here they're worn by great black heavyweights who have so much gold about their bodies, the gold rope around the neck is almost a minor accessory. Haven't sussed out these bods yet . . . just seen them from the safety of the company car.

Anyway, as I said at the start, the big news is AusGeo has landed the management contract to whip the bauxite mine into some sort of order so the Guyanese can privatise it and earn some money. God knows they need it. Give Mum and Dad a hug next time you go up and I expect

*news of your imminent arrival here. By the way, the phone
works most of the time, but the fax is very erratic. Pigeon
post might be more reliable. Luv-ya-lots . . .'*

Madison carefully refolded her brother's letter and
headed resolutely back along the crowded footpath.
Without hesitating she walked into the resort wear shop
and pointed to the model in the window. 'I would like to
buy that outfit. Size ten please.'

'The safari set? Very well, but I'm sorry the hat is just
a prop, it's not for sale,' said the assistant who was
dressed in a gold and silver painted sweatshirt.

'Never mind, I'll get my own hat,' grinned Madison.
'I'm sure I'll find one in the wilds of Guyana somewhere.'

The woman nodded sagely. 'Oh, you must have a
decent hat in Ghana, that African sun . . . ferocious . . .'

'It's Guyana, actually,' began Madison but seeing the
blank stare from the saleswoman, nodded in agreement.
'Yes, I'm sure I'll find something suitable.'

A short time later she was standing outside the shop,
bags in hand. The clothes fitted, the boots fitted, and
they'd felt and looked good. Madison glanced up and
down the street.

'Guess I'd better find a travel agent.' There was one
across the road and as she waited for the lights at the
pedestrian crossing, she wondered if she should wear this
new outfit to the office when she announced she was
quitting.

She had reached this decision so easily, without even
thinking about it. Whatever the reason it felt right. A
sense of recklessness that she found exhilarating swept
over her.

*

Roger George, looking every inch the suave hotel general manager smoothed his Jerry Garcia tie, a small gesture towards frivolity and flamboyance that relieved the conservative starkness of the pinstripe Zegna suit. 'My dear Madison, I am very distressed about your decision—on one hand. On the other, I have to say I am not surprised. You know your talents and abilities as well as we do and I'm sure you'll have offers to choose from. It's the nature of the hotel industry to wish to circulate to the, shall we say, more prestigious or challenging hotels in a network.'

'Challenge. That's what I'm after. Definitely. A challenge. I haven't the language skills for the Georges Cinq,' she gave a teasing smile in case he thought she was seriously considering the best hotel in Paris, 'but I would like to see what I can achieve in, say, one of the boutique hotels in the UK or Asia.'

'Aren't we challenging enough for you?' He lifted an amused eyebrow. 'Seriously, Madison, I'm sorry to lose you because you've done an excellent job here. You've pulled off some spectacular events and done more than I ever anticipated could be done in the marketing of this hotel. You have a big future ahead of you and it is natural that you wish to spread your wings. I will of course be happy to recommend you to our hotels abroad.'

Madison stared at him, wondering why no one in the hotel administration had ever bothered to tell her before that she was this good. Or was it just smooth talk to ease her way out the door?

'What if I change my mind? Would you take me back on board?'

His demeanour remained unruffled. 'If there is a slot here, we will always take you on, Madison. You have proved yourself.'

That was smooth, thought Madison. He doesn't say

what slot might be available. He could take me back in the housekeeping department and not be breaking his word. She shuddered, remembering the week she'd spent working in various sections of the hotel. Changing sheets had not thrilled her.

'Just testing,' she grinned and then became serious. 'I intend to break through the plastic veneer of front of house and rise above the chandeliers to the walnut doors and cedar halls of senior management. I intend to run the place one day.'

'Run this place?' For the first time the unflappable Roger George looked somewhat taken aback. 'You plan on managing a large hotel like this . . . well, perhaps in some Third World country . . .' He gathered himself and gave her one of his patronising smiles. 'That's the spirit, think big and who knows where you might end up.'

Madison rose. 'I'll end up at the top, Roger. The top is the only place I plan to go.' She stretched out a hand. 'Goodbye, and thank you.'

'Thank you, Madison. And good luck. Wherever you end up.'

'Thanks, Roger. I'll always keep a slot for you too.'

She left the wood-panelled office pleased she'd got in the last word. Petty it may have been, but he'd annoyed her. She wondered why she'd always felt intimidated by the GM's private school old boy charm. Still, he had given her a glowing reference and contacts to look up in England and Singapore.

Madi's colleagues from the hotel took her to dinner at the end of the week. They went to a Paraguayan restaurant where great slabs of lamb were hacked from a carcass on the asado barbecue pit and served with potatoes and spicy sauce. As the meal wore on, carafes of red wine were passed up and down the table. Madi was initially amused at the envy of her bold move, and the comments by her workmates that it was just what they expected of her.

'You have "star" written all over you. You're going to be big, be a big success, Madi,' said Frank the accountant.

'You're going to be swinging from the chandeliers, not just crashing through the glass ceiling,' said Louise from personnel. 'We all knew you'd be the one.'

'Be the what?' said Madi feeling rather confused. She'd dismissed earlier compliments as the wine talking, but now she sensed these people she'd worked with for five years knew something about her that she didn't.

'Typical Madi, so modest. You're going to be a *huge* success. *Huge.* You've all the right ingredients. You just walk into a room and people pay attention to you. It's like actors. Some have it, some don't.'

'Hope you'll give us a job when you're running a hotel chain in Europe or America,' added Tony who ran the kitchen staff.

Madi laughed it all off. However, that night as she lay in bed and thought about what they had said, she felt a slow resentment build up inside her. She did have a lot of fun qualities and career skills. Other people thought so too. Yet all the while she'd been married to Geoff, he had been telling her she was a sham. Faking her way through a job beyond her capabilities.

Whenever she'd told him of a marketing or promotional plan she was about to propose for the hotel, he'd sneer. 'And whose idea did you borrow for that?' And when she'd told him about the successful campaigns and events which she'd created and developed, he'd doubted her. 'Yeah, you and how many others thought of it? You can't fool me, Madi. I know you better than anyone. You're going to fall, fall flat on your face. You'll be found out one day.'

And as tears sprang to her eyes, he'd turned away looking pleased with himself. Finally she'd say, 'Find out what? What am I supposed to have done? Why don't you believe me?'

Now she was appalled that for so long she'd caved in to the assault of his verbal abuse. It had taken a counsellor to make her realise how he'd used her to counter his own inadequacies. As Matthew had said, it somehow empowered him to destroy a person like her who was an achiever, a decent and good person. Dr Geoffrey Churchill had embarked on a career as an arts administrator, after switching from academia at the University of Sydney where he'd completed his PhD and lectured in fine arts. Right from the start he'd found it hard to adjust to life outside the protective cloisters of the university. They'd met at a tennis club and looking back now, tennis was probably the most they'd ever had in common. He had courted her with a serious itinerary of opera and art gallery visits. Then he'd expounded at length on the background and finer points of the artists and performances in what he'd described as her introduction to the 'better facets of culture'.

Madi knew his knowledge far exceeded hers, though she found this assumption of his role as teacher and hers as student a little condescending. But she didn't let it show because he took such pleasure in teaching her. He also gently criticised her dress sense and suggested she wear her hair pinned up in a smart French roll rather than the casual style she favoured. At first she enjoyed being 'looked after', even when he took to going shopping with her to choose her clothes. He also ran the finances and made decisions on where they should go for holidays.

Madi had been attracted to his caring, nurturing attitude, so like her father and brother. He was an attractive man who was admired by other women, and she suspected he had an adoring ring of female students who found their charming and erudite lecturer very appealing.

In those first months Madi had tried to change him, persuading him to go on picnics and hikes. He'd gone along with an air of indulging her rather than sharing the experience. He'd stopped such 'frivolous' activities within months after their wedding. At the same time he began to spend long hours at his new job. In leisure time at home, he'd play his treasured collection of classical CDs and watch obscure foreign films. They each became absorbed in their own interests. As time went on, she sensed he suffered low self-esteem because of his career demons, perceived or real. But in the privacy of their marriage, he refused to discuss his problems. Instead, he would assert himself over her and suck the energy out of her. Then he'd sail out to face the challenge of another day.

After a night of insults, Madi was left drained and emotionally wrung out. She cried often in the car on the way to work, wondering what had happened to the dreams that had led her in a frenzied dash to the altar six years earlier. But once she drove into the dark pit of the underground garage beneath the hotel, she'd blot her eyes, take a deep breath, and by the time she reached her office she'd have a cheery smile for all.

Each morning in the shower, Madi would stand and let the hot needles of spray bounce off her neck and shoulders and wonder what she was doing with her life. Then one morning she got up and decided it was time to go. Walk out the door. She did what she did every morning. She ironed his shirt and hung it on the bedroom door knob. She squeezed fresh orange juice and left it by the coffee pot while he was in the shower. She dressed carefully and opened the bathroom door and stood there holding her briefcase and an overnight bag. 'I'm going, Geoff.'

'So?' He peered through the misty glass. 'You have some flash meeting on, some plush lunch, some marketing do?' His voice was critical, sneering. 'Not like the rest of us hoi polloi who grab a sandwich or eat in a coffee shop.'

'You told me you'd joined Tatt's Club. Oh never mind, it doesn't matter any more. I'm going.'

'So? Go. Or are you telling me you won't be home till late . . . some function or other so I should go ahead and eat, is that the reason for this touching farewell?'

'Geoff, I'm going. For good. Leaving you. I'll stay tonight at the hotel and we can talk about it tomorrow.'

She quietly closed the door and took a deep breath. And another, realising she was close to hyperventilating.

She was halfway down the hall when the bathroom door was slammed open. He grabbed her shoulder and spun her round. 'Oh no you don't. You don't walk out of here after a comment like that. Just what do you mean?'

'What I said. I'm leaving you.' She spoke in a tired, resigned voice, avoiding looking at the dripping, furious man clutching a towel.

'Like hell you are. What for? If you're having it away with someone else, fuck you. Two can play at that game. Don't think for one minute you'll get out of this lightly. You won't do this to me.'

'There's no one else, Geoffrey. We're miserable. Have been for ages. Why go on like this? I can't see things changing.'

'You're the miserable one.' He jabbed a finger in her shoulder. 'You're the one who needs to change.'

It suddenly struck Madi he was right. She needed to change, to get back to how she used to be, and the way to do that was to make a fresh start. In a flash of clarity, she saw there was no way forward together. This relationship was at an end. Had been for years. She looked at him without expression. 'It's too late for us, let's face it.'

He dropped an arm about her shoulders. 'Hey Madi, you're just having a bad time right now. If you want to get counselling, I'll help you. It'll be all right, don't go to pieces.'

Madi squirmed away from his arm, stunned to discover his touch made her recoil. Taking another step towards the stair, she said quietly, 'I'm not going to pieces, Geoff. I feel very calm about this. It's sad, I'm sorry, but it's over'.

'You're a bitch, Madi. A screwed-up bitch. You won't get a bloody penny out of me,' he shouted at her as she went down the stairs.

'It's *our* money and I don't want your money. And I've never felt less screwed up in my whole life,' she called back.

He leaned over the banister and shouted a parting shot. 'You're sick in the head, oh yes you are. You're just like your mother. She's never even pretended she liked me. I bet she put you up to this. Other women aren't like you. Believe me, I know. Don't think there aren't plenty of women who will jump into your place in bed.'

Madi reached for the front doorknob. 'Have them lined up, do you?'

'Yes! As a matter of fact I do. And have had for some time. You're not the only one who works late at the office, fucking on the floor!'

Madi pulled the door shut, too shocked and hurt to slam it in anger. Moisture stung her eyes as she got in the car, backing it out of the driveway by habit. But within a block she pulled over and burst into tears. It hit her for the first time that her husband had been sleeping with other women. Too many small incidents came to mind which she had chosen to ignore over the past few years. The late nights, the business trips away for a weekend. Phone calls where someone had either hung up or a girl had asked for Geoffrey and after a Yes–No conversation he'd dismissed it as a query from a girl at the office. Now it seemed so obvious. What a fool she'd been to put up with him for so long. But what hurt most was his assumption that she had been having an affair.

It was true she had longed for someone in her life. Someone she could cuddle and laugh with, who made her feel happy, who told her how clever and wonderful she was, someone to enjoy sex with. Their sex life had dwindled to desultory Sunday morning interludes. She was left unsatisfied and lonely as he'd leapt from bed and gone off on his newly acquired mountain bike. They never kissed or talked during sex and for the past six months he hadn't touched her. When she'd made advances he'd turned away. As Madi continued on her drive to the city, a slow anger took the place of self-pity and fuelled her conviction that she was doing the right thing.

The twelve months formal separation had been a nightmare. The arguments, the accusations, the hassles over the property settlement. At first he'd tried to be civil and placatory and said he'd handle everything with their family solicitor. But Madi quickly realised she was being treated as the cast-off incapable female and so she'd hired her own lawyer, pleased at how angry it had made Geoffrey. She'd always overlooked his cautious and careful ways with money, realising now he was downright mean. With no children things had been fairly straightforward, the house sold, profits split, possessions shared, although all with acrimony. He'd continued to try to weasel advantages but she'd stood her ground, finally producing evidence of her income, her contributions to joint expenses showing she'd paid more of the household bills while he had spent money on personal indulgences. He'd finally backed down and Madi enjoyed a moment or two of satisfaction for having won a round where he would normally have expected her to cave in to his emotional bullying.

She found it hard being on her own again even though she recognised she was a different person to the girl who'd married so young. But something told her that once over this bumpy patch her life would improve and she'd fly like an eagle. She hadn't experienced that soaring lift-off yet, but she was learning to like herself, enjoying her own company. She'd been incredibly lonely outside working hours sometimes, but now . . . having made the decision to leave the safety and security of her job and fly away to Guyana, even if into the protection of her brother, she felt she was on her way to a new life at last.

The United 747-400 soared into the clear blue sky over Sydney, banking to the east to give a spectacular view of the harbour. Then it slowly climbed to thirty-seven thousand feet for the nonstop flight to Los Angeles. In LA, Madison sat in the Red Carpet Lounge for an hour enjoying a Californian chardonnay and the latest US magazines before boarding a United 767 to Miami.

After disembarking, she found the Guyana Airways flight to Georgetown had been delayed till the following day. The Guyanese girl at the desk was charming but could only offer a smile and a shrug, pointing out it was not unusual. Her relaxed manner gave Madison an inkling that this attitude might reflect the Guyanese approach to life in general. She checked into an airport hotel and attempted to phone Matthew in Georgetown. There was no answer at his house, though the phone made such a strange sound she wasn't sure if it was working or not. She fell across the double bed and slept for a few hours.

Later she showered, pulled on a pair of jeans and a white T-shirt and tried again, unsuccessfully, to reach Matthew. Finally she rang the mine number he'd given her and was relieved when he came on the line. Quickly she explained she was on tomorrow night's flight.

'I'm glad you caught me, Madi. I have a problem out here and can't get back into town. But a friend I've made here is going to meet you. I'll get onto him with your flight details right away. His name is Connor Bain and he's an expat Aussie who's thrilled to have more Australians here.'

'What was his name? Spell it.'

'C-o-n-n-o-r. Got that?'

'Yes. Unusual name.'

'He'll take you to the house and I'll be back the next day. Just rest up. Really sorry about this, but I'm so glad you're on the way.'

Madi tried to hide the disappointment that her brother wouldn't be at the airport. 'How will I know this guy?'

'Don't worry, he'll find you, I gave him a photo of you. Besides, you'll probably be the only blonde in the entire country!' The line crackled and dropped out for an instant then Matthew was back shouting over the phone. 'So don't worry, Connor will look after you.'

'What if something happens, what if the plane is late or delayed again?'

'He'll wait. This line is bad. Take care, see you soon. Luv ya.'

'Bye, Matt.'

Madi hung up. She was a seasoned traveller but for the first time she knew she was flying into something way beyond her experience. The casual airline staff and appalling phone line did not create a very appealing first impression.

She ate in the rooftop restaurant looking over hotels, a shopping mall and looming aircraft. In the distance, the city of Miami did not call to her. She scanned the menu offering Tex Mex, Surf and Turf, and a variety of chilliburgers, and felt a depression settling over her. This was not how she imagined her grand adventure would start. Then she caught herself and wondered why she'd thought of this trip as a grand adventure. She was going to see her brother who happened to be in a Caribbean/South American backwater of a country that sounded weird and had something of a turbulent history.

She ordered an omelette and salad and a glass of wine as the sunset-streaked sky faded to murky twilight and she thought about travelling. She'd always loved travel books. Best of all she loved travel books written by lady travellers of the Victorian era. She'd found her first intrepid lady traveller book one Saturday when browsing in a secondhand bookshop. Since then she'd built up quite a collection.

Her hobby had provided a pleasant diversion while Geoff played his CDs, reducing the need for conversation which invariably turned to conflict. Her friends made fun of this literary indulgence but they also enjoyed hearing occasional anecdotes gleaned from the writings of women like Beatrice Grimshaw in Papua New Guinea, Jeanne Bare who disguised herself as a young man and went to sea in the eighteenth century with French botanist Philibert de Commerson, the adventures and writings of Mary Kingsley, Isak Dinesen, Violet Cressy-Marcks.

These women had inspired in Madison a passion to travel to exotic places. She'd once told Matthew she'd been born a century too late and would have made a wonderful intrepid lady traveller discovering lost Egyptian tombs, chasing butterflies up the Amazon or studying stone age tribes in inaccessible jungles and deserts. To be sitting in an airport Holiday Inn on the edge of Miami wasn't quite the same. Still a journey has to begin somewhere, she rationalised. And the important journeys she had already made in her life had almost always begun tremulously.

She recalled the weak-kneed walk to her car the day she'd closed the door on her marriage and the nervous introspection she'd felt the next day while wandering along Manly Beach. At first, she wished she'd taken the path out of her marriage earlier. But then she'd adopted the Buddhist approach of seeing each experience as a process without necessarily having a beginning or end. 'Go with the flow,' as her mother had said when they'd discussed what she should do after she left Geoff. She decided this was the attitude needed now—she must let herself go. Madi relaxed at last and ordered a second glass of chardonnay.

The flight was not one of her most enjoyable. Crammed between two large Jamaican men, who talked across her in accents thick with reggae rhythm and peppered with 'man' and 'yo', Madison slunk down, closed her eyes and slept till they touched down in Trinidad. As the men groped for bags and hats, they gave her wide smiles.

'Yo weren't very good company, Mary.'

'Still, it was nice sleepin' with yo,' quipped the other.

Madison couldn't help smiling back at them.

The stopover was only forty-five minutes and as any view had disappeared under the dark sky, Madison decided to stay in her seat.

The stewards, slim, dark and handsome, exuded a warm charm. Madison was struck by their affectionate physicality. They touched their passengers—discreetly and inoffensively—patting an arm, gently adjusting a head on a cushion, and when conferring with a stewardess they would give her arm a friendly squeeze or touch her hand to make a point. It was such a refreshing change from the slick professionalism that ran off most airline staff and made you feel you were made of plastic, as they waved their pots with the litany . . .'Tea? Coffee?' There was a genuine warmth and naturalness about these men that made up for the dried bread roll snack and melting chocolate bar.

On the intercom before takeoff, the pilot advised the flight was on time. Arrival at Timehri airport, Georgetown, Guyana, would be approximately 10 pm.

An hour after the plane landed, Madison wished she'd never thought of coming to Guyana. Straight off she could see that frustration, irritation and discomfort lay ahead of her. She was standing in a straggling line with forty other tired passengers in a hot tin shed with a single fan slowly churning as rain pummelled on the roof.

She eyed the one immigration official with growing annoyance. He stood secure behind his podium apparently enjoying the knowledge that he represented Authority and Power, while in front of the wooden counter everyone waited for him to pass judgement. He took each passport in his fingertips and slowly turned page after page, looking at every stamp ever entered there. Occasionally he glanced up at the cowering owner of the little book before languorously turning its pages again to find a suitable blank space. With closed fist he smoothed the page open so it stayed flat. He lifted the Official Rubber Stamp, checked its details in case they had miraculously changed in the past few minutes, pressed it firmly and carefully onto the ink pad, checked the bottom of the stamp again and, with a last glance at the passport holder, he lifted his arm and stamped the page with a mighty and impressive thud. The book was then thrust at its owner while the immigration official looked to his next victim.

Nodding at the five deserted immigration podiums, Madison asked a South American businessman behind her, 'Why don't they have more officials doing this?'

'It's midnight. Who wants to work at midnight?' He shrugged and almost smiled in amusement at her question.

Madison struggled to control her exasperation. 'But all flights get in at this hour. You'd think they'd have a better system.'

The man raised both his hands in a dismissive gesture. 'This is Guyana.'

He was a man in his fifties, olive-skinned with dark eyes, hair greying at the temple. He was slightly paunchy and looked a little worn around the edges. He seemed the type nothing would faze, a man who'd travelled and seen a lot in his time.

The line moved up one. Madison yawned and was suddenly concerned about Matthew's friend. Would he still be out there? 'How far are we from town?' she asked the businessman.

'It's an hour's drive, more maybe in this rain. Have you got a hotel reservation?'

'No. I'm being met, I think. I'm supposed to go to my brother's, but he's out of town.' She suddenly felt a little nervous. Guyana so far had the feel of a place dominated by Murphy's Law. If something could go wrong, it would.

'The decent hotels are full because there is an international tariff conference on in Georgetown,' he explained. 'Don't worry, my wife is meeting me and if your friend's not here, you can stay at our place and we'll take you to your brother tomorrow. I'm Antonio Destra, by the way.' He shook her hand and Madison felt at ease and surprised herself by trusting this friendly man immediately. He exuded a rather fatherly air. 'Here's my card. I've been in Miami on business.'

'You're Guyanese?' She glanced at his card. 'Oh, you work for an American company.'

'Yes, we sell new and used equipment to the mines and construction companies. I'm actually Colombian,' he added. 'And you?'

'I'm Australian. Madison Wright. I've come out to visit my brother—he's on assignment here at the Guyminco bauxite mine.'

'Ah, we do business with them . . . one way or another. Sometimes there is no money at Guyminco,' he shrugged. 'They're having problems.'

'Yes, my brother's company AusGeo is trying to sort them out. How do you do business with them if they don't have money?'

'We take payment in bauxite then sell it on the open market. It's just a matter of shuffling commodities. Business is business,' he beamed. 'So what are you going to do while you're here?'

'I'm not sure. What do you suggest?'

'You should see the Kaieteur Falls—the jewel of Guyana.'

They talked some more and Madison felt herself warming to this friendly and outgoing man.

Suddenly she was at the top of the line, enduring a blatantly sexual assessment by the immigration officer before he embarked yet again on his slow and deliberate passport inspection routine. Eventually the stamp fell with the official approval and she passed through a doorway to a messy hall where the luggage was piled. She finally found her bag and took it to a large powerfully built, black woman customs officer who glanced at Madison's small carry-on bag and asked with economy of words, 'Duty free, house goods, food, liquor, shopping?'

'I don't need any of that stuff, I'm just here on holiday with my brother. Please take a look if you want.' Madison was trying to be polite, trying to disguise her growing impatience.

She was waved through and, dragging her bag on its wheels, she walked into a brightly lit bare area that served as arrival and departure waiting space, opening onto a crowded carpark where the rain continued to teem down. Madison stopped in confusion, surrounded by bustling, pushing, shouting taxi drivers and porters looking for business.

At that instant a hand grasped her elbow. She spun around to push the offender away and suddenly, she was looking up at a well-dressed man with reddish hair and blue eyes. He gave her a swift smile and spoke with a pleasant Australian accent. 'You're Madison. I'm Connor Bain. Let's get out of here.' He took the handle of her suitcase and still holding her elbow began to walk her swiftly through the throng.

A shout made her stop. 'Hey, Madison!' Antonio hurried up, a pretty, small, dark-haired woman beside him. 'Madison, this is my wife Celine. You okay or do you wish to come with us?' He glanced enquiringly at Connor who held on to Madison's arm and was frowning.

Madison made swift introductions and thanked him. 'Connor is a friend of my brother. Thanks so much anyway.'

'Telephone us next week and tell us how you're going,' Antonio called as Madison plunged into the rain-drenched parking lot, propelled by Connor's hand still on her arm.

'Better hurry, it's wet.'

'I can see that, but we didn't have to be quite so abrupt, did we?' asked Madison as Connor pushed her suitcase onto the back seat of his car and held the door open for her.

'I'm trying to beat the travelling circus from the tariff conference. They come in for a conference and take over the town. City streets are blocked off when they travel anywhere. So who was that fellow anyway?'

'I met him during the boring wait in Immigration— thanks for waiting for me, by the way—he works for an engineering company.'

'Thought I recognised him. Colombian, I think.' He glanced at her in the darkness. 'Do you make a habit of picking up men in planes and airports?'

Madison was tired and snapped more than she meant. 'He was very helpful, and in case you didn't notice, that was his wife who met him. I thought he was a decent bloke.'

'Decent bloke.' Connor gave a short laugh. 'Doesn't take you long to make up your mind about people.'

'Feminine instinct is a powerful tool.'

'So? How do I rate so far?'

She refused to look at him. 'Too early.'

He chuckled, but as the car threaded through the crowded, unlit parking lot he suddenly groaned. 'Oh, no. Damn.'

'What's up? What are those blue lights? An accident?'

'No, they are Georgetown's only two police cars escorting the convoy of tariff officials. By the way, if you are in an accident or need a police officer, do not call the police. Instead drive yourself to a police station, collect the required officer and return to the scene of the crime. Then you'll be expected to ferry him back again.'

'You're joking. Why are the police going so slowly? Do all the cars only go at forty ks an hour as well?'

'No. Driving slowly gives them the regal status they feel should be accorded them. That's the Guyanese for you,' he laughed as if that explained everything.

'It's dark, it's pouring rain and it's the middle of the night. Do they expect the populace to line the road and cheer?'

'You're getting the hang of the place already. This is going to be a long trip. Tell me your life story.'

'I think I'd rather sleep.'

'Go ahead, drop the seat back,' replied Connor affably, thinking how incredibly young and innocent Matthew's sister looked in her jeans and T-shirt with her gold hair tied in a teenager's ponytail. He gave her another quick glance as she settled back. It would be nice to have an attractive, easygoing Aussie girl around for a bit. He began to think of places he might take her dancing and dining.

Madison had a million questions but felt she'd get only cynical replies from this man who seemed a bit brash and slightly superior. He was altogether too confident the way he'd steered her by the arm through the carpark. Not that he was impolite, just very sure of himself and what he was doing. And she'd had enough of overbearing men. Still, he certainly was handsome.

She opened her eyes as they hit a pothole and saw through the rain, bars of fluorescent neon lights shining on a wet canvas awning where a painted sign said Disco. Sitting incongruously next to it was the dome of a small squat mosque, cotton flags on bamboo poles sagging in the rain. She closed her eyes again.

The sound of the car horn awoke her with a start. Iron gates swung open and Connor parked most of the car underneath a white weatherboard house. 'We're here.' He touched her arm again, then called out. 'Singh, where are you? Get the bag out of the back seat.'

Madison stumbled from the car, still half asleep. Connor took her hand luggage from her and opened the front door. A light was burning above a flight of wooden stairs. The house was silent. At the top they turned right and he opened a metal grille door across a hallway. 'I won't bother you with the Fort Knox details right now. Second on the right.'

The room looked plain but comfortable. A small bedside lamp was lit between the single beds, one of which was turned down and had a mosquito net draped over it. Connor clicked a dial by the door and the overhead fan began to slowly revolve. 'I'll bring your bag up. Bathroom is across the hall. The pump is on. Hyacinth will show you how it all works tomorrow.'

Madison dropped her jeans and T-shirt on the spare bed, picked up a towel from a chair, found the bathroom and washed her face, too tired to bother with teeth brushing or careful make-up removal. It was 1.30 am. Connor had left her bag inside the door. She unlocked it and groped for a clean T-shirt or anything near the top that she could wear in bed. There was a tap at the door just as she was finishing dressing.

'Here. Welcome to Guyana.' Connor burst in offering a china jug which held magnificent bird of paradise flowers and two stems of white ginger. Their perfume was overpowering and exotic. He stood the jug on the dressing table. He was dripping wet and she realised he had been raiding the garden to gather the flowers for her.

'Things will look brighter tomorrow,' he grinned. 'The rain will be gone and Matthew should be back by lunchtime.'

'Thank you so much for picking me up and waiting . . .'

He reached out and intimately rubbed his thumb under her eye. 'Smudged mascara. You look like a raccoon. Good luck, Madison.'

He headed for the stairs as Madison lifted up a corner of the mosquito net and fell onto the bed, wondering what to make of this man, so domineering . . . yet apparently still soft enough to smell the flowers.

FIVE

Madison slowly awakened but did not open her eyes. She lay listening to unfamiliar birds, the soft clack clack of the overhead fan, the rhythmic scratching of a handheld twig broom, voices in the street, the cheerful lilt of an unfamiliar accent. There was the drag of a metal gate across concrete, then it slammed shut.

'Good day, Singh.'

'How be it, Hy'cinth?'

'Adch, man.'

A dog barked. Other dogs in the street chorused and Singh bellowed at them to hush up.

Madison rolled over. She opened one eye and saw the jug of flowers through the veil of mosquito netting. Sunlight streamed into the room and a breeze wafted the perfume of the ginger towards her and faintly rattled a glass louvre.

The rich perfume of the white ginger brought back memories of the previous night and Connor, damp from the rain and wet garden, handing her the heady flowers. That gesture had shaken her first impression of him as a confident, slightly cynical, career-oriented achiever. The fact he was prepared to drive an hour in the rain late at night to meet his friend's sister meant he and Matthew must be good friends. She supposed he was typical of the kind of man Matthew mixed with over-seas—ambitious, adventuring types working their way up the international ladder of business. He was good-looking in that open Aussie kind of way, red gold hair and frank blue eyes, not so tall but with a broad chest and shoulders. She had no doubt he'd have a killer charm with women.

Madi sat up and ducked out from under the mosquito net, annoyed with her straying thoughts. She was here to see her brother, experience a very different country and she was certainly not looking for any kind of relation-ship. Connor Bain was one of her brother's friends, and she hoped they'd all get along without him or anyone else making sexual overtures.

The shower was a mere trickle and cold so Madison decided against struggling to shampoo her hair. She walked into the kitchen to find a buxom black girl with an electric frizz of curls busy kneading dough on a floured bench. She wiped her hands on her apron and gave Madison a happy smile.

'Welcome, mistress. I be Hyacinth. You sleep good?'

'Yes thank you, Hyacinth. I'm Madison Wright.'

'Ah, you sister to Mr Matt. You want I show you how tings work?'

'Yes indeed. What's wrong with the shower? It was fine last night.'

'Oh my, you have to learn ever'ting.' Hyacinth unpinned her apron. 'Come, I show you.'

Forty minutes later Madison had washed her hair and mastered the diabolical routine of the Georgetown water supply and a few other domestic complexities. Her mind was buzzing with the water pump instructions: when to turn it on, off; how to prime and start the diesel generator that provided electricity when the public power system collapsed, which was almost daily; where to find the large portable gas bottles for the stove; and how to unlock the padlocks on the gates.

Inside the house she understood why Connor had referred to Fort Knox. Folding metal grilles were pulled across the bar area that housed liquor and the stereo and CD player. With a ringing clank Hyacinth showed her how the hallway to the bedrooms was sealed off at night by yet another grille. In the bedrooms, safes held personal effects. 'Mr Matt and Mr Kevin got the numbers for the dials, I no know dem.' And with a flourish Hyacinth produced a bunch of keys from her pocket. 'Dese be keys to pantry and food stores. And doubles for gate and so on.'

'I see, I think. Why so much security in the house? It makes me a bit nervous.'

'Teefs no can take away tings, eh? All dis Guyminco company idea. Other houses same way.'

'Who lives around here? Are all the people from the mine?'

'No. Down road *reech*, very reech, Portugee and Indian people. Business people. But some of dem one time just simple folk like me.' Hyacinth headed to the kitchen.

'So how did they get so rich?'

Hyacinth leaned down and pulled a tray smothered in freshly roasted coffee beans from the oven. 'Well, I couldn't say anyting 'bout dat.'

'That coffee smells delicious. Could I make some? Where does it come from?'

'I do for you. Dis be local coffee.' Madison was shooed from the kitchen.

Matthew rang a short time later. 'So you're really here, sis. I can hardly wait to show you this amazing country.'

'I'm sitting on the balcony with fabulous coffee and homemade coconut cookies. When am I going to see you?'

'Tell Hyacinth not to bother with lunch for me. I'll be there about three. I have a meeting. See you then. You get settled in. Has Hyacinth shown you the water pump and so on?'

'God yes! Rather quaint.'

He laughed. 'Local colour, Madi. We'll hit the town tonight, okay?'

'Sounds fun. See you when you get here.'

Madison unpacked and Hyacinth hovered. 'You got some washing, ironing?'

'Not really, thanks Hyacinth. Only my travelling clothes.' Though with the heat and humidity already high, Madison could tell she was probably going to change outfits more than once a day.

'Primrose come and do wash and iron, help me. She my sister. She work for Mr Bain so she have only one person to look after.'

Madison was almost going to ask just how many

more servants were going to materialise but thought better of it. 'Oh, I look forward to meeting her. Do you have brothers too?'

'No, just be me, Primi and Rose.'

'Your mother liked flowers I think.'

'She like English tings. She give us girls fancy names, but we no turn out English!' Hyacinth laughed at her joke. 'Guyana not England, dat's for sure,' she added as she turned, swaying her hips, giving a saucy laugh and singing a snatch of a calypso ditty as she went to the kitchen.

Later in the morning Madison marched downstairs carrying a shoulder bag and wearing a hat and sunglasses. Hyacinth introduced her to Singh who was sitting on a shaded bench outside the kitchen in his singlet and shorts. He rose and shook her hand, giving her a warm smile, not at all uncomfortable about his informal attire. 'You going somewhere, mistress?'

'Yes, I thought I'd go downtown, change some money, get orientated. I need a map of the place. When I asked the cambio money change lady in Miami for Guyana dollars, she hadn't heard of them. So much for international money exchange.'

'How you go, mistress? You have a friend coming to drive you?'

'No, I called a taxi. There are a couple listed in the phone book.'

Hyacinth looked concerned. 'You go to town in a taxi? Why you don't wait for Mr Matt? What taxi yo ring up?' she asked, a cautious note in her voice.

'I don't know, the first one I saw. Speedy Taxi, I think.'

'Ee-eio, ooh, ma'am!' Hyacinth wailed and clutched her head and Madison stared in astonishment. 'Eeah, dem is *bad* men. Bad men. Dey cheat you, dey take you bad place. No good taxi.'

Madison found it difficult to share the flamboyant concern. 'Dear me,' she said with a smile as a car pulled up at the gate. 'Well, it can't be helped now. Here it is. Singh, open the gate please.'

'You take care, mistress. Hang on to yo purse,' Hyacinth warned.

Madi walked boldly to the car but underneath she felt intimidated and nervous as she reached the driveway. She slid into the back seat of an elderly, forlorn Hillman. Calypso music blared and the driver hid behind large dark glasses. A striped T-shirt was pulled tightly across muscular shoulders which rippled as he glanced up at her in the rear vision mirror, with a look that was a question. 'Where yo go?'

'I want to go to the bank, and then a bookshop, I guess.'

'Which bank?' He reached over and turned the music lower as he pulled away.

'Oh, I don't care.' She hesitated to give her reasons.

'Yo want to change money?'

'Why do you say that?'

There was a flash of white teeth. 'Yo look like yo be a new visitor.'

'You mean I look like a tourist?' Madison had hoped she looked like an expatriate wife.

'Are yo from Australia?'

Madison sank back in the seat. 'I guess my cover is blown, huh?'

The driver chuckled. 'I've met a few Aussies here. I recognise the accent. So, yo want me to wait at de bank and den take yo to de bookshop?'

He glanced at her over his shoulder and Madison saw that his smiling face was a mixture of Indian and African. Like so many people here he was 'all mix up' as Hyacinth had put it during the tour of the domestic arrangements. The driver was a handsome and tidily dressed man and he exuded a cheerful confidence. She felt her fears melting. Certainly she had no experience of this strange country yet, but this local didn't look 'a *bad* man'.

Madison couldn't believe how long it took to change her money even though the bank had the outward appearance of a modern financial institution. Its efficient architecture belied the languid approach to the business of banking by its earnest multitude of staff. Madi went through three different queues before reaching the cashier. She was finally handed a slip of pink paper. 'Where's my money?'

'Go to the teller. Give them this.'

She sighed. Four people in four different sections had calculated on four different pieces of paper the exchange rate for US to Guyanese dollars. At last the teller finished counting the notes and handed her a giant wad of money. Madison burst out laughing. 'Good grief. Have you given it all to me in one dollar bills?'

The lady teller gave her an icy stare. 'No.'

Madison peeled off the top five hundred dollar bill. 'Can I break this? Give me some small change.'

'We do not have coins in our currency.'

Madison gave up. The newsagent or bookshop assistant would have to cash the bill so she could pay the taxi.

Outside she looked up and down the street before spotting the taxi with the driver waving to her from halfway down the block. Clutching her bag she hurried along the footpath. When she reached the car she was already perspiring freely, the humidity and heat seemed to have soared while she had been inside the air-conditioned bank. The driver was leaning against his cab, chatting to a man whose head was crowned with dreadlocks and a coloured beanie, and who was carrying a string bag of wooden carvings. The driver waved. 'Sorry I couldn't park close to de door. No space. But I watch out fo yo.'

Madison held her shoulder bag close to her body, feeling she was carrying a fortune.

'Yo want to buy a carving? Dis friend of mine, he do good work.'

'No thanks.' But then glancing at the carvings through the string bag she was struck by their craftsmanship. She fingered one the artist held out and glanced at the carver with admiration that was not just for his work. He was a giant African who looked as if he too had been carefully carved from the finest ebony.

'All Guyanese wood, me do de work ma'self,' he said, offering another carving to her to examine.

'It's very good. But I'm not ready to start buying anything yet.'

'But dis de best. I no come t'town. I be in de bush. Dis mean is good time fo yo to buy from me,' he cajoled.

'No. Not today.' She shook her head.

He slapped his head with his free hand. 'Man, yuh 'ard ears.'

Madison glanced at the driver, who chuckled. 'He say yo is stubborn, ma'am.'

'You don' even ask de price. I make very good price. Listen, I have something I know I mek it jist fo yo.' He delved into the string bag looped over his shoulder.

'No, really,' Madison reached for the taxi door which

the driver opened and she slid into the seat. The wood carver thrust his hand through the window and opened his palm. A small frog nestled in it. Madison glanced at it, then looking more carefully she picked it up as if it were a fragile treasure.

It was made of pale polished wood, gleaming like gold. Its legs were neatly tucked beneath it and the texture of its skin was hinted at in the artist's fine strokes. But there was a strength and a liveliness to it and for an instant she felt it could leap from her hand. Its wooden face was expressive, a slight grin lurked at the wide mouth, a faint amusement in its round carved eyes which surprised her. It appealed to Madi immediately. She looked into the quizzical dark eyes of the artist through the window. 'You know dat I mek dis fo you. Dis be yo luck. Dis frog be yo destiny.'

'How much?'

'One thousand. He only a small one. But he be a mighty spirit.'

'Five hundred.' Madison reached into her pocket and showed him one of the bills she'd tried to change in the bank. 'This or nothing.'

She hoped he'd take it. Suddenly she desperately wanted the tiny frog.

The man took the note. 'I only take dis because I know dis one belong to yo.'

'Be seein' yo, bro,' said the driver starting the engine. And as they swung into the traffic he went on. 'Dat man is good. One of de best I know. He hardly ever come down to town. Yo lucky day eh?'

'I just love it. I feel this little frog is symbolic for me.' She recalled the carver's words that she had ignored as the spiel of a salesman. Strange he should say that, she thought, repeating the words to herself. 'You know dat I

99

mek dis for yo. Dis frog is yo destiny.' She wondered how that could be.

'It ain't just any frog. Dat one is gold Kaieteur frog. He be . . . what yo call it . . . not many left now.'

'Endangered? This species is in trouble like America's eagle and Australia's koala?'

'I couldn't say about dem. But our gold frog is a rare creature. Most beautiful in de world. But all de frogs is disappearing everywhere in de world.'

'I think it's the same back home. Why is it, do you suppose?'

'Dey say de water, de air, de land, all be poison. Here de jungle is being wrecked many many places. Government has let in logging companies and now dere's a big gold mine called Columbus. All dat sort of action. No good for de Amerindian people or de forest where dey live. But dis country got ta make money somehow. Like all of us.' He returned to his recollection. 'Man, seeing dat little frog was someting. It got eyes like diamonds I saw once.'

'Where was that?'

'On a tributary of de mid-Mazaruni River.'

'What were you doing there?'

'I'm really a pork-knocker.'

'What's a pork-knocker?'

The driver laughed. 'He be a man who looks for diamonds. Used t'say dey lived on wild pigs. Most are up de big rivers. Some of dem are wild men, dey don' come out much. Dey meet in camps and de buyers fly up. I do a bit of gold prospecting too. I got malaria so I've bin workin' in town doin' dis while I get better. I'll be goin' out again. De interior calls yo. I like bein' in de forest and on de river. And I hope I make a big find and den I can send my boy Denzil to a good school. Now, here's de bookshop, what yo looking fo?'

'Maybe a book or two about Guyana. And I need a couple of maps. One of the city and one of the interior. Who knows, I might go exploring. Everyone keeps telling me how beautiful the interior is.'

'But it's hard to get around. Especially for a lady. I don't tink dey'll have de sort of maps yo mean.'

The Universal Bookstore was a small shop by Australian standards and there were few books about any subject beyond the Americas. Madi was interested to see a wide range of locally produced poetry books and novels by Caribbean writers. She picked up two novels by Roy Heath and V.S. Naipaul. Next to them was a book by Shiva Naipaul. She opened it at random and her eye fell on his description of the thinly disguised fictional country he called Cuyama . . . *'a mongrelised ghost of human beings living in a mongrelised ghost of a country . . .'* Did this apply to Guyana today?

She went to the boy perched on a stool in the doorway, and asked if they had maps. He directed her to a girl behind a counter who looked blankly at Madi. She went to another girl leaning by a stand of school supplies and repeated the question. The girl slowly shook her head as if this seemed to be an odd request. 'Then I'll just take these.' Madison handed her the three novels and was immediately directed back to the girl behind the counter. The blank-eyed girl laboriously wrote out the names and authors of each book in full, copying the detail carefully, before writing the price beside each one. She handed the paper to Madison who looked at it, clearly puzzled.

'So what do I owe you?'

'Take it to the cashier, please,' said the girl, pointing at yet another girl ensconced in a small cage-like structure. This cashier added up the cost of the books, wrote the amount in the space on the docket and showed it to Madison. 'Three thousand and twenty, please.'

Madison paid. But before she could collect the books, a stamp had to be glued to the docket, initialled by the cashier and handed back with the change. Madison took the docket back to the girl behind the counter. The docket was then checked before the books were handed over. Madison smiled incredulously as the sales ritual concluded. 'Do you have full employment in this country?' she asked, trying to keep a straight face. The sales assistant just looked at her uncomprehendingly.

Madison stepped out into the searing sunlight and reached for her sunglasses. Across the street a big open-air market was bustling with sellers who squatted before heaps of fruit and vegetables. Leaning wooden stalls were hung with cheap brightly coloured household wares like brooms and plastic bowls. Madi's eye was caught by a hammock strung across the front of a stall.

'What's the market called?' she asked the driver who materialised beside her.

'Dat's Bourda Markets. Good for food tings. Yo want to go and look?'

It suddenly occurred to Madison that she hadn't seen a taxi meter in the cab. 'How's my bill running with you? Is this going to cost me a fortune?'

He smiled easily. 'No, I make a round trip, fair price. Don' worry yo'self. Come, I'd better walk with yo in there. Watch yo bag.'

'I was looking at those hammocks.'

'Ah yes, from Brazil. Yo'll need a hammock if yo're going to de interior. Tie 'im between trees. But dere's a better place to buy dem. I can take yo to de Amerindian shop.'

'As I'm here, maybe I could walk around for a few

minutes.' She liked the idea of having a tall burly man in tow as they walked through the narrow lanes formed by the vendors. 'Look, my name is Madison Wright. Maybe we should introduce ourselves.'

He smiled widely and offered his hand. 'Dat real nice, Miz Wright. I be Lester Styles.'

They turned into another lane crowded with baskets of food. But there was not a huge variety of fruit and vegetables. 'What are those?' She pointed to a lump of pale brown legumes spread on a grass mat.

'Cassava. De bread of de Amerindians.' Lester explained how cassava was starchy and the staple food of the tribes. There were no potatoes, just edoes and yams and breadfruit, and a large pale fruit called a plantain that looked like a banana. 'Yo fry or boil dem to eat. Some people mash dese ones. De Amerindians make many tings with de cassava, strain de juice for a drink, very strong, and make flour or eat like potato.'

Madison picked up a bunch of long green snake beans. 'I like the look of these. What's the most common dish people eat here?'

'Oh, souse, pepperpot, black pudding and pepper sauce on ever'ting.' He picked up a handful of red chillies. 'Dese make pepper sauce. Very hot.'

'What else goes into pepperpot and souse other than chillies?'

Lester liked the idea of being a tour guide and warmed to the task with smiling enthusiasm as they headed back towards the taxi. 'Pig face, ears, pigs' feet, cassareep, cow heel. Very strong smell. Cassareep comes from cassava, pepperpot is Amerindian dish.'

Madison grimaced. 'It doesn't sound very appetising to me.'

'Oh, and yo must eat labba and drink de black water,'

Lester added encouragingly. 'If yo do dat, yo den come back to Guyana.'

'What is it? Some magic potion?'

'Labba is about the size of a small dog, like a big rat. Black water is creek water. We call it black because it's dark, from the minerals and roots. But it's clear, it's sweet, good for drinking.'

Madison looked dubious. 'Don't know that I'm into eating rats. But clearly I have a lot to learn about this country.'

When they reached the taxi, Lester opened the door and Madi slid into the back. 'Yo want to learn about Guyana, heh?' He spoke seriously and gave her an earnest look.

Madison looked at this man she'd met only two hours earlier and who now seemed like an old friend. 'Yes, I think I do.'

'Okay, we go to de library,' he announced. 'Don' worry, won't take long.'

The taxi swung around a corner and Madison gasped as she stared out the window. 'Wow, look at that!'

'What, where?'

'There! Those flowers, the waterlilies in the canal!'

A broad canal in the middle of the street divided the traffic. It was choked with massed pink flowers, their proud fat heads on long stems bobbing above the flat sea of green leaves that smothered the surface of the rank water.

'Dey be lotus.' Lester swerved into the side of the road and stopped.

'Do the lotus have a perfume?'

'Don' know. We see. I show yo someting.' Heedless of

the passing traffic he leapt out of the car and skipped to the edge of the sloping verge, followed by Madison. Lester leaned over to reach for a flower, slithered and slipped a little and squelched into black mud that covered his gym shoes.

'Ooh, be careful.' Madison kicked off her sandals. 'Wait, I'll help you.' She inched along and went to Lester who was ankle deep. She held out her hand. 'Are you stuck?'

'A bit. I was trying to get dat bud, see de green pod.' She held his arm as he reached far out and grabbed the cup-shaped pod with its seeds sewn in slit green sacks. Cars honked but they ignored them. 'Look in here, de seed . . .' He squeezed a plump seed from its hole and peeled away the outer layer to reveal a white kernel which he popped into his mouth. He took another. 'Here, yo try.'

Madison bit into the seed. 'It tastes like a nut, a cashew, sort of. Very nice. Thank you so much. Very kind of you to go to so much trouble for me.'

Back behind the wheel Lester took off his muddy shoes and socks and wiped his feet with a rag from under the seat. Madison sat in the back picking the seeds from the lotus pod. 'They are stunning. Those flowers are as big as soup bowls.'

'Wait til dey dry, den try dem.' He put on his shoes minus the muddy socks.

The library was a beautiful white colonial building. They went to a reception desk where a girl checker took their bags and gave them a numbered receipt. 'Keep yo money with yo,' whispered Lester.

They walked up a sweeping staircase to the upper

level where shelves of books were protected by small mesh barriers. One of the librarians in a drab mud-coloured uniform approached them. 'What yo interested in, politics, animals, history?' she asked conversationally.

'What do you have on travel in Guyana, like to the interior?'

The girl looked blank. 'Yo don' know de titles of de books?'

'No.'

'Man, how I know what to get when I don' have no names?' Her head rocked from side to side in exasperation.

'Can I just look along the shelves?' asked Madison stepping through the small opening in the mesh towards the shelves of books. She had to step around a bucket, one of many scattered along the aisle between the books. Glancing upwards Madison saw damp patches on the sagging ceiling.

But the lethargic girl suddenly sprang into action, barring her way. 'No public in here.'

'Why not?'

'Rule. I get de books, dat de rule. Wot yo want?'

'I don't know! I just want to look and see what looks interesting.'

'No titles, no books. Dat's de rule.'

Madison looked to Lester in desperation. He pointed at a book. 'Dere, dat blue one. Dat's one. Give us dat.'

'Dat blue one, dere on de shelf?'

'Yeah man. Dat one, de blue one up dere.' Lester spoke as she did, pointing at a book. He gave Madison a wink as the girl reached for it. Flipping through pages, Lester stopped and made an extravagant reaction. 'Yeh, man dis be de one. Hey, yo photocopy, okay?'

With the pages carefully memorised, the girl disappeared into a back section to photocopy. 'Okay, yo go look.' Lester propelled Madison into the musty rows of books. 'See what yo can find.'

This seemed like madness but she swiftly glanced up and down the racks and was soon immersed in a collection of colonial and pre-Independence books on Guyana. In the travel section there was little and what there was seemed very dated. Obviously no one in recent times had bothered to write about the delights or otherwise of travel in Guyana. She noted that most of the contemporary books were political, extolling the virtues of former socialist leader Forbes Burnham's government, and had been published by his government.

She was about to turn away when a title caught her eye. *On the Diamond Trail In British Guiana* by Gwen Richardson. It was an old volume and Madi blew a small cloud of dust from it before opening the copyright page. She saw that it was published by Methuen of London in 1925. She turned to the mildew-spotted title page to reveal a grainy black-and-white photograph of a young woman that made her gasp lightly in amusement and, she realised at once, admiration. It was clearly a studio photograph taken in the staged style of that period, but there was something more about the image that captured Madison's complete attention.

The young woman was handsomely attractive but it was her dress that made the picture exceptional—a long tweedy but stylish black skirt, high boots, a pocketed blouse, a bush hat set at a slightly rakish angle, a scarf at the throat and a Colt .45 held confidently in her hand.

'Whacko, Gwen!' exclaimed Madison softly and Lester stepped forward to look over her shoulder.

'Oh man, dat some lady dat one,' he said with exaggerated melodic intonation that made Madison smile. 'She a real colonial lady to be sure.'

'Colonial lady?' queried Madison.

'Oh yes. Guyana people know colonial people real well,' he laughed. Madison let the remark pass but she knew there was a sub-text to it she didn't understand. 'Yo want to be like dis lady?' he asked smiling.

Madison felt a little annoyed at the question, not so much that it implied something slightly absurd, but because Lester had seemingly read her thoughts. Yes, she actually did have an instant liking for the woman, or at least for the bold individualism and sense of adventure the image conveyed. 'Why not?' she asked looking him in the eye and closing the book more firmly than she had intended.

'Ohhh,' he crooned and raised both hands in front of his face in mock defence. 'If yo really want to go into de jungle like dis lady, den yo do it. Dat way yo will really get to know dis country. Maybe still find something colonial dere,' he added, then quickly changed the subject. 'Yo want to borrow dis book?'

'Yes. Can I become a member of the library?'

'No worries. I'm a member. Yo can use my card.'

They walked down towards a desk where a handful of people queued to record their borrowings. 'You're a surprising man, Lester.' She tried to imagine a Sydney taxi driver lending her his library card.

'Ah well. I'm one of de lucky ones. Got some education, but got de gold bug too. Driving, I can take up and put down any time I like. Maybe one day I'll get what yo First World people have lots of—ambition.' He paused and smiled. 'But maybe not. Ambition is not a big ting in Guyana.' Madison had already reached that conclusion.

The library clerk studied the book and the card carefully and looked from Madi to Lester. She opened the book to put in the date stamp but then paused and turned to the page with the picture of the author. She examined it and grinned, then looked at Madison. 'Hey, yo going after diamonds too?'

Madison forced herself to remain even tempered. 'Who knows? It might be fun.'

Finally the date stamp was impressed on the slip of paper attached to the cover, recording the first borrowing of the book for thirty years.

As they reached the car Lester opened the door. 'If yo do go after diamonds, be sure to take yo frog with yo.'

Madison was slightly surprised to see that he was quite serious and she was about to question him when he went on. 'How about taking a look at a real local hammock. Dey be ideal for de diamond trail.' He grinned and gave a deprecating shrug to take the bite out of the quip. 'At de same time yo can meet some more of de locals. Amerindians. Dey spend enough time in dem, so dey should know how to make dem.' He laughed again. 'Hammock be an Arawak tribe word. Dey spun de cotton which was grown by de Arecunas and de Macushis made de hammocks. Now it be more a town business,' he added.

'Will it take long? How far is it? Not out of town I hope?'

'No. I'll take yo to the Amerindian hostel where de people stay in Georgetown. Still have yo back in time for lunch.' He raised both hands in a gesture of openness. 'Trust me.'

Madison couldn't help but smile and agree. 'Okay. Lead on. You haven't led me astray yet.'

They left the main streets and began travelling down narrow potholed and garbage-littered back streets. The smell of poverty drifted into the car, which was emitting a significant number of loud rattles despite Lester's efforts to avoid the worst of the potholes. Madison felt

109

obliged to raise her voice, 'What exactly is an Amerindian?' she shouted over the rattles.

'Ah, I give yo another lesson, dis one about where de natives come from. I was taught at school dat de Indians came from Asia to America over de Bering Strait which was den a sort of bridge between de two continents.'

'Well that must be going back some time.'

'Many tousands of years ... and dey kept moving south till dey reached South America. Over de centuries Amerindian civilisations sprang up all over ... de Aztec and Pueblo in North America, de Maya in Central America and de Inca and Chibcha in South America. Dere descendants make up de nine tribes in Guyana today.' He gave her a cheeky grin. 'Someone yo might know of befriended de Amerindians when he was here looking for de gold of El Dorado.'

'I know. Sir Walter Raleigh.'

'Top o' de class. He one smart man. He treat de Indians good and dey help him. De English and de Dutch get dem on dere side and protect dem and in return de natives hunt down de runaway slaves. Lot of Negroes still don' like de Amerindians because of dat.'

'How do you feel about them?' asked Madison bluntly, since he was being so open.

'I have good friends up de river. In de villages dey lead de life like dey always have, dat's okay. But now tings be changing in some places and it's hard fo dem. Dey should have same tings as everybody else, but de government mess tings up—fo everybody. But I spend time with dem and I can see de tribes getting radical. Soon dey make a voice in dis country and not stay quiet in de forest.'

Lester spoke with some heat. 'All we Guyanese want is fairness fo everyone. It's not right people with de power make corruption and take money. De poor people see dis and cheat and teef to get money to get a better life or get out. Who goin' t'make dis country strong, eh? Amerindian people no can go and live happy in Miami like some of us. Dey only want here.'

'It's a problem all over the world I think, Lester,' said Madi quietly. 'But what can we do about it?'

'Sometimes, some of us have to find a way to help. No good everyone wait fo someone else t'fix tings up.'

They pulled into the yard of a simple rambling double-storeyed building. A broken truck was sunk in weeds and a tethered goat lay in the shade of a tree. A small shop flanked the entrance to the Amerindian hostel and a shy dark-eyed young girl peeped from the doorway.

'Who stays here?'

'Children be chosen from various villages and brought down to experience de city and get a better education. Dey stay for a year. Den go back to de village.'

'Don't they find it hard after what they've seen in Georgetown?'

'I've got Amerindian friends whose children be homesick. Some go back early. But dey all go back eventually taking experiences dat can help de village. Most of dem don't like de city. Some come down to stay 'cause dey sick. Dey come for treatment in de hospital and with specialist doctors. Malaria, typhoid are big sickness dat send dem down here. Most times dey look after demselves. Forest medicine. Take a long time to get specialist doctor from Georgetown up to de interior. Another reason, de Amerindians getting organised.' He nodded towards the upper floor. 'De big chief is up dere.'

'Organised, you mean politically?'

'Yeah. Dey be a gentle sweet people. Dey mind dere own business, keep to demselves. But now, big business, logging, de mines, de trouble in de rivers, no good fo dem.'

111

'What do you mean trouble in the rivers?'

'Sick fish. Poison in de water, trees cut down, big diggings round de hunting grounds. Dere old life gone.'

'Is the environment a big issue here?'

Lester continued in his thick patois. 'Man, we all know dat word. De calypso boys sing 'bout dat, oh my yes. We know 'bout dat en-vi-ro-ment right enough.'

They walked into the small shop. It was colourful and cluttered, filled with baskets, mats, decorations, fish traps, ornaments, mostly made from woven grasses and wood. Lester watched Madison admire the strong intricate floor mats. 'Dey made from tibisiri, taken from de heart of de Eta palm. Wear a long time.'

Strung around one wall was a selection of string hammocks. 'Dese be de best ones, very soft, very strong. Can get wet, won't rot quick,' said Lester. 'See even bebbe ones.' He held out a mini baby hammock.

'Oh, that is adorable.'

'Yo got babies?' asked Lester.

'No.'

He lifted down a pale string hammock. 'Here, dis one be good for yo. Yo tie it up like dis.' He showed her how to knot the strong twine ropes around a pole. He gave a tug and the knot slid into place, holding firm. 'Yo sleep deep in dis one, de sides come up and almost cover yo. Keep out bad boys.'

'What?'

'Insects. Yo take a mosquito net and waterproof sheet and yo be set to sleep in the jungle.'

The memory of the picture of Gwen with her gun and her bush outfit came to Madison's mind. 'Right, I'll take it.'

They left the shop and walked across the compound as two young boys strolled past them, swinging schoolbags, speaking a language Madison had never heard. They exchanged shy smiles and disappeared into the building.

'Can we look around?'

'Dere be nothing to see. De dormitories, de dining hall, some offices. Dis place be very basic.'

Madison felt there was more behind the facade of simple buildings than she was being allowed to see. And whatever it was, she suspected Lester was part of it. Could this be the seat of a new political movement?

As if to support her thoughts, a man came through the gate and hailed Lester as they reached the taxi. Lester exchanged greetings and shook hands. The man was a striking-looking Amerindian with coppery olive skin, a broad flat face with wide dark eyes, a finely sculptured nose. His sleek dark hair was woven with red threads falling in a long tightly bound braid down his back. He wore a coarse cotton shirt with a geometric design woven into it.

The brief exchange between the two men meant nothing to Madison until Lester waved a hand in her direction. 'Madison Wright, a new visitor to Guyana. She be goin' to look for diamonds in de interior.'

Madison gave an embarrassed laugh. 'Well, it would be nice. I'm not quite sure how to go about it all . . . I'm actually here visiting my brother.'

'I am Xavier. Xavier Rodrigues.' The Amerindian man flashed her a wide smile showing perfect even white teeth. 'You're not English.'

'Australian.'

'Ah. Another outpost of the former British Empire. I hope you do come to the interior, Miss Wright. We are persuading visitors to our country to come and see for themselves.'

As Xavier grinned, Madi noticed behind him a business-suited man hurrying into the hostel. For a minute, he reminded her of Antonio Destra, the man she'd met at the airport. Then two bright-eyed girls came out of the building carrying half-finished woven baskets and sat on the ground under a tree, chattering softly as they began weaving the long strands of dried grasses. As the men talked about a meeting planned at the hostel, Madison reached into her shoulder bag looking for her camera. She put her books and the tiny carved frog on the ground beside her bag and lifted out her camera, giving Lester a querying look.

'Sure, sure it be okay. Dey making tings for de shop.'

She crouched down before the giggling girls and took their photo. When she turned back Xavier was holding her wooden frog.

'Where did you get this one?'

'I bought it from an artist friend of Lester,' she said. He handed the carving back to her and stared at her intently. 'You chose well. The golden frog will always look out for you.' For a moment Madison felt something quiver inside her, a hint, a portent, that this would not be the last she'd see of this intriguing man.

Matthew's car was in the driveway when they pulled up. Madi paid Lester and took the scrap of paper on which he wrote his home phone number. 'If yo need to go any-where, phone me, okay?'

'I will. Thanks so much, Lester. It's been a great morning.'

'Enjoy de day.' He drove off with a wave as Singh held the gate open.

'Mr Matt back. He worried where yo be, mistress.'

Madison ran to the door and was halfway up the stairs as Matthew came down and they met on the small landing in the middle, hugging effusively. 'Hey, Madi. You had us in a bit of a stir.'

'I'm sorry the time got away, I had such a fascinating morning. Oh Matt, it's so good to see you.' She hugged him again and he grinned at her.

'I'm glad you're here, sis.' He only called her 'sis' in moments of extreme affection. Holding hands they went upstairs.

Hyacinth appeared in the kitchen door. 'I figured dat taxi man spirit yo away,' she said with a relieved smile. 'Yo call other taxi next time.'

'No, no, Lester was great. I'm going to hire him all the time.'

'Where did you go, what took so long?' asked Matthew. 'Come on out on the balcony. Hyacinth, bring us some tea and Madison's lunch please. So what news from home?'

'I've brought you Vegemite and Vita-Weats and Mum and Dad have sent you a new beach towel.'

'A beach towel? Have you seen the beach!' Matthew laughed. 'God luv 'em. Are they well?'

'Fighting fit. Now tell me, what's happening with you? AusGeo won the management contract, but what does that mean?'

'It means we have to get the mine producing more bauxite more efficiently. Kevin has to get the whole system working better so I can sell it off. The local boss Lennic Krupuk has departed. Gawd, we're starting to uncover some ludicrous expenditure and waste. You must come out and have a look around. It's a great trip up the river. We went in the luxury company cruiser Krupuk bought. Now that and the weekender he bought for the company are being sold. Bit of a drive but not too bad.'

They talked while Madison ate her sandwiches and cake.

Matthew laughed heartily at her story of the money-changing and the devious way Lester had managed to get her access to the bookshelves at the library. She showed him Gwen's book and he glanced quickly at the photograph. He smiled and handed it back to her. 'It sounds like *Annie Get Your Gun*. Should be a fun read at least.' He stood up and looked at his watch. 'I'm going to the office in town so I'll see you later—about five. Kevin will be home tonight and a few of our new friends could drop in for a drink before dinner. You'll meet some really fun people here.'

'Terrific. But I'm feeling utterly exhausted at the moment.'

'It's the climate. The humidity gets you. Have a shower and a kip and you'll be right.'

'I might try out the hammock on the verandah off the bedroom.'

'Great idea. Everyone gets the hammock habit here. Some, I reckon, never get out of it.' He gave her a kiss on the cheek. 'Glad you made it, sis,' and bounced down the stairs.

She woke up two hours later, amazed she'd slept so soundly. She went into the kitchen and cautiously plugged in the kettle, nervous at the shredding electrics. Cords were frayed, plugs went into adaptors that sort of fitted the sockets. 'Jiggle dem' had been Hyacinth's advice. Meatballs and what looked like crisps were set in bowls under a cloth. She tried one of the crisps, which looked like a hard banana slice dusted with chilli. It tasted spicy but tangy. No one seemed to be about, so she had a cup of tea, showered and changed. She decided to start a letter to her parents and got lost in her description of her first day in Guyana.

Then Matthew was home calling to her and introducing her to Kevin Blanchard who was staying down for a couple of days before going back to the mine. Matthew called to Singh to bring ice and glasses and picked up a bottle of rum. 'There's rum and coke, rum and water, rum and ginger, rum and milk, rum and ice, or rum punch made with some ghastly bottled cordial.'

'Doesn't Hyacinth know how to make proper punch? We should keep a jug in the fridge,' said Kevin. 'Madi, bring the hors d'oeuvres.'

They trooped through the kitchen, down the back steps and through the garden to the small gazebo where Singh was setting out the glasses and emptying ice trays into a plastic bowl.

'Ah this is the life.' Matthew settled himself and Madison sank into an old cane chair. Kevin handed her a rum and coke.

'I'm having just ice, so I'll have the ten-year-old,' said Matthew as Kevin picked up a different bottle of rum. 'Smooth as silk this, Madi. Try some.'

She took a sip. 'It's like a liqueur, an old brandy.'

'Aged rum, can't beat it. Cheers. Welcome to Guyana, Madi.'

At that moment there was a 'Hoy!' and Connor joined them, giving Madison a grin. 'I see you're right into it.'

'The rum?'

'No, life in the fast lane. I saw you earlier today standing in a drain with some black fella. Stealing flowers by the look of it.'

*

Soon others arrived including Sharee and Viti from the scavenger hunt. Madison found herself thoroughly enjoying the group's company. John and Ann da Silva were neighbours down the block. John was of English and Portuguese descent, born in Guyana. His wife was English and both were sophisticated, worldly, well travelled. Madison took an instant liking to their unpretentious and bubbling personalities. Both were passionate about Guyana.

'We love it, but we aren't blind to its problems which can drive you crazy. We have a wonderful lifestyle here. I go back to see my family in London. And all John's relatives—dozens of them—are here,' grinned Ann.

John ran the City Garage with his brother, and Madison soon realised Ann knew as much about cars as he did. 'Is that because of the business?'

'No, I race them,' she answered. 'I've just come back from a rally in Belgium. Jolly good fun. Would have been more fun if I hadn't blown up and lost my leading position.'

'Let's not run the race again,' groaned John good-naturedly. It turned out they'd met when Ann had been competing in a car rally in Guyana.

Madison leaned over to Ann. 'Would you give me a few pointers some time? I've always had a secret ambition to race a car.'

'You have?' Matthew raised an eyebrow. 'As well as chase butterflies up the Amazon?'

'You're going into the interior, of course,' said John, passing the rum.

'I'd really like to but I'm not sure how to go about it on my own.'

'You don't go into the interior on your own!' exclaimed Connor Bain, joining the conversation.

Then Ann, who gave the immediate impression of being a strong, organised and no-nonsense woman, turned to Madison. 'We will fix a trip, don't worry. If you haven't gone up the river and out into real country, you don't know Guyana.'

Madison raised her glass. 'Thanks, Ann.' And she had no doubts Ann would fix something.

Madison was feeling very relaxed, maybe it was the rum, but she decided she wasn't going to get hassled about Connor Bain's abrupt comments or anything else. She had the distinct impression things would simply 'happen'.

'Six o'clock,' came an exuberant and united chorus and everyone laughed. Madison stared around the group, looking for the joke. No one had looked at a watch. She picked up Matthew's arm and glanced at his watch. 'All right, I give up. What was all that about?'

'The six o'clock bee! Listen. Quiet everyone,' ordered John.

And there, buzzing loudly around the lush garden, flew a large fat beetle-like bee.

'It appears at six on the dot,' he continued. 'It's sort of an alarm clock to start the evening. All the other noises will start now, frogs, night jars and so on as they wake to the night. And others are singing good night as they head home to bed.'

Madi stared at John but realised he was stating fact.

'This country is amazing,' Madi laughed.

'I'll drink to that. Pass the rum,' said Connor.

The six o'clock bee continued on its rounds in the garden, its buzz now drowned by the clink of ice and laughter. The sun began to sink behind the huge bougainvillea-covered fence and the breeze from the sea cooled the garden at last.

SIX

As Madison piled her golden hair on top of her head, small tendrils, blown by the overhead fan, flew around her forehead and high cheekbones. She dabbed at her damp upper lip and checked herself again in the mirror, pleased with the crisp white sundress she'd chosen to wear. The overall effect was cool and classy even if she did feel warm. The temperature was in the mid-thirties and very humid.

She was looking forward to this lunch with Connor. She'd surprised herself by impulsively saying yes to his invitation when he casually suggested they lunch at the Georgetown Club. He had annoyed her on a couple of occasions with his patronising attitude yet she had to admit there was also something about him she liked.

Somehow she felt safe in the company of this strong West Australian who always said what he thought.

But there was also a slight feeling of deja vu, which wasn't so different from the first feelings she'd had when Geoff had swept her off her feet in the early days of their relationship.

Now in her thoughts she wondered, when did a relationship change? And how did one know what would last? But she had no intention of stumbling into that trap again unless she was very, very sure.

Madi and Connor had been paired at several dinner parties they'd gone to with Matthew and Sharee, Kevin and Viti. But this lunch would be the first time they'd been alone together since the trip from the airport. Well, she reasoned, this would test whether she liked him or not.

Singh held open the gate for them with a smart flourish and a cheerful salute. 'The shorts, barefeet and singlet spoil the effect a bit,' grinned Madi. 'Singh seems pleased with himself. Some days he's only half awake.'

'Depends on the rum intake, I guess.'

On the way to lunch she asked Connor if he was going to attend the American Ambassador's reception which she had been invited to as Matthew's partner.

'Yes, I'll be there working the room. All in the course of duty.'

'Working over cocktails is a nice way to work.'

'In Guyana, it's absolutely essential. The usual rule book doesn't apply in countries like this one.'

'Banana republic rules, eh?'

'That's right, Madi. You're catching on fast. But it makes the job interesting.'

'What exactly is your job? I've only really got a vague

idea that it's something to do with the International Funding Organisation, a bank that specialises in Third World country projects in conjunction with the United Nations. You work out of New York and you're subsidising Matthew's company to prepare the mine for sale.'

Connor sighed. 'Heavy stuff for midday traffic in Georgetown, but in a nutshell I'm a supervisor on projects designed to kick-start development in countries like Guyana. Through the banking network I can get the backing of big companies and big money if the project warrants it.'

'Sounds a bit risky. What if you get it wrong?'

Connor leaned back and raised his hands in a gesture of mock horror. 'Get it wrong? Don't even suggest the possibility.' He became serious again. 'No, so far no major disasters. We have built-in checks and balances, but yes, there are mistakes sometimes because we're dealing with places like Guyminco and also a gold mine here called Columbus, that usually don't have enough skilled workers and administrators. And there's been a lot of power plays—mostly crooked. These countries are vulnerable to a lot of very shonky wheelers and dealers in business circles.'

'You mean some businessmen are criminals? Why is it like this?

'Well, in the case of Guyana there were too many cooks for the broth. The educational infrastructure just hasn't been there to cope with the development of mineral resources that's now heading the agenda here. The real action in Guyana is just beginning. If they don't get the right help now, and learn to handle their finances properly, corruption and greed will ensure that all this bauxite and gold mining will make a few rich people richer and leave the poor wondering what the hell it was all about.'

'And that's where you are making your contribution?'

'Yes, but it's hard to get across sometimes that the income from natural wealth needs to be invested in essential infrastructure to make the economy attractive to foreign investment. You may have noticed a certain laissez-faire attitude about the place.'

'Yes, it's quaint the way they can complicate the simplest task and find extraordinary ways of going around in circles.'

'Nicely put,' said Connor as he did a U-turn in Main Street. 'Here's the club, and let's change the subject to something a little more digestible for lunch. Right?'

'Your turn to pick the subject then.'

Connor gave her a quick approving glance. 'I have a splendid subject. Details later. By the way I'm glad you're wearing a skirt. Ladies in trousers, even smart silk ones, are not welcome.'

'You're joking.'

'This is the Georgetown Club, a bastion of conservative attitudes, class snobbery and discrimination.'

They drove into the members' carpark to be greeted by a uniformed guard. At the top of a small staircase leading into the club, a plump, dark woman welcomed them in fruity English tones. 'Will you be taking a drink before luncheon, Mr Bain?'

'Yes, we will, thank you.'

'You shall be called when luncheon is served.'

Madison lifted an amused eyebrow as they walked through onto a spacious airy verandah with deep cane lounges and chairs grouped on highly polished timber floors. The sloping wooden shutters stood angled open, channelling the breeze and screening guests from the gaze of passers-by in Main Street.

They drank Banks beer and chatted easily about people

they now knew in common and the coming long weekend trip to the Essequibo River where they'd all been invited by Colonel Bede Olivera—a former politician, now turned political commentator.

'I've heard some wild stories about the Essequibo resort area where the high flyers have their holiday places,' said Connor. 'It's called New Spirit but some call it "Happy Valley" like the place in Kenya where the Brits had their escapades in the 1930s.'

'*White Mischief*, the murder of Lord whatshisname,' said Madi. 'Wasn't that a movie starring Greta Scacchi? Good grief, are we going into that sort of colonial scene?'

Connor laughed. 'I doubt it. Most of the colonial trappings in Guyana have been replaced by the fashion called Miami high life, it seems to me.'

The waiter informed them lunch was served and on the way downstairs to the dining room they paused to study the old framed photographs from the early days of the club; cricket teams, past presidents and committees, all male, white, British and socially elite. Women appeared in photos at balls and social functions. 'Looks like something out of the Raj,' said Madison.

'Those days are gone,' came a pleasant voice behind them. Madison swung around to find Antonio Destra standing there. She realised she'd been too busy to call him.

'Hello there. How have you been?' she asked.

'Busy. And you? Discovering all the attractions that make up this interesting city, eh?'

'Yes indeed. In fact, didn't I see you down at the Amerindian hostel?'

Antonio's expression didn't change. 'No, I don't believe so. What were you doing there?'

'Just buying a hammock,' said Madi lightly. 'Do you

remember Connor Bain?' The men nodded and Connor touched her elbow, 'Our lunch is ready. Excuse us, Antonio.'

'Enjoy your lunch. I shall see you tonight.'

'Of course,' said Connor over his shoulder. 'Always the same mob, only the gossip changes.'

'Right on, pal,' called Antonio with an endorsing guffaw.

'He's a charming character, isn't he?' said Madi softly. 'Latin charm, I suppose. What does he do really?'

'Turns up everywhere,' said Connor with a grin. 'No seriously, he is the largest supplier of heavy machinery to the mines. And spare parts. Seems to be very well connected in politics too, with people like our weekend host, the colonel. But then if you aren't, you're dead in business in countries like this.'

Connor and Madi took their seats in what looked like a set for a film depicting India in the days of the British Raj, circa 1920s; heavy mahogany chairs, silver cutlery, bone china dinner service, starched linen serviettes. Soup was served immediately.

'Set menu?' queried Madison with a professionally raised eyebrow.

'Fraid so. Part of the charm of the place.'

The 'charm' extended to a main course of roast beef and three vegetables with gravy, accompanied by cut crystal holding black sauce, mustard and pepper and salt.

'So what is the interesting conversational subject you promised for lunch?' prompted Madi as they settled into the main course.

'You.'

'Boring.'

'Can't be as boring as my economics lecture in the car.'

'Well, you know the basics. Hospitality industry. Married young, divorced, sadder and wiser, now having a wonderful holiday, and hoping to make the big time in London, or equivalent.'

'Now a dedicated career woman.'

Madison sipped her boiled ice water to consider that one. 'Well, yes and no. I can't see why one can't be organised enough to have the best of both worlds. I suppose it depends on getting the right man and the right job. That's a big ask these days.'

'And what is your definition of the right man?'

'Someone very different from the last one. He's got to be straight up, honest, communicative, and above all respect me for who I am and what I aspire to.'

'Where do they make them like that?' quipped Connor.

'I'm not sure, but I'll keep my eyes open this time.' She put down her knife and fork, leaving much of the course as a comment on the overcooked food. A waitress quickly removed her plate and Madison put her elbows on the table and leaned towards Connor. 'Tell me about your love life.'

Connor choked on the baked potato he had just taken and there was a flustered grasp for a serviette and glass of water. He regained his composure. 'I see what you mean about communicating and being straight up, as you put it. Do I have time to compose the right answer?'

'Right answer for you, or for me? And . . . do we know each other that well?' grinned Madi.

'The downside to my job is the travel—which I love— but it isn't conducive to permanent relationships. I guess I've chosen career—'

'Men always do,' interjected Madi but Connor ignored the barb.

'So like you I'm keeping my eyes and options open. Anyway, that's not the sort of personal question a professional career woman should ask. Why are you interested in my love life?' he countered with a grin.

'Human nature interests me. Priorities are changing. It's hard to know where one fits these days . . . if one cares to know, that is. My mother grew up in the age of the superwoman who went for it all. She gave up her visions, dreams and expectations to raise a family and has felt resentful that she missed out in some way. That's just surmising, she's never actually said so. But she and Dad are starting a business together and they're very happy.'

'But hence your desire to make good?'

'Is that how I strike you?'

'No, actually you don't. I'm only going on what you say, not what you present. You seem somewhat vulnerable, understandable after a divorce, I imagine. But despite your plans to run the Pierre or Georges Cinq, you come across as a bit unfocused about your future. What's your real passion in life?'

Fortunately for Madi the dessert arrived. 'Steamed pudding and custard,' she exclaimed with delight and dismay. 'I don't believe it.'

'Obviously you'll be able to dine out forever on the story of the menu,' said Connor, clearly disappointed that she'd changed the subject. 'As I said, it's all charm. I'm absolutely delighted that the lunch is such a roaring success.' Madi noticed a touch of sarcasm in his voice. So what had she said wrong this time, she wondered.

Sampling the dessert gave Madi some moments to consider the conversation and whether she wanted to discuss with this man what he called the passion in her life. Her work, she realised, evoked enthusiasm and challenge and satisfaction, but never passion.

And there was no passion in her private life. Her marriage had been a disaster. For the first time Madi was forced to acknowledge she wasn't passionate about anything. She owned up. 'A good question, that one about passion, Connor. I've got to admit that I really haven't got a driving passion, if you exclude an enthusiasm for doing well at my work.'

'No causes to follow?'

'Nothing you'd call passionate. I'm for the environment, though. How about you? What cause are you championing?'

'I'm lucky. I'm absolutely passionate about my work. I really feel that I'm in a position to do some good for a lot of people like the Guyanese. New York is an exciting place to be based in, and the rest of the world is full of new challenges. Being on the move so much is a bit of a drag, but there is a constant intellectual challenge as well as the adrenalin charge of making sure I never lose a cent of the organisation's money.'

Over coffee Connor talked more about the assignments he had supervised in recent years and Madison had to acknowledge to herself that he was right. He really was passionate about his work. He really believed it was helping the people of Third World countries. That, in his own way, he was having a beneficial impact on social justice in the world.

Yet at the same time she found it all a little disturbing, despite the admiration she was beginning to feel for the handsome, suave, capable man across the table. There was something wrong. She couldn't put her finger on it, but there was just something about all that unqualified devotion to work that made her feel uncomfortable.

Well, maybe it was just that old paranoia raising its head again.

The bill arrived on a little tray in front of a garish plastic and rhinestone brooch on an extraordinarily large bosom. At least that was what Connor first saw, before his eyes rose to meet those of the beaming Guyanese woman who was the luncheon maitre d'.

As he signed the chit, Connor stole a quick glance towards Madi and he caught the smile in her eyes. He'd enjoyed Madi's company over lunch and hoped he'd see more of her during her visit. He would plan places to take her—dates with interesting women had been his pattern when opportunity presented itself in these outposts.

Madi intrigued him more than most and he couldn't help wondering about where she might end up. Would she be a tough hotel executive working long hours, going home to a lonely apartment? Or would she throw that over if she met the right man and settle down and raise a family? It suddenly struck him she would make a fine wife and mother—good-humoured, easygoing, and warm was how Matthew had painted his sister. He and Madi appeared to come from a secure and loving middle-class background.

Connor gave little weight or attention to Madi's comment that she might have both career and family. Women he'd seen do that ended up exhausted and frustrated because they never seemed to have enough time to do either job properly. And it certainly wasn't possible for the wives of men who had to move from country to country like him.

As they left the club Madison noticed Antonio Destra was now sitting with a group of expensively dressed women of several races, all chatting and laughing. 'There's Antonio,' she whispered, nudging Connor.

'Working the room, as always. He's indefatigable that man. All the women are the wives of big players in this town, so you can bet your life he's not just making social chit chat. Their gossip will be of some advantage to him. God knows what, though.'

'Maybe he just likes women, although he seemed happily married.'

'Practically every male in South America likes women. Now there's a popular passion for you.'

'That's stereotyping.' She gave him a sharp dig in the ribs.

Connor sent her home in a taxi because he had an appointment in the city and Madi decided to rest during the afternoon to be fresh for the evening reception. She found the humidity of the country quite exhausting and usually looked forward to her afternoon siesta. However, today she felt exhilarated after the lunch and decided to take her library book with her to the hammock on the verandah, happy to have some idle time to start reading the story of pistol-packing Gwen Richardson.

She flicked open the book and looked at some of the pictures. Gwen and her pistol featured in the frontispiece. Then for most of the time she'd stayed out of the pictures, acting as photographer to record the book's scenes of Georgetown, the river, and the boatmen and crew who dragged her small boat around the rapids. Madi was entranced to read that Gwen had hired a maid from Georgetown to travel with her. Gwen described Leonora as '. . . a young girl from the Demerara River . . . her mother is pure Indian but she could speak English . . . but was so wooden and stolid that I thought at first she would prove to be stupid but she was far from that . . . her *unresponsive demeanour was a mask she often adopted to hide her jolly nature'.*

Then a shot of a handsome man in a uniform caught Madi's eye. Despite his stern expression, he was a real Errol Flynn type with moustache and all. Major Maurice B. Blake was all the caption said. I wonder if Gwen took him with her into the jungle, Madi thought. God, on looks alone I'd follow him to the source of the Amazon. I think there's more to Gwen's little adventure than the title suggests.

She flicked to another photograph, this time of a camp in the jungle with Gwen looking totally at home in her solitary setting. The description on the opposite page caught Madi's eye:

'Now that I had my own landing and such good material to work on I was ambitious to make my camp as beautiful as possible. None of the trees or underbrush along the bank was cut, and they looked very decorative against the dark, gleaming water. From my tent door on the crest of the hill I could see over the tree-tops to the opposite bank, where there was a little creek cutting inland; sometimes before dawn, a long wraith-like wisp of white mist, following its curves, lay on the soft tree-tops, like a great spirit so weary of the night's revels that it was caught still sleeping, when it should have vanished before the first grey hint of dawn . . .

'I built a babricot table and benches of straight, fragrant saplings that gave out a delicious scent as I peeled off their outer dark cover and revealed the real cream and gold of their wood. No ancient Gothic banqueting hall was ever made more dignified nor more lovely than mine . . .

'At night the full moon gave the camp an air of deep mystery, and the pillars and arches, fading away in the

gloom, seemed to lead on forever. Through the trees the Kurupung caught the moonlight and broke into a million glittering pieces. In my dining-hall the solitary, narrow moonbeams that turned the leaves to virgin silver were slanting ways for fairies to climb to the leafy tree-tops.

'Never can I love any place more than I did my king-dom on Terry Hill. I hope to return there some day and have the Indians build me a house of forest timber and roof it with palm leaves. I shall gather orchids and strange flowering creepers and hang them from that fra-grant roof. On a nearby hill I shall have a garden of veg-etables and fruit trees. I shall have an Indian hunter and a lot of hens and chickens, and there I shall live in per-fect contentment and peacefulness.'

'Go, Gwen!' thought Madi, already swept up by her description. 'I wonder if she ever went back and fulfilled her dream.'

Spellbound, Madi turned back to the beginning of the book and started to read, occasionally reaching out for an iced lemon squash on the table beside the hammock.

She was putting the glass back on the table, while reading the book, when she got her first big surprise. Indeed, it was such a surprise that Madi dropped the glass and the squash spilt over the table so she had to scramble to stop the glass rolling off and breaking on the floor.

'Well, I'll be dammed,' said Madi out aloud and she ran inside to the telephone and dialled Matthew's office number.

'Matthew Wright.'

'Matt, Madi. Guess what?'

'The Sea Eagles have won the Grand Final.'

'Rubbish, Matt. No, I've discovered Gwen is Australian!'

'Gwen who?'

'Gwen Richardson. Pistol-packing Gwen, the Guyana diamond hunter.'

'Really.'

'Yep. From Ballarat. Because her book had an English publisher I'd assumed she was English. Her father was Scottish and he'd migrated to the goldfields in Victoria. How about that?'

There was silence at the other end of the line.

'Matt . . .?'

'Yeah. I was trying to think of something to say.'

'Oh.' Madi was clearly disappointed. 'Matt, you know that I have been reading about women adventurers all my life. Now here is one from close to home who did some extraordinary things right here in Guyana. It has really inspired me, Matt.'

'To do what?' he asked cautiously.

'Well, explore a bit of Guyana. Everyone keeps saying I must go to the interior.'

'Yeah, well, they meant on a tour or something, Madi. Not with a pith helmet and a pistol.'

'Matt, stop being a turn off. I find it very exciting, and I'm going to bore you with lots of Gwen's adventures from the book. Bye.'

'Don't pack a rucksack until I get home. But keep reading. Maybe she comes to a sticky end. And stay out of the sun. Bye, sis.' He hung up.

At the American Ambassador's reception she covered the essential small talk with her American hosts and, observing custom, she circulated and found herself in a group that included Antonio Destra and his wife, Celine, who was talking to another woman. Antonio turned to Madi and kissed her hand.

'Dear Madison, how lovely to see you again. Enjoy your lunch with Connor Bain? He is such a talented man in his field. I think he is going to help this country quite a bit.'

'Yes, it was nice. First chance I've had to talk to him properly. How about you? You were clearly outnumbered at the club.'

Antonio roared with laughter. 'All part of the rich tapestry of life, Madison. Look I'd like you to meet a friend of mine. He's in your line of business.'

He steered her across the room to a very distinguished-looking, impeccably dressed man in his mid-forties. Madi smiled to herself. Hotel management type to a 'T'.

'Madi, meet Sasha St Herve, manager of the Pessaro Hotel. Madison Wright, Sasha. She's one of your tribe.' He laughed loudly again. 'Excuse me if I leave you to compare notes on room service. I have to talk business with your brother. Catch you later, Madi.'

'Thanks, Antonio.'

'One of our city's characters is Antonio,' said Sasha, his accent immediately identifying him as Swiss. 'I was speaking to your brother a few moments ago and he told me you have been working in the hotel industry. Promotions, I believe.'

'Yes. Marketing and promotions. I'm hoping to move on and work in London.'

'You wouldn't like to do a little freelance work while you're here?'

Madi laughed, 'Well . . . it would be different, I guess.' Her expression changed. 'Are you serious?'

'Indeed yes. Expertise such as yours is not readily available here. I have a very bright young man from Barbados as marketing manager but he lacks entrepreneurial skills. And especially the ability to target women.

I'd like to get the local women into the hotel for lunches and cocktail parties. After all, they are the social organisers in this town. Perhaps we could discuss this further. Would you consider it inappropriate to sit on the terrace for a moment and talk more? This is the Guyanese style of doing business. Naturally if you would prefer to meet at the hotel . . .'

'There's no harm in talking. I'd be very interested in the logistics of running a hotel here.'

They settled themselves in smart white patio furniture covered in bold flower prints and took an hors d'oeuvre and a glass of champagne from a passing waiter.

'As you can imagine, being the only international hotel in the country we have to maintain certain standards, which can be a bit of a challenge. Things have improved dramatically here since the old socialist days, but there is still a stigma that our hotel is just for foreigners. I'd like to break down that barrier and attract more of the local population. Once they cross the threshold and feel comfortable, I hope they'll become regulars.'

'Are your prices a factor in keeping people away?'

'Possibly, but a lot of people here have money now. Some surprising types have a surprising amount of money,' he said, glancing at Madi to see if she'd caught his meaning.

'Are they the, er, types, you want in your hotel?'

'Naturally we don't want the rowdy element from down the rougher parts of town. But we have a good band playing by the pool, a dance area, outdoor dining, as well as the formal restaurant and a coffee shop.'

'I'd have to look at the hotel and get a more detailed briefing, do some research, and look at the timing because I hadn't planned to be here all that long. But I can say now that it could be interesting as a one-off project. And rather fun.'

Sasha St Herve leaned over and clinked his glass gently against Madi's. 'Come and join me for lunch at your convenience. You can make up your mind after that.'

Madi returned to the party and seeing Matthew in deep conversation with a well-dressed Guyanese man, headed towards him. Then catching the slight frown and negative look that crossed Matthew's face, she realised he didn't want to be interrupted. Business undoubtedly.

Matthew was relieved Madi had caught his signal. His conversation with Ernesto St Kitt was disturbing him and he wished Stewart Johns would materialise. Across the room, the CEO had been aware for some time of the intense conversation taking place between his marketing director and the government official who was proving to be a valuable link between the intricate workings of the political powerbrokers and AusGeo's task of saving the mine. St Kitt had emerged as an honest official who showed integrity and a sincere desire to see Guyana back on its feet.

But Ernesto St Kitt was a troubled man. 'My predecessors in the mines department were notorious for not keeping records, it appears,' he told Matthew with a wry smile. 'But one name keeps cropping up. That of a company called El Dorado. I thought you might like to know that a lot of missing funds from the Guyminco mine were apparently channelled through this company.'

'What sort of funds, what sort of money are we talking about? The mine has very little cash flow. It's been operating for some time by paying its bills with bauxite or holding them against future sales.'

'It's big money, and over a long period of time, starting during the Burnham regime. Looks quite systematic, really.' Ernesto was very English in his use of the language, a legacy of his years at the London School of Economics. 'Some of it relates to equipment purchases, spare parts, things like that. But the paperwork is very suspect, very inadequate by any commercial standard.'

'Even by Guyanese standards?' asked Matthew.

'Even by Guyanese standards.'

'What do you know about this El Dorado company?'

'Nothing—yet.'

'Working on it?'

'Of course.'

'Keep in touch, mate.'

'Most assuredly.'

They shook hands and as Matthew turned he bumped into Antonio Destra.

'Hi there, buddy. Just introduced your sister to the boss of the Pessaro. Nothing like a common interest to move things along.'

Matthew had met Destra once before, but only briefly, at one of the dinner parties soon after his arrival in Guyana when the AusGeo team was being introduced to a wide range of Georgetown identities. At the time Destra had indicated he had a few dealings with Guyminco and was well known to the now deposed Lennie Krupuk.

'That was kind of you, Antonio. They will no doubt compare notes on the catering tonight.'

'Right on, mate.' Destra was adept at picking up national characteristics of speech. 'This is really good news for Guyana that your company is sorting out Guyminco. Long overdue, I can tell you, but you probably don't need telling. Maybe I can help in some way?

I've been out of the country again or I would have made contact before this. How about lunch next week?'

Matthew was cautious. 'I'm a bit busy, Antonio. Got to go back upriver to the mine shortly. What did you want to talk about?'

Destra finished fussing with a big cigar and lit it with a flourish of his gold cigarette lighter. 'All things machinery-wise. I do a lot of work for the major mines. I've swung a deal or two with Guyminco in the past, but nothing big because they always seemed strapped for cash. But if you're going to get that place airborne you're going to need some new machinery and that's my line.' He puffed on the cigar then gave Matthew a sharp look. 'And maybe we could exchange a little bit of mining gossip.'

Matthew got the message. They exchanged business cards. 'I'll call you when I check my diary,' said Matthew.

Connor had claimed Madi for most of the evening and they were sharing one last drink when Matthew with Kevin beside him signalled it was time to bail out.

Connor declined Matthew's offer of a lift, as Madi excused herself to make a polite farewell round of several of the ladies, including the wife of the ambassador.

As they waited with Connor for the valet to fetch their cars, Matthew whispered to Madi, 'Get many offers from the over-sexed, over-here embassy staff?'

'The information guy was very attentive for a while. He might come good,' she said light-heartedly.

'You never know your luck in a big city,' returned Matthew. It was one of his pet expressions and Madi loved it.

'Funny you should say that. I got offered a job tonight.'

'Hey, everyone, Madi has been offered a job. Doing what, pray?'

'The top dog of the Pessaro is interested in my marketing skills.'

'Celebration called for,' shouted Matthew exuberantly. 'Everyone to the Palm Court for a nosh up. You can tell us all about it over dinner. You go with Connor and meet us there, okay?'

Clear of the embassy grounds Matthew turned on the car's tape player. 'Time to get a cultural fix, cobber,' he said to Kevin. John Williamson singing *Cootamundra Wattle* flowed from the speakers.

When the song finished Kevin turned down the volume a little. 'Pick up any quality goss, Matt?'

'Matter of fact I did. Does the El Dorado company mean anything to you?'

'Not unless it's connected with Sir Walter Raleigh and his little dream of riches.'

'No, but the symbolism may be spot on, Kev.'

'What do you mean?'

'Fill you in tomorrow. I'll brief Johns at the same time.'

'How about you? Gossip-wise?'

'The Americans are very, very interested in what we're doing with Guyminco. I rather fancy they might have some parties who would like to get their hands on it after we've smartened it up. The commercial attache really worked on me tonight.'

'I think we're going to make the CEO's day. Good news and bad news.'

'Who goes first?' chuckled Kevin.

Matthew smiled. 'We'll let the CEO make the choice.'

SEVEN

The motor launch moored at the stelling on the out-skirts of Georgetown was named *El Presidente Good Time*.

Colonel Bede Olivera stood on the landing, hands behind his back, sucking on an unlit cigar, smiling in welcome as his party of guests tumbled from the car.

Matt and Sharee, Kevin and Viti, Connor and Madi started unloading their bags.

'Leave that for the boy,' called the colonel. 'Get to it, boy,' he called to a wiry black teenager balanced on the stern of the launch. With a grin the youth leapt onto the wharf and headed for the pile of overnight bags.

Matthew introduced Sharee and Viti to the colonel, who gave them an appraising glance, took the cigar from his mouth and shook their hands. 'Glad to have you with us, girls. Been up to New Spirit before?'

They shook their heads. 'We're looking forward to it,' said Sharee with a big smile. 'It was very kind of you to invite us along. Matthew has assured us you men aren't going to spend all the time talking politics and mining.'

'You betcha.' The colonel looked pleased. 'There'll be plenty of fun, you can be sure of that. New Spirit is a special place. Unique in Guyana.'

The colonel was fond of sweeping statements and big gestures. He had extended the invitations in a manner where refusal would have been an insult. And as he'd pointed out to his male guests, it would be a very useful networking exercise. Stewart Johns was on a quick trip to Canada for an international mining conference and when Matthew had raised the invitation at their last meeting, the CEO had encouraged them to go. 'I hardly know the guy,' Matthew had said. 'Seems a bit strange. What do you suppose he's after? It might be a social weekend but there'll be a reason for it, for sure.'

'There's always a reason behind everything in this place, no matter how innocent it looks. But we need favours too. So if some of this damned bureaucratic red tape can be smoothed out by a pleasant weekend upriver, go for it I say. Apparently the New Spirit development is very lavish. Senior government officials and well-heeled business people have purchased leases and built weekend retreats there on the Essequibo River.'

'It's not exactly rustic. And no one seems to have asked where the public servants got the money.'

'Maybe you'll find out,' the CEO had grinned. 'Have a good time, but keep your eyes and ears open. I want a report when I get back. And not just on the fishing and waterskiing.'

Matthew and Kevin exchanged a quick grin watching the colonel escort Sharee and Viti on board *El Presidente Good Time*. He was living up to his reputation that ranged from ladies' man to powerbroker. A former Guyanese officer in Forbes Burnham's socialist army, he had changed sides and become a politician in the first democratic government. Then he had lost his seat and developed a penchant for outspoken criticism of his fellow politicians, including those in his own party. The final expulsion from favour came when he walked out on his plump African wife and seven children for a blonde stewardess. The colonel now spent part of the year in Guyana and part in New York where his wife preferred to live. He also made a living as a TV commentator and writer.

Connor had first met the colonel in New York. 'He's a big lump of a man but don't be taken in by his size,' he confided to Matthew. 'He's very fast on his feet when it comes to spotting a deal, detecting shifts in the political wind, and knowing how and what power plays are being made. He writes quite well too.'

Colonel Olivera, dressed in shorts that strained around his girth, expensive American Lacoste knit golf shirt, plastic sandals and Yankee baseball hat, bounced around the cruiser organising the storage of bags, chairs under the awning on the afterdeck, and the first round of drinks. Madi felt he was at pains to present himself as an affable cog in the machine with no regrets over losing his former position close to the hub of the system. There were flashes of ego tempered with bonhomie, and they all watched with amusement as he shouted orders to the teenage deckhand, the only crew, to release the mooring lines.

'What's your name?' asked Connor as the lad untied the final mooring down aft.

'Andy, boss. Andy Rodin.' He gave a little salute and they all burst out laughing as he added, 'Me is very handy.'

'Handy Andy,' they chorused in unison. 'And Rodin to boot,' chortled Connor, explaining to Viti who gave him a questioning look. 'Rodin, the sculptor—famous for his hands.'

Looking the part with his multicoloured crochet beanie perched atop his thicket of curly hair, calypso band T-shirt, faded shorts and bare feet, Andy clicked his fingers to show he was pleased with his new nickname.

The laughter was drowned by a throaty gurgle of the motor which the colonel flamboyantly accelerated and they roared away from the stelling.

They soon passed the suburbs and tatty little riverside townships that seemed to Madi very unhealthy and depressing.

Handy straddled the bow crooning to himself, tapping a tune on the wood of the bowsprit, his feet dangling over the side.

Madison sat on the deck behind him, her back against the wall of the cabin, hugging her knees and watching the unfolding vista of the broad river. She had left the main party on the deck aft so that she could experience her first look at the countryside without distraction. For the first time she felt she was seeing the real Guyana. Although it wasn't the deep heart of the country that Gwen had described in her book, already she had a taste and smell and sense of it.

The enormous width of the tannin-tinged river lapped the mysterious shadowy tangle of undergrowth that rose in a solid screen along the banks. She longed to explore beyond this tantalising green wall, visualising small villages and towns scattered along dirt tracks. And further inland, she imagined, were creeks and rivers that swept through near impenetrable jungle, hiding waterfalls and rapids and overlooked by mist-covered mountains.

The thick tropical growth edged the water for long stretches, then they'd round a wide sweeping bend and come across a small cluster of boats, a crude stelling, a clearing where thatched roofs were visible. Near one such village, a young boy in a small wooden canoe rested on his paddle to watch the luxury vessel from Georgetown speed by. Madi waved and was delighted when the youngster lifted his paddle in acknowledgement.

The colonel directed Kevin to open a cooler which was packed with ice and bottles filled with homemade rum punch. 'Speciality of the house,' he announced boisterously. Plastic cups of punch were passed around, the sweet juice mix barely disguising the powerful measure of rum. Madi came back to join them holding onto the handrail as she edged cautiously along the gunwale. Connor helped her down and offered her a drink. 'Well, I can think of tougher ways to spend a Saturday morning. What do you think of the scenery?'

'It's magic. Absolutely enchanting. Exciting, just as Gwen described it in the book I told you about. But my God it's hot out there in the sun.'

'Ha. Remember what Noel Coward used to sing, only mad dogs and Englishmen go out in the noonday sun.'

'Right on, buddy,' shouted the colonel as he handed the wheel over to Sharee. 'Follow the river, sweetie, you can't go far wrong . . . just don't run into the bank.' He blasted the boat's siren, attracting the attention of the deckhand on the bow. 'Hey, Andy, Handy Andy. Get in here and keep an eye on the lady.'

'Here's to the good life,' said Kevin and they raised their plastic cups in unison. 'Bloody strong, isn't it?' he gasped after a long drink. 'Reckon Guyana Airlines could fly planes on this stuff.'

'I'm working on it,' guffawed Olivera. 'Yeah, it's a good life Kevin, if you're on the right side of the track.' His expression changed and he became serious as he settled into a big deck chair boldly labelled *El Capitan*. 'Some people in Guyana talk about the good old days and mean when the British ran things. Even today lots of older people would like to see those times back. They didn't see it as colonial oppression, they simply believed the empire was good because it was British. God ordained it that way.'

'One could say the same about the Brits' influence over Australia a few decades ago,' said Matthew.

The colonel sipped his rum punch. 'My heritage is Portuguese with a bit of Indian thrown in. We look down on Africans as descendants of slaves even though the Portuguese and Indians were brought in as indentured workers, which was just a small step above being slaves, believe me. The Portuguese quickly moved from the canefields to commerce. But even though they were European, they spoke differently and had different cultural affinities than the British so they weren't classified as whites.'

'There's always a desire among immigrants to preserve their national identity and maintain their family and cultural roots,' said Connor. 'Unfortunately it can also be alienating.'

'In order to succeed in British Guiana, we had to adopt English ways and language. Today the Amerindians are really the only ones who have held on to their traditional ways. And that is only due to their isolation.'

'Is that changing now?' asked Madi.

'They're being forced to move more into mainstream society. In some villages they have vehicles and buy western food. The government programs are well intentioned but they also help dismantle the Amerindian's traditional lifestyle. However, the Amerindians are becoming more active in seeking a better share of the country's wealth. In some quarters they are now regarded as troublemakers.'

The Australians looked at each other. It was a familiar story.

'Race is such a divisive matter,' said Madi. 'Why can't the world just accept we are all one race—the human race.'

Olivera rolled his eyes. 'Ho, we have a dreamer in our midst.' He smiled almost condescendingly at Madi. 'Try telling that to the people in any country with a racially mixed population. Everyone believes theirs to be the superior race.'

Matthew decided to change the subject. 'So how is the country adjusting to the new democratic regime?'

'It's hiccupping along, as you would expect in a Third World country waking up after a long sleep. The government is trying. But among my old friends in government the understanding of egalitarianism doesn't quite mean we are all equal. And when it comes to free market thinking, opportunities are hard to resist sometimes, if you get my drift.' He gave the side of his nose a nudge with a finger.

'In other words corruption is rife, the rich get richer and the poor are getting the rough end of the pineapple,' said Madi.

'Nicely put, young lady. Could not have expressed it more succinctly myself. Rough end of the pineapple, eh? Is that a peculiarly Australian expression?'

Madi was disarmed. 'Yes, I think so . . . not widely used in polite conversation, though.'

'Say, I'll remember that. Figure I can use it some time.'

'It seems to me the economy is still rocky, times are tough for the average family,' said Kevin. 'Why doesn't the government make things easier for developers to increase the wealth of the place? You must admit the red tape is discouraging,' he added candidly.

Olivera was unfazed. 'You don't change an ingrained system overnight.

'But it's a rich place, really, mineral resource rich, that is.'

'Sure, Kevin. You're right. Guyana is rich in untapped resources and if we are truthful, the Amerindians hold the rights—historically if not legally—merely by being the indigenous population.' Olivera gave a shrug. 'Such comments are not popular with my esteemed colleagues.'

'Or developers, or investors, I imagine. So whose side are you on?' asked Madi.

He laughed. 'My dear girl, I was an idealist and I believed in socialism and the concept of the people's rule. A lovely ideal. An unfortunate reality. Now I am on my side. I look out for me. It's very fashionable in Guyana today.'

The colonel looked at his watch. 'Hey, I'd better check the bridge.' He swallowed the remains of his drink and threw the plastic cup into the river.

Connor realised Olivera had switched back to playing the affable host. The colonel's recognition of the Amerindian claims to the land and resources surprised Connor. It sat uneasily with the self-interest the man espoused. It certainly would not increase his popularity among the country's powerbrokers. And where, thought Connor, did all this fit with their invitation to spend a weekend up the river? He looked at Madi, who was engrossed once more in the jungle that embraced the river. She's got spirit, that girl. Real spirit.

'Hey, Madison.' It was the colonel, his head around the cockpit doorway. 'What you got to realise is that every man has his price. Some come cheaper than others. What's important is who is doing the buying.' He paused briefly. 'Think about it.'

Madi continued to stare across the river as he bustled back to the wheel and sounded the siren long and loud, signalling to a scatter of buildings in expansive gardens on a high bank of the river. He turned the boat and steered it towards a white jetty.

Manicured lawns ran right down to the water's edge. A pathway lined with palms and tropical shrubs climbed the bank to a large house that even from a distance reflected an impressive grandeur. There were barely visible rooftops of smaller residences scattered around the grounds.

'There are six houses in this section and a little beach and another small stelling round the bend. It's got water on three sides,' said the colonel as Handy leapt onto the wharf with a rope.

A middle-aged couple, smiling shyly, came to greet them. 'That's Rohan and Aradna, they'll take care of everything. The guest cottages are over there. Andy, get the gear. Right, my friends, up to the main house and let's find the others. Lunch is ready, Aradna?'

She nodded. 'We serve up soon as you say, master.'

The group straggled along the grass carpet, gazing up at the huge double-storeyed plantation style weekender. This was scarcely roughing it.

The other house guests, who'd arrived the day before, were spread along the spacious verandah, lolling on cane furniture and enjoying pre-lunch drinks. Antonio Destra was first to greet them. Then Lennie Krupuk, the former

148

head of the mine, waved a hand. Matthew glanced at Kevin who shrugged and said, 'Is Roxy here?'

''Fraid not. Busy supervising the packing back in Georgetown. We leave for Canada in a week.'

The irrepressible Lennie had been swiftly and laterally ejected from Guyminco as the cost overruns attributable to him became increasingly obvious. He resigned before he was pushed, an arrangement that suited everyone.

They then exchanged handshakes and warm greetings with the mines department official Ernesto St Kitt before the colonel launched into the rest of the introductions.

Here at New Spirit was an impressive coterie of senior officials, government ministers' men who made things happen in finance, trade, immigration and development. 'All from the right side of the track,' whispered Matthew to Madi.

She gave him a nudge in the ribs. 'By the way, I saw you bridle when I fired a salvo at the colonel.'

'It'll take more than that to sink the colonel.'

'I'm sure it will.'

Madi found the women were mostly girlfriends, decorative and unthreatening. Two more mature women quickly distanced themselves from the others, explaining they were private secretaries to two of the officials present. Madi was not sure how this was to be interpreted. The whole culture was unlike anything she'd experienced before, but she told herself it sure was interesting and it gave the weekend an unexpected edge.

Finally a woman in her sixties appeared from inside the house. She had a stunning smile, broad forehead and strong chin, wide mouth and eyes that sparkled with laughter. She had once been a very beautiful woman. The remains of her beauty were now lost in rolls of glistening black fat and addled skin that spoke of too much liquor, smoking and an indulged life. Her dark curly hair had a dramatic band of grey in one single swathe from the centre of her forehead down one side. She wore a loose African print shift, her feet were bare and a series of carved wooden bangles rattled around her arms as she came towards them.

'This is Lady Annabel Markham, just call her Annabel. If you want to know anything about horticulture, she's your girl,' boomed the colonel, introducing the group from the boat.

'Girl' wasn't quite the appropriate word, thought Matthew as he gallantly rose and took Her Ladyship's hand. 'Very pleased to meet you.'

Annabel had a deep throaty voice and a musical laugh. 'And I too. What a devilish handsome boatload you've brought us, Bede.' And she added, 'I can call him Bede, in fact I can call him almost anything I like . . . and I have in our time, eh?' she chuckled. 'I'm his ex-sister-in-law. The last remnant of his earlier incarnation.' She spoke with a very British accent and turned to Madi. 'And which of these fellows is lucky enough to claim you as his pretty girlfriend, eh?'

Madi bridled. 'None of them is so lucky, I'm afraid. I am Matthew's sister. I'm visiting him on my way to work in London.'

'Congratulations, Madison! In one stroke you have put me in my place, told me you are nobody's dolly bird, and that you are a professional woman. I salute you.' Plump as she was, Lady Annabel bobbed in a graceful curtsy and Madison grinned. 'Where are the drinks, Bede? You're falling behind in your duties as host.' She waved a hand, jangling her bangles and taking Madi's elbow, propelled her to a chaise and matching footstool further along the verandah. Her Ladyship put up her feet and spread her bulk along the chaise, indicating Madi perch on the footstool.

Madi did as she was bid, finding herself fascinated and also repelled by the imperious dame who seemed something of an anachronism in the present company.

She eyed Madi. 'I thought I'd rescue you from the damsels up there. Pinheads most of them. Now let's talk about London. I adore London. I was schooled there then came back here, which was a bit of a waste . . . though it was a very social place in my time you'll probably be surprised to hear. Very social. I married well . . . chose better than my sister,' she chuckled again, looking at the colonel, 'though the old bastard is good to me, seeing as I'm now a bit down on my uppers. He has to be nice to me, I know too much about him.

'Anyway, I married a diplomat, Guyanese, very bright, quite a bit older than me—I recommend older men, by the way, provided they have their own money and teeth. We spent many years in London. Haven't been back for yonks now. When he died I stayed on but the money ran out so I came back here and cared for my dear father till he passed away.

'I'm all on my own now. Once Bede and my sister split up, she took off for Canada with their tribe—God, all those children, I thank my lucky stars I'm a long-distance aunt, couldn't bear to have them around. And I stayed on and now in a strange way Bede Olivera, my ex-brother-in-law, is all the family I have.'

'Don't you get lonely?' asked Madi, thinking Lady Annabel probably had a fund of stories to recount.

'I used to rattle around in Daddy's old house—where I grew up—I'll take you there one day. Bede paid me out and did some deal so I at least have a small pension now. The house is only used occasionally. And I live in a flat behind

Bede's house. He spends a lot of time in New York, the second wife doesn't want much to do with Guyana or me. Can't imagine why. I can be quite entertaining, you know.'

'I can see that,' laughed Madison.

The colonel came over. 'Now, Annabel, stop holding court and boring Madison. Here's a drink.' He handed Lady Annabel a rum and coke. 'More punch, Madi? Or something else? We have spirits, beer . . .'

'A cold beer would be great. That punch sneaks up on you.'

'Everything sneaks up on you in this place,' observed Lady Annabel. 'It's one of Guyana's charms . . . the unpredictable.'

At lunch they sat along two big tables set on the verandah. A cool breeze wafting from the river below was fragrant with frangipani blooms. Aradna served large platters of baked fish, savoury rice, spinach salad and plantain fritters. Fine French and American wines appeared and later came brandy and port with a coconut mousse served in half shells sprinkled with brightly coloured shreds of coconut.

'If this is a casual weekend lunch, what do you dish up on posh occasions in town?' asked Kevin, leaning back in his chair and savouring the port.

'The difference is that in Georgetown you have to listen to me pontificate over brandy and cigars, here you are allowed to head for the nearest hammock,' joked the colonel.

The group scattered slowly, Lady Annabel going into her bedroom, the others to their rooms or shady parts of the gardens where hammocks hung and lounge chairs were placed facing the river.

'We're going to play mah-jong, or maybe cards,' said one of the girls, and Viti and Sharee were quick to agree to join them.

Antonio wandered off with a couple of the senior public servants to a set of chairs at the far end of the garden.

Matthew and Kevin opted to join the girls.

'Feel like a bit of a walk?' asked Connor.

Madi nodded. 'I need to walk off that lunch.'

'Stay on the track,' advised the colonel. 'There are nasties out there!'

They followed the path that wound through the land-scaped gardens where the guest cottages were dotted. 'It's a pretty lavish setup, bit like a resort,' commented Madi. 'Where do you suppose he got the money?'

'Need you ask? So, what do you think of our host, Colonel Olivera, and friends?'

Madi was thoughtful for a moment. 'Well, I'm not as familiar with the place and people as you guys are, but there are strange vibes beneath the surface. I have to say I find it all a little uncomfortable.'

'You felt it too. I assume it's the smell of power and corruption. That group could swing any deal they wanted. Most of all I think they're out to cream off what they can.'

Madi looked up questioningly at the man walking beside her. 'You don't seem too offended by it?'

'Seen it all before, over and over again. It's the way of the world, or at least a big slab of it. Power corrupts. Always has, always will. It just does so much better in a hothouse environment. Thrives, like a rainforest.'

'But it doesn't bother you?'

'Of course, Madi. But there's very little I can do about it, except to try to make the deals I'm involved in as clean as possible, but even they are going to end up a little grubby, you can be pretty sure.'

'Like the colonel . . . always looking after Number One. I suppose you're right. It's the same to some degree everywhere, I guess. It just seems distasteful when there are poor people struggling to give their kids a slightly better chance. People like the Amerindians Lester took me to see. They're good people, but they can't get ahead because they're not part of the system.' They walked silently for a while then Madi went on. 'It just seems so wrong when all I hear you men talk about is the wealth of this place.'

Connor put his arm about her shoulders, almost a consoling gesture. 'It's pretty rough and ready out here, just thinly disguised by sophisticated days like today. We're still trying to assess why Matt and Kevin and I were invited here with the bureaucrats who could get the mine on its feet.'

'You mean you're all here to make deals?' asked Madi.

'Not really. It will be a more subtle play. Did you notice Destra going off with a couple of those government officials? God knows what deal he's trying to pull. Ernesto—he's a surprise guest—the odd ball player, but he'll have his ear to the ground for more clues to the mysterious El Dorado company that he told Matt had been siphoning off money from the mine. Possibly with Krupuk's knowledge. I want to bend the ear of some of these government blokes. You see, Madi, so many of the people we need to help make the mine viable for sale are the same people who have been profiting from it. We are still having trouble getting approvals from government departments. Obstacles appear for no reason, files get lost, meetings get adjourned indefinitely. And there's no way the AusGeo team will tolerate shonky deals, not while Johns sets the standards. He's vintage crop, that man.'

'Three cheers for some good news. But how is AusGeo going to get the job done under these circumstances?'

Glancing at Madi's worried face, he took her hand. 'Don't worry. It's nothing that can't be solved. You're here for a good time. Let's go exploring. Let's leave the beaten track.'

They turned onto a little used trail into jungle where the sunlight was shredded into thin shards as it penetrated the canopy above. The forest floor had little undergrowth yet they could barely fit on the path side by side. 'Shall I go ahead, frighten away the snakes?' said Connor.

'You do that!' Madi laughed, realising Connor would always be the sort of man who looked after a woman, whether the woman wanted to be looked after or not.

He dropped her hand and stepped forward, and as he did so he leaned down and lightly kissed the top of her head. Surprised, she looked up at him and seeing his soft smile and the rather yearning expression in his eyes, caught her breath. In a second their faces drew close and he held her by the shoulders and kissed her lingeringly on the mouth. When they drew apart it seemed as if ages had passed. 'Why did we wait so long to do that?' he whispered, then squeezed her shoulder and stepped in front of her. 'Okay, follow me, Macduff.'

The trail weaved through rainforest trees and ferns, vines looped from branches and aerial roots stretched towards the dank moist ground.

Connor stopped and craned his neck upwards. 'Look at those trees, bloody magnificent. The country has millions of them.'

'I wonder how old these trees are?' Madi spoke softly, afraid to break the spell. The light about them seemed pale green, the air was heavy and wet, leaves the size of dinner plates drooped in the steamy atmosphere.

'This is real Garden of Eden stuff . . . unbelievable, right on the doorstep,' said Connor. 'Strange I've never been in a rainforest before.'

'Never been to North Queensland to see the Daintree?' said Madi incredulously.

'Went to the Blue Mountains in my bushwalking youth, but no, I missed the rainforest experience back home. Been spending too much time in the jungles of Tokyo, London and New York.'

Madi was overcome by the impact of this place. She had read that there come moments of recognition in life where your soul connects with the place you are in, and she understood this to be one of those moments. She turned to Connor. 'I don't know how to explain this, but I've just had a sort of flash, a sense that this place is special, as if it holds a message for me.'

Connor looked puzzled, but she seemed profoundly moved so he stilled the quip that sprang to his lips. 'You mean like a premonition, or deja vu? And why this place?'

'I don't think it's this particular spot, it's more the forest or jungle itself. It's the sort of thing Gwen talks about. She says if you feel at home, then it's right you should be here. It's the trees, the sheer wilderness, knowing this has been here so long . . .'

'Madi, half a mile back there's a mob sitting in the lap of luxury, we're scarcely in total wilderness.' Connor wrapped his arms about her. 'Don't take it so much to heart. Guyana is having a strange effect on you, I suspect. Or is it just because you're at some personal crossroad?'

She clung to him. 'I don't know, Connor. Lady Annabel said things just creep up on you in Guyana.' She sighed, looked up into his eyes and smiled. He kissed her again and as they drew apart she looked about her. 'All I know is, I have to go into the country—the interior. Up the rivers, see Kaieteur . . .'

'Like Gwen,' he said gently then looked at his watch. 'I think we'd better get back. I'd like a bit of time with a bloke from Treasury who's one of the guests, to see if he can help me get a decision out of them occasionally.'

She hugged him roughly. 'How bloody romantic.'

While Connor and Madi picked their way through the rainforest, the mid-afternoon lassitude and stillness had settled over the estate. Matthew swung lazily in a hammock under the thatched overhang outside the two-room cottage that he shared with Kevin. A slow footstep and shadow caused him to lift his head. Ernesto St Kitt was standing there.

'Were you sleeping?'

'No, just hanging out . . .' Matthew struggled to sit up, the hammock rocking to and fro. 'Come and join me, there's a chair in the shade. Hottest time of day, I reckon. Maybe a swim might be in order soon.'

'Yes, be a good idea.' St Kitt settled himself in the chair and stretched out his dark legs. He looked like he was ready for tennis in immaculate white shorts and white short-sleeved shirt.

He nodded his head towards the bedroom. 'Kevin with you?'

'Kevin's trying to consolidate his position with Viti. Connor's out walking in the rainforest with my sister.'

St Kitt drew up his legs and leaned forward. 'Good,

then we can speak. The El Dorado company . . .' he left the sentence unfinished.

Matthew looked at him. 'Have you found out anything?'

'Yes and no,' he said then chuckled. 'Been the story of my life lately. I find a clue, then I find I'm in a blind alley. It seems that everywhere I turn some information is mysteriously missing. Apparently quite a few people know I've been digging around, even though I've tried to be careful. Files disappear from cabinets and computer systems. One of the secretaries remembered seeing references to El Dorado, then suddenly told me she must have been mistaken. Soon after, she quit her job.'

Matthew leaned forward to encourage him. 'Any hard facts?'

St Kitt looked around as if expecting someone to be watching them, then replied. 'Your mine is, I suspect, just one of many sources of funds for this El Dorado organisation. I don't know who is behind the company as it is little more than a name with nominee shareholders to conceal the real owners of the operation. Even so, my file on it is growing very nicely and sooner rather than later I expect some names to fall into place. It's like an invisible funnel. Money goes in but where the spout empties out, I don't know. One thing I do know is that El Dorado has good connections with the government. It has been issued licences for a series of major development projects.'

'What sort of licences?'

'Mining, logging, export.'

'And one assumes a fee was paid for these licences?'

'Yes, but the real income for the government will be from royalties. I don't know the details. Of course, licences with royalties are licences to print money.'

'And no names? Would any of the government officials here this weekend know anything?'

Ernesto St Kitt nodded. 'I'm sure they do, but getting these bureaucrats to admit to anything is another matter altogether. Still, one doesn't know what one may just stumble across in chats on a weekend like this.' He leaned back as if in resignation and put his hands behind his head. 'This El Dorado business smells, Matthew. And it's disappointing. I had such hopes that new and better days were upon us.'

'What do you think is really going on . . . just between you and me.'

St Kitt shifted in his seat. 'This is pure speculation. But there has to be more than one important person involved. It must be a tight-knit group who have been milking funds and ruining companies like Guyminco. And I don't believe those at the very top of government are fully aware how bad it is. And I suspect some new players have moved in for a slice of the action. All this talk of Guyana taking off economically and getting international aid must sound like the original El Dorado revisited to some of the crime barons of South America.'

'Olivera? Is he clean?' asked Matthew. 'This place didn't come cheap and you don't make a fortune writing political commentaries about Guyana.'

'Olivera is not alone in this development. New Spirit is owned by a group of business leaders from Georgetown. It was originally meant to be reserved by the government for the Amerindians, you know.'

'Great!' exclaimed Matthew. 'I wonder if Lennie Krupuk knows anything about El Dorado? Surely he must because the payments El Dorado received from Guyminco occurred during his regime.'

'I think it is appropriate to ask him. Now that he no longer works for the company, he might think he is off the hook.'

'He is certainly not going to give me the time of day when it comes to questions like that,' said Matthew. 'Why don't you give him a go?'

'Of course. It's worth a try. Now he's planning to leave the country he may just be willing to feed me some crumbs from the table. Perhaps I may imply that I have a little leverage on the subject.'

'You're a good man, Ernesto. We have a saying at home, *"someone has to keep the bastards honest"*. You're trying hard to do just that. I hope you succeed. There are probably too many well-intentioned blokes who gave up long ago and subscribed to the *"if you can't beat 'em, join 'em"* theory.'

'You're very kind. Thank you. Hopefully right will triumph. It sometimes does, you know. See you at dinner.'

Matthew watched him break into a jog as he went across the lawn. There was something about St Kitt's parting remark—'*Hopefully right will triumph*'—that disturbed Matthew. The public servant didn't sound too convinced when he said it.

Dinner couldn't have been more jovial. Several of the men were amusing raconteurs and their retelling of some high level diplomatic manoeuvres with Fidel Castro in Cuba kept the guests entertained. The meal lasted a long time with everyone adjourning to the verandah for liqueurs and coffee.

Afterwards some settled down to watch a movie, relayed via Olivera's satellite dish; others played billiards, and a small group including Lennie Krupuk, Antonio

Destra, the colonel and some of the bureaucrats noisily played liar's dice for substantially high stakes.

It was the early hours of the morning when Madi awoke feeling thirsty and, wrapping her sarong about her, padded silently to the water bottle she'd left in the bathroom. She unscrewed the top, took a sip, then stepped out onto the dark verandah of her little cabin. She looked briefly into the sky, marvelling at the clarity of the stars, then absently took another drink, suddenly aware of the warm clammy air on her skin. At the same time she noticed that on the verandah of one of the guesthouses several people were talking in low voices, occasionally laughing lightly. Curious, she stepped quietly across the lawn, and listened, then moved closer. As her eyes adjusted to the dark, the candlelit gathering came into focus.

The activity around the table was deeply concentrated. On a second table closer to her, rows of white powder waited to be sniffed through a straw, a jar of tablets stood open and rolled cigarettes lay ready to be used. There was a cough, a snort, the striking of a match.

'Christ, they're into drugs. Hard stuff,' she whispered to herself as if the sound of her voice was necessary to determine reality from a nightmare.

Frightened, she shrank back and stumbled as she hurried to her cabin and locked the door. She sat on the bed in the darkness, hugging her shoulders to stop herself shaking and tried to replay the scene she'd witnessed, trying to put faces to the figures she'd been unable to see in the shadows.

Eventually she calmed down enough to crawl back under the sheet but it was some hours before she fell into a fitful sleep.

EIGHT

Like a bad dream shrinking in sunlight, the scenes of the night before seemed less scary to Madi when she awoke. But she still couldn't shake a sense of something sinister. While not feeling threatened herself, the knowledge that so many of the people sharing her weekend holiday were associated with hard drugs was deeply disturbing.

She wondered if she alone knew about it as she went to Matthew's room to suggest they walk over to breakfast together. Her brother was quick to see her mood. 'So what's bothering you?'

Madi quickly described the scene on the verandah the previous night. 'What do we do, Matt?'

'Do? We do nothing, Madi. It's nothing to do with us.

If that's their scene, let them be. It's not our bag, that's for sure, and they probably know that. They come up here to get into this sort of thing, I suppose. They're not inflicting it on us so don't worry about it.'

'Do you think anyone else knows?'

'In our group? I doubt it. The girls went to bed before us and Connor, Kevin and I weren't far behind. It's best we carry on as if we know nothing. It's their country, their scene and, as I said, they didn't try to inflict it on us.'

'It made me uncomfortable though. I've never had anything to do with drugs. Have you?' Madi asked.

'I smoked some pot in my wild youth and in Mexico a few years back I tried some sort of magic mushroom which was such a horrible experience it turned me off completely.'

'What happened?'

'A bad trip—hallucinations, weird and ghastly visions, no idea of time or space or place or who I was. I kept looking at my body and seeing parts of me melt or explode. It was like turning inside out—my skin was sucked inside and my entrails fell outside and sort of blew up and splattered. It was like drowning in your own innards.'

'Ugh!'

'Yeah. I don't recommend it. But these people are obviously snorting coke and using hip designer drugs. More socially acceptable than injecting yourself in a public loo,' Matthew grinned.

Madi digested this for a moment, pausing to pick a flower from beside the path and smell it. 'I guess there is a big drug scene here. You hear so much about drug cartels in South America, drug war lords and the like. It's just that I simply hadn't given a thought to the idea that I'd find it on my doorstep, so to speak.'

Matthew shrugged. 'I don't know how big it is. You don't get offered drugs in clubs or in back streets from what I've seen. I'm sure I would have been approached by now. But we are in South America and Colombia isn't all that far away.'

They reached the main house which was quiet, sun dappled and welcoming. Matthew squeezed Madi's arm. 'Let it go, Madi. Forget what you saw and enjoy yourself. And say nothing to the others at all.'

'Not even Connor?'

'I'll talk to him later, when we're back in Georgetown. By the way, do you remember exactly who was there, taking part?'

They paused at the bottom of the wooden staircase. Madi closed her eyes, trying to visualise the shadowy scene of the night before. 'Not really. I recognised two of the government guys. I heard a girl laugh.'

'Was Lady Annabel there? Or Ernesto?'

'I couldn't tell.'

The house boy Rohan approached, full of morning freshness, his hair slickly oiled in place. 'Good morning. You are the first awake. Will you take breakfast now?'

Matthew and Madi settled themselves at the table set for breakfast on the verandah as Aradna appeared with a shy smile and put papaya juice in front of them.

By the time they were eating their banana pancakes, Kevin, Connor and the girls had joined them and they all began describing how well they'd slept despite the barrage of mites and mosquitoes outside their mossie nets.

'We had little geckos all over the walls,' said Viti. 'Presumably they feasted on the mosquitoes.'

'Noisy little things though,' said Sharee, breaking into an imitation of their 'chuk-chuk' call.

164

'Are we the only ones up?' asked Connor, finishing his juice.

'The others must have partied on a bit,' said Matthew, working his pancake around in the brown sugar syrup. 'Well, they're missing the best part of the day. I just love these tropical mornings before the heat and humidity start sapping the energy.'

Madi leaned back in her chair and looked out into the jungle around the resort and sighed. 'You're right, Matt. It is a lovely part of the day, but more so up here than in Georgetown. Absolutely enchanting really. It's the closest I've come to being in the environment that captured Gwen's imagination and I can understand how easily she was seduced by it.'

Matthew laughed. 'That's what I like about you, sis, always the romantic.' He pushed back his chair and stood up. 'Okay, while you're finishing Sharee and I'll get Handy Andy organised with the boat to take us up the river for our day out with John and Ann da Silva. Everyone down on the stelling in forty-five minutes. Okay?'

As they threw bags of swimmers, towels and bottles of drink into the boat, Lady Annabel appeared on the balcony of the guesthouse. She gave them an Aussie cooee call and waved furiously.

'She's a real card, that one,' observed Connor as they waved back, laughing at her gesture to multiculturalism.

'I feel a bit sorry for Lady A,' said Viti as Kevin helped her aboard the launch. 'She must be lonely. Seems to belong to an age that left her behind.'

'I think she was quite a party girl in her time,' added Matthew. He turned to Madi. 'You should get her to show you through the old family home. She knows the scandal about most of the families in town.'

'Maybe I'll do that,' said Madi seriously. 'I'm finding this place more and more fascinating by the day.'

It was a half-hour trip in bright sunshine and as they rounded a bend in the river they came across John da Silva waterskiing behind a boat driven by Ann. Their speedboat raced across alongside and John swung dangerously close. Calling out a cheerful greeting and lifting a hand, he pointed out the small wooden A-frame house close to a high bank.

There was a small strip of grey sand in front and Handy swung the boat towards it, cutting the engine and letting the momentum carry them gently to shore where they leapt out into the shallow water. Handy dragged the anchor up onto the beach as John spun in almost to the shore, stepping out of his skis.

'Morning and welcome. Who's next for skiing? Water is perfect but, be warned, Ann drives boats only marginally less dramatically than racing cars.'

'I'll have a go,' said Kevin quickly as he pulled off his shirt. 'Got my cossie on ready to blast off. Did my apprenticeship on the Hawkesbury River in Sydney,' he said, grinning at Matthew and Madi.

Ann called from the boat, telling them to drop their stuff in the cabin and help themselves to food and drink.

'We just had breakfast,' Connor shouted back.

'Right, then come and meet the others and have a cold beer,' said John as they reached the house. Madi was amused to find that he wasn't joking about the beer so early in the morning. As they relaxed on the verandah of the house where the da Silvas were staying, John made sure they all had drinks, then fell into an easy chair.

'All very romantic,' he said. 'As tourism takes off here, a place like this would be a top spot for visitors.'

'Will tourism really take off here?' asked Connor of no one in particular.

'Has to,' replied John confidently. 'Everyone is on the lookout for the new tourism experience, trying to find the last unspoiled frontier. It won't be long before the operators discover that we've got something different in this country that's worth flogging to travellers. Despite its shortcomings, Guyana is still relatively stable and safe, you've got to agree.'

'There doesn't seem to be much infrastructure to support large-scale tourism,' observed Madi. 'It's no good promoting a destination with a difference if you don't have the right accommodation and services that tourists demand.'

'Right on,' agreed John enthusiastically. 'We've got to get that into the minds of our politicians. Most of their thinking is limited to mineral resources. Cut it, dig it, export it, seems to be their basic policy.'

At that moment the peace was shattered by the boat roaring into shore with Kevin giving a long triumphant shout as he glided stylishly across the water to reach the beach. The group on the deck cheered his performance and he acknowledged them with an exaggerated bow.

Sharee took up the tourism theme. 'This country may never be a Sun City, Miami or Hawaii, that's for sure, but it has a lot to offer that's different. The environment, for one thing. It's still largely unspoiled and we've got more rivers and rapids and waterfalls than you can count. Sure, there's little in the way of tourist infrastructure yet, but that takes investment. And there's plenty of ready cash here, even if it's not obvious,' she observed.

'What do you mean?' asked Madi.

'Certain people here have access to big bucks—mostly

gained illegally of course—but they don't spend it or invest it here. They're quick-dollar people who take the money and run or live lavishly on long holidays.'

'They look out for Number One,' observed Madi with a hint of cynicism. 'Just like the colonel's creed.'

'Ah yes, Olivera the unpredictable, the great survivor,' observed John, pausing to acknowledge the arrival of his wife and Kevin, carrying the skis. 'How's your visit with the great party-giver across the river?' he asked with a grin, pressing a finger to the side of his nose and sniffing. 'Any . . . you-know-what going on?'

'John!' admonished Ann with mock seriousness. The others laughed.

'It's not exactly a secret,' her husband responded.

'What?' asked Viti.

'Drugs,' said John. 'A lot of the folk who weekend across the river are into snorting coke.'

Viti gave a little gasp of surprise. 'I haven't seen any drug-taking at New Spirit. But then there are drugs everywhere these days. But I can't say I have noticed it getting any worse of late in the city.'

Matthew and Madi said nothing as John launched into anecdotes of the fast-developing drug scene in Guyana. 'The Colombian cartels are having it tough, so new routes have to be developed,' he said. 'If we're not careful Georgetown will become a gateway for cocaine and heroin dealers from other South American countries. In our back door and out our front door to Miami.'

Ann nodded. 'It has the potential for a local disaster if the police don't stop it soon.'

'Trouble is, some of the big boys in high office are involved as well, at least according to local gossip,' said John.

'It's not obvious on the streets,' remarked Kevin.

John leaned back in his deck chair and flicked the top off another bottle of beer. 'Haven't you seen those big black guys dripping gold and driving flash cars? Where do you think they get the cash?'

Madi was glad the subject of drugs had moved away from the drug-taking at New Spirit.

As she took in the beauty of the river, the bordering jungle, the mountains rising in the distance, the thought of this lovely country being taken over and controlled by drug lords appalled her. She resolved to talk to Lester about it. He was street smart and would probably have an accurate picture of the real scene.

'What do you think, Madi?' Connor interrupted her thoughts.

'About what?'

'Boy, you were far away. I mean about waterskiing . . . want to brave it?'

'Why not?'

They took turns skiing and falling up and down the broad Essequibo, everyone's efforts accompanied by shouts of good-natured derision or applause.

They finally pulled the speedboat onto the narrow beach and headed for the house for pre-lunch drinks. John was first to break the bad news.

'Friends, we have a crisis. Due to a discrepancy in logistics for the weekend, we are almost out of booze.'

The men looked at each other with bemused expressions. This was serious. 'No booze, on a Sunday morning in the middle of nowhere,' exclaimed Matthew.

'Fear not,' announced John with authority. 'We will sally forth to the nearest village and replenish our stock. Volunteers?'

Matthew and Kevin instantly put up their hands. Connor glanced at Madi.

'I'll come,' she called enthusiastically. 'Give me a chance to see my first local village.'

Matthew laughed. 'We will expect a full assessment of its charm and tourist promotion potential over lunch, Madi.'

She screwed up her face and poked out her tongue at him.

Connor stepped forward. 'I think I should also check out this local tourist attraction. Might find something the IFO will consider worth funding.' He doubled over in mock pain as Madi dug him in the ribs.

The expedition roared along the river for about ten minutes until they came to a village sprawling on a high bank with the dense jungle bearing in on three sides. A scatter of river boats and a couple of small ferries were moored to the stelling where a group of laughing children were doing 'bombs' into the water.

The village consisted of a main street half-sealed with a crumbling strip of bitumen, and several blocks of dirt roads lined with mainly unpainted wooden houses. There was a general store, an electrical and mechanical workshop, a petrol bowser, a shabby community hall, a white-painted Baptist church, a scatter of hawker stalls, two small dim cafes and a liquor shop.

Madi found it rather depressing. 'Whatever do they do here?' she asked John.

'God knows why it was built in the first place. Now it's providing labour for some of the logging companies working the area, and the shops flog a lot of stuff to the Amerindians living in the jungle or upstream. There are places like this along most rivers in the country.'

A well-dressed group gathered outside the church waiting for the service to begin. With them was a tall, thin, black man, dressed a little incongruously, Madi thought, in a three-piece black worsted suit, an old brocade waistcoat and garish patterned tie knotted under the curling, almost white collar. He held a black umbrella in one hand and a battered Bible in the other.

John led the little party into the liquor shop and while they negotiated their purchases Madi wandered along the street which opened onto a small town square, grassed in the centre with several large shade trees. Under the trees sat a group of some fifty Amerindians, men, women and children. They were listening attentively to a man who was clearly Amerindian. Madi squinted into the sun trying to see him more clearly. Yes! It was the same man she'd met at the Amerindian hostel in Georgetown, the man Lester had introduced her to. What was his name again? Ah yes. Xavier Rodrigues.

'C'mon, Madi,' called Matthew. 'Back to civilisation.'

She looked again at the meeting of Amerindians, then turned and ran after the men who were each carrying a case of beer.

As they passed by the church the last of the congregation were entering with the black-suited man bringing up the rear. He paused under the portico at the top of the steps, his attention caught by the group coming down the road loaded with liquor.

His face was running in sweat and his eyes popped with feverish passion as his voice rose in singing octaves . . . *'Oh yes, I hear de Lord and he speak to me and he say, here come de devil . . . Yes sir, de devil come and get inside dese poor people and send dem wild and crazy . . . crazy for de demon drink.'* He shook his umbrella at the party. *'You all gonna rot in hell, only de Lord Jesus can save you, yes siree, you is in big trouble with de Lord Jesus.'*

Only John responded, the others feeling a little

171

embarrassed. 'You may well be right, sir,' he said. 'Only time will tell.'

The afternoon, lubricated with rum and beer, passed at a leisurely pace. The girls followed John and Ann down to the little beach to have a cooling dip and see how successful they were at fishing. 'Might catch a passing apapraima,' John joked. 'One of the biggest freshwater fish in the world.'

'Are there really fish out there?' asked Sharee.

'Just piranha mainly,' said John casually.

Madi jumped, '*Just* piranha. You're joking! You mean we've been waterskiing near them?'

'The speedboat keeps them away,' said Ann, but as soon as she spoke John was pulling in his line, dragging a piranha over the grassy bank.

The girls clustered around the fish as it flapped on the grass. Madi studied the wide pointed mouth with the sloping rows of fine teeth.

Memories of reading thrillers where packs of flesh-stripping piranha dispatched hapless victims in seconds made her shudder.

Sharee picked up a stick and poked at the fish which promptly and savagely snapped the stick in half causing her to squeal and jump back.

Chuckling, John carefully held the fish, twisted the hook from the side of its mouth and tossed it back into the river with a strong bowling action.

'You've now met a sample of Guyana's wildlife, Madi,' said John.

'I saw a jaguar once,' said Sharee. 'I was driving to Brazil with my family. It was beautiful.'

Madi pounced. 'That's what I want to do.'

'Drive to Brazil?' asked Connor, who'd come down with Matt and Kevin to view the catch.

'Anything. Just to get out into the interior to see the real country and the people and the animals. I'd especially love to go up the Mazaruni River.'

'She's been reading Gwen's book again,' sighed Matthew.

'Whose book?' asked Ann.

Madi quickly filled her in on the story of the adventurous young Australian woman and her diamond-hunting expedition in the 1920s.

When she had finished, Ann asked Madi, 'Would you like to climb up to the falls?'

Viti glanced at the tall and striking Englishwoman. 'Falls? Which one?'

'Kaieteur, of course. There are lots of fabulous waterfalls in Guyana, but Kaieteur is special.'

'Oh it is. I've flown there,' said Viti with enthusiasm. 'But you can only stay about two hours because of the cloud cover and mist closing in. I'd love to go back and spend a day there.'

'That's the beauty of going overland,' said Ann, and added thoughtfully, 'I promised you I would organise a trip. I'll do it when we get back to Georgetown.'

Madi's eyes shone. 'That would be fantastic!'

'Let's talk it over with the others,' said Ann, leading them back to the verandah.

'How long does the trip take?' asked Connor.

'A week. Longer if you have problems,' said John.

Matthew looked concerned, sensing this discussion was getting serious. 'What sort of problems?'

'Accidents on the rapids, vehicles breaking down, Amerindians forgetting to leave a canoe at pick-up points, or all of those things.'

'When could we go?' persisted Madi.

'She's dead keen,' said John with enthusiasm. 'Ann, let's do it. It's been years since I went. I'd love to do it again.'

'How many can go?' asked Connor, who'd been following the conversation as intently as Madi. 'If Ann is willing to get the trip up, I'm keen to be in it.'

Ann shrugged. 'It's not just me. John has to get the vehicles. We'd need two four-wheel drives that can tow a trailer with gear. We have to take everything we need—petrol, water, food and so on.' Ann was suddenly businesslike. 'This would be a good time to go—before the rains.'

'Oh Matt, do come too!' exclaimed Madi.

'I can't, sis, I'm working, remember?'

'Yeah, me too,' said Kevin dolefully.

Madi flashed Connor a glance. 'You can get time off?' A warmth spread through her at the prospect of Connor sharing this special experience.

'Yes. In a strange sort of a way it could be classed as work. Count me in, Ann? I'm willing to push, pull and paddle.'

'That's more than likely too,' said John.

Sharee spoke up shyly. 'Could I come too? I've never been to the interior.'

'But you grew up here,' exclaimed Kevin.

'My parents always took me to Barbados or Brazil for holidays and we've never been far out of Georgetown. Guess they couldn't see any reason to.'

'Of course you can come if you're prepared to rough it a bit,' smiled Ann.

'That's going to be half the fun,' said Madi, remembering Girl Guide camps as a kid and teenage treks in the Blue Mountains with her university bushwalking club.

Connor tweaked her hair. 'You're a real surprise,

Madi. Sophisticate of the international hotel scene one moment, plunging into the jungle the next.'

They passed the next hour on the river bank leaning against the trunks of the trees which brought welcome shade and discussing details for the now highly anticipated Kaieteur trip.

Wearing sunglasses and holding a cold drink in one hand and trailing her fingers in the sand, Madi caught Matthew's eye. They exchanged a swift warm smile that said what they were both thinking. 'Now *this* is a good day.' Madi couldn't imagine any place on Earth she'd rather be.

Ann and John were still discussing practicalities for the trip to Kaieteur.

'Matt and Kevin can ask Hyacinth to cook food like pepperpot and curries and bake roti. The rest will be tinned and dry goods like rice,' said Ann.

'I can bring curries and pickled meats, they keep. And pepperpot, of course,' said Sharee.

Viti wrinkled her nose. 'I'll bring anything you like but pepperpot. I hate it.'

'That's unpatriotic, it's your national dish,' admonished Kevin, laughing.

'So which way do we go to Kaieteur?' asked Madi, thirsty for details.

'A day's drive to Kangaruma then into longboats to head up the Potaro River. There are three sets of rapids and others we have to walk around.'

'And we carry everything?' asked Sharee.

'Afraid so,' said John. 'Amerindian helpers are usually available, but sometimes they don't always appear on time.'

Ann grinned. 'That's my job. You send messages by the jungle telegraph and the tom-toms go into action. You cover every base then hope for the best.'

'The canoes tend to get older and leakier as you go upriver,' added John. 'It's all part of the adventure.' He roared with laughter and Sharee looked dubious.

Ann gave her husband a playful shove. 'For God's sake, John, stop trying to scare everyone. It's really a breeze—more or less. It's ages since we did something adventurous. I'm really looking forward to it.'

As the afternoon drew in they changed and settled themselves on the deck with rum punches. Madi wished they didn't have to go back to New Spirit. She enjoyed the company of this congenial group and was thrilled Connor would join them on the Kaieteur trip. His dry wit would counterbalance John's jovial and hearty manner. Ann, ever pragmatic and sensible, was also a delightful raconteur.

This unpretentious couple loved Guyana. They viewed it with the objective eyes of people who had lived abroad. They could understand the reasons for its flaws and appreciate its benefits. Admiring their positive attitude, Madi concluded that tolerance, optimism, patience and inventiveness were needed to enjoy life in Guyana.

Eventually they farewelled the da Silvas, boarded the boat and headed back down the river, which glinted like smooth silk in the late golden light of sunset. Back at New Spirit, Aradna and Rohan helped Handy unload their bags while the group headed across the grass.

The colonel cupped his hands and called to them. 'Sundowners are ready to be poured.' As they reached the balcony, Madi glanced back at the golden river and saw a path running along part of the river bank.

'I think I'll give the sundowners a miss, Matt. Had too much booze today as it is. I'm going to take in the sunset with a stroll along the river. See you at dinner.'

'Remember it's early tonight. We're leaving for Georgetown as soon as the moon is up.'

'No worries.'

Madi really enjoyed being alone for the first time that day. She walked slowly, pausing occasionally to take in the view or to find a flat stone and skip it across the surface of the water, just as she used to do as a kid on those treasured Christmas holidays with the family. She reached the end of the New Spirit complex then noticed a slightly overgrown path punched through the green wall of jungle. She paused and looked at it. Like a magic garden really, she thought. Step through the invisible gate and you're in another world.

She had walked for about twenty minutes in the quiet gloom of the dense undergrowth when she came to the edge of a small stream that flowed into the river. There were a couple of crude stools made of bush wood on the bank. She sat on one of them and gazed around. A lovely spot to meditate on nature's beauty, she told herself. Then something in the water caught her eye.

For reasons she could never explain she looked around and found a long stick. Leaning carefully over a log that lay half in the stream, she poked towards a dark shape barely visible in the murky water. The stick caught on something and she pulled gently, slowly dislodging and lifting the heavy object away from the log.

Her scream pierced the tree tops sending birds screeching in flight. It was a scream of horror. A gold watch glinted against a black arm, the hand hanging limply in a gesture of defeat. The body moved in the current and she screamed again, before letting go of the branch. Then she stood paralysed with shock as the body, responding to unseen forces, bobbed to the surface and rolled over before sinking again. But it was time enough for her to stare into the unseeing eyes of Ernesto St Kitt, his right temple clotted with blood.

Madi ran blindly along the jungle track and river bank to Matthew's cabin, praying he would be there. It was empty. So was Connor's. She tapped at another door and Viti opened it, hairbrush in hand. Her happy smile vanished as she saw white-faced Madi.

'Madi, is something wrong?'

Madi breathed deeply and slowly. She spoke with unnatural precision, in short gasps. 'Viti, would you please quickly find Matthew. Ask him to come over to my cabin. Don't make any fuss about it. Try to get him on his own.' She drew another deep breath.

Viti wanted to ask more questions but Madi simply whispered urgently, 'Please'. Then she turned and hurried away. Viti put down her brush, flipped her long black hair over her shoulder, closed the door and ran towards the main house.

In a few minutes Matthew opened the door to Madi's bungalow without knocking. 'What's up, I got some strange hissed message from Viti.' He stopped as he saw her sitting on the bed, her arms folded around her shoulders, staring at the floor. 'Sis . . . what's up?' As Madi lifted her stricken face, he hurried to her and wrapped his arms about her. 'For God's sake, Madi, tell me. Are you all right?'

'It's not me, Matt, it's Ernesto. He's dead. He's in the river.'

Matthew recoiled in shock. 'Dead? What do you mean?' He held her at arm's length, gripping her shoulders.

'He's drowned. He's in the river by a log. Down the path.'

Matthew sprang to his feet. 'We'd better get help, get people up there quickly.'

'Matt. No . . . wait. I mean, yes, we have to do that, but it's just . . .'

'Just what?' Matthew sat down beside her again. 'What, Madi?' he asked gently. The impact of it was starting to hit him, the fact that, of all the people there, the man who was trying to help him was dead.

Madi spoke slowly and softly. 'I don't know what happened. He didn't have any clothes on. Just his watch. And there was a big cut and lump, a bad one, on his head. He was caught by a log.' Madi stopped as if exhausted by the effort of talking. She shook her head. 'Matt, I'm scared.'

Her brother wrapped his arms around her again. 'Hey, come on now, sis. Chin up, as Dad used to say. Look there's nothing to be scared of, even though it must have been a horrible shock for you. It was probably just a terrible accident.' Matthew tried to comfort her but his words trailed off. 'You haven't said anything to anyone about seeing the drugs last night?'

She shook her head.

'Keep it that way. I don't know if it's connected, but I'm pretty sure Ernesto would not have been part of this drug scene. He was invited here for some other reason, like we all were.' He paused for a moment thinking fast. 'Look sis, we'll have to report this without any more delay. I'll go and tell them what's happened and that you're in a bit of a state and are resting. Stay here. I'll send one of the girls down to be with you.'

'And Connor.'

'I think Connor and I should go with them to . . . stay

with the body till the police come.' He kissed her quickly. 'I'm sorry this happened to you, it's horrible. But let it go, Madi, it's over.'

'Oh no, it's not,' she murmured as Matthew raced back to the big house.

Madi changed and lay on the bed hearing events unfold—loud voices, shouts, an engine starting, a boat roaring up the river.

There was a tap at her door. 'Madison, may I come in?'

Madi hesitated before answering, 'Yes, Annabel, of course.'

'My dear girl,' she came and sat on the edge of the bed, 'how ghastly for you. What a tragedy this is.'

Madi didn't answer. Lady Annabel was deeply concerned. 'Poor Ernesto. What a shock. What happened, do you suppose?'

'I have no idea.'

'Come and have a stiff brandy.'

Madi rallied and stood up, 'Yes, I think that's a good idea. Thanks, Annabel.'

They joined the others who were all gathered on the balcony talking quietly. As Annabel poured the brandy, the girls and Kevin hugged Madi, asking gentle questions. But Madi kept her answers brief and made it obvious she didn't want to talk about the incident.

Antonio Destra came over to join Annabel and Madi, who were leaning on the rail, not speaking and staring out over the dark river. 'Goddamned nasty business for you, Madi,' he said gruffly but sympathetically. 'Not the sort of thing a girl expects on a holiday. You feeling better now?'

Madi forced a little smile. 'The brandy is helping.'

'Unfortunate accident. Most unfortunate. Can't understand what possessed the man to go swimming right up there. I'd been looking for him all day for a talk.'

Madi stiffened slightly. 'You mean you didn't see him all day?'

'Yeah. He wasn't at breakfast, so the staff told me.'

'Then perhaps he drowned last night,' said Madi almost as if thinking aloud, then bit her tongue.

'I had a nightcap with him about midnight, maybe a little later. He said he wanted a relatively early night,' said Lady Annabel. 'Charming chap really. Very decent. Quite extraordinary at his job, so I hear. Hardly the sort of fellow one expects to go skinny-dipping in the middle of the night, Madi.'

'No, of course not,' agreed Madi, but there was something about this conversation that made her once again feel a chill of fear ripple down her spine. 'I think I'll have another brandy if you don't mind.'

As Annabel went to the bar Madi turned to Antonio and asked with forced casualness, 'What were you going to talk to him about?'

Antonio was caught off guard. 'Talk to him? Oh, yeah. You know, the usual,' he said, slightly rattled. 'Business chat. Gotta keep in with these public servants, you know. They're the real powerbrokers in this place. The politicians are just the front guys on the stage. Anyway that's how I see it.' He cocked an ear towards the river. 'I can hear the police helicopter coming in. I'd better go down and direct them to the stream.'

Standing on the river bank beside Annabel, Madi was the first to turn away as the dark shape was lifted from the boat and dropped onto the little wharf with a thud. A rug was quickly thrown over the body. Connor and Matthew came up looking grim faced, leaving the colonel and Antonio on the wharf. Aradna quietly asked if anyone wanted dinner but was sent away to bring more drinks.

Finally Colonel Olivera appeared with the two police officers from Georgetown. 'I know you all planned to leave this evening, but this unfortunate incident has of course changed matters. You'll each be required to give a statement, nothing to worry about. Straightforward accident I'd say.'

Madi and the girls threw nervous looks at Connor, Matthew and Kevin. The colonel continued. 'I'm sure you'll want to help clear matters up as soon as possible for Ernesto's sake and for his family's.'

'Of course. We'll do everything we can to help,' said Matthew. He gave a quick nod to his sister, who was standing nearby with Connor holding her hand.

Connor squeezed her fingers and spoke quietly in her ear. 'You all right?'

'Sort of.' She gripped his hand and turned him around so they faced the river, their backs to the rest of the group. 'You don't think they'll keep us here tonight, do you? Please get us out of here after we've talked to the police,' she whispered urgently.

Connor kissed her on the side of her head. 'I'll fix it with Matt. Don't worry, Madi.'

Half an hour later, everyone was gathered on the balcony again. The colonel came out with a safari-suited senior police officer and a junior uniformed officer.

The police chief smiled politely showing large, yellow old-dog teeth. 'Ladies and gentlemen, I am Inspector Palmer and this is my assistant, Frickdern, who will take notes. I realise this is distressing for you all so I will try to keep matters as brief as possible. If further information is required we will contact you back in Georgetown.'

He then asked to speak to Madi first as her statement would be the most important. Inside the house, Madi sat on a hard leather chair facing Inspector Palmer on the lounge. Frickdern sat to one side making notes on his lap.

She told exactly what she had done and seen, trying hard to keep her voice as neutral as possible, adding when she finished, 'It has been a great shock, I'd like to get away and forget the whole thing as soon as possible. I'm just here on holiday'.

'All very understandable. Of course it has been a shock. A nasty one. Have you ever seen a deceased person before?' he asked in a conversational manner.

'No, I have not,' she answered almost curtly.

'Difficult. Especially when a friend meets a tragic accident.'

'Ernesto was scarcely a friend. I only met him twice,' she snapped back and was about to ask why everyone was so readily convinced the death was due to an accident but stayed silent.

'Anything odd happen during the weekend involving the deceased, anything that sticks in your mind?'

Madi forced herself to stay calm. 'No. We've just been having a good time mainly. Some of the men had little businesslike chats. Our lot spent most of the day across the river.'

'And do you have any theories as to what might have happened?'

'Me? Theories?' Her eyes were wide and innocent. 'No. None at all.'

The smiling softness disappeared from the inspector's

face. 'Very well, Miss Wright. Thank you. Will you be staying in Georgetown much longer? I'll quite possibly have more questions for you.'

'I'll probably be staying on for a while.' She flashed him a brief half smile. 'I'll be very interested to know exactly what happened.'

'So will I, Miss Wright. So will I.' Madi was leaving the room when the inspector threw a final question at her. 'Oh, Miss Wright, did your brother have one of those little business chats with the deceased?'

Madi was taken aback and turned around stunned. 'Er . . . yes, I think he did.'

'Thank you, Miss Wright. Please ask your brother to step in.'

By the time everyone had been questioned, a buffet of cold food had been spread out on the verandah and the atmosphere had relaxed a little. Matthew and Connor went to the colonel, who was getting quite drunk but trying to hold himself in check with a bit of a struggle. 'Colonel . . . Bede, we're going to head back. Andy is confident he can handle the boat in the dark. He spoke to Rohan who has agreed to accompany us and help bring back the boat, if that's all right with you.'

Olivera's sober and formal demeanour melted abruptly and he leaned back in his chair, waving his drink which slopped on his hand. 'Please yourselves. I'm sorry the weekend ended so badly. Next time, eh?'

'Indeed, next time,' said Connor graciously. They both shook the colonel's hand. The girls muttered their farewells to the group in general and they all headed for the boat in such haste that Madi almost smiled.

As they were stepping from the stelling, Madi suddenly looked down and in the waving torchlight caught a glimpse of a slightly damp patch on the decking beneath her feet. With a shudder she realised she was standing where Ernesto's body had lain.

Once settled and travelling down the river in the silver path of the moon no one felt a need to speak. Everyone was tired and Madi felt drained. Connor dropped his arm around her. 'It won't seem as bad in the morning.'

She tried to still her mind but the more she thought about Ernesto's death the more questions and fears came to her mind until, utterly exhausted, she fell asleep on Connor's shoulder.

NINE

The AusGeo driver pulled up to the Pessaro Hotel and a tired Matthew and Kevin got out and headed for the small meeting room on the first floor. Stewart Johns, who'd arrived back the night before, had set up a breakfast for heads of departments from the mine and the Australian team. The group assembled and were served coffee by waiters standing stiffly to attention at one side. Kevin reached for a pastry.

'Five hours sleep last night after that big weekend is poor preparation for a session with the CEO,' he moaned over a black coffee. 'Have you talked to him yet?'

Matthew shook his head. 'No one has seen him, apparently. I'm wondering what all this is about. Why bring in the fellows from the mine?'

'Probably wants them to feel involved. What was he doing in Canada anyway?'

'Some international mining meeting of bigwigs, the future for the industry given the economic and environmental climate and so on.'

At that moment Johns strode into the room with a man they'd never seen before. The CEO looked fresh and buoyant. The other man was large, solid and fit-looking. Muscles bulged beneath his pale blue shirt despite his advancing age.

Johns glanced around the room. 'Good morning, gentlemen. This is Gordon Ash, Guyminco's new general manager. Please feel free to speak frankly in front of him.' He let this piece of news drop into the stunned silence, then continued. 'Okay. Report time. Fill us in on the past week or so.'

The reports went around the table, the mine people recounting production figures and technical problems. Some had been solved as best they could, other decisions were awaiting clearance or an alternative suggestion. Gordon Ash leaned forward, his big beefy hands clasped on the table in front of him, sometimes making notes as he followed every report with such intense attention that it caused the speakers to turn their eyes away from his unnerving scrutiny.

Eventually it was Matthew's turn.

'So, how was the social weekend with the backroom boys? Pick up anything of interest?' asked Johns.

Matthew spoke quickly and concisely filling him in on the death of Ernesto St Kitt.

'Good God, what a mess. Damned shame. There goes our best informant and helper in the government. Do you think it was an accident?'

'They're claiming it was.' Matthew kept silent about the drug-taking. 'I have my doubts though.'

'Nasty for your sister. What's the next move then?'

Matthew was reluctant to speak too openly outside their small Australian team, particularly when this gathering included Guyanese nationals. You never knew where loyalties lay or who knew whom. 'We gave statements to the police, they might want to see us again.'

'I see.' Johns moved on, getting little more out of Kevin but understanding he too was holding back. He then briefed the gathering on Gordon Ash, outlining his background as a solid mining executive who'd worked his way up with hands-on experience both in underground and open-cut projects, then moved to administrative status and ultimately to senior executive level. He'd worked in mines in many countries and was a problem solver who understood men, mining, technical and bureaucratic red tape. He would stay on as GM after the Australians had left, until the mine was sold or his two-year contract ran out, whichever came first.

Gordon Ash then made a short relaxed speech in his soft Canadian accent saying he had an open door policy, he expected to know about problems before they happened and would keep in close touch with the department heads. 'I like informal briefings. I jog every morning so I invite each of you to take your weekly turn of keeping me company on my early morning runs as a means of keeping me up to date. Healthy bodies and healthy minds lead to healthy productivity. Keeps the brain cells fit as well.'

He gave a cheerful smile and leaned back in his chair as the impact of this statement sank into the men, who were already feeling weary at the mere thought of running beside this man who was built like a rugby forward. *Breathing* would be difficult, let alone talking facts, figures. There were discreet raised eyebrows exchanged among the Australians as Johns broke the meeting into an informal meet-the-GM session while the buffet breakfast was wheeled in. He drew Matthew to one side.

'Nice surprise souvenir from your Canadian trip,' remarked Matthew with a smile.

'He was on my shortlist so I set up a meeting while I was away. He took the job immediately so here he is. He can be a bit abrasive at times, but he's bright and knows mining inside out and the men will respect him because he's one of them. He'll run a tight ship.'

'Good choice.'

'Can't afford to let our good work go down the drain. So fill me in. What didn't you say at the table just now?'

'I had a serious talk with St Kitt before he died. He sought me out, said he had been working on finding out who owns this mysterious El Dorado company, but hadn't been able to pin it down yet. But he had some suspicions that were pointing in a certain direction. I never found out more than that.'

'You think it was an accident?'

'No.'

'So it follows that if certain people were concerned at his probings, he was removed from the picture. Which means—'

Matthew completed the thought. 'That someone at New Spirit could have killed him, probably on Saturday night.'

'It doesn't make sense to invite a bunch of outsiders to a planned murder.'

'Maybe it wasn't planned.'

Johns raised his eyebrows and glanced across at the group clustered around Gordon Ash. 'I'd better get back to our new GM. Keep your eyes open, see if we can find another insider that might help us, but don't waste energy or take risks. We're not here to find out what happened to missing monies and shonky deals before we took over. We're here to clean up the mess. I'll need you and Kevin at the mine for a few days to help with Ash's orientation. And I've asked Connor to come out as well for a meeting with Ash re the money side of things. He needs to be clued in on the IFO deal we've made with Connor. At the end of the day, it may be the two of them that sign off on the Guyminco sale.'

The news of Ernesto St Kitt's death quickly spread through Georgetown, generating shocked gossip and speculation.

That evening Hyacinth bustled in before serving dinner, looking distressed, asking if it was true that Mr Ernesto had been murdered.

'My sister Primrose worked for them for little while. Dey nice family. He be an honest fellow. Who kill a good man like dat?'

'We were told it was an accident,' said Kevin quietly.

'Toosh, I don' believe what dem government people tell us. Mr Ernesto look after our people. He be honest, not take money like de rest of dem.' She turned towards the kitchen. 'Dis be bad ting. And we never gonna know.'

'Never going to know what, Hyacinth?' asked Madi as she came in and took her seat at the dining room table.

'Hyacinth, let's wait and see what the police find out,' said Matthew.

'You gonna be waiting till we git snow in Guyana, Mr Matthew,' she sniffed.

Madi stared at Hyacinth's retreating white uniform. 'She doesn't think we're going to find out what happened? What did you tell her?'

'We didn't tell her anything, she arrived with full details, including the news it was no accident.'

'What does she know?' Madi looked concerned.

'It's only gossip and there's going to be a lot of it. Ignore it and say nothing,' advised Matthew. 'Kevin and Connor and I are going out to the mine for a few days with the new GM. Too bad, as I had it in my head to go to the meeting Ernesto had set up.'

'What meeting?'

'I haven't mentioned this to anyone, except the police inspector. He's a cunning operator, by the way. Ernesto told me during our talk that he had a mid-morning meeting at the Blue Toucan on Wednesday with someone who had information about El Dorado, something about dealings with a bank.'

'That's all he said?' asked Madi.

'We were going to talk again after the meeting. Well, we'll have to forget that. Now, are you going to be all right on your own, Madi?'

'Yes. I'll be fine. I have to meet with Monsieur Sasha St Herve from the Pessaro Hotel. We arranged it at the ambassador's party.'

'That's right. He offered you a job. Are you going to take it?'

'I did have my sights set on London,' admitted Madi. 'But this sounds like a one-off campaign and there's nothing to be lost going along to listen. Might pay some expenses, like the Kaieteur trip.'

'You're still going on that?' asked Matthew somewhat surprised. 'I thought what happened the other day might have changed things a bit.'

'Why? If anything I think it's what I need, an adventure to distract me. I haven't been much of a tourist since I got here, more of a party girl. It's been fun,' she added, 'but I really feel a deep need to see more of the wild beauty of this country.'

'Well at least Connor will be going along to keep an eye on you.'

'I don't need anyone to look out for me. I can manage quite well on my own, thanks. Gwen did.'

Matthew grinned, pleased to see Madi back in independent form again.

On Tuesday morning at breakfast Madi opened the local morning paper and let out an indignant shriek. 'My God! Listen to this: *Government official found dead—drug overdose suspected cause of accident.*'

Matthew was just as astonished. 'Drug overdose? They're joking. You said you were sure Ernesto wasn't on the verandah that night. And Connor and I both agreed he didn't seem the type. I'm sure he was on our side.'

Madi stared at Matthew, seeing in her mind's eye the drug-taking scene on the verandah and the face of Ernesto in the river.

'"Sides", what do you mean "sides"? Just who are we dealing with?' Madi asked quietly.

Matthew rubbed his forehead. 'I wish I knew. Read the rest of the article.'

In a low voice Madi continued: '*An adviser to various government departments and a former lawyer, Mr St Kitt had achieved mid-level status in the service of the Government of Guyana. In the words of the Deputy Prime Minister, "he was a valuable and worthy professional employee. I did not know him socially but we are all sorry to hear of his sad demise under such circumstances".*

'It is believed Mr St Kitt had taken an as yet unnamed drug for recreational purposes on his own while visiting friends at New Spirit on the Essequibo. He went alone along the river, telling friends he was going for a walk and a swim. It is believed that while under the influence he fell, struck his head and drowned.

'He is survived by a wife and three children.'

Madi was furious. 'It's all bullshit, Matt. What a cover-up for Olivera and his government cronies. All distancing themselves very nicely.' Madi's eyes sparked in anger.

'Madi, think carefully,' Matthew said calmly. 'Is there any chance it could have been like they said?'

She thought before answering. 'I'm trying to be as objective as possible. I didn't know Ernesto well so I don't have any strong emotional need to try to protect him. I don't know anything about forensic science. I don't know why I am so sure about this, but there are some things you know in your bones are true. And I just know Ernesto didn't die like they're making out. It looked like he had been hit on the side of his head.'

'Well, it mightn't stand up in court, but I understand what you're saying. Even in the darkness I had the same impression.'

Madi stared at her brother. 'So he was murdered,' she said. It was a statement not a question.

'I see a horrible scenario emerging.' Matthew paused. 'He was asked up there out of the blue because he never socialises with those people. Then he sought me out to tell me he had suspicions about government deals that were being funded by some mysterious company called El Dorado. I think everything is tied up with whatever he was unearthing about El Dorado.'

'What had he found out? Did he tell you? Because if

he did . . . oh Matt, you could be in danger too!' Madi was suddenly fearful.

Her brother was quietly reassuring. 'As I said, he didn't have very much to tell me anyway. That's what was bothering him, the fact he could find out so little. He was convinced El Dorado had influence in high places. Files about the company had disappeared. That sort of thing.' A car horn sounded from the driveway. 'That's the company car. Look, I've got to get out to the mine. See you later.'

Matthew hugged her and Kevin called out goodbye from the bottom of the stairs. Madi finished her breakfast then called Lester to pick her up in the taxi. She needed to buy sunblock and a backpack for the hike to the falls.

Later sitting in a coffee shop with Lester she decided to pour out the whole story of the weekend, relieved to be able to share it.

'Man, dis be a bad story,' he shook his head. 'Dat Ernesto St Kitt be a good man. I don' think he bin ambitious, no grabbin' for power, but he wanted to make change. Good change. Now dey try to dirty up his name.'

Madi then told Lester she'd called him for another reason. 'What's the Blue Toucan?'

'It be a coffee shop in Charlestown, nuttin special. It be all right for a cup of coffee or a beer. Why? Yo want to go dere?'

'Yes.' Madi told him what Matthew had said about the meeting Ernesto had set up for Wednesday mid-morning at the Blue Toucan.

'So yo is gonna go, right? I knows it. I'm acomin' too. But who we gonna meet, Madison?'

'I don't know, I figured I'd just see who drifted in and out. Can't hurt.'

Lester chewed his lip for a moment before answering. 'Can't do no harm. Just keep yo eyes walkin round de room. But what yo gonna do if dis person find yo? Mebbe he know yo be a friend of Ernesto.'

'No one could possibly connect me with him. So, are you going to have coffee with me at the Blue Toucan?'

Lester heaved his shoulders. 'I gotta keep de eyes on yo, dat's for sure.'

They sat in silence for a moment, then Madison slapped the table. 'Lordy Lordy, Lester . . .' she cried mimicking him. 'I didn't tell you the good news!'

'You got good news after dis weekend? What might dat be?'

'I'm going to Kaieteur Falls . . . overland. Our friends are setting up a trip. I'm so excited, Lester.'

He grinned at her light cheerful change of tone. 'Dis be good for yo. So, yo get to see someting yo lady friend wrote about, huh? Now yo watch out for de jumbi,' he kidded. 'Be warned, nobody come back from Kaieteur de same. It changes people. It has a secret.'

'What's that?'

He grinned. 'If I tell yo, it no longer be a secret!'

He drove her back home and Madi was surprised and pleased to see Connor's car in the driveway. She waved to Lester and confirmed she'd see him tomorrow. As she hurried up the stairs he called out in a hearty voice, 'We got to get yo outfitted proper. Yo can't walk in de jungle without de gear!'

Connor dropped the newspaper and rose from the lounge, reaching her in the middle of the room and embracing her in a solid hug. Then loosening his embrace he stared earnestly into her eyes. 'Are you all right? I'm on my way out to the mine to meet the new GM. Matthew filled me in on the drug-taking at New Spirit and the conversation he had with Ernesto. It puts a whole different light on the man's death. I'm sorry you got involved, Madi.'

He leaned down and kissed her softly and at the tender touch of his lips, Madi found herself kissing him back ardently and strongly, suddenly overwhelmed with her physical need for support and caring. She drew away but stayed in his arms, holding on, unable to stem the tears as the pent-up shock, fears and sadness of the past weekend caught up with her.

'Let it out, Madi, and let it go.' Connor tightened his arms and held her till she felt better and gave a half smile as she pulled away wiping her cheeks.

'Sorry, but that feels better. I guess I needed to do that. Thanks for being such a good shoulder.'

Connor stared at the soft blondeness of Madi and for a minute he felt like he wanted to be more than just a shoulder to cry on. Madi always radiated such strength and independence and yet he knew that underneath this veneer she was still fragile and unsure of herself, her future. He also knew this was not the time to push himself forward too much. With a girl like Madi, patience was required. This thought surprised him. Patience meant time and who knew how much time they had together. He and Matthew had discussed the idea of encouraging Madi to go on to London but he knew she would never go until she had experienced the Kaieteur trip, and he was pleased.

The Blue Toucan was a simple coffee shop marked by a large wooden cutout of a painted blue toucan swinging by its curved beak. Madi and Lester arrived a little before ten o'clock and ordered coffee. They passed the next half hour talking about the interior of Guyana. Lester told her at greater length the saga of Sir Walter Raleigh who made two trips to Guyana in the sixteenth century in search of his El Dorado to lay gold at the feet of his beloved Queen Elizabeth.

'El Dorado, the fabled city of gold,' said Madi.

'El Dorado once be a person, not a city,' Lester told her. 'It means "de gilded one". He be a prince who be covered in gold. A Spanish conquistador who be captured by Raleigh in South America told him de story. How de Indian tribe save dis explorer. Dey blindfold him and lead him in de jungle and up de rivers to dis place where de warrior king and all his men be covered in gold dust and all about dem be a gold city, El Dorado. Raleigh be under de spell. He never want to rest till he find dis place, but he don't find it.'

Madi was fascinated and added another story about Raleigh. 'In history at school we learnt that Sir Walter spent years in the Tower of London and was eventually beheaded. He was most famous for throwing down his cape for the Queen to walk on, I think. Very gallant fellow, so the history books say.'

She sipped her coffee, thinking how lucky she had been to find Lester so early in her stay. Quite remarkable really, she thought, that they were both so comfortable with each other, yet poles apart in profession and culture. She realised with a little surprise that he was the first black man she had ever spent time with, talked with, felt like a friend with, even though she paid him for the taxi's waiting time.

She plunged back into history, 'I wonder if it was just greed that drove Raleigh on?'

'Mebbe, but he treat de Indians right, not like de Spanish, and he be really rapt about de natural beauty of Guyana. Like yo lady Gwen he love de birds, de forest.'

Lester's expression suddenly changed and Madi glanced over her shoulder towards the front of the coffee shop. Antonio Destra stood in the doorway looking round the small room. Seeing them he came towards Madi, taking off his sunglasses and quickly turning on a big smile. 'This is a surprise. Checking out the grass roots colour of the big city,' he laughed.

'You might say that,' she said a little coolly. 'Meet Lester Styles. A friend of mine. Lester, Antonio Destra.'

'I be her adventuring adviser,' said Lester with a grin as they shook hands.

'Is that right? So I hear you're really going to climb Kaieteur, eh? Few get to do it.' He turned to Lester. 'You going along too?'

'Been dere, done dat,' he replied with another big grin.

'Umm,' Antonio gave Lester a penetrating look.

'Are you meeting someone?' asked Madi, catching Antonio's eye and glancing round the near-deserted coffee shop.

He paused for a fraction then shrugged. 'No, had some business down this part of town and thought I'd have a snack. The place has quite a reputation for their black cake. Would you care to join me?'

Madi debated for a split second then shook her head. 'Many thanks, but no thanks. I have a meeting at the Pessaro. We were about to leave.'

'More your style, Madison,' smiled Antonio. 'Well, all the best.' He reached for her hand. 'I hope you have recovered from the weekend's unpleasantness,' he said, lowering his voice.

'As much as one can, Antonio.'

Lester nodded to him, Madi paid the bill and they headed into the street. Once in the car and on their way Lester said one word, as if he had read her mind. 'Coincidence?'

'Perhaps. Matthew didn't broadcast the info he got from Ernesto about the meeting.'

'Mebbe if he found out some way, he having a look to see who turn up to meet Ernesto, just like yo, Madison. Maybe he tink it yo. Maybe it be him. Strange he show up.'

'Antonio seems to have a habit of doing that, showing up. Let's go, Lester. I really do have an appointment at the Pessaro.'

Sasha St Herve settled Madi by the swimming pool at an umbrella-shaded table. The trainee waiter was nervous as he set out coffee for the manager, tea for his guest. Madi gave him a warm smile as he backed away. 'Who trains your staff?'

'We have two staff recruitment and training people. Those who show a bit of style and competence we send over to our sister hotel in Barbados for a bit of a polish and experience in dealing with picky travellers.'

'Guests here aren't so fussy?' grinned Madi.

'Well, we try our best but circumstances being what they are . . . If guests expect the same service, food, cooking and obsequiousness of a top European hotel, they will be disappointed. Guyana is a different experience . . . and frankly that is what I wanted to talk to you about.'

'Marketing a unique experience?'

The suavely dressed manager leaned back and gave a soft laugh. 'Spot on, Madison. Actually, that's exactly what I'm proposing. I have a concept—well, it's not totally my idea. And it's further down the track than a concept because we already have the important component, financial backing.'

'So who are you trying to sell the concept to if you already have the finance? Surely not the public at this stage.' Madi sipped her tea and looked at him. 'Who are you pitching to and what would I be selling if I take up your offer?'

Sasha also paused before answering. 'You're smart and obviously know this business. Very well . . . naturally what I tell you is in confidence.'

'Of course.' Madi was intrigued now as this sophisticated man was not the sort to trifle with insignificant details. He might only be the general manager of a four-star hotel in a Third World country but she could recognise the ambitions of a man who was aiming high in this competitive field.

'You haven't been to the mountains, the interior yet?'

'I'm about to go on a trip to Kaieteur Falls.'

The hotel manager was obviously delighted to hear this. 'Good. That will give you some idea of why this concept is so stunning.' He drew a breath. 'What we are proposing is a casino and wildlife lodge that is so spectacular it will rival the top theme complexes in the world. It's to be called Amazonia and it will give clients a one-off experience of the jungle, the animals, the rainforest all within the comfort and safety of a five-star hotel. High rollers will be flown in mainly to gamble, but there'll be golf, whitewater rafting, rainforest walks, flora and fauna parks, fishing and hunting. And a touch of local culture. We'll set up a kind of theme village where tourists can see how the Amerindians live and buy souvenirs and artefacts. But the key is the gambling.

That's what the guests will mainly be there for. The other attractions are a bonus. It will be the most spectacular casino in the world.'

Madi stared at him. 'Where would you put this . . . concept?'

'We've chosen a location in the south, so we can fly in the Brazilians, Colombians and Venezuelans as well as the Americans, Canadians, Brits, Japanese and other Asian tourists who would come in through Miami and Trinidad.'

'How would you supply, staff and run a huge complex in the middle of nowhere?' said Madi, thinking this sounded pie in the sky stuff.

'All it takes is money. I agree it will not be easy. You understand what is involved in the smooth running of a large complex.'

'You must have access to a huge amount of money. May I ask who is behind this?'

'Let's just say a consortium. As you are aware, profits from a successful casino can be immense. The backers feel it's worth the investment.'

'So where do I come in?' Madi's mind was racing but she wanted as much information as she could get before making a decision.

'We need the outline of a general promotional and marketing campaign, the PR side of it, to sell the concept to a few more offshore investors, the government, tourism and airline people and other parties we need to have on our side.'

'A glossy sales brochure prospectus pitch, eh? The rewards, benefits and pluses for all concerned,' said Madi with quiet authority.

'You have the picture.'

'Has the government given the go ahead?'

'The relative departments and ministers have indicated there's a green light on it.'

'But nothing is set in cement.' Madi wondered how sure this deal really was, but thinking quickly, decided that wasn't her concern. She could see fast and relatively easy money. 'I'd need to go to the location, get the feel of it, talk to the people involved . . .'

'Of course, we can fly you down south any time. As for information, I can give you everything you need, facts, photographs, artist's impression, plans . . .'

'But you're the spokesperson. Is the Pessaro chain involved?' Madi wondered why the backers and investors wished to remain anonymous. They'd chosen a perfect front man in Sasha St Herve.

'Indirectly. Package deals will involve clients coming into Georgetown and staying here before flying to the casino. Confidentially, it so happens my contract will be up for renewal at the same time we anticipate the Amazonia complex opening, so I could make a lateral move.'

'Turn down Europe for the jungle?' Madi gave the suave European an amused glance. He had the grace to look a trifle embarrassed.

'Money compensates for certain compromises and hardships. I can always fly to Europe for my vacation.'

Well, they've bought you, thought Madi. Then she said, 'I'm intrigued by the whole idea, of course. But I would like to think about it. Could we meet when I come back from my trip to the interior?'

'Of course. A perfect arrangement. You'll agree I'm sure that this country has huge potential for development.'

They moved on to talk about the hotel business, promotional successes and internationally known personalities in the hospitality industry. Madi enjoyed their talk but couldn't help feeling her involvement in the hotel business now seemed part of a previous life.

She finished her tea and thanked Sasha. As he escorted her through the lobby past shops displaying raw paintings of local scenes and 'Amerindian Artefacts For Sale', she saw Antonio Destra coming towards her with a wide smile. He stopped and shook Sasha's hand. 'I'm pleased to see you took my advice,' he said to Madi.

Madi turned to Sasha. 'Antonio ran into me meeting a Guyanese friend in a less than salubrious coffee shop in Charlestown this morning. He suggested I should frequent the Pessaro instead.'

'I have to agree, of course. You were out experiencing the other side of Georgetown, eh?' said Sasha smoothly.

'Only coffee with a friend. My big experience is yet to come.' She said goodbye to them both and went to the entrance, nodding to one of the two Pessaro taxis. Glancing over her shoulder she was surprised to see Antonio and Sasha engrossed in conversation.

It only took a week to assemble the expedition to Kaieteur Falls and on the night before their dawn departure the party of six gathered at the da Silvas' home for a barbecue and final checklist. John had two trailers to be towed by Land Rovers. Each had hollow sides which formed an extra petrol tank. Each carried spare tyres, ropes, tools, oars, water in heavy plastic barrels, cooking fuel, hammocks, tarpaulins and personal bags. Food was stored in a borrowed airline in-flight food container. Madi had followed the advice to pack as little as possible because they had to carry their own gear as well as extras.

As the final equipment was stowed in the trailers under John's supervision, Madi perched on the portico beneath a weak-bulbed light and read the appendix in Gwen's book. Gwen had listed all the items she had ordered for her expedition. Rations were served out each Sunday morning, each item being weighed in front of her men.

'So what does Gwen say we should have?' asked Connor teasingly.

'She recommends keeping the sugar soldered in a kerosene drum so it doesn't get wet or punctured. Among her medicines she says Maorix is a wonderful liniment— *a secret acquired from the Maoris of New Zealand who have knowledge of herbs, the secret of whose healing properties is unknown to Europeans,*' she read.

'What's it cure?'

'*It immediately alleviates the irritation of mosquito bites and stings.* Which reminds me, do you have repellent, Connor?'

'Where's the list.' He pulled a scrap of paper from his shorts pocket. 'Toilet paper, toothbrush and paste, hard water soap, mossie repellent, headache and tummy pills, plastic bags to keep everything in.'

'Sensible shoes that can get wet,' added Ann.

'I'm bringing my camera and extra film and a note-book,' said Madi.

'You going to write a book too?' asked Sharee.

'No, but I think it's nice to keep a journal. You forget things, so it's good to write impressions as they strike.'

The travellers, joined by Matthew and Kevin, slept in sleeping bags and on furniture and hammocks at the da Silvas' house, and at 4.30 they were roused for hot coffee and sweet rolls ready for the 5 am takeoff.

Matthew hugged Madi in the dawn light. 'Now don't

do anything stupid, heed Gwen's advice, and have a good time.' He kissed her cheek. 'I hope it's all you want it to be, sis.'

'I'm doing it, Matt, that's the main thing.' Her golden hair plaited into its thick braid sat shining on her shoulder beneath Matthew's favourite canvas fishing hat. She wore cotton jeans, a T-shirt under one of Matthew's cotton shirts, and thin cotton socks inside her tennis shoes.

Matthew turned to Connor and shook his hand. 'Keep an eye on the kid, mate.'

'No worries there, Matt. If I can keep up with her. When we get to the falls she'll be sprinting to be first to the top, I bet.'

'No one sprints up that climb,' said Ann. 'Besides, there's a lot to see on the way up, wonderful plants and ferns.'

More farewells, Kevin and Matthew giving Sharee and Viti quick hugs and then the six of them walked to the two packed vehicles, Ann, Madi and Connor getting into one, John, Sharee and Viti in the other. The engines gurgled with a throaty roar as Kevin and Matthew held open the gates, and the Land Rovers passed through.

Matthew looked up at the first streaks of dawn in the sky.

'Don't worry about her, sport. She's a strong hombre that sister of yours,' said Kevin, seeing the wistful expression on Matthew's face.

'I'm not so worried about her safety. I just hope she finds what she's looking for. She's been a bit lost in life and she seems so sure she's going to find whatever it is that will make her happy up those falls.'

'Good a place as any to start a fire,' said Kevin in his laconic Aussie way.

'What do you mean?'

'Dunno how to explain it. It was something my dad

who was a scoutmaster used to say. You have to start a fire in your belly and your soul before you get anywhere in the world and find your passion in life.'

'I've always thought the best times were sitting round a fire,' added Matthew thoughtfully.

'Well, let's hope the falls light Madi's fire. I'm going back to bed.'

As the gold red ball of the sun rolled over the horizon, the travellers sped down the new highway past the turn off to the Guyminco mine. When they hit the dirt road, a cloud of red dust billowed behind the first vehicle. Madi leaned across from the side bench where she was sitting to shout at Connor on the other side. 'Makes me think of the outback!'

'I was just thinking the same thing. You been around Australia much?'

Madi shook her head. 'Most of the capital cities. But I haven't been to the top end yet.'

'Shame on you.'

'I know. I'll rectify that one day. What about you?'

'All the top spots, Mt Isa, Weipa, the Pilbara, even Rum Jungle.'

'Work or pleasure?'

'Both. Interesting places. The IFO has money in various corporate developments out there.'

Madi wanted to talk more but the rattling trailer bouncing over corrugated ruts made conversation impossible.

The thin curtain of greenery on either side of the road thickened slightly and Madi felt at last she was leaving civilisation. The heat began to rise and she took out her notepad and fanned herself. Hearing the engine slow and stop she jumped out to stretch her legs.

The two vehicles had skittered down to the landing where they waited for a car ferry which was ploughing its flat wooden snout through the water towards their side of the river.

The Land Rovers were squeezed in between two massive timber trucks. As the ferry punted back across the river, Sharee handed out bacon and egg rolls.

'Never thought I'd enjoy a cold fried egg so much,' commented Connor.

The road on the other side led straight up a rutted incline. Ann passed the wheel to Connor and joined Madi in the back, stretching her legs. Red dust had turned her tanned skin and shorts a streaky orange.

'We drive straight through to a place called Kangaruma now. Let's hope we get there by dusk. We'll camp at a guesthouse there,' she said.

Madi nodded, thinking it would be a welcome relief. The bouncing in the back of the Land Rover was shaking every bone in her body.

Then without warning they sputtered to a stop. 'What the hell . . .' Ann swung over the side and went to Connor. 'What's up?'

'Don't know. She's stopped.'

'I can see that,' retorted Ann in her racing driver's manner as she lifted the bonnet.

She started tinkering while Connor and Madi sat on the side of the road.

'I'm not very mechanically proficient so I won't offer to help,' said Connor.

'Good,' said Ann from under the bonnet.

Birds smashed through the trees with almost sightless abandon, insects hummed and large black flies honed in on them. 'They're Kubowra flies, they sting, watch them,' advised Ann.

In seconds Connor and Madi were slapping at their arms, legs and necks as the Kubowra attack continued.

Ann announced that the ignition was shorting out. Each time the dash panel was screwed back on, it shorted again.

Ann swore under her breath. 'We need some sort of insulator,' she said.

Connor thought for a second then scrambled in the back and opened a box of rum. A bottle was pulled from its carton. Flattening the carton he handed it to Ann. 'Here, try this to steady the panel.'

It worked and they set off again. Before they'd gone a quarter of a mile they ran into the other Rover, which John had turned around when he realised they were not behind them.

Both vehicles were now driven as fast as their loads would allow to make up time. They lurched and bounced across the rough troughs in the road, the trailers shimmying and sashaying. Madi and Connor hit their heads on the roof one minute then crashed their bottoms on the metal seat the next. Madi untied a pillow from someone's belongings and sat on it, which helped a little.

'This is worse than my first riding lesson,' shouted Connor.

The road was narrow and overhanging sapling branches poked through the open sides of the Rover.

Then without warning, the second Rover stopped again. Cold dead.

This time it was serious. John drove back to them and conferred with Ann. Viti and Sharee joined Connor and Madi by the roadside.

In the late afternoon light, Madi looked along the road admiring the clumpy low plants lining the edge. As dusk fell, they lifted their heavy velvet green leaves towards the sun, displaying brilliant burnished red gold undersides.

Darkness fell. It seemed to Madi that it happened in less than a minute. Now the jungle loomed high either side of the road and it seemed to creep towards the group huddled by the two vehicles. The stars gave no light, the moon had yet to rise above the fortress of trees.

By torchlight John and Ann began to rewire the panel. With surgeon-like precision they worked in silence, occasionally requesting more light or 'pass the red wire through here'.

Madi stood to stretch her legs as the others sat on the road, leaning against the second vehicle. As she moved around the vehicle with her back to the jungle, she felt a spine-chilling, hackle-raising sensation that someone or something was behind her. She spun around and gasped as she came face to face with an Amerindian who was watching the proceedings with great interest. He was short, dusky-skinned and wore only loose khaki shorts. His hair was cut in a black fringe and he held a handful of tall spears. He was barefoot and gave her a friendly smile. 'Broke down, eh?'

'Yes,' replied Madi, still a little stunned, not expecting her first encounter with an Amerindian in the forest to be quite like this.

John pulled his head out from under the dash where he was half lying on his back.

'Big re-wiring job, know anything about engines?'

The Amerindian shook his head and grinned. 'Just outboard motor. Good luck. I go hunting now.'

'We are on the right road to Kangaruma?' asked Ann suddenly.

'Yes, many hours yet.' The hunter disappeared into the forest as soundlessly as he'd arrived.

For two hours they worked, stripping down bits of wire from here and there to rewire and bypass the ignition, wiring direct from the coil. Finally John straightened up and looked at Ann. 'Well, we have no lights, she won't idle, but she'll go.'

'Right, let's move,' said Ann and they all piled back into the vehicles. The engine turned over and kept revving and they took off into the darkness.

The night was inky and eerie. The track fell away into massive holes and hollows, or was barred by fallen trees and deep piles of sand, the lights from John's Rover in front barely helping.

'This is bloody impossible,' yelled Ann as they crashed over another log. 'Can't see a thing. Get a torch.'

Connor shone the torch from the passenger window. But it was little help.

Madi shouted to Connor to hand it back to her. 'I'm light, I could go on top and shine it down onto the middle of the road.'

'Well, hang on,' said Connor, handing her the torch. Ann slowed as Connor helped Madi climb the small ladder onto the roof where she lay flat, one arm linked to the roof railing, the other shining the torch onto the track ahead. It was only a pinlight of brightness but Ann yelled out it was doing the job.

They edged up the mountain, then began the descent, the slopes of the ravine dropping away on either side. Then away in the moonlight, glowing white against the jungle, Madi saw the small arch of a suspension bridge over a stream. The water moved slowly, glassy black, the near full moon lit the sandy bank like a luminous pearl.

'Not long now,' called Ann. She could now drive by moonlight, and Madi climbed down into the Rover. Connor rubbed her aching back.

'Having fun yet?' he asked in her ear. Madi was too tired to answer.

They followed the red tail-lights of John's vehicle as he gave a blast on the horn and turned left. Peering out of the side Madi saw a polished wooden signpost that pointed to *Guesthouse*.

They'd arrived at their first official stop. Connor glanced at his watch. It was just on midnight.

TEN

Shining in the moonlight, the Land Rovers passed a small thatched hut and came to a log fence which marked the yard of the guesthouse. A squat simple building loomed in the silvery light. All was dark.

'Well, we were expected at sunset and it's now past midnight,' said Ann. 'No wonder the caretaker is in bed.'

'Door's locked,' said Sharee in a tired voice.

'Find a window,' directed Ann.

Sharee pulled the old flyscreen off an open window and climbed inside to open the door. Lanterns revealed basic accommodation: three rooms with bunks, a kitchen, a screened verandah with a long wooden table and chairs.

'The fridge is broken and there's no oil for the stove,' reported John.

'And the water tank is leaking and empty,' finished Connor, who'd longed to wash the dust from his face and hands.

'This place is way below anyone's minimum standards,' declared Viti.

More lanterns were lit and a cooler was carried in with fresh fruit and beer chilling in the melted ice. Dust was thick, roaches scurried and the mustiness was choking. They flung open windows, even though some weren't screened. Madi peered down the hill from the verandah. 'What's down there?'

'The river, but I wouldn't swim, there are quite a few piranha. Better fill up some buckets for washing,' said John.

Sharee, Madi and Connor volunteered to bring back the water.

At the river's edge they tied a rope to the bucket handle, threw it out and hauled the water in. Madi took one look and, in the darkness, pulled off her shirt and tipped the bucket over herself. 'Ah, that's better,' she laughed. Connor didn't bother taking off his shirt and simply dumped the water over his head. Sharee modestly splashed herself and they each carried water back to the house where Ann and Viti had assembled a hasty supper of fruit salad, cheese and breadrolls. John downed a beer, did a U-turn and fell onto the nearest bunk.

The bunks were unmade, just old horsehair mattresses, but after the jolting of the past twenty hours, Madi welcomed anything that was motion free. She lay in the darkness, hearing the light breathing of Viti in the bunk above her, grateful for the cotton sari Sharee had loaned her as a sheet.

Wrapped in her colourful cocoon Madi tried to sleep but she was overtired, and the scrabblings and scratchings of what sounded like small feet bothered her. Turning on the torch she spotted a mouse but couldn't locate the crunchy noises. She closed her eyes. Hearing a thump and muttered curse from the next room and then noises on the verandah, Madi crept out to find Connor throwing a pillow onto the dining table.

'I'm sleeping here. That mattress is harbouring life.' He lay on his back and put his hands under his head on the pillow, crossed his ankles and shut his eyes.

Madi crept back to her room, eyeing her bed. She turned on the torch and flung back her old mattress. She couldn't help the small shriek that made Viti sit up in alarm.

The underside was a crawling, crunching, seething sea of cockroaches, inches thick as they oozed over each other's metallic bodies in a heaving black wave. Madi ran for the verandah and, after checking the cushions, curled up in an old armchair. Viti also fled and found refuge on a sagging lounge at the other end of the verandah. Connor snored peacefully on the dining table, oblivious to the arrival of his extra roommates.

In the morning some order was restored and the caretaker appeared. He was a vague old man who found oil for the stove, but scratched his head over the water situation.

'We need to conserve our drinking water, so just use it for cooking and drinking, river water for washing,' said Ann.

As the group had decided to stay until the following

214

morning, Madi, Sharee and Connor unpacked the hammocks, wishing they'd taken the time to do it the night before. John, Ann and Viti drove the few kilometres into a nearby town to visit the young district commissioner who issued permits to travel into Amerindian protected country. They came back with the required documents and a bag of grapefruit from the commissioner's tree.

John checked the trailers and with Connor moved them down to the river for gear to be loaded into the boat the following morning.

That night the boat captain, who was to take them up the Potaro River, arrived with a crate of cold beer from the rum shop he owned 'down the track'. Throwing off wet sacks covering the bottles he quickly named the local beer price. Connor raised his eyebrows at the near double cost of beer here compared to Georgetown. 'Freight and availability,' explained John.

'So how's it looking for tomorrow?' asked Connor of the slightly bowed, white-haired older man who had introduced himself as Captain Winston Blaise.

The captain rubbed his snowy white hair. 'She's low but we'll pass. We'll have to leave early, mind.'

After a dawn breakfast of porridge, Connor made two trips down to the river with the gear then walked back down the incline with Madi and the last load. 'Your brother's boss would approve of our boat,' he said.

'You mean it's not the *El Presidente Good Time*?'

'It's certainly not pretentious,' he grinned.

Madi's jaw dropped, then she burst out laughing at the ancient wooden longboat. Open and unlined, revealing its skeleton hull, it had a series of simple wooden planks serving as seats. The captain directed the stowing of the gear and then the passengers clambered in, sitting where he directed them to evenly distribute their weight.

'Dis boy assist me.' He pointed to the childish thirteen-year-old Amerindian who gave a shy smile then skipped to the bow and perched in its nose. Another man stepped forward, a tall strong African wearing a battered Panama hat with its sides rolled up cowboy style, a clean shirt and trousers cut off at mid-calf. The captain introduced him as Royston.

'We give him a lift upriver a little bit.'

They had no sooner set out with the outboard motor sputtering than water began to ooze steadily into the bottom of the boat.

'Water's coming in!' cried Sharee.

At the stern, tiller against his thigh, Captain Blaise glanced down. 'She do leak a bit,' he remarked laconically. 'Been outta de water. Soon seal up.' He pointed to the empty powdered milk tins. They got the message and started bailing.

Within an hour the seams appeared to have expanded and the steady trickle of water slowed to an imperceptible seepage.

Royston moved from where he'd been squatting and bailing and sat next to Madi, lifting his hat in greeting. 'What are you doing upriver, Royston?' she asked.

'I'm a pork-knocker.' He pulled a slip of paper from his top pocket and handed it to her.

She read his full name, birthplace in Guyana and age, forty-four. This slip of paper, it stated, gave him the right to mine for minerals for one year from the above date.

'When I'm not up the river I run a nightspot round D'Urban Street in Georgetown. But there's good money to be made if yo is lucky.' He pointed to the sides of the river banks where the earth, softened from rain, had partially collapsed. 'Some fellows dug twelve thousand dollars worth of gold outta there three weeks back. I've nearly saved enough for my own dredge so dis gold an' diamarns be jes waitin' fer me.'

'Do you work alone?'

'I got two partners and a fellow to cook.'

Madi smiled and nodded. The stories of porkknockers in Gwen's book and what Lester had recounted came flooding back. They were a strange breed of men, locked in a battle with themselves and a desire to find the wealth they believed would set them free. Small, even large strikes were often squandered, waiting for 'de big one'.

It was peaceful with the breeze in their faces. As they chugged along they were all wrapped in their own thoughts. The river was more than a kilometre across and smooth and apart from a flash of wings dashing across the water from the jungle on one side to the jungle on the other, they saw little sign of life.

Then up ahead the dark shape of a dredge loomed midstream. Royston pointed and the captain nodded, turning the tiller towards it.

Alongside, Royston heaved his hammock and his haversack with a packet of Foam washing powder protruding from it onto the mining dredge which would be his home for the coming months.

'Good luck, Royston,' called Madi.

'And to you,' he answered and lifted his hat as they moved away. They soon passed other dredges, flat barge affairs with equipment, generators, small cabin-style houses and plastic roofs to shade them. The plastic reflected and refracted in the sunlight on the water. Some of the dredges were moored in the shadows of the banks and all looked deserted.

'Where is everyone? Are they diving or ashore?' wondered Madi out loud. One had some tattered washing strung out to dry beneath a tarpaulin roof but it still looked abandoned.

'Down in Georgetown for the cricket,' said Captain Blaise. 'When de West Indies play, ever'ting stop.'

Madi glanced at the young Amerindian boy, who was now keeping a wary eye on the water.

'What's he looking for?' asked Connor.

'Tacubas, partly submerged logs, or sharp rocks just below the surface,' replied Ann.

John pointed at the stream of foamy white bubbles that began to appear on the surface of the river. 'Rapids ahead.'

'How far ahead?' asked Sharee, sounding worried.

'Time to turn ourselves into mules and packhorses,' grinned John.

They nosed into shore and unloaded everything including the engine. Connor helped Madi on with her backpack. 'You okay with this? John said it's about a kilometre.'

'Give me the other bag and my hammock, I'm fine.'

'Atta girl.'

The trek around the rapids, which were obscured by trees, was steep with a shaky log bridge to be crossed. Madi could hear the crashing rush of water over rocks and wished she could see the tumbling rapids.

At the end of the trek, everything was loaded into a second canoe which was waiting for them. Then they sat on flat rocks at the edge of the river and ate lunch.

Connor, beside Madi, watched the Amerindian boy throw a fishing line into the swirling water. 'I wouldn't want to fall in there.'

'Gwen had some close calls in the rapids. In those days they had to paddle all the way up the river,' said Madi, who was finding the heroine of her travels coming more and more into her mind as they travelled further towards Kaieteur Falls.

'Have you seen the canoe? The boats are getting smaller.'

'You mean we're all going in that one! I thought there must be two canoes. How are we going to fit?' exclaimed Madi.

'Snugly,' said Connor leaning against her and putting his arm around her shoulder to give her a hug.

Madi grinned at him. 'This is fun. Aren't you glad you came?'

'Bailing a leaky canoe, dragging gear up hill and down dale, wondering what danger and drama waits around the next bend?'

'Exactly,' laughed Madi.

Captain Blaise pushed the canoe into the rushing water, jumped in and yanked at the outboard, but nothing happened. The captain yanked again at the cord of the outboard, getting only a rheumatic gurgle in response. The boy pulled out a paddle and began to work it furiously. John, closest to him, took the paddle from his small arms and dug strongly into the water. The captain tried to nose back towards the bank or find a rock to anchor against. But the overloaded canoe drifted backwards with the current as the captain struggled with the engine and John paddled fruitlessly.

Madi reached for Connor's hand. 'I might get my wish to see these rapids. When do we bail out?'

'Now, now! Gwen would ride the rapids. Ever been whitewater rafting? It's fun.'

Madi shook her head, but at that moment the outboard roared to life and they surged forward to everyone's relief.

When Captain Blaise finally berthed upriver, they were all glad to see a somewhat larger and sturdier longboat waiting to take them on the final leg. Now they headed steadily upstream in the stillness of the early afternoon. For Madi, the scenes Gwen had described were coming vividly to life.

Viti passed homemade guava juice and lemonade and they chatted idly as the afternoon melted slowly into the river and forest on either side of the broad smooth water.

Captain Blaise spoke quietly. 'Soon be able to see him.'

'Who? You mean the falls?' asked Madi, excitement welling in her.

'Are we that close?' added Connor.

'Long way off,' grinned the captain, 'but from this next bend in the river you look up dat way, you see Kaieteur.'

Everyone in the boat craned to where he pointed. 'No matter how often you see it, the thrill never fades,' said Ann quietly. In silence they all looked upwards at the steep green hills as the boat moved up the middle of the river.

'There's water, is that it?' cried Sharee. 'To the right.'

'No, that be Grandmother's Armchair. They little falls,' said Captain Blaise.

Then in the crease of the hills they saw it and a shout went up. There was no mistaking the width of water dropping, dropping, down into a hidden gorge. A distant silver ribbon that was quickly, tantalisingly, lost from sight. Until around the next bend in the river it appeared again, an incredible length of distant sparkling silver hidden in the folds of impenetrable jungle-clad hills. They stared in silence at the far off sight, trying to imagine how awesome it must be close up. Then it was lost from sight again.

'We won't see it again till we get to the top,' said John.

'Looks a hell of a hike,' said Connor.

'It is,' remarked Ann. 'Walk at your own pace. It isn't a race.'

By late afternoon as the sun began to slide behind the high hills they glimpsed in the distance a white speck ahead on the edge of the river. 'That's the base camp for Kaieteur,' announced Captain Blaise.

'We'll have a warmer welcome than last night,' said Ann. 'The Bells are a dear old couple who have been caretakers here for years.'

'Nothing much has changed in three decades,' added John.

Slowly the little white speck grew larger and revealed itself to be a simple house, windows open, standing behind slips of dark figures who waited on the sandy strip of beach.

Captain Blaise cut the engine and they glided in, the boy leaping out and pushing the canoe into the shallows till it jammed on the sandy bottom. They all jumped out to cries of welcome and greetings.

'I be Roy Bell,' beamed the gnarled old man. His happy plump wife enfolded Madi, the first to reach her, in a hug. 'And I be Hilda.'

John and Ann greeted the Bells warmly. 'We bring messages, some mail and supplies.'

The resthouse was whitewashed, cool and clean and perfumed from the garden. Two sets of bedrooms stacked with bunks went to the left and right off the main room. 'Boys one side, girls t'other,' announced Ann.

Madi quickly rolled back the mattress, relieved to find it unoccupied by wildlife.

A long table was set outside under an awning. As the unpacking and organising swirled around her Madi stood to one side taking in her surroundings. Behind the resthouse was a little cottage belonging to the Bells—with an outdoor kitchen under a thatched roof. Their farm was behind that and off to the right was the gorge that led to the base of Kaieteur five kilometres away. Water from the falls bounced into rapids, then partly ran off into a stream that gurgled and rushed, and finally calmed and gently melted into the still water before the house.

Flat rocks led out to the deep water which was backed by dark hills in the distance. In the middle a rocky islet looked like an easy swim. Between the shore and the islet the water looked cool and inviting. In minutes everyone had found swimsuits and raced into the sunset waters to wash away the rigours of the journey. Connor produced his hard water soap and was amazed to find it lathered. Madi untied her hair braid, loosening her golden hair into the water. Connor reached for her and soaped her head, rubbing her scalp with his strong fingers. She lay back in his arms wondering if Gwen had ever felt as happy as this.

'Rinse off,' he commanded, pushing her beneath the

water and laughing as she came spluttering to the surface to try to push him under.

Refreshed they all settled around the outdoor table for their first civilised meal since they had set out, glad that an antique kerosene refrigerator offered some degree of chill for the food and drinks.

Mr Bell came by and quickly accepted an offer of rum. 'You want to make punch, dere's a big tree out de back full of ripe limes.'

'Sounds good. Who's for a little fruit picking?' asked John.

'I will,' offered Madi.

'I'll help. There's a bucket in the kitchen.' Connor followed her across the moonlit open sandy soil to the tree.

'Umm, this smells good,' Madi sniffed at the tangy fruit and the few sweet blossoms still on the branches. They both reached for the same fruit and their hands touched. She turned to Connor and in the moonlight beneath the lime tree they kissed, each stunned at the passion the kiss aroused. Connor caught his breath and drew back. 'We'd better be careful, this place is magic I think,' he said softly.

'Frightened of spells?' Madi smiled in the darkness. 'Lime juice is guaranteed to cure them.'

She reached her arms around his neck and firmly pulled his head to hers until their lips were touching again. And she held him until their kiss almost took their breath away. Surprised at herself for being so in control of the moment, she finally let him go and turned towards the lime that still hung on the branch. 'You can pick that one,' she grinned.

Together they filled the bucket and holding it between them walked like Jack and Jill to the house. Madi glanced at the water. 'Looks very fishy. I love fishing, do you?'

'I've been known to throw a line in now and again.'

They asked Mr Bell if there were fish in the river and he nodded emphatically. 'I get lines, you catch breakfast.'

'Finish your drink first, Mr Bell,' Connor added.

Connor and Madi cast their lines then settled themselves on a blanket on a small strip of coarse river sand between two low rocks. A full moon rose from behind the ring of hills turning the water to a gleaming pewter grey. And over those hills could be heard the wash coming from smaller falls called Old Man's Beard.

It was Madi who suddenly noticed a small moving light. 'What's that? Is it someone far away with a torch? Oh, it's gone off.'

They watched and waited and in seconds the little light flicked on again followed by another and another, small dancing lights that appeared to be in a line.

'Min min lights,' laughed Connor. 'No, they're fire-flies.'

They watched, entranced, as the glowing conga line swerved and swayed out across the water.

'How magic, like dancing fairies,' sighed Madi. 'I'm going to remember this all my life.'

'Me too,' breathed Connor reaching for her.

The fishing lines lay ignored as they wound their arms about each other, mouths and lips burning with an intensity that swept away all barriers and shyness. In minutes, each knew they had passed the point of no return.

Connor slowly and gently fumbled with Madi's clothes, sensing a shyness and hesitancy on her part, kissing her lightly all the while. Madi stiffened for a moment, then melted again under the passionate touch of Connor's lips. There could never be a more romantic setting, never a more perfect moment to make love, and she surrendered to it all. Thoughts of being emotionally hurt again were swept away and she sighed with pleasure as he kissed her breasts. With equal ardour she began to take off his clothes. While not retreating from the moment, in the back of her mind came the realisation that she'd never experienced this elation and surge of desire before. The first time she'd had sex with Geoff he had taken her in the back seat of his car around the corner from the tennis courts. It had happened before she was aware of what they were doing and afterwards had felt slightly taken advantage of, though she knew she could have stopped him if she'd insisted. In retrospect she'd realised all his lovemaking was selfish, it never occurred to him to ask about taking precautions either.

Madi shyly drew back from Connor for an instant. 'Connor, shouldn't we be careful? I mean, I hadn't exactly planned on this happening.'

'Me either, despite what you might think. All I can say is that I've been careful and taken precautions. I haven't had many different women. I don't do one-night stands,' he added quietly.

'Is this a one-night stand?' asked Madi seriously.

'I hope not. It's up to you, Madi. I've been a bit confused about my feelings for you over these past weeks. At first I thought it was just lust—you're so attractive, not just your body,' he kissed her nipple lightly, and continued with sincerity, 'but your personality, your strength of character, so many other things started to grow on me. I'd like to think there was something special between us.'

'Not just a holiday romance?' Madi hugged him to her. 'I had one fling after my marriage broke up—more to reassure myself I was still appealing as I'd felt so rejected. But that was safe sex all the way. There hasn't been anyone for a long time. I just can't separate the physical sensations from my emotions . . . they say men can do that.'

'That's not true. So, do you have any feelings towards me?'

'I have to say, I have strong feelings for you too, Connor.'

They lay in each other's arms feeling close and loving, each digesting the remarks of the other.

'You don't suppose we're being swept away by the magic and romance of this place?' asked Madi finally.

'What I feel for you started at the airport when I met you, Madi. I went to meet a mate's little sister and was knocked out by this incredible lady. And it wasn't the blonde good looks either. Do you believe in chemistry between people?'

'It's not a matter of believing, it's fact.' Madi began to shiver.

Connor covered her body with his. 'Are you cold?'

'No.' Madi couldn't explain the sudden shaking that had swept over her as the full implication of what Connor was saying sank in. 'I'm not ready for any sort of commitment, Connor. I wish I hadn't met you so soon. But I do feel drawn to you too . . . I don't know what to think.' She buried her head in his shoulder.

He held her tightly, struggling to control the passion she aroused in him. 'Don't do anything you don't want to, Madi . . .' He began to kiss her again then recoiled with a sharp 'Ouch!' and sat up.

'What's up?' Madi stared at him in concern as he began slapping at his back and bottom.

'Damned midgies or something are biting me like crazy. I didn't put repellent on this part of my body. I didn't expect to be out here naked.'

Madi began to laugh as he danced about slapping and scratching. 'Quick, put your clothes on, I've got some rub-on stuff in my jeans pocket. Pass me my jeans.'

'God, talk about cooling the fires of passion. Ouch, why aren't they biting you?' complained Connor.

Madi suddenly felt a sharp sting on her shoulder. 'They are!'

As they hurriedly dressed in fits of giggles, both fishing lines zinged and began to unreel. Madi had her reel in her discarded shoe but Connor's went rolling along the sand as the fish on the other end raced away with Hilda's cassava dough ball. 'Bloody hell.' With one leg in his shorts, he stumbled after his line while Madi began pulling hers in as she continued to laugh.

In the torchlight they peered at their catch. 'Gawd, catfish. Watch that spine on its back, it's lethal,' said Connor. 'Well it can do for bait, let's see what else is out there.'

In ten minutes they had fifteen catfish then the catches stopped. 'That must be all that's running at the moment. Let's call it a night. I'll clean them and we'll use them for bait in the morning.'

As they returned to the house where John and Ann were the only ones still up, the twosome were subjected to some good-natured ribbing.

'So where are the fish?'

'We heard some jollity down there.'

'Pretty romantic spot, huh?'

'It was till the fly attacks started and there are more than a dozen catfish of decent size waiting to be turned into bait to catch breakfast,' retorted Connor.

'Hey, don't use them all for bait,' said John. 'Mr and Mrs Bell will eat them. Put them in a dish and leave them by their door.'

*

This time Sharee had taken the bottom bunk. Viti and Ann were in double decker bunks on the other side of the room. Madi climbed up, trying not to disturb Sharee, pleased to find Mrs Bell had made up the bunk with clean if well-worn sheets and a thin coverlet.

Madi lay down thinking about Connor, trying to analyse how she felt. She did find him physically attractive and she liked him. She enjoyed his company and his sense of humour, and she knew if she let herself go she could fall wildly in love with him. The longing to be in love, to have someone love her back, who respected and liked her, was immensely appealing. But she'd been badly hurt and she'd promised herself that in the future she'd proceed with caution.

She had met Connor under somewhat unreal circumstances. Would their relationship be the same if they were living more normal lives in a boring city? And besides they were on different paths at the moment. Guyana was merely an interlude for her and, wonderful as it was, it would soon end. She'd come here to mend a fragile heart and restore her self-esteem, hoping to find a new and positive direction for her life. She certainly wasn't going to leave here with her life again in tatters. This time she would let her head not her heart dictate her actions.

But creeping into her thoughts came the memory of Connor's touch, the fresh smell of his skin, the fine red gold hairs on the back of his wide hands that were strong and bony like a bushman's, but caressed so tenderly. Was she glad the stinging flies had rescued her from a situation that might have compromised their friendship? Or had she been saved from plunging into a ravine when she wasn't ready?

Madi finally fell asleep, thinking of the bewitching fireflies that had danced on the water and enjoying the growing sense of anticipation and excitement that welled in her knowing she was so close to achieving her goal. Her last thought was that out there in the darkness, above the gorge, the mighty Kaieteur was waiting for her.

It scarcely seemed she'd been asleep a minute when a scream, an agonised wail, made her sit bolt upright in her bunk, banging her head on the ceiling. 'What the devil . . .?'

Ann rolled over and mumbled, 'Howler monkeys, they'll stop soon.'

Madi lay in the moonlight listening to the distant sobs and cries of the little rusty monkeys as they raced through the jungle canopy calling to each other—in warning, play or anguish, she couldn't tell. Then, as though a conductor had raised his baton, they all stopped simultaneously. She waited, thinking it was like waiting for the other shoe to drop. But then she remembered nothing else until bright sunlight, sleepy voices and the tantalising smell of coffee and toast awakened her.

Mr Bell and Captain Blaise decided after breakfast that the climb to the top of the falls should wait a day because clouds were moving in and it would rain during the afternoon. They predicted the following day would be 'wash clean'.

'Right. Rest day,' announced John.

Clothes were washed and spread on rocks to dry. They swam out to the little rocky islet and looked at the fast running current on the other side. Viti took Mr Bell's small wooden canoe for a paddle into the creek. She came back remarking how pretty the start of the walk to the falls looked.

'Let's go for a walk after lunch even if it is raining,' said Madi.

But after their meal of pepperpot stew, enthusiasm for the walk dwindled. Hammocks had been strung between trees and under the outdoor eating area and Madi was tempted by the appeal of sleeping off lunch in the cool breeze.

'I think hammock resting is going to be my greatest souvenir of Guyana. A comfortable soft hammock, a breeze and I'm out like a light,' said Madi.

'But you're still going on the walk,' said Connor.

'Yep. Who's coming?'

Sharee and Viti were the only volunteers. The three girls put on their walking shoes and set off onto the shadowy track that wound along the creek before taking a right-angle turn towards the gradual incline. They could see it would get steeper as it wound to the top of the falls.

They explored around the creek, Viti scratching at the gravel and pebbles with a stick and, deciding it held the possibility of gold, she filled her hat with mud and gravel to be washed in Mr Bell's gold pan later.

They came across small pretty blue flowers on a vine that weaved and trailed up and down trees and Madi picked a spray and tucked it in her hair.

Sharee, who was staring intently at the ground, called to them. 'Come and look at these amazing ants.'

Madi didn't see them for a moment, then she saw half a green leaf marching along the trail, followed by others. 'Leaf cutter ants,' cried Madi. 'I read about them in Gwen's book.'

'I've always called them umbrella ants,' said Viti. 'It's a bit like carrying an open tent on your head.'

230

They followed the marching procession of munched-off green leaves along a distinct trail the ants had made to a hole where they disappeared beneath a bulge on the surface. Madi reached into her backpack and took out her camera to shoot a close-up of the ants' nest and its parade of umbrella-carrying inhabitants.

'Oh, I just happen to have Gwen's book in my backpack. Let's see if I can find the bit she wrote about ants.' The other two good-naturedly rolled their eyes and while Viti continued to fossick with her stick, Madi and Sharee perched on a fallen log and Madi read from Gwen's book:

'Among the most remarkable forms of life are the ants, which differ from the English variety in having stings like wasps. The first I especially noticed were the Drogher or Cousis ants; they are small and harmless looking enough, but in reality are a power to be reckoned with, as they are capable of cutting into and carrying off a half-bag of rice in one night. The Droghers I saw on Maripi Island were in a procession of millions; each one carried a piece of leaf several times its own size, and from the appearance it presents while doing this is often called "the umbrella ant".

The procession passed over a long trail, down into a hole that must have been already very deep, judging by the fat roll of earth that surrounded it; the excavation party was still bringing up large pieces to add to the fortification. I have often seen a bare patch about six inches broad worn by these ants right through the thick layer of leaves that covers the ground of the forest, a sort of Piccadilly of ant-land, only proportionately very much broader.'

'Heavens, how fascinating and alarming!' declared Sharee.

'Ja. Quite so,' agreed a strange voice from behind them and the three looked up in surprise to see a man emerge from down the track. He was tall and fair with a thick blond beard and pale blue eyes. He wore a grey shirt and brief shorts, thick socks, solid boots and a canvas hat. He hung on to a haversack on one shoulder and gave them a friendly wave with his free hand.

'Good afternoon, I am Pieter Van Horen. The ants are interesting, yes? You know there are about ten thousand species of ant and none of them is genetically the same.'

They introduced themselves and all shook hands. Their new friend squatted on a small rock beside Sharee and Madi.

'You just climbed down from the top?' asked Viti.

'Ja. I have been camped up there for several days. I'm going back down the river to my second camp.'

'How was the weather?' asked Sharee.

'Misty with clouds, but it will be fine tomorrow, I suspect. Are you going up soon?'

'Tomorrow. I do hope it's clear,' sighed Madi.

'You must stay there for the sunrise and the sunset. They are spectacular,' said Pieter.

He smiled a lot and had an enthusiastic manner of speaking with a strong Dutch accent. Madi warmed to him immediately.

'Are you travelling about Guyana?' asked Sharee.

'In a manner of speaking. It's part of my work.'

'What do you do?' asked Madi curiously.

'I'm an ethnobotanist. I'm working for an institute in the US which is studying the benefits of plants used by the indigenous people here.'

'You collect and classify specimens and send them back?' said Madi.

'That's the botany part, ethnobotany involves studying

232

the people of many races and how they use the plants for medical and other purposes. At the end of the day it means we can produce a product to help other people. Guyana's Amerindians have lived in harmony with their land and we have much to learn from them.'

'That's like in Australia, where I come from,' said Madi. 'We are just starting to understand the rich knowledge our Aborigines have about caring for and using land. Spiritually and emotionally they understand it, as well as physically.'

'What were you doing at the top of the falls? Are there special plants up there?' asked Sharee.

'All plants are special to me,' chuckled Pieter. 'I also investigate insects and snakes and toads and frogs. They too hold the answers to how mankind can protect itself and survive. There's a marvellous secret here at Kaieteur . . . as well as spectacular plants.'

'Do tell us what it is,' said Madi. 'This might be my only chance to get up there and I'd hate to miss it.'

Pieter gave a good-natured laugh. He opened his haversack and emptied out its contents as he looked for a pen and small sketch book. A camera, plant press, an all-purpose knife with lots of blades, small containers and bottles wrapped in cloth were put to one side as he fished out a little book and drew a rough map.

'At the top you come out here, then there are two tracks to the falls. Take this one which is further back but it gives you a better look at the falls before getting to the actual top where the river drops over. This spot is very good for photographs,' he added with a grin. 'But here,' he drew a series of small Xs, 'along here is a row of bromeliads.'

'Why are they special?' asked Sharee.

Viti was now peering over Madi's shoulder at the

sketch pad. 'I know bromeliads. They're those waxy, spiky plants.'

'Yes, and they hold the little secret. They hold water from the mist of the falls and living in them is a tiny creature called *Colostethus beebei*. You only find them in these particular plants.'

'What are they?' asked Sharee.

'A frog. A little gold frog. First named scientifically by G.K. Noble from the American Museum of Natural History in 1923.'

'I saw an old documentary on the frogs on television!' exclaimed Sharee. 'That British nature series by . . . what's his name . . . Sir Gavin Rutherford.'

'Right,' said Pieter. 'So, now that I have checked my *beebei* friends, I can continue on.'

'Why were you checking on the gold frogs?' asked Madi.

'Ah, there is a belief among scientists that these frogs—this handful of living gems—hold the timepiece to the future.' He looked around the group who were listening with interest. 'These frogs don't croak as you would say in English. Instead they cry a sweet sad song. They sing of beauty and the balance of nature. While they sing, all is well with our world. They are the harbinger of the state of health of our planet. So you see, if the frogs stop singing, it means the planet and all that is on it is dying.'

'Is there a chance that the frogs could die?' asked Madi. 'We worry about the hole in the ozone layer and acid rain and the fact some of our frogs in Australia are disappearing.'

'We assume time is on our side, but we must use it wisely and try to make sense of the war between greed, politics, stupidity and ignorance,' said Pieter. 'Now I must be moving on, the day is waning. I have a small boat and outboard along a little further. I'm on my way back to my river camp, then I'm going down towards Brazil.'

'Stop and have a cold beer first,' said Sharee, 'while we have kerosene to run the fridge. Mr Bell is running low.'

'Thank you, but no. It's getting late and I want to be back before dark. By the way, they sell kerosene at the pork-knockers' village at the top of the falls,' said Pieter. 'It's five times the price of anywhere else. That is, if you feel up to carrying it back down the track.'

'We can manage that for the Bells,' said Sharee.

'There's a village at the top?' exclaimed Madi. She was a bit disappointed. Civilisation at Kaieteur didn't fit in with her mental image of the remote falls.

Pieter heard the disillusionment in her voice. 'It's just for the pork-knockers working the diamonds up the Potaro River. Don't worry, there are no souvenir shops yet.' He gave her a big grin. 'I hope you enjoy the experience of Kaieteur. It is a special place. You know the legend?'

When Madi shook her head he smiled at the three girls. 'Old Kaie was an elderly Patamona tribesman living up the Potaro River. He had become a burden to his relatives, so they put him and his prized belongings into a woodskin canoe and launched him downstream. The old man was hurled to his end over the falls. Soon after, the Patamona say, his woodskin appeared in the shape of a sharp rock and to the west of the basin his belongings took the form of a huge square rock. You'll see them from the top. So after he'd met this tragic fate they called the falls Kaieteur after him.'

'How sad,' said Sharee.

'Imagine being pushed over the falls just because you're old,' said Viti.

'It's the way some still choose to die,' said Pieter. Then seeing their sombre faces, he added, 'But I know you'll find that Kaieteur will stay in your hearts'.

He picked up his haversack and turned back to Madi. 'Be sure to say hello to my golden friends.'

ELEVEN

Madi didn't go back to sleep after the howler monkey alarm just before dawn, but lay there excited and for some reason slightly apprehensive. At first light she heard one of the men lighting the gas in the kitchen. She slipped quietly from her bunk and picking up the bucket by the back door went down to the river and dipped it into the refreshingly cool water to wash herself.

At breakfast everyone was slightly subdued and Madi sensed it was not the early hour. It was more a contemplative atmosphere as they prepared for this special day.

Connor noticed it too. 'Feels a bit like troops preparing for the day of battle,' he whispered as he extracted a piece of toast from between the hand-held metal griller.

'How would you know that?' asked Madi.

'Don't be a pedant, my dear. Don't you have days in your job where you know it's going to be a war day?'

'I'm unemployed,' she reminded him, then grinned. 'Yeah. I know what you mean.'

The group assembled outside as Roy and Hilda Bell came to see them off. Mr Bell produced a gift for each of them. He had carefully chosen and smoothed branches from the surrounding forest which he'd whittled into walking sticks.

'Walk with a stout stick and keep your eyes down and you be jist fine,' he advised.

Madi was touched at the old man's gesture. 'I'm going to keep this as my favourite souvenir of Kaieteur Falls,' she said warmly.

'Walk with a stout stick. That's sound advice for life, Mr Bell,' said Connor, shaking the old man's hand.

'Snakes, slippery rocks, loose footholds, steep sections. You'll need dem stout sticks,' said Captain Blaise, joining the Bells to see them off.

John lifted the empty drum of kerosene. 'We'll bring you back a full one tonight,' he promised.

The sun was barely above the hills as they set off in straggling single file. The start of the walk was like a trail through English woods, a carpet of fallen polished wet leaves, lichen-crested logs, soft light hazing through misty straight trees climbing forty metres above. They crossed an ancient stone parapet across a docile stream gurgling over fat stones that looked as polished as gems.

Ann reminded John of the last time they had done this when the stream had been a raging torrent forcing one burly fellow, a sufferer of vertigo, to crawl over on shaking hands and knees. 'Needless to say, he didn't hang over the edge of the falls when we got there,' laughed Ann.

'What was the point in his going up then?' asked Connor.

'You'll see,' said Ann.

They lapsed into silence and as the discernible track had disappeared, it became a matter of picking where to place their feet as it got steeper. Twigs cracked under foot, birds called, and then came the faint whoosh of a stream for the next mile. In the enclosed humid atmosphere the heat rose and glimpses of the distant cool stream were tantalising.

They wound upwards in S curves, taking even more care where feet were placed, grateful for the support of Mr Bell's stout sticks.

Madi paused to look at the varying stratas of growth that reached from ground to canopy crown. It had taken an adjustment period for her eyes to discern the subtleties of the rainforest growth. All her senses were engaged. She bent to study the almost aquatic minuscule world flourishing in dribbling rock at her feet. A miniature waterfall trickled alongside tiny ferns and flossy plants less than a finger long, where dwarf grasses and pearl-sized pebbles were scattered. Emerald moss sponged over a rock and Madi pressed her hand on it, collecting the cool water that oozed out to smooth over her heated face.

The dimly lit life of the ground cover was thin but of immense variety. The dank rich mouldy smell and the rustle of unseen tiny insects were fascinating and she knew if she stayed on her knees here for the rest of the day she wouldn't tire of observing this miniature world. She lifted her eyes and studied the layers of plants on plants rising above her, each one a multitude of different textures and surfaces and shapes. The buttress roots of the massive trees formed walls around a world of rotting vegetation. Inside that was yet another eco system of plant and animal life, a nursery of shooting seeds and rich nutrients.

Looking at the looping lianas that linked trees together, Madi imagined one tree damaged by termites could bring down several, ripping a hole in the solid canopy above. The entwined tree tops that formed the roof of the rainforest became a bed for the ardent vines and flowers that made it up the thick trunks to loll on the canopy and explode in bloom in the sunlight many metres above.

Madi realised the others had gone ahead while she'd stopped to look at this verdant world and she felt suddenly fearful. Then turning around she saw the boat boy. The young Amerindian was waiting for her, a faithful shadow with a shy smile carrying the empty kerosene tin.

Ten minutes later as she concentrated on a particularly tricky incline it levelled slightly and she saw Connor sitting on a rock. 'I've been waiting for you to catch up. Are you okay?'

'Oh, absolutely. I've just been so fascinated with it all. I keep looking at the plants and losing track of time.'

'I don't want to rush you, but the others are quite a way ahead.'

Madi shifted the weight of her backpack, which seemed heavier. She determinedly brushed past Connor and strode forward, digging her walking shoes into a crevice and climbing up the hill to forge a shortcut. 'No one waits for me.'

Connor glanced back at the boy, grinned and followed Madi, eyeing her lean strong legs protruding from her cut-off jeans.

'Madi, check where you're putting your feet, this next bit seems unstable. Prod with your stick,' advised Connor, who had stumbled slightly.

Madi was about to make a rude retort but the ground looked deceptive. She prodded a covering of dried leaves between two rocks, where she planned to step, to take her weight and boost herself upwards. The stick disappeared through the leaves into thin air—a hidden crevice with a flimsy cover could have meant a broken ankle. She steadied her pace and decided to pay more attention.

Finally the climb lessened and the walking levelled out. Connor tapped Madi on the shoulder. 'Listen.' Above the abuse of disturbed birds she heard a low drone, like an incoming plane.

She turned around to Connor, noting his flushed face and shortness of breath. She was glad that with the rivulets of perspiration between her breasts and the weight of her backpack and pulled calf muscles, she was not alone in her suffering. But that was soon forgotten as the steady drone registered. 'It's the falls,' she whispered. 'We're getting close.' With renewed energy she strode to where the rest of the group was sitting and catching their breath.

'Johnson's Peak is where we have to get to, down this way,' said John.

They walked through slightly open country with water everywhere, running between the rocks and dripping from trees. They passed intriguing plants and three-metre-high bromeliads with bizarre spiky flowers. Suddenly Madi glanced down and gasped in delight, avoiding stepping on an exquisite cluster of wild orchids.

They ducked under an overhang of rock where a

small dry cave offered shelter to animals. Then just a few clambering steps and they emerged into the open onto a big flat rock. The sound of the falls was deafening. They had arrived.

Madi closed her eyes and turned her back to the sound. Shrugging off her backpack, she dropped it, and slowly turned around to face the falls.

She opened her eyes.

And there it was before her, a frontal view so close that she was overwhelmed by the realisation that all those millions of litres of water from the Potaro River were melting over the edge to the far away depths of the gorge. She thought she would be prepared for the sight she'd seen on postcards. But the grand scale, the momentum and gravity with which nature had created this spectacle with no outside influence was breathtaking. There was no indecision in the water's course, no wavering of the solid volume of river that slid effortlessly over the lip of the falls to crash into oblivion.

This was God's creation, but for what cause was this geological manifestation? The answer was too difficult to comprehend while her eyes were held by the sheer splendour and magnificence of it.

Connor's hand touched her shoulder, and Madi reached up, squeezed his fingers and felt a wave of gratitude that he was there to share this unique experience with her.

'Makes you feel pretty insignificant, doesn't it?' he murmured in her ear.

'No. It makes me feel important because we are here and we can share this and realise together how wonderful nature is. I feel privileged,' said Madi firmly.

'Well, it's nature's five-star standard up here. This is pretty amazing,' declared Connor. 'No architect, landscaper or technocrat could have conceived or created this. It's the rawness of it, the sheer simplicity that knocks you.'

'It's not a monument . . . yet it's a symbol. I wish I understood more why I feel the way I do,' said Madi.

The rest of the group were grinning at each other, sharing the delight of confronting this awesome sight.

'Photo time,' said Sharee, delving for her camera.

Madi suddenly turned to Connor. 'The frog. The gold frogs—I must see them.'

She gripped Connor's hand. 'Remember last night I told you about Pieter? The ethnobotanist? He said if the gold frogs disappear, it will be a sign the planet is dying.'

'Well, that sounds a bit extreme. Sounds a bit of a radical greenie . . . they're always forecasting the end of the world is around the corner.'

'But Connor, we have to heed these little omens. You can't just go blindly forward, tramping over everything, assuming all will be well. We've already messed up so much of the environment. When you come to a place like this it makes you realise how beautiful the world can be. That the songs of little gold frogs are important.' She spoke quietly but with great intensity. He held back the flippant remark that had sprung to his lips. He didn't want to dampen her enthusiasm and she was right, places like this were rare and special.

He pointed to the far edge of the flat rock that faced the falls. The gorge dropped away and on the edge of the rock were clumps of small waxy green bromeliads. Madi hurried to these as the group photographed each other with the falls as a backdrop. Connor crossed his fingers that the little frogs she seemed so keen about were actually there.

Cautiously Madi parted the fat succulent leaves, peering down the length of their spiky arms to the heart of the plant where a puddle of water had collected. The leaves were wet and looked slimy but they felt smooth and cool and she was reminded of snake skin. She detected a slight movement and looked closer. And there, balancing and clinging to the base of a leaf was a tiny flash of gold. As her eyes focused, Madi saw clearly the almost blinding glitter of the small frog. Sucker toes spread from each foot grasping the leaf. Its head tilted as if it was listening to her breathing. An eyelid blinked. 'Hello, little frog,' said Madi softly. 'I've come a long way to see you.' The frog didn't move, and Madi parted several other leaves in the same bromeliad before she found its identical mate—gilt-dipped, as shiny bright as new gold, no longer than her thumb.

She felt Connor's breath on her neck and she moved her head as she held the leaves apart so he could see the brilliant little creature.

'What do you suppose would happen if you kissed your frog prince?' he asked.

'Trust you to think of that,' she admonished him.

'They're pretty amazing though,' he admitted.

The rest of them came over and glanced at the frog and made admiring noises, but were more interested in moving on to the crest of the falls.

'Connor, do you realise how significant these are?' said Madi. 'These particular golden frogs aren't found anywhere else on the planet, just here in these plants in this place. It's like they are some sort of guardian angel.'

'And you say the day they aren't here we're in deep shit?'

'Sort of. Pieter said the Amerindians have a more poetic way of putting it.'

'In Australia there are dozens of theories about why the frog populations have decreased, from removal of their habitats to the hole in the ozone layer, acid rain and pesticides washing into the rivers,' said Connor.

'How do you know that? I didn't think such things would interest you.' Madi sounded pleased.

'I haven't lived in the rarefied corporate atmosphere or in Third World backwaters all my life. At home in Perth we had a green frog that lived in our letterbox for years. Mum used to make sure the birdbath next to it was always filled with rainwater. I wonder how many green frogs still live in the city suburbs to delight young boys and scare the girls?'

Madi kissed the tip of his nose. 'Connor, that story is very endearing. I'm more impressed to know you cared for a little green frog, than the fact you talked the IFO into funding an agricultural water project in Africa.'

'Hey come on, you guys, let's make for the headwater. You can see it fall straight to the bottom,' Ann called.

'I'll be there in a tick.' Madi was delving into the pocket of her backpack and Connor watched her curiously.

From it she drew out the small wooden frog she'd bought with Lester from his artist friend in Georgetown. It was roughly carved but it still bore a striking resemblance to the frog they'd just seen.

'Where'd you get that?' asked Connor. 'I didn't know you were a froggy fan.'

'I'm not. I mean I don't despise them or anything. I've never had a pet frog. But when I saw this it just . . . appealed to me.'

Connor looked at it, turned it over and then gave it back to her. 'It's nice to have a lucky talisman.' Giving a lopsided grin he reached into his pocket and drew out a beige stone bandéd in even rings of chocolate brown.

'That's beautiful,' declared Madi. 'I've never seen anything like it.'

'It's a zebra stone from Western Australia. My grandfather gave it to me. He picked it up in the Kimberley, I think. He was a bit of an amateur geologist. Got me interested in minerals and collecting bits of rock. Taught me to look under my feet and above my head. We used to go camping and from him I learnt rudimentary astronomy. He was a terrific man. Simple, down to earth, never went to a university but incredibly wise in his way.'

Madi handed the smooth stone back to him and decided she liked this man who'd kept a pet frog and walked about with a lucky stone from his granddad.

Connor and Madi caught up with the rest of the group as they wove through the wet track, ducking under rock overhangs and threading their way past exotic flora. 'My gosh, look at the size of that. Quick, Connor, take my photo!' exclaimed Madi.

She stood beneath a five-metre bromeliad. 'I have one with a spiky pink flower in a pot in my garden but it's just kind of small and clumpy. How old do you suppose this one is?'

'Yonks. I couldn't say. You look cute though.' Connor clicked the shutter.

In twenty minutes they had curved around to the actual top of the falls. Here the broad Potaro River slithered past small jutting boulders and clumps of razor grass to the unexpected drop over the great bite from the cliff face that was the ragged edge of the falls. The golden water surged over the lip in white foaming waves that fell two hundred and twenty-six metres.

'Watch a section of water come down the river and over the edge and try to follow it down, then you get an idea of the power and speed,' said John.

Mist drifted up from the gorge obscuring the base of the falls. The sheer weight of the water crashing below obscured its actual landing. They were standing on the left-hand side of the falls and each of the men lay down and hung over the edge, looking below into the gorge.

Sharee shook her head. 'I'm not doing that. What about you, Madi?'

She still couldn't drag her eyes away from the immense swaying curtain of water. Then as she stared, a rainbow appeared, melting out of the mist to arch from halfway down the falls back up to the river behind. At the same time a cloud of small, black swifts, the sharp-winged birds that roost behind the falls, darted out and, swept by the updraught, sailed and soared in formation before sweeping across the rainbow to disappear into the forest.

Tears sprang to Madi's eyes at the sheer magnificence of it.

'Awesome, eh?' murmured Connor beside her. She squeezed his hand. 'Come and peer over the edge, it's quite a sight.'

She lay on the rock and Connor held her ankles, but the drop, the roar of water, the spray on her face was too overwhelming, and she got to her feet.

'There's a little ledge you can stand on, right by the drop, makes a great photo,' said Ann.

'You know what's amazing too,' commented Connor. 'There are no touristy things—like safety rails, warning signs, protective barriers. It's utterly natural, wild, like it's always been.'

They paddled in pools at the edge of the Potaro, throwing in sticks and watching them sail over the edge. They took photos, and they sat and simply looked at it. Every moment it changed. 'When no one messes with nature, perfection is what Mother Earth does best. No human being could create something as beautiful as this,' said Madi thoughtfully.

It was getting close to lunchtime and John suddenly commented, 'You know what it looks like?' They all turned to him as he studied the falls.

'Beer. It looks like the world's biggest beer fountain.'

'John! You're impossible,' declared Ann.

'A cold beer would go down well,' sighed Connor.

'It's only an hour's walk to the pork-knockers' village,' said John, a gleam in his eye.

The men were on their feet, picking up their backpacks and tying on shoes. 'It'll make a longer walk back down, but worth it, I maintain,' said John.

'And think of the icy rum punch sitting in that old fridge back at the Bells' house.'

'Oh, Gawd, the kerosene! That fixes it, we have to go to the village.'

They called to the boat boy who was sitting in the shade, eating a piece of fruit Ann had given him. 'Where's the kero drum?'

The teenager gave the thumbs up and pointed behind him.

'Right, let's go.'

Madi hung back. 'Do we come back this way?'

'No, there's a shorter track from the village that meets the track we came up,' answered Ann. 'Why?' she asked, seeing the expression on Madi's face.

'Well, after what Pieter told me, I thought I'd like to stay up here and see the sunset and sunrise.'

'On your own?' asked Sharee.

'Why didn't you say so? We could have all arranged to do that, I guess,' said John, thinking of the cool drinks and swim waiting back at the Bells' house.

'Did you come prepared?' asked Connor.

'Sort of,' she said, patting her backpack.

'Good. So did I.' He grinned at her. 'I had a feeling you might be hard to drag away. I'll stay with you. It'd better be worth stale sandwiches and warm water.'

'Oh, Connor.' She hugged him.

Ann picked up her pack. 'You'll probably be able to buy food at the village. Come on then.'

They passed a deserted guesthouse which John said had been built for former Canadian Prime Minister Pierre Trudeau and seldom used since because few dignitaries roughed it overnight at the falls. An hour's visit and they would fly back to Georgetown by late afternoon.

It was a hot walk to the village, the girls chatting quietly, the men half listening to the girltalk and thinking of the welcome beer waiting for them. 'What if they've run out?' said John.

'Don't even think it,' said Connor.

Behind them the Amerindian boy swung the empty drum, singing a folk song to himself. To Madi the unfamiliar dialect and rhythm seemed as much a part of their surroundings as the strange plants and trees and the feeling of remoteness, yet all was strangely comfortable and connected. Was it because, like Gwen, she felt herself drawn into this country? As if following her train of thought Connor suddenly asked, 'Did your friend Gwen climb Kaieteur?'

'I don't believe so. She didn't write about it. She just went after diamonds up the Mazaruni River.'

'No more readings from Gwen's book then?' asked Viti.

'Did she find diamonds?' asked Sharee.

'Yes. But just when things were looking up she received a message sent upriver and she rushed off to New York. We don't know why she went to New York. She doesn't reveal anything of her personal life. It's very frustrating. I'd love to know more about her.'

'You'll have to go to Ballarat where she was born and try to find out,' said Connor.

'Was she married?' asked Ann, who was beginning to count Gwen as an invisible guest among them. 'Maybe she had to go back to see the old man.'

'What husband would let his wife go off into the wilds in those days?' asked John.

'There've been women adventurers who have done that, even disguising themselves as men in the 1800s,' said Madi.

'Don't get her going. Women adventurers are her hobby,' grinned Connor.

'So what's Gwen's story?' asked Viti. The girls had to admit they were becoming intrigued with the romantic idea of attractive, well-to-do Miss Gwendoline Richardson heading out from Australia and ending up panning for diamonds on the Mazaruni in Guyana in the 1920s.

'The British Guiana Government wouldn't give a woman alone a permit to take an expedition upriver,' Madi explained. 'So Gwen fell in with a Brit—a Major Blake—who had a holding up there, and he agreed to lease her a portion and act as her sponsor. But it was Gwen's show all the way.'

'Chauvinistic bastards. Hope she made a fortune,' said Ann.

'Was there any hanky-panky with the major?' asked John.

'Well, she didn't write about that. It all seemed very

above board. Once or twice she pays him a compliment about his ingenuity in saving them from a sticky situation. But Gwen could manage—and did—quite well on her own. She was the expedition leader.'

'Oh God, is that a mirage or do you see it too?' said Connor, stopping in his tracks. They all stared ahead and burst out laughing. Across a sandy clearing stood a small thatched hut. On top of its roof was erected a fading, bent tin sign in red and yellow—BANKS BEER. Beside the hut, which served as the local store, was a rough thatched shelter over wooden tables where several men were sitting, watching their approach. A few shanty shacks formed a sort of makeshift main 'street'.

'Looks like the wild west in miniature,' said Connor, laughing.

The bottles of beer were cold enough and four times the price in Georgetown, but no one argued. They joined the pork-knockers under the shelter and exchanged greetings. The men, young and old, dark-skinned and unshaven, smiled at them but there was a wariness that was not encouraging.

John explained they'd climbed up and the men nodded. 'We do it if we have to. Most times we fly up. Strip's back there.' They pointed to a distant cleared stretch of dirt.

'So you look for diamonds up here?' asked Viti. 'Are there lots in the river?' Her sweet naivete was disarming. John and Ann knew the men didn't discuss their finds—even with each other. Buyers and agents flew in to buy from the pork-knockers. Some of the men preferred to sell their finds down in Georgetown. But there they ran the risk of blowing their profit on the city's nightlife.

There was little to spend their money on up here except rum, beer and card games.

Madi was intrigued and began asking how they went about dredging and what the diamonds looked like. 'I mean, are they hard to see, like gold?' She remembered a gold-panning weekend with her parents at Hill End in New South Wales, which had been very frustrating to an eleven-year-old. Matthew had found the only little nugget.

One of the young men laughed. 'Dey sparkle with fire, girl. No mistake dem.'

'Could I see one?'

The man responded to Madi's eager gaze and bubbling enthusiasm. He reached into his shoe and drew out from his sock a blue and white Vicks VapoRub inhalation tube.

'Christ, I haven't seen one of them for years. My granny was always making me push one up my nose when I got stuffed up,' laughed John.

'We have it in Australia too. But it comes in a jar, greasy stuff you had to rub on your chest,' said Connor.

The young man unscrewed the plastic top and shook the contents into the palm of his hand.

A coarse sprinkling of rough stones showed many colours, each glinting with a hint of the fire and light within.

They pored over the diamonds in fascination and then one of the other men produced a balled sock from his hip pocket and showed his cache. In minutes they were all talking and the pork-knockers, long deprived of an outside audience, attempted to outdo each other with their stories. Another round of beers and the men began discussing the pros and cons of the democratic government. Connor glanced at Madi as the death of Ernesto St Kitt was mentioned.

'We hear it on de radio. Man, dat how dis country bein' run, mebbe de bosses didn't throw him in de river, but, man, dat be a murder for sure. He was making speeches 'bout helping de man in de street and helpin' git dis country going straight. I don' believe dat fella a druggie. My sister know he's wife. Dey a good family.'

The other pork-knockers nodded in agreement.

'De city can be a bad scene, man. Up here, you only got de bushmasters and your neighbour to knock yo on de head,' joked another.

'A bushmaster? Gwen mentions them. A poisonous snake, right?' said Madi.

'Very poisonous,' said John. 'But you Aussies would be used to that.'

'Mind where you sleep at the falls tonight, Madi,' said Sharee with a wink.

'I have my hammock rolled in the bottom of my backpack,' she answered.

'I think we should be making a move. Let's get the kerosene. Madi, see what food you can get. Are you sure you two will be okay?' asked Ann.

'Of course. It will be an adventure,' Madi answered quickly.

Connor rolled his eyes. 'You and your adventures.'

In the makeshift store they found a packet of Kraft cheese, biscuits, cans of Coke, some peanuts and candies. 'Pretend we're at the movies,' said Connor handing over cash for the small feast.

The Amerindian boy struggled across the road with the full can of kerosene. 'John, he can't carry that on his own,' cried Ann.

'Don't fret. I've got a plan,' said John, sliding Mr Bell's stick through the handle. Ann took one end and John took the other. The boy looked around and reached up for their backpacks. 'Take it for awhile, we'll trade you part way down.' Sharee patted Ann's shoulder, glancing at Viti who nodded her head at them.

The young pork-knocker offered to sell Madi a diamond but she shook her head. 'I'd like to find my own.'

It was the parting of the ways. Connor and Madi farewelled the rest of the group and headed back the way they'd come towards the falls. 'You sure you can find the way back down in the morning?' called Ann.

'If we're not back by afternoon . . . give a hoy,' called Connor.

'Connor, you don't have to stay if you don't want to,' said Madi. 'I'll be fine. I think.'

'Rubbish. You're not doing me out of this . . . adventure.'

By the time they got back to the falls the day was fading. Connor eyed Trudeau's old guesthouse. 'Do you reckon we could bust in and make ourselves at home?'

'Connor, that would defeat the reason we're here. To experience the falls.'

They set up a small camp, strung their hammocks between trees set back from the mist of the falls, and pooled their resources. Connor had brought a torch, Madi insect repellent. They each had a hammock and thin plastic sheeting. Madi had thrown in Sharee's cotton sari as a cover and Connor had a knife—'to slice the cheese'. His final offering was a small bottle of rum and they both had water.

'Wait, something else,' Madi pulled out a lime. 'Thought it might be a thirst quencher. Be better with the rum.' They made themselves a rum and water and went back to the falls to watch the sunset. Madi sighed. 'I see what Pieter meant. Look at how the water changes colour with the sky.'

The river was burnished red and gold, seeming to glow with an incandescent light. The surging white crests of the tumbling river flashed like molten gold as they went over the edge.

'Imagine this after massive rains and floods. This is just a normal season,' said Connor.

Madi watched the movement of the river as it slid to the falls and exploded downwards. 'I wish I could compose music. Can you imagine a symphony that captured all of this?'

'That's what's missing, music . . . What music would you play here if you could . . .' They talked of music, of dreams, of passions, of things they'd like to try. They talked of friends, and places, and families. And slowly the sunset melted into the hills and all was luminous dark.

'Let's eat supper and come back and watch the moon-rise,' said Connor.

They ate their picnic by torchlight. 'What I wouldn't give for a hot cup of tea.' Madi untied her cotton anorak from round her waist and slipped it on as the evening coolness settled on them.

'Glad Ann told us to bring plastic in case of rain during the climb. It will be dewy, I guess,' said Connor spreading his thin plastic sheet over his cotton hammock.

With a rum to fortify them they went back to their viewing rock and silently watched the glimmer of light behind one of the distant mountains grow brighter until the rim of the moon showed above the peak.

Majestically it rose, turning the churning waters to silverplate and casting a metallic and friendly light around them. They could now distinguish other sounds above the water and Madi cocked her head. 'I heard something. Let's walk away from the falls a bit.'

They headed back towards the bromeliads, picking their way by the beam of the torch, Connor going first and reaching back to help Madi and shine the torch at her feet. It took longer than it had earlier, but then they came out on the rocks set back from the falls. The clutch of bromeliads glistened in the moonlight, their greenness frosted with a silvery sheen from the moon.

Both heard it together. A resonant, rich, throaty song. It rose and fell like heartbeats that lingered. Silence, then it began again. This time a chorus, a chuckling joyful song, that echoed and reverberated across the ravine.

'The golden frogs . . . they're singing,' whispered Madi. She held onto Connor's hand as the trembling notes bored into the fibre of her soul.

Connor kissed her head. 'Then all is well. Let's go back and sleep.'

Madi thought of last night, and now she wanted to kiss him again with the joy of all they'd shared on this memorable day. But he kissed her lightly on the top of her head like a doting father, and virtually tucked her into her hammock with another quick goodnight kiss.

Madi woke before the sunrise, an eerie foggy light swirling about the dripping trees. She felt damp, her hair and face were wet. Glancing over at Connor she could see rivulets of dew running off the plastic cover spread over him in his hammock.

She walked quietly back to the edge of the falls and sat hugging her knees and watched the fog and mist swirling up from the ravine and across the surface of the glassy Potaro. Like Salome's veils slowly lifting, the layers of mist began to melt in the streaky pastel shades of the coming dawn.

She hurried back to fetch Connor. 'I can't let you sleep through the sunrise.' She shook him gently. 'Come on.'

Together they watched the colours of the river and falls change as the red, fat ball of sun rolled into view, rising higher, the red glow becoming hard-edged, white gold that hurt their eyes.

'It really makes you understand the words, a new day dawning . . .' said Madi.

'Anything seems possible when you see something like this. It's very renewing.' He wrapped an arm about her shoulders. 'I'm glad we shared this, Madi.'

'It's something that I'll never forget. Connor, we should make a vow, whenever things seem hard, or we get depressed and sad, we must remember this.' She waved her arm out towards the panorama of pristine rainforest on the mountains around them, wreathed in the last shreds of mist, the velvet strip of sparkling river, the spread and drop of the remarkable falls.

They sat a moment or two longer and Connor's arm tightened around her shoulders. Madi turned to him and lifted her face to his kiss.

If ever there was a moment, a place where passion was matched by its surroundings this was it. Connor and Madison made love in the first rays of the sun, their heated bodies cooled by mist, the roar of the falls matching the pounding of their hearts.

Madi lay back on the mossy rock as Connor gently kissed the length of her body. The beauty of Madi, the feelings she aroused in him, the magic of this place, swept over him and he struggled to find words to express it. 'Do you feel what I do, Madi? I just can't describe it . . . I'm gone . . . over the falls, all is lost.' He buried his face between her breasts, the sweet smell and sensation of her skin crushed against him. She smiled and rubbed his head. A contentment and a glow spread from her toes through her body. 'It's wonderful, Connor . . . I can't find words either. Let's just share it.' They lay there in silence, bodies pressed together but Madi was trying to make sense of her feelings. Connor had given her a wonderful gift—he had given her back to herself. She felt a woman again, whole and magnificent and adored. She had an energy, a sense of power, not over Connor but because of him. She knew whatever the future held, she would be all right. She was strong again. The failed marriage, the insecurities, the indecision about her future, all slipped away over the falls. It wasn't because a man had made love to her and become smitten. She had given herself and she suddenly saw how, by giving oneself, so much came back in return. It had been a shared experience, but for her it was also a milestone in her journey to discover who she really was. This was for Madi her moment of revelation and she would always thank Connor.

She smiled into his blue eyes. 'You don't know how wonderful you've made me feel . . . for lots of reasons.'

'Good. Hang onto that, Madi. I feel it too.'

They arrived back at the resthouse to find Mrs Bell hanging washing out.

'Did you find it gooood?' she asked in her singing accent.

'Unbelievably beautiful, Mrs Bell.'

'There be cake and coffee with Mr Bell,' she said, pointing to where he was sitting with the rest outside the house.

Ann was first to spot them walking over. She called out and Connor and Madi raised their walking sticks in acknowledgement.

Over Mrs Bell's cake they described the sunset and sunrise with bubbling enthusiasm, finishing each other's sentences, trying to describe the impact it had on them. Watching Connor and Madi, it was obvious to each of their friends, though no one said anything, that they had undergone some subtle change in the way they related to each other.

After a swim, they all went fishing and Madi caught more catfish. The rest of the day was spent relaxing. That night over fresh fish curry with chilli and lime relish, they agreed it seemed they'd been away from the city for weeks.

Next morning they set out with Captain Blaise. They all felt fit and relaxed and pleased that each had met some personal challenge in making the trek and climb. It had been hard saying goodbye to the Bells. The old couple stood holding hands, their white heads shining in the early morning light, gap-toothed smiles creasing their finely wrinkled skin. They were grateful for the kerosene and Ann had carefully packed a plastic bag containing letters the Bells wanted posted to friends and family in Georgetown.

Madi had been first up and had said her own private farewell to the elderly couple whose simple life, love and caring for each other, and whose faith and trust in the world around them, had touched her. She wished she had a gift for them and wondered how she might send them something. Then she thought of her little carved frog. She loved it dearly. She stroked the little wooden creature and decided she would get Lester to find another. Then she

259

offered the frog to the Bells as a gesture of thanks for their kindness.

Mr Bell turned the little carving over in his bumpy boned hands. 'This be a very good fellow,' he said softly, then handed it back to Madi, pressing it between her fingers. 'But dis fellow got your name on him. He be made for yo. Thank you, but we can no take him from yo.'

Heading up the river the girls discussed what they might get for the Bells that would be practical and how they might get it to them. They settled on a box of tinned and packaged luxury foods.

'Captain Blaise will see they get it,' said Ann. 'There'll be someone going upriver, one of the pork-knockers perhaps.'

There were no breakdowns on the way back and late that night Connor kissed a sleepy Madi as Singh held open the gate. 'I'll call you. Take care, my sweet.'

She nodded, handed Singh her backpack and, holding tightly to Mr Bell's stick, walked to the darkened house. 'You had a good trip, Miss Madi? Where you go?' asked Singh as he pushed open the front door and turned on the hall light.

'I had a very good time, Singh. I climbed Kaieteur.'

Singh gently closed the door behind her. 'Well now, dat be some ting. Some ting indeed,' he muttered in awe.

Madi splashed her face, brushed her teeth and fell into bed as Matthew padded down the hall and tapped at her door. He peered at his sister beneath the shroud of mosquito net.

'Was it worth it, Madi?'

'Oh yes. Oh very much.'

'Good. Sleep tight. Talk in the morning.'

'You have to do it, Matt,' she called sleepily.

She was asleep before Matthew reached his bed and she dreamed of Kaieteur, of Connor's kiss and touch, of the cascades of water, of rainbows and little black birds, and heard again in her dream, the singing of the little gold frogs.

TWELVE

Water Street, the commercial end of town, was jammed, choked and chaotic. A normal state of affairs. The mixture of races—black skin and Chinese eyes, fine-boned Hindu faces topped by crinkly hair, African, Portuguese and Amerindian blends—normally delighted Madi. But now they crowded in on her. After the beauty of the trip to Kaieteur, the noise, the putrid smells, the sense of danger from what Lester called the street choke and robs, made her clasp her small bag to her chest and hurry after Ann.

'You all right? You seem distracted. Singh is waiting for us outside Stabroek markets,' Ann said.

Madi was relieved to see Singh, who took the

shopping basket from Ann and opened the door of the Toyota Landcruiser.

Madi leaned back in relief in the air-conditioning. 'I think I'm going through some sort of adjustment. Like a mild form of culture shock. I'm mentally and emotionally still back at Kaieteur and the river. I can't cope with this city madness.'

'How are you going to be in London or Sydney?' said Ann.

Singh nosed the car through the stalls and shoppers outside the main markets, narrowly missing a man carrying a carcass of beef across the sunbaked square.

'I'm not ready to move on yet. In fact I want to go back up the river. Further into the interior. Now that I've had a taste, I want to see more. I'm absolutely fascinated by the place.'

Ann glanced at her. 'You sound as though you've eaten labba and drunk creek water. That means you'll always have a yearning to return to Guyana. That's the local belief, anyway. But I understand how you feel. It happened to me too.'

'It did?'

'Oh yes. I came out here for a car rally, met John, fell in love, went back to England and couldn't wait to get back here. John was part of it, of course, and it took me a while to differentiate between my feelings for him and the extraordinary pull the country had on me.'

'How did you adjust?'

'I travelled around as much as possible. John made that easy, knowing people everywhere. I still don't quite know what the magic is . . . it was so different from England. So exotic . . . the jungle, the way you can have a magnificent garden, a fabulous and quite privileged lifestyle. The people are marvellous—incredibly warm, as I'm sure you've

263

discovered. There are so many frustrating things, of course, but in a strange way, that's part of its charm too. You can always manage to laugh at adversity here. In the UK, you tend to get tight-lipped.' She gave a hearty laugh.

'You don't miss England?'

'How can I? I'm lucky enough to go back a couple of times a year.'

Madi stared out at the street of such unfamiliar faces to those she saw at home, the colonial buildings, the tropical trees, the undisciplined jumble of cars, bicycles, trucks and carts. 'Strange, I've never thought of living anywhere but Australia. I never imagined I would be drawn to any other part of the world.'

Ann gave her a steady look. 'Get it out of your system, then see where you are and you'll probably have a clearer idea of where you're going.'

She didn't elaborate on what 'it' was, because they were now outside Guyana Stores.

'Right, let's raid the supermarket.'

It intrigued Madi that the main store of Georgetown could so regularly run out of things. Drippy freezer cabinets with open lids held nothing save for a squashed plastic bag of squid pieces. Shelves that should have had tinned provisions were empty and where a pile of just-arrived items was being unpacked, shoppers grabbed three and four at a time, scarcely noticing what they were buying.

'The old days of shortages when you had to queue for the basics are still remembered. People's shopping philosophy is, if it's there grab a couple and figure out what to cook with it later,' said Ann dropping tins of mushrooms, canned soup and packets of dried haricot beans in her shopping basket.

*

'My dears, what a pleasant surprise! Doing the provi-doring, I see.'

Lady Annabel, resplendent in African print caftan, dark glasses and a long sienna scarf wrapped around her head, sailed towards them. 'Dear Madison,' she leaned forward and kissed her cheek. 'How did you find Kaieteur?'

Madi grinned. 'It was magnificent. Words fail me.'

'I doubt that.'

'So, what are your plans?'

'For today, next week, or next year?'

Lady Annabel took off her glasses and studied Madi. 'I was thinking of today. Like in the next hour. Would you care to go for tea somewhere? Actually, I was about to go over to my old house. Madi, would you like to come? Ann?'

'Can't thanks, Annabel. Got to get the food back and meet John. But, Madi, why don't you go? You'll find the house interesting. I'll send Singh back to pick you up.'

'Would you, Ann dear? That would be lovely. Madi?'

Madi shrugged. 'Sure. I have no special plans this morning.'

Madi reacted in some surprise at the size and haunting splendour of the old mansion. High-standing and double-storeyed, it rose in peeling paint like an ageing grey shadow from the tangled garden. The area under the house had been glassed and closed in, a modern addition which looked like a new bandage on an old body. 'That's an office for Colonel Bede,' said Lady Annabel as the car delivered them to the wrought-iron fence and gate. 'He trundled in a desk and filing cabinets but doesn't seem to use it much. Holds a few meetings there, he told me. At least someone is occupying the place occasionally. Whole place is a bit of a white elephant,' she said in a sad voice.

Ann waved goodbye. 'Singh will be back in an hour or so.'

They walked through the overgrown garden, past the choked pond and hibiscus and bougainvillea, once regularly pruned and now sagging with overlong tresses. A knotted and twisted flambeau tree rose up on one side of the house reaching beyond the upper verandah. 'I'm going to take some cuttings back and pot them up for my little garden. I just like to check the place every few weeks.' Annabel went to a side entrance, unlocking a thick door which led to a staircase leading to the verandah. 'Used to be the servants' entry.'

Madi caught her breath at the musty odour that reminded her of old clothes, mothballs and mouldy carpet. Strips of sunlight fell through the closed wooden shutters but Madi could make out the bulk of mahogany furniture crouching darkly in the large sitting room. There was a faint aroma of old wood, or was it furniture polish? Annabel opened a set of shutters which revealed dusty leather, ornate and heavy chairs, sofas and sideboards and a dining table of baronial proportions. On the walls were misty scenes of the English countryside which seemed faded and insipid, or was it just the contrast of the hot sun and bright colours outside the windows.

'You've never moved or sold anything?' asked Madi. 'What's going to happen to all this?'

'God knows. Where would I put it? I can't afford the upkeep of this place. Bede owns it all now. I'm quite comfortable in my little flat across town but this does bring back memories. Daddy entertained many notables here.'

They walked through other rooms with four poster beds, massive wardrobes and bureaus, old paintings and family portraits.

'There's so much personal memorabilia here,' exclaimed Madi. She refrained from voicing her impression that it seemed like a living mausoleum, as if Daddy had been carried out in action, brushing his teeth or combing his hair, or asleep in his bed, and no one had set foot back in the house and nothing had been moved since. She knew without asking that his clothes would still be hanging in the closets.

'How long has it been like this, closed up?'

'Ten years. Bede made a legal agreement for me. I really don't understand it except I have somewhere else to live and an allowance from the estate.' Lady Annabel shrugged. 'We can have tea . . . if you don't mind tinned milk. I keep supplies here and occasionally pop in for a solitary tea party with Daddy.' Madi didn't know how to react as Lady Annabel seemed quite serious about her occasional teas with a ghost.

'Have a browse around while I pop downstairs to the kitchen. Won't be long. There's a side balcony off the games room which is quite pleasant. Make yourself at home.'

Madi tried to imagine Annabel as a child growing up in this now musty and museum-like relic of a bygone imperial era. The buzz of cars, cyclists and traffic outside was muffled by the garden. Had it ever been a gay, light-hearted place, Madi wondered.

She peeped into large, elaborately tiled bathrooms with massive brass-tapped tubs and willow-patterned toilet bowls with varnished wooden seats and tarnished brass chains. She opened the floor-to-ceiling doors of a bathroom closet and recoiled in surprise at the dusty and slightly musty assortment of toiletries, personal effects and towels, untouched for years.

The main verandah was filled with a clutter of fat rattan furniture covered in faded brocade print. Between the living room and entrance to the verandah, a flight of stairs led to a small landing that turned at right angles down to the main reception area. Madi peered over the railing, glimpsing what appeared to be a library to one side of the large front door and a sitting room to the other. In the sitting room a small bookcase caught her eye and she glanced along the row of titles of old mouldering British crime novels and history books.

As she stood there studying the titles, she heard footsteps coming up the staircase. At first she thought it was Annabel, but the lopsided step, one footfall seeming heavier than the other, caused her to lift her head. Someone coming up from the colonel's office, she wondered? Holding a book she'd just drawn from the bookcase, Madi leaned over the balustrade and saw an elderly man resting on the landing, shirtsleeves rolled up, a Fair Isle vest over his white shirt and tie. Madi smiled at him, thinking he must work about the place, then she turned her attention back to the book and wandered along the verandah to a wicker chair. Straight away she was absorbed—*Being The Discovery of the Large and Bewtiful Empire of Guiana by Sir Walter Raleigh*.

She thumbed through the facsimile edition of Raleigh's enthusiastic account of his search for El Dorado. Immediately images of his adventures in the interior flashed through her mind. Despite the quaint language she was soon marching beside him, thrilled by his reckless expedition into the unknown in search of a prize beyond description.

'Tea is ready, darling,' called Annabel brightly. Madi

carried the book to the enclosed verandah where Annabel had opened a window and set out a teapot and cups of Royal Albert china on a tray beside an opened tin of evaporated milk.

'Annabel, this Raleigh book is utterly fascinating.'

'I know. Poor Raleigh, he tried so hard, came so close, one suspects, and still lost his head in the Tower of London.' Annabel poured the tea. 'Like Raleigh, Daddy was quite convinced that there is a fortune in gold out there somewhere. He used to tell me the legends about it as bedtime stories when I was a little girl.'

'You must have had an unusual childhood.'

'It was very special.' Lady Annabel smiled softly. 'No other time in my life has ever matched it. No man was as special as Daddy. Everyone at court and in the diplomatic world adored him. He was a very good diplomat, I've been told. After Mummy died, I was surrounded by a devoted father, adoring uncles and aunties and now . . . all gone.' She handed Madi the cup and lifted a hand towards a wall where framed photographs hung.

'They were grand days really,' she said with affectionate nostalgia. 'Such times we had when we all got together. Christmas was magnificent. We always tried to come back here and have Christmas and see out the old year in BG. We were British Guiana and proud of it.' She stressed the word British.

Madi glanced at the rows of faded photos in walnut and tarnished silver frames. 'No other cousins or family?'

'Some of the children are back in the UK. I used to see them infrequently, at the obligatory tea with mad Aunt Annabel.'

'That's a shame . . . that you only see them infrequently, I mean.'

'God, no! They are the most boring and stuffy bunch

you can imagine. And the children have no manners. Another reason for making my escape back here.' She laughed, but Madi sensed it was a hollow laugh.

Madi looked again at the wall of photos of lost relatives and found her eye captured by a sepia shot of men in golfing attire posing with clubs and Indian caddies. She put down her cup and stood to look at it more closely.

'Annabel, this man, who's that?'

'Oh, that's Uncle Eric. He lived here with Daddy during the brief stint of my marriage.'

'Doesn't he live here any more?'

'Good grief no. He passed on years back.'

A shiver went through Madi. 'Annabel, I just saw him on the stairs. I heard him walking up the wooden stairs. He had a sort of lopsided step, a limp perhaps.' It suddenly occurred to Madi the man she'd seen hadn't come upstairs nor had she heard his distinctive step go back down.

Annabel replaced her cup on the tray. 'Come with me.'

Madi followed her through the house to one of the bedrooms. Annabel pushed the door open. It was obviously a man's room, and it looked as if the occupant had just stepped out.

Annabel went to the closet and opened it, revealing tweedy jackets, cotton shirts and a row of walking sticks. 'Uncle Eric had a gammy leg, Boer War. Walked with a bad limp.'

Madi felt faint. 'But I saw him on the stairs, as clear as day,' she whispered hoarsely.

Annabel shut the closet door quietly, unmoved by Madi's announcement. 'Don't worry about it. You just saw a jumbi, my dear.'

'Annabel, you don't see a ghost in the middle of the day. And it wasn't a ghost, it was your Uncle Eric!' Madi's voice had risen. This house was more than giving her the creeps now. How was a sophisticated, sensible woman like herself supposed to simply accept this explanation? Ghosts! She was the last person to be visited by some apparition. She'd never been to a clairvoyant, tarot card reader or dabbled in any spiritual or new age psycho babble. Not that she would totally dismiss the idea of ghosts . . . she supposed.

Annabel flicked her scarf over a shoulder and reached out to touch Madi's arm. 'Madison, this is Guyana. You must accept such things here. That shouldn't be difficult for an Australian since you all sing endlessly about the ghost of some swagman. I understand that Matthew and Kevin are rather noted in certain local circles for their party duet of your unofficial national anthem.' The two women exchanged understanding smiles. 'Jumbis, ghosts, spirits, call them what you will, we believe in them and accept them. Have no fear, Madison. He means no harm. This was his home. Let's have another cup of tea on the verandah.'

Madison silently contemplated this casual acceptance of the ghost's residential status in the old house as Annabel topped up their cups. 'Dear girl. There are many things here you might not understand. Don't fight them, merely accept there is a reason. Don't challenge and pry, just go forward and follow your own path. It is safest that way.'

Madison picked up her cup, trying to digest the casual remark but feeling that behind Lady Annabel's words there was a warning. She wondered if this was a reference to Ernesto's death or their visit to New Spirit.

Madi doubted she'd be making a return visit to this

house. How could she explain seeing a ghost to anyone else? It wasn't the sort of thing you could tell just anybody. 'Oh, by the way, yesterday morning I saw a ghost. Uncle Eric with the bum leg.'

But she did tell Lester as he drove her to the bank the next day.

He gave her a sly knowing smile. 'Ah, a jumbi visit yo, eh? Dis be good, Madison. Yo be tuning in. Yo gettin' on de Guyana wavelength. Soon yo be playing de drums.'

'Don't joke, Lester, it was very unnerving.'

'See, yo don' say it was scary.'

Madison thought for a moment. 'No it wasn't. Only because who's going to be scared of an old man with a bad leg. What could he do to me?'

'Dat true. But yo don' deny it be a jumbi.'

'I saw the man, I saw his photo and he's been dead for years. It was the same man. I've never disbelieved in ghosts, I just wasn't convinced one way or the other. But this seems all too . . . well, silly, in a way. Yet I know what I saw.'

'Jumbis be good an' bad. De obeah man can put a spell to keep dem away. But if yo see a bad jumbi yo tell him buzz off and go see dat Uncle Eric,' he chuckled.

Madi wondered how such a story would go over at a dinner party back in Sydney and she burst out laughing.

'Wot so funny, Miss Madison?'

'Just a private thought, Lester.'

He gave her a shrewd glance, then changed the subject. 'So how was Kaieteur? Yo found de secret . . . saw de frogs?'

'I did! They're magic.'

'And did yo sleep good in dat hammock we get?'

'It's the best. I can't adequately describe the hideous beds I nearly slept in along the track.'

Madi launched into stories of the trip and Lester listened with satisfaction, delighted that she so deeply enjoyed the experience. 'So now yo seen dat, what next? Yo go to London?'

'Lester, that was just the beginning. I'm hooked. I want to explore so much more of the interior.'

'Now dat good news, but I ain't gonna be round here for a little time to hear yo stories. I'm going up to my holdin'. Time to look for de fire in de river again.'

'Looking for diamonds,' exclaimed Madi enviously. 'You're going up to work your holding?'

'Yeah. My mumma gonna look after my boy. I save some money so I'm seeing if I can make a bit more stash.'

Madi hated the idea of not having Lester around. He was reliable, honest and fun company in the car, happy to share confidences with her and interpret the Guyanese way of life.

While she shared her experiences with Connor, Matthew and Kevin, it was in passing, and they laughed or listened with a slightly indulgent air. To them, Madi was filling in time, they enjoyed having her around, but didn't see her visit here as anything more than a holiday. She tried not to think about her relationship with Connor. He was fun, she enjoyed his company and she didn't want to think of it as just a romantic interlude. But neither of them was prepared to plan much beyond the next dinner, the next party.

Madi sensed that in her desire to explore and travel into the wilderness, she was following an essential inner journey, even though she had little idea of what she might discover. But she had a disturbing feeling that she had to respond to these bold new feelings or she wouldn't be at peace with herself.

After the banking she invited Lester to have coffee with her. It had become something of a regular feature of their outings. At first Lester charged waiting time, but now he regarded the coffee break as time off for friends to chat and he didn't add the time to his fare. He enjoyed Madi's genuine egalitarian attitude towards him and came to appreciate the increasing depth of interest she was showing in his country. Despite his ingrained happy-go-lucky approach to almost everything he was initially a little uncomfortable at these coffee sessions, but now he enjoyed them, despite the good-humoured roasting he got from the other drivers.

'Yo be lookin' restless. Yo got man trouble, eh?' asked Lester with a shrewd grin.

'Not really. I'm trying to avoid thinking too far ahead on that score. No, it's me, Lester. I just have this compulsive urge to go back into the interior.' Madi fiddled with a tendril of hair by her cheek. 'I never felt so . . . driven about anything before. And I really don't know why.'

Lester nodded. This lady has been reading too much into that old book, he reasoned. He looked into his cup and took a satisfying sip of the heavily sweetened brew.

As he put his cup down Madison leaned across the table. 'Lester, I want to go with you to your holding. I want to hunt for diamonds.'

It was a calm, quietly delivered proposition and it totally rattled the taxi driver. For a moment he stared at her blankly then slowly a big white-toothed smile took over, although it failed to restore the power of speech.

'I'm not joking, Lester. I want to come, for a couple of weeks, say. I won't get in the way. I want to help you. Get in there and do it, just like Gwen did.'

Lester gaped at her and struggled to speak. 'Well, dat be one crazy idea. Course not. Wot people say? Yo is from t'other side of de track. Wouldn't be proper. Hell man, every pork-knocker on de river be sayin' tings 'bout me. An' yo,' he added with emphasis.

'I'm serious, Lester. Wouldn't you like the company? And anyway, I don't have to apologise for how I choose to lead my life.' She was a little surprised at the firmness of her stated resolve, and she thought how her new-found confidence would have really shocked her former husband.

Lester was still looking at her in shock, then Madi smiled broadly and in almost a whisper pleaded, 'Please consider it, Lester. Please'.

He finally broke out into his usual infectious laugh. 'Man, yo is full of surprises. Wot yo bruddah gonna say ... hey, bro, I is goin' up de river to de jungle wit dat fella Lester. Now come on, Miz Madison Wright, wot he gonna say?'

'Well, bruddah, he gonna say I is one mighty mad gal,' Madi retorted in her best Creole. 'Seriously though, Lester. Why not? You know what you're doing, you've been looking out for me here in the city. I trust you ... and you said you were gonna be my Guyana bruddah, eh?'

Lester still looked stunned at the idea. Madi went on. 'I'll pay my way, plus something extra. A bit more stash as you put it. I won't be a handicap. I'm prepared to get muddy, work hard, do whatever you do.'

The offer to pay him made an impact but he was still unconvinced. 'Better talk it over with yo bruddah and yo boyfriend,' said Lester calmly. Confident no more would come of this crazy plan, he looked at Madi. 'Sure, I'd like yo company. It can git lonely up dat river sometimes, depressin' when dere ain't no fire 'bout. Sometimes yo dredge and wash for days and days and find nothin', den next day yo see dat little twinkle, dat little fire in de bottom of de pan and oh man, dat be one great feelin'.' His eyes danced and his grin widened.

'That does it, I'm going to come. I'll bring the gear I took to Kaieteur and you'll tell me what supplies and stuff I need, right?'

Lester shook his head and looked bemused at the very notion of it all, but added in a conciliatory voice, 'After yo talked to yo Mr Matthew. Now, I gotta go see one friend'. He was desperate to restore some sort of sanity to the day. 'I take you back now, okay.'

Madi tried to pick the right moment to discuss the idea with Matthew but, despite lolling on the cane lounge with his feet up after work and a rum in his hand, his reaction was neither relaxed nor understanding. His jaw dropped degree by degree as Madi gushed out the detail of what she proposed.

'It's crazy, Madison. For a start it is totally inappropriate going bush with a black bloke up some damned remote river and camping in the scrub. Imagine how that piece of gossip would go down around the cocktail circuit.'

'Matt, people like that will always gossip. I don't care.'

'But I care. Connor will care,' he added angrily, then calming a little, added, 'Look, sis, the climb to Kaieteur was one thing, this is far different. It's not a holiday trip. They don't have a Club Med up there, you know. The man is trying to scratch a living in probably the hardest way possible in this country. He

276

doesn't need a tourist along . . . and a woman, to boot'.

Madi's mouth tightened. 'That's a pretty sexist remark, Matt. Tourist I may be, but I want to get into really working, really looking for diamonds. I'm prepared to get my hands dirty and I do have some idea of what to expect,' she said stubbornly, indicating Gwen's book sitting on the coffee table.

'Get real, Madison,' exploded Matthew picking up Gwen's book and flipping through the pages. He stopped at a photograph of the handsome Major Blake. 'See, she had a white bloke in charge . . . and don't tell me there wasn't any hanky-panky, eh?' He chuckled and Madi snatched the book from him.

'Gwen was in charge and I don't believe there was any such hanky-panky, as you call it. Why can't you accept that a woman, even back then, could want adventures and experiences that were radically different to prove herself?'

'Is that what you're doing, Madi? Trying to prove something. What, for God's sake?' asked Matthew quietly.

Madi didn't answer. She went to her room and softly shut the door. A few minutes later, Matthew knocked. 'You're putting me in an awkward position, sis,' he said gently. He walked over to where she was sitting on the bed and kissed her cheek. 'Let's sleep on it.'

Matthew could feel his socks getting wet as perspiration ran down his legs while he jogged beside Gordon Ash around the oval opposite the Pessaro Hotel. The general manager insisted on his morning 'conference run' in Georgetown as well as at the mine. Matthew was grateful there was a slight sea breeze and that it was still early. In two hours, the heat would be ten degrees higher and the humidity a killer. He was beginning to dread these Georgetown visits from Gordon Ash and he always tried to escape the regime when he stayed overnight at the mine.

'We're meeting Johns for breakfast with your mate Bain from the IFO.' Ash quickened the pace. 'I've been through this caper a few times before in Third World situations. Must say I can't agree with this propping up of poor countries by international funding organisations. This place is never going to get on top of itself under those conditions. Too many Third World governments just keep servicing the debt which keeps ballooning.'

'So what's the answer?' Matthew matched his stride to the older man. 'I agree outside funding places enormous hardship on the local people, but without some outside aid and influence what is their alternative?'

'Maybe they should repudiate the whole idea of their debt.' Gordon Ash was blunt and somewhat self-opinionated, thought Matthew.

'That surely would incur retaliation.' Matthew glanced at the rough, tough fighter beside him. 'You must create a bit of havoc in boardrooms.'

'I've been known to speak my mind.'

That's just what we need at this moment, thought Matthew. An idealist. Ash obviously didn't fully appreciate the subtleties of the mine's financial situation. 'Guyminco's been raped and rumour has it the funds were siphoned off into a phantom company,' said Matthew, wondering if Gordon had heard anything about El Dorado.

'I've heard the gossip. Made it my business over a few rums in the first week. You know what I think?'

Matthew shook his head.

'I think the government and bureaucracy are now relatively clean,' Ash said. 'They're into fringe perks, not big cash payments. If there's a villain it's someone with access to cash flows outside Guyana who needs to launder money in a country like this where no one takes too much notice.'

'Any suspects?' Matt asked.

'Hell, I'm the new boy on the block. I'm just theorising.'

Matthew decided not to push the subject further.

Connor heard of Madi's plan to go diamond hunting as they sat in the gazebo at the bottom of Matthew's garden. A gaudy macaw, impossibly bright in blue and yellow feathers, flew into a nearby tree with a loud screech.

Connor sipped his rum. 'Madi, I have no right to tell you what to do, but as a friend—a good friend, I hope—I ask that you think this through very carefully.'

'I have, Connor. I've considered the pros and cons quite seriously.'

'So what are they?'

Madi sipped her drink. 'I won't go through them all, but I assume one negative factor is me taking off into the jungle with a man I hardly know, coloured, and a nobody by our standards.'

'That had crossed my mind. But that's your decision. You say you can trust him and I respect that.' But he gave a lopsided grin. 'Though I have to admit to slight pangs of jealousy.'

'Of Lester, or of me going bush?'

'Both, I guess. Safety is another concern.'

'Crossing the road in Georgetown is dangerous. I can't live in cotton wool. I now realise I've spent most of my life mouthing politically correct attitudes, hiding behind the safety and security of my job, my family, my lifestyle and even using my broken marriage as a reason for not stepping off the cliff.'

'You can get through life quite well without hurling yourself into an abyss, you know, Madi.'

'Are you telling me you've always played it safe? Never taken a risk?' She leaned over and kissed him on the cheek. 'This is more than just exploring the wilds of Guyana, it's a little journey of self-discovery.' She spoke lightly but meant every word.

'Matthew told me he wouldn't try to stop you any more, so all we can do is point out the pitfalls and let you choose, and you've done that. I hope you find whatever it is you're looking for, Madi.'

'Only way to find out, right?' They both turned as a large black bee hummed loudly into view. Connor glanced at his watch. 'Right on the dot.'

Madi brightened now that Connor seemed content to accept the decision. 'Poor Lester, I don't know who was more stunned that I had decided definitely to go, he or Matthew. They both kept looking at me and saying, "Are you sure?" like a pair of mother hens. Anyway, someone will be taking supplies up to Lester. I can come back with them.'

Connor leaned back in his chair and lifted his arms in a gesture of resignation. 'Right, sounds like you've covered everything. What more can I say?'

'You could wish me luck and tell me to have a nice time,' she said softly.

Connor reached over and awkwardly wrapped his arms about her. 'I do, Madi, but I'll worry the whole time. And I'll miss you.' He kissed her hard on the mouth.

A week later Madison was sitting in the centre of a small, open aluminium runabout with Lester at the tiller and supplies and gear stacked high around them.

Madi started to feel excited. It was early morning on the river and she was entering a whole new world. It seemed that every nerve in her body, all her senses, were switched on to absorb and respond to every detail of the adventure. She wore a broad-rimmed Akubra and sunglasses to combat the tropical sun and she had splashed suntan oil over her exposed arms and dabbed white zinc cream over her lips and face, much to Lester's amusement.

'Puttin' on de Australian war paint, eh? Scare de Amerindians, eh.'

Madi accepted the good-humoured jibe with a broad smile. She was happy beyond belief. In just a few hours she felt she'd crossed an invisible border that divided the safe and known from the remote and unpredictable. Already the energy of the jungle was making itself felt, the thickness and impenetrability of it crowding down to the water's edge.

Occasionally they passed minor assaults into its flanks as loggers dragged greenheart trees to the water's edge and onto barges.

Lester told her of the strength and durability of these magnificent trees that soared forty-six metres straight and true before throwing out branches at the top of the rainforest canopy.

'Dey be a valuable tree, de wood lasts long time in de water. But dey can't grow dem anywhere else. Dey only grow where nature put dem.'

'They can't transplant them or grow them from seedlings?'

'When dey gone, dey is gone.'

The musky smell of the rainforest earth, an occasional drift of wood smoke from an unseen Amerindian village, the calls of strange birds, drifted across the water to Madi who inhaled deeply, imprinting all of this on her senses.

Lester was also reflective, wondering again at his madness in agreeing to bring a foreign white woman up to his rough and remote holding. But she was different from any woman he'd ever known. She had real spirit. She didn't seem to be like so many of her own kind, polite but condescending. He couldn't imagine any of the expat ladies he drove around in George-town undertaking such a trip. He grinned to himself, remembering the meeting Madi had set up between himself, Matthew and Connor. Although he'd met them before, there had never been any sort of social exchange. They'd sat down rather stiffly in the lounge room with a cold beer and discussed the whole idea and it soon became obvious. Lester wasn't for the trip any more than they were. It had been Madi's persuasive, passionate and persistent arguments that had eventually won the day, and Lester just didn't have the heart to keep saying no.

They made slow progress up the river due to the weight of their supplies and eventually reached a small island, one of many, where a solid open boat made of greenheart was tied to a tree. Lester nosed in calling out, 'Jacob . . . yo dere, man?'

Madi could see a tent and small camp set up in the trees and then a figure tumbled from a hammock. He was a short, deep copper-skinned man, with powerful arms and shoulders.

'Dis be Jacob, he half Amerindian, half Negro like me. Dey call dese river men bovianders.'

'What's that mean?'

'Cause dey live above yonder, boviander mean short way t'say, above yonder,' Lester explained with great logic. 'Dey be de best captains and bowmen on de river. He help us get de boat up de rapids.'

'Not this boat, I hope,' said Madi looking at the little freeboard of Lester's craft.

'Hey, yo Jacob,' shouted Lester, stepping out and pumping the man's hand. He got a cheerful gap-toothed grin in return. 'Miz Madison, dis Captain Jacob.'

He gave her a small salute and became unexpectedly decisive. 'So we is ready, water lookin' good, Lester. We load dem up, yeh?'

Jacob spoke in a deep hoarse voice and soon the two men were busy transferring everything to the solid long-boat, Jacob stowing the gear to distribute the weight evenly in the six-metre craft. The boat was powered by a huge marine version of a car motor mounted on a long propeller shaft that could be readily lifted clear of the water.

Madi tried to help by handing things from the run-about. 'What's wrong with his voice?' she asked softly.

'He lose his proper voice shoutin' and singin' at de river men fo' years. De crew men got to row in de old days. Singin' help dem get the verse.'

'I read in Gwen's book that the crews used to sing shanties while they rowed,' said Madi. 'I remember one about a chicken jumping over a fence?'

'*I bought a chicken for eighteen pence...*' Lester began chanting and Jacob swiftly joined in. '*Hurrah boys, hurrah! I bought a chicken for eighteen pence, and the son of a gun jumped over de fence . . .* ' they sang.

Lester grinned, 'Jacob know some songs all right.' He eyed the laden boat. 'Dis one heavy greenheart, it no get smashed up on de rocks.'

'Today's good news,' quipped Madi more to herself than to the others, but they nevertheless smiled in acknowledgement.

After a snack they pushed off towing Lester's empty boat, its outboard stowed in the main craft. Madi sat in the centre, Lester in the stern at the tiller and Jacob stood in the bow with a long solid paddle. Madi wondered how Jacob and Lester would be able to control the ungainly and heavily laden craft should they get into difficulties in rough water.

Reading her thoughts Lester was reassuring. 'Don' be nervous, Miz Madison, dese just small cataracts, not big falls we goin' down.'

Jacob entertained them with another hoarse shanty.
'Juliana my dear, Juliana my love.
The girl from over the mountains.
Juliana so fair with her black curly hair,
The girl from over the mountains.
Blue mountains so high that the barley rot dry,
The girl from over the mountains,
Blue mountains so high that a sailor can't climb,
The girl from over the mountains . . . '
Soon they were in the white water. Not a big set of rapids, but there was still a lot of white water roaring around visible rocks. Madi tensely gripped her wooden seat and marvelled at the skill of the bowman in keeping the boat clear of danger. Shouting steering commands in Creole to Lester and using his paddle to steer the bow into clear water or to push them off the rocks, Jacob

guided them through the cascade to the smooth, deep, clear-flowing water upstream.

'How 'bout dat one, Miz Madison?' shouted Lester above the motor.

'Great,' she shouted back. 'Fun, isn't it?'

Lester simply raised his eyebrows and rolled his eyes. Wait till we hit the big ones, he thought.

Soon the keel was scraping over rocks again and the water around the boat was churning and foaming and the boat was proving almost impossible to handle. Then it suddenly became wedged between two rocks. The motor was cut and Jacob grabbed the bow rope, leapt over the side and pushed the boat free, then thigh deep in water, with the rope over his shoulder, began hauling the boat, slowly step by step. On board, Lester used a paddle to push against the bottom and rocks. Madi felt utterly useless, and at times a little frightened when Lester slipped and the boat was momentarily out of control. Frightening episodes she'd read in Gwen's book came to mind. But she refused to think about them and eventually they made it through the rapids. Using the engine and the paddle, Lester swung the boat and steadied it as Jacob climbed back on board. Madi marvelled at the old man's strength and skill and saw why the river men were so esteemed.

But she barely had time to relax before they were into the next set of rapids. After that, it was easy motoring and Jacob lit a cigarette, only occasionally signalling or calling a direction to Lester to keep the boat clear of shallow, submerged rocks.

Madi, leaning back into a pile of gear, had started to doze when she suddenly heard Lester shout, 'Dere she be'.

A landing, a couple of boats, an unpainted wooden

shack and several shelters—thatched roofs on poles—
were visible.

'Where are we?'

Lester grinned. 'Dis be civilisation, man. Our corner
shop.'

It was a crude shack with a hand-painted wooden sign
advertising the services of The Trading Post.

*Boat and mining supplies. Beer. Rum. Foodstuffs.
Goods bought.*

Madi thought the latter service rather enigmatic.

The proprietor was an old pork-knocker with a short
plump wife.

'Hey, Sammy,' hailed Lester, 'back agin to mek me
fortune dis time, man.' They both laughed uproariously
at this.

'Hey, Lester, you still workin' dat dud claim of yours?'

'Sure ting. Dis time got luck with me, Sammy. Meet
Miz Madison. She Australian visitin' friend of mine in
Georgetown.' It was only a slight distortion of the facts,
but it got around a lot of likely questions and boosted
Lester's prestige somewhat.

Sammy eyed her with interest and rather self-
consciously tucked in his grubby old singlet. 'So you
really lookin' for diamonds? I can sell you some. Good
stones. No government tax. Like to see?'

'Yo keep yo rubbish stones, Sammy. Miz Madison
goin' to bring us big luck, yo just see.'

Madi broke into the good-humoured bantering.
'Thanks for the offer, Sammy. Perhaps I will look at your
stones one day soon—just to compare them with what
we find.'

Lester was jubilant. 'See. Told yo so, Sammy. We got
luck wid us dis time.' Lester then dropped his voice and
spoke quietly. 'Any finds?'

Sammy shrugged. 'You know how 'tis. No one talk less they have to. Or after rum dey open de mouth and de story jump out. Been okay. Some good fire comin' up.'

Madi tuned out of the conversation, enchanted by the quaint atmosphere of the remote riverside store and its amazing range of merchandise. Tins of food, packets of soap powder, bags of flour and sugar, dried food, weedy fresh vegetables grown by Sammy's wife, hats, boots, nets, tents, mining tools, and several tanned animal skins.

Lester and Jacob had reloaded the gear in Lester's boat and checked that the outboard was still firing. Jacob tucked the money Lester gave him inside his hat band and jammed the hat on his head.

'Thanks for making the trip such fun. You going back now?' said Madi as she shook his hand.

'No, ma'am. I wait a day or so. Dere be someone wantin' a ride back down de river.'

The old shopkeeper came out with a couple of glasses of rum and gave one to Jacob and they both squatted by the river to watch Lester and Madi set out. They waved their glasses in salute and Madi waved her Akubra.

'Wot yo' mek of dat white lady an' Lester?' asked Sammy.

Jacob pondered over his rum and took a slow deliberate sip. 'She nice, but mus be bit strange t' come t' dese parts. Mebbe she be lucky, like she say. Mebbe.'

Sammy nodded in agreement and smiled. 'Reckon Lester eat better dis time now he got woman cook.'

Out on the winding river, the little trading settlement was quickly lost to view and the jungle crowded in on the narrowing waterway. Suddenly Lester tapped Madi on the shoulder and pointed to a gigantic tree. 'See dat tree and dat mountain top wid de bump on de right. Get dem in line and dere be de door to our creek.'

He steered towards the tree and sure enough there was the narrow and almost concealed entrance to the stream. Madi felt a fresh surge of excitement. It was everything she had imagined it would be and as they slowly turned in, she reached up and pushed aside the hanging branches. Within a few yards the stream widened and she was able to glimpse the sky above the towering forest canopy. She noted that the sun was low and hoped the camp site was not far off.

Lester stood, while holding the tiller, throttling back to dead slow. 'Look out for sunken logs.'

Madi soon saw what he meant as they scraped past a rotting tree trunk just below the surface, then a few minutes later Lester cut the engine. Their way was blocked by a fallen tree.

Lester cursed. 'Damned swamp tree. All time dey fall down.'

'You mean we have to go in there? Past that tree?'

'Yep. Unless yo want to drag dis boat cross de swamp.'

'Can't we cut through the tree?' Madi stood to look ahead and saw that the tree blocked the entrance to what seemed to be a small lake.

Lester was fiddling in a tin box. 'Okay, we fix him.' He manoeuvred the boat up against the tree and went to the bow. Leaning over the side he tied a stick of dynamite to the trunk and handed the fuse to Madi. 'Unwind dis as we back up.'

She fed out the fuse line as they headed back towards the river before sheltering close to the bank. Lester cut the engine. 'Get down low in de boat.' He lit the fuse and crouched beside Madi, who had her hands over her ears.

The explosion shattered the old tree, chunks of wood spearing in all directions. The jungle screamed back in protest at the disturbance. As the acrid black smoke began to drift away, Lester gave the outboard an energetic tug and they inched ahead to the calmness of a tiny lake. At one side of the topaz water was a small strip of silvery sand which Lester made towards with a cheerful whistle.

'This is so pretty. How on earth did you find it?'

'Mebbe luck, mebbe accident, mebbe meant to be, eh?'

Madi jumped onto the gritty sand, glad to stretch her legs again. She was drenched in sweat and exhausted by the heat and humidity. But the tiredness was barely noticed as she took in the idyllic setting of the camp site, even though it was heavily overgrown with weeds and shrubs. Under a thatched roof on four poles was a rough table and stools. A fireplace of blackened river stones was nearby. Tools, sluice boxes and other equipment were intact under a weighted tarpaulin almost totally covered in vines. When Lester pulled back the tarp, Madi burst out laughing at the sight of an old tin hip bath.

'Yo bones get sore n' stiff doin' de work, we be glad of hot bath, b'lieve me, Miz Madi.'

'I believe you. Very civilised, Lester, very civilised indeed.' If Matthew could only see us now, thought Madi happily.

'We take turns and be private, okay?'

'Thanks Lester, that will be very nice.'

Together they worked quickly as a team to unload the boat, set up two tents, string hammocks, store food and light a fire. Lester used a machete to slash back the undergrowth around the central part of the camp, leaving the bulk of the site for the next day when he was refreshed and had more light. Already it was time to light the kerosene lanterns and to cook dinner.

Lester was crouched before the fire while Madi sat on one of the bench stools sipping strong black coffee, watching him stir tinned stew in a saucepan.

'Smells good. I could eat the proverbial horse.'

Lester chuckled. 'Dis horse come outa de tin. Best stew in Georgetown supermarket.'

They ate without saying much, both feeling quite exhausted. Madi yawned and Lester stood. 'Okay, Miz Madi, hit dat mattress in yo tent. Now, yo not gonna be 'fraid in de night if dere be spooky noises?'

'You mean animals and so on?'

'Could be. Could be de water mama singing too.'

'Okay,' she said with resignation. 'Who's that? Another jumbi?'

Lester gave a crooked grin. 'It be a woman with long hair and magic power. She live under de water. Sometimes she sit on a rock and try to lure de men.'

'Like a mermaid?'

'Yeah, she can be big trouble. More even dan de matchikouri.'

'All right, I'll bite. What's a matchikouri?'

'It be like a man, but big and hairy with flaming red eyes, webbed feet and fire coming from his chest. He grab people and rip dem in pieces to eat.'

'Gee thanks, Lester. Just the sort of bedtime stories I wanted to hear.'

He shrugged. 'Yo got t' know de stories of dis culture. But ah think yo is too sleepy to bother if dem come wandering by, eh?'

'You're right. I'm so tired I couldn't care if they all

carried me off.' Madi took her plate to the bucket of water by the fire and washed it. 'Goodnight, Lester. I'm really thrilled to be here. Thanks so much for letting me come along.'

'Yo sleep good, Miz Madi.'

She slipped out of her shorts and top and pulled on a cotton shirt of Matthew's. She fell onto the air mattress and blew out the small lantern. The light from the oil lamps outside quivered, causing shadows to move on the canvas of her tent. But she wasn't frightened, despite Lester's tales.

She tried to isolate the sounds around her, of Lester retiring, of the soft rustle of trees, of distant water tumbling over rocks, of strange nocturnal noises from small jungle animals abroad in the bright moonlit night. But soon she was sleeping soundly and deeply, feeling safe and contented, embraced by the jungle around their camp.

THIRTEEN

It was midday, the heat and humidity were oppressive and the glare from the sun reflected off the river and seared like a laser beam. Madi had a splitting headache despite Matthew's old floppy white cricket hat. This was only their first proper working day and Madi was beginning to realise that the adventure was going to involve a lot more hard work than she ever imagined. But no way was she going to give in to her aching back and arms. If Gwen could do it in the 1920s, she would do it today.

Very early the first morning they'd walked all over the accessible parts of the claim. The lease and surrounding area were thickly covered by jungle in most parts, but laced with narrow animal trails and a network of little streams, and there was also a small swampy area. With the enthusiasm of a born naturalist, Lester pointed out the indications of possible diamond and gold country, the shape and colour of rocks, the grand towering trees, a mixture of soft and hardwoods, and manicole palms. 'Dose palms are edible cabbage trees, make good hats, too. Good country,' he said with warmth and pride. 'Good country.'

'How did you ever find this spot?' asked Madi as they pushed through undergrowth, both slashing away with machetes.

'All round de big rivers like Essequibo, Potaro, Demerara yo find good country. De best way be de old maps. Dem British geologists made good maps. You can buy at de Lands Department.'

The camp was crudely fenced with posts and wire and the claim's perimeter was marked by a metre wide boundary line of cleared underbrush, now somewhat overgrown. 'We have to clear dat back, it be de law.'

A roughly painted wooden sign on a post gave details of Lester's claim, his name, prospecting licence number and description of the location and area. Madi estimated that the claim was about the size of a couple of city blocks. 'How much do you pay for this, Lester?'

'Dis cost me one thousand Guyana dollars a year to work.'

'A real bargain, I'd say, provided you find gold or diamonds.'

'Dat be de gamble.' Lester grinned. 'Diamonds be rascals to find. Sometimes better luck with de gold.'

Lester worked in the old-fashioned way with a minimum of modern technology. His sluice box—'pork-knockers call him a tom box'—was made from a steel drum with the top and two sides cut out. A piece of wood was slotted into one end—the head—and a drum with holes bored in the bottom was attached to the top end. Sections of board were slotted across the bottom as traps. It was tipped on a downwards slant and gravel and water were shovelled and bucketed into the drum with a constant stream of water. Occasionally he would create a small dam in the creek, set the tom box in the water, remove the dam wall or block and let the slurry of water and gravel flow continuously through the tom box. Then it was lifted out and the heavy sediment and stones trapped in the bottom were rinsed in the pan or picked out.

He taught Madi to pan. 'Okay, yo be de jigger man workin' de tom box. Now take dat battel—dat what we call de gold pan—and do like dis.' He handed her the shallow V-shaped dish and showed her how to squat at the water's edge and swirl the fine mesh tray inside the outer tray in a circular motion, trapping the bits of gravel, gold and diamonds in the centre.

It took Madi only a short while to get the hang of it. She became excited at a silvery flash but it turned out to be small and valueless crystals glinting from their sheen of water. Other pretty little stones, like garnets and smooth dark toffee jasper speckled with cream spots, she put to one side. Lester had explained to her the different gemstones and crystals found in the area and was amused by her treasuring of stones he regarded as rubbish. But he did nothing to dampen her enthusiasm, saying that her little finds showed promise of something better.

'We call dese sweetmans. What yo do with dem, eh?'

'Maybe have them made into jewellery. I almost have enough bits of jasper to make a necklace of graduated stones. Polished up and the backs cut flat, they'll be beautiful.'

'A gold 'n' diamon' necklace or ring be better, eh?'

'Of course! Lead me to the diamonds, Lester. This is hard work . . . but I'm loving it,' she hastily added, for despite her aching back, headache and tired arms, she was totally absorbed in this work. Each time she twirled the sieve she expected to see the sparkle of a real gem.

Then had come that first brilliant flash of gold and she'd squealed in wild excitement. That tiny nugget, the size of two pin heads, had been enough to keep her at the hot, back-breaking work for hours. She figured the headache had come from staring too intently into the metal tray at every speck, fearful of missing even the smallest gem.

Lester let out a rebel yell of delight when Madi shouted, 'Gold, Lester! A nugget. A real nugget. Honest. Look'. She stumbled across the rocky creek bed to where he was digging.

Lester leaned on his shovel and smiled at the sweat-soaked woman, wide-eyed and almost speechless, who held out her pan for his inspection.

He carefully poked at the little nugget. 'Congratulations, Miz Madi,' he said, nodding his head in appreciation of the find. 'Well, like I said, tings were startin' to look good. I reckon it a good time to stop for lunch 'n' we have little celebration, eh? The tom box is nearly empty, dat's good.'

Lunch was pickled pork on cold rice with a chopped yam sprinkled through it. Madi was hungry and didn't mind what they ate so long as it was filling and renewed her energy. She marvelled that such simple food could taste so good. Memories of barbecues and picnics reminded her how much better food tasted in the open

air or by a campfire. As soon as she finished her mug of
tea she jammed the old cricket hat on her head and stood
up. 'Right, I'm ready.'

Lester didn't move. 'Middle of de day be siesta time.
Better we rest, den work.'

It was unbelievably hot so she followed Lester's example and lay in a hammock in the shade of some trees. In
minutes she was dozing.

When she slowly began to wake she was dripping perspiration and sleepily thought it must be hot enough for
the rocks to melt. Suddenly she was imagining the scene
transformed by a surrealist painter—sloppy rocks melting over each other, lava hissing into the river with foamy
bubbles steaming. Weirdly shaped trees bending drunk-
enly with rubbery trunks. A river that ran uphill, peeling
backwards over rapids to expose the river bed like a tin
of sardines. Flowers that opened and shut like time-lapse
photography.

She dreamily recalled Gwen's description of giant cup-
shaped lilies filled with spongy emerald moss out of
which grew smaller flowers of amazing colour and variety . . . of flowers that sprouted from the trunks of trees
. . . of frogs and lizards and butterflies as brilliantly
coloured as enamelled jewels—bright red and green, silver and black, turquoise and yellow. She imagined a
plague of gold frogs scattered like glittering tropical
confetti.

Madi felt like Alice in an abstract wonderland and
shook her head to clear this strange vision. The scene at
the camp settled back into focus—the slowly flowing
stream, solid rocks and the reassuring figure of Lester
hunched over the wooden sluice box. Watching him

Madi felt a surge of fondness for her Guyanese friend. They had exchanged few personal revelations before this trip but there was a bond between them she could not easily identify. It was not romantic or physical, nor brotherly, nor the bond that girlfriends share. For the first time she realised she had a good male friend without any complications. They had vastly different lives and backgrounds, and what now bonded them was this country. Thinking back she realised how lucky she was to have met him. Lester had given her the keys to the door of Guyana.

She joined him, glad to paddle in the cooling creek. 'Here, dig down through de dirt an' sand till you get to de gravel. Take up de gravel and wash in de pan and we see if him look good.'

They found flecks of gold in the first few pans and Lester decided to dig further into the bank, first tipping a bucket of gravel into Madi's pan.

Suddenly Madi let out a shriek. 'I've found one!' With her fingernails she lifted the shiny but opaque stone, barely a quarter of a carat, into the palm of her hand. Lester hurried over.

Madi was almost breathless. 'It's real, isn't it, Lester? Is it a real diamond?'

'Yep, dat be one. Guyana diamonds be very hard, very bright. Good quality. Okay, find some more like dat and we be in business.'

Within an hour they'd found two more and Lester decided they should concentrate their efforts on this part of the claim.

Side by side they worked, saying very little, concentrating on what they were doing, a sense of rhythm and purpose in their movements. There was something about this sheer physical work, as opposed to talking, thinking, interacting with other people, as she did in her normal work, which Madi preferred. At one point she had the strange sensation of rising out of her body, being high above and looking down at the two figures—one tall and dark, the other shorter and blonde—just two small specks beside a sliver of slipping water, dwarfed by the jungle all around.

Once or twice Madi and Lester exchanged a look, a swift smile, a murmured comment but didn't pause in what they were doing.

Mid-afternoon Madi just had to plunge in the creek to cool her hot and aching muscles.

Lester kept washing the gravel through the sluice box. 'De last box,' he shouted to her. 'Always de best, I say every time. Even if nothin' dere it de last box of de day and dat good news, hey?'

She watched as he took the shaker pan with the final mix of gravel. He carefully washed away the sand pan and poured in a portion of mercury, then raked through it with a finger, giving a satisfied grunt. Madi peered into the bottom of the battel to see a cluster of gold nuggets and gold flecks sticking to the mercury.

'Now how do you get it out?'

Lester took a handkerchief and put the residue from the pan in it and squeezed. The mercury ran out through the cloth into a jar, leaving the gold behind.

'In town I take de gold to de Gold Board and dey clean it up wit a blow torch to get rid of impurities. Weigh him and pay me. Easy, eh?'

Lester was hugely pleased with the day's work. He handed Madi a small glass phial with a cork top. The diamonds rattled in the bottom.

Madi held it up to the light and turned it slowly. 'It doesn't look much for such a hard day's work.'

'Like yo say, Madi, no worries. We add more to dese tomorrow, eh?'

'I hope so.' She looked at the small stones again, almost hypnotised by the pieces of compressed and crystallised carbon. She now understood the lure and obsession that drove Lester and all the other pork-knockers. She could appreciate why men—and women like Gwen—would endure the hardship and deprivation of the interior and take the gamble involved simply to find specks of light hidden by nature for thousands of years.

Lester smiled at her. 'Be careful, Madison, yo have the light of diamon' fever in yo eyes.'

She laughed and handed him back the phial which he put with his handkerchief into his pocket.

Lester went ahead to the camp, asking Madi to tidy up the workings ready for the next day. When she'd finished she walked a little distance along the stream. The last sunbeams stuttered through the canopy of green twilight. With her gym shoes slung around her neck Madi waded through the shallow creekwater, treading on a soft carpet of sunken brown leaves.

It was a dim, enclosed world and Madi found herself pausing to study lizards and insects, delighted as a blue morpho butterfly fluttered away. Gingerly she prodded strange mossy growth looking at tiny plants and flowers with total absorption. She stared in amazement at the world around her, so very conscious of how her focus and interest had narrowed to pinpoints in the immediate world that embraced her. Georgetown seemed far away, Sydney seemed like it was in another galaxy. She reached in her pocket for her carved frog, rubbing her fingers over its smoothness, and felt content. She believed her frog—her replica of the golden frogs of Kaieteur—was her lucky talisman, the guardian of her destiny.

She became aware of the smell of wood smoke and on reaching the camp found that Lester had filled the old tin bath with buckets of hot water. He greeted her with a grin. 'This be yo reward for de first day! Man, yo sure pulled yo weight. I din' think yo'd make it through. Enjoy de bath. I'm goin' check de traps, maybe we catch something tasty like a marudi, a brush turkey, eh?'

Madi eyed the bath. 'Oh, Lester! What a treat! Thanks. You're a real gentleman.' He gave her a courtly bow and another of his big smiles, collected his rifle and a haversack and strode off into the jungle.

The hot water eased her stiff muscles and she had to giggle to herself at the picture she must present, hunched in the tub in the open air by the tent and campfire in the middle of the jungle. 'Hey, Gwen, this is the life, eh?' She spoke aloud, invoking the spirit of that other Australian woman who had fallen under the spell of diamonds, the river and the jungle of Guyana.

The days became a cycle of physical work that toughened Madi's muscles amazingly and strengthened her back. The labour was broken by periods of beauty and tranquillity, moments of high excitement and drama. It was such a totally absorbing new world that she gave little thought to anyone or anything away from this immediate environment.

Lester was full of admiration for her dogged efforts to stick at it when she was tired or when days passed without any finds. She was a worker but he recognised she was genuinely fascinated and enjoyed what they were doing and where they were. His worries about the rough conditions and how she'd cope had long gone and he realised he'd miss her company and very able assistance.

Gradually they fell into the habit after dinner of sitting around the campfire sharing a tot of rum and talking. Most of all she loved to hear Lester talk about Guyana. He spoke from the perspective of a man who had made up for his minimal education with extensive reading. He was prepared to accept the blemishes and stumbles of his country's past and he optimistically believed Guyana could go forward to a better future.

Sometimes Lester and Madi just fantasised about how they'd spend a lot of money if they had luck and found a fortune of diamonds.

'Man, I'd set ma boy Denzil up. Put him in a good school, take him away . . . to America.'

'What happened to his mother? Where is she?'

Lester shrugged. 'She ran off wit a Canadian man. Miner fellow. She never write. We jes live together and she didn't take to a baby. Good-lookin' woman wit education and she catch eye of a miner at de office where she work. My mumma take de boy over when she take off. Man, I live for dat little boy.'

He took a long sip of his rum and lit a cigarette. 'What 'bout yo, Madi? . . . Yo bin married, but no babies. Yo is a career gal, eh?'

Madi didn't answer straight away and leaned forward to poke at the fire with a stick. 'I assumed I'd have babies eventually, but the marriage didn't work out. We were in the two-incomes-no-kids set and life was mainly about having a good time. My husband never saw me as a real achiever. I had a job and did it well, wanted to achieve more, but he kept putting me down, saying there was no big future for a woman in hotel management. But I'm not prepared to just stay home and be a mother and wash a man's socks either.' She paused and looked up as sparks from the fire swirled into the night sky. 'But that's another world. I'm not missing it one bit, Lester. Not at the moment anyway.'

Lester chuckled. 'Seem to me yo got to find a passion in life, dat ting dat drive yo on. Some ting dat give life some meanin, yo know what I mean?'

She looked across the campfire at Lester, now lounging back against a log, hands behind his head and taking his turn to follow the sparks up into the jungle canopy and the night sky.

'I've never had that grand passion you talk about, Lester,' she said quietly, still a little amazed at his reading of her life. 'I can't imagine that. But I can feel something changing in me. Something has happened to me since I've been here. It's like I'm really being my real self for the first time.'

'I go long with dat. De way yo talked us all into letting yo get up here . . . yo is one strong lady, Madi.'

She returned his smile, remembering for a second Geoff's constant criticism of her. 'Lester, that's the nicest thing anyone's said to me for ages. A real compliment.'

They talked about their childhoods. 'I had one good set o' clothes I wore to church every Sunday and dey got put away de minute we got home, to keep dem good. I used to love dem stories in de Sunday School. Mebbe dat got me started on de readin'. And de stories my mumma told me . . . like de gilded man. Mebbe dat start me on de gold huntin',' he grinned.

'The Walter Raleigh story? If he really came here looking for the city of gold . . . where is it? Legends spring from some grain of truth they say.'

'Dat fo sure. Dey say it be here, in de lake where de man o' gold comes up.'

'Here? Is it near here?' she asked urgently.

Lester chuckled. 'No, not here. In de south. Dey say El Dorado be in Lake Parima on de Rupununi plains. Man yo should read dat Raleigh's book yo found at Lady Annabel's. He write about dis country, de birds, de life in de forest. He be a good man, he treat de Indians good, he respect dem and dey help him. He believe dat like de blood flows round our body in all dem little rivers and streams, so be de same here . . . de way to de heart be up de river. De bloodstream of de body and de waters of de world go to de heart.'

They spent most of their days undisturbed, except for some harmless wild animals wandering into camp. But several times Amerindian hunters dropped by and Lester always squatted down for a talk, often sharing a tot of rum with them. Once two Amerindians equipped for hunting called into the camp and, from the way they sought out Lester and spoke to him, Madi deduced that they were doing more than passing the time of day.

Characteristically, they didn't stay long.

That night by the fire, she casually brought up the visit. Lester nodded his head thoughtfully. 'Tings getting stirred up round de settlements. De captains goin' to have a big meeting.'

'What's that mean?'

'It mean that it about time fo' some changes in Guyana, and our Amerindian friends are going to mek things change.'

Madi was mystified. 'Like what?'

'Well, dey want a big say in where dis country goin. Dey want t' share in wealth of de land, like de mines. Dey say de country belong to dem really.'

'It sounds just like Australia and the Aborigines. Land rights and all that sort of thing,' Madi said.

In the early light of the next morning she lifted the flap of her tent and, seeing Lester still asleep in his hammock under the tarpaulin, headed for the creek to bathe. There was a deepish pool where she could squat in the crisp water up to her armpits. She brushed her teeth, dressed and sat on a log to towel her hair dry.

Maybe it was because her attention was diverted, her head covered by the towel, the fact she had bare feet and legs or that she simply put herself in the wrong place at that moment, but suddenly she felt a scratch on the side of her calf. She didn't cry out, it didn't hurt that much, but when she looked down her voice stilled in her throat as she saw her attacker. Solid and deadly black, the creature was about a hundred millimetres long with a barbed and curved tail. Its sting was armed with the erect barb, and it quivered with agitation on the ground by her foot. She had never seen a scorpion before, but there was no mistaking its lethal shape. It was between two rocks by Madi's leg and as she moved it scuttled under one of the rocks and disappeared.

Madi's heart was beating rapidly and she tried not to let panic overtake her as she hurried back towards their camp calling out to Lester.

He examined her leg. 'It be a scratch, not a big sting, yo is lucky. Dey is normally only out at night.' He had a first-aid kit and rubbed an ointment on it, making Madi wince. 'We better get de piaiman look at it.'

'A what man?'

'Piaiman be de Amerindian medicine man. Dere one in de village near here. Best go now. Take some tings, maybe we stay dere a day or so.'

Madi was in too much discomfort to discuss this idea

so she grabbed a few clothes and her toiletries, threw them into a shoulder bag and headed for the boat. Her leg was throbbing and a slight redness and swelling showed around the surface of the scratch.

The trip took about half an hour, and Madi sat back with her eyes shut, trying to block out the pain. A dog barked and a child called out and Madi opened her eyes as the boat bumped into the bank at a small village. She could see several round thatched huts with tall grass spires and people running down to greet them. Lester helped Madi out and spoke quickly to one of the children to alert the village.

In a short time Madi was sitting on a wooden stool in the shade of a tree with her leg being treated by the piaiman. He was a wizened, stocky old man, with a shock of shiny black hair, cut short above the ears and combed forward to hang down above his eyes. He wore frayed shorts and a faded T-shirt. He had teeth missing and smiled a lot, speaking softly in his tribal language as he lit a tobacco pipe. She glanced at Lester, wondering at the man's casual attitude, and he whispered, 'De smokin' be part of it. He say we should ha' brought de scorpion so he can rub its guts on de scratch.'

'In Gwen's book she said she was able to tame scorpions,' said Madi weakly, trying to distract herself. 'She had them walking all over her without attacking.'

'I heard of dat,' said Lester.

The piaiman's demeanour now changed and he began to chant, rocking to and fro, blowing the tobacco smoke around and over Madi, shaking a small rattle.

'What's he doing now?'

'It be a sort of tareng, dat be blowing, dey believe de

breath and spirit be one,' explained Lester. 'It a kind of spell, don' worry.' Seeing Madi's shocked expression, he smiled reassuringly. 'Even we coastlanders know 'bout dis. He be sendin' away de spirit dat make yo feel bad. De medicine men have very powerful magic.'

The piaiman finished his ritual and two women with long glossy braids came and rubbed a paste made from lime juice on Madi's leg which hurt a little where the surface of her skin was highly sensitive. She was also given a strange-tasting herbal brew to drink which for a moment she was fearful of swallowing, but Lester allayed her fears. 'Just folk medicine, it be safe fo yo.' In minutes she began to feel drowsy.

'Dey say yo must rest here a little time. Keep your leg up,' translated Lester. They made her comfortable. A shy young woman with copper skin and almond eyes, wearing a cotton dress, propped a small wooden stool under her foot. Madi gave her a smile then dozed, leaning back against the tree.

An hour or so later she was served a meal of fish and what tasted like tapioca pudding.

Lester helped her to her feet. 'How yo feel?'

She took a few cautious steps and rubbed her leg. 'Good. It feels fine. Are there going to be any after effects?'

'No. Yo only had a little brush with dat one.'

'But where is the piaiman, I must thank him, pay him something.'

'All done. I fix him up. Come on round and see de village. We is gonna stay tonight. Someting important goin' on.'

Looking around the quiet village, men idling or sleeping in hammocks, kids playing, women working quietly in craft or around fireplaces, Madi was unable to imagine that anything of any consequence beyond daily chores was stirring anyone, but she was pleased at the invitation to look around her first Amerindian village.

'And what is this important event all about?'

'Xavier Rodrigues coming t' speak to de village. He go round all de country explain' tings to de people. He getting de people to support him so he can speak for dem in town.'

'Georgetown? You mean, it's a sort of political rally? Out here?' she said with mild astonishment.

'Yeah. But not like in de ole Burnham days when de speakin' go on and on and all dat other rubbish—gettin' the school kids out to cheer him and dance and so on. Dis be for de Amerindian people, get dem all agree to push for better tings.'

'You mean more government assistance, better conditions and so on?'

'Dey don' want handout from de government, dey want to run tings for demselves. Xavier tell 'em dey got to get power and dey decide what dey do.'

'And do they know what they want?'

Lester shrugged. 'I can' say anyting 'bout dat. But dey look to Xavier, he be de leader and he smart in dealing with de coastlanders and de power men.'

'How did Xavier get to be the leader of all the different tribes all over the country?'

Lester pondered this for a moment. 'I don' know 'bout dat. I s'pose 'cause he been talkin' and talkin' and travellin' round and tellin' em what dey want t'hear. Dey tink de time is come. Now we walk dat sore leg and we go round de village.'

They stopped where the women were cooking and pounding out thin flat rounds of cassava bread. They showed Madi how it was made, first grating the dried white yam-like root on a board studded with nails. Then they pushed it into a long cylindrical tube-like basket that was stretched and squeezed by a child sitting on a pole attached to its base. One of the women explained in halting English that the juice from the cassava was poisonous but when boiled it became a safe flavouring which was used in pepperpot stew—cassareep.

'We use cassava to mek drinks . . . Cassiri and paiwarri. Men drink and . . .' she rolled her eyes and gave a little lurch when she couldn't find the word.

'Get drunk,' said Madi laughing. 'I hope that the poison and the drink are always clearly labelled.'

At a wide shallow pool in a nearby stream Lester and Madi sat quietly and watched a man and his young son, both carrying bows and arrows, studying the water. After a whispered exchange the father pointed to where the boy should stand and the lad took his bow and arrows and waded carefully until he was knee deep in water. The bow was almost as tall as the boy and it took an effort for him to pull back the arrow as he stood motionless for several minutes, poised to shoot as he watched the movements of a fish moving slowly into his range. His father went a little way upstream and set a fish trap, a narrow basket baited with a small piece of meat. He returned and squatted on his haunches with Madi and Lester.

'Poison not allowed no more,' said the father. 'Some pork-knockers use barbasco and haiari juice.' He grinned at Lester who held up his arms defensively. 'Not me.'

'What's that?' asked Madi.

Lester explained that it was a poison the Amerindians extracted from the roots of particular plants and they put it in the water where fish were likely to be. It stunned the fish which floated to the surface to be picked up.

The Amerindian pointed to his son, now proudly holding a quivering fish on the end of his arrow. 'Dat de best way.'

Madi lifted her hands above her head and clapped in appreciation of the boy's achievement, winning big smiles from both the boy and his father. 'Do they use many poisons and medicines from the forest?'

'Course. Traditional medicine be very good. Man, dese people bin figurin' it out since twelve tousin' years before Columbus saw South America. Coastlanders like my mumma use de old folk medicines. Dey even in de cookbooks. Can't get all de plants in Georgetown but dey know de Amerindian people got de knowledge.'

'That sort of knowledge should be preserved.'

'It should be looked at better by de scientists. Yo ask Pieter. He be comin' tonight.'

'Pieter?' she queried. 'You don't mean Pieter Van Horen?'

'He be de Dutch plant man you meet at de falls. Clever man. He lookin' for de medicines from de trees and so on. Yo'll be glad to see him again, I be tinkin'.'

As the day developed, the preparations for the visit of Xavier began to look like some sort of celebration. A lot of food, including a roasted pig was cooked, the ground outside the main hut was cleaned with brooms, and tibisiri mats were spread around. The women appeared to do nearly all the work while the men lazed in hammocks or sat and smoked and talked in small groups.

In the late afternoon, Amerindians from other nearby jungle villages began arriving, coming in groups along the many trails and some along the only road to the village. Women carried babies in soft woven slings across their breasts and the men carried basketweave warishi

309

backpacks suspended by a cloth band wrapped across their foreheads.

It was just before sunset when a noisy scatter of children and dogs heralded the arrival of the two men in a small but powerful boat. Xavier, lithe, dark and handsome and neatly dressed in shorts and a shirt, the sleeves rolled above his muscular arms, was accompanied by the tall fair-haired Dutchman.

Madi could immediately feel the charisma Xavier exuded as he was welcomed by village leaders. A powerfully built Amerindian with painted markings on his face, shoulder length hair, and dressed in western clothes, seemed to be the official greeter, shaking Xavier's hand, pummelling his shoulder and talking rapidly as the villagers clustered around him. The women hung back smiling shyly as the community 'captains' came forward, followed by the older men.

Lester and Madi stood back as Xavier moved through the crowd, touching the children and acknowledging the women. Then he came towards them, smiling. Lester explained he was showing Madi diamond country.

'You're a long way from home. Are you doing field work of some kind in Guyana?'

Madi grinned. 'No, I'm just visiting my brother. Lester has kindly taken me under his wing. I wanted to see the interior very much.'

'It's good that you can see the real Guyana. What is your brother doing here?'

'He's a management consultant . . . at Guyminco, the bauxite mine.'

'Ah. I see,' said Xavier with what Madi thought inferred a reservation about her brother's work. Xavier turned to the white man who smiled at Madi as he joined them. 'You have met Pieter Van Horen, I see. He is a man very respected by the Amerindians. Pieter is travelling with me to explain to our people how important the forests are.'

'Well, that's part of the mission in its most basic form. I have a lot more to say than that,' Pieter chuckled in his thick Dutch accent.

Xavier gestured towards one of the open-sided shelters. 'Come, let us sit down, the women have some refreshments ready and we must not disappoint them.' He led the way to one of the mats and several of the men sat in a semicircle around them. The women hurried forward with calabashes of cool drink. Pieter sat next to Madi, a little to one side of the group around Xavier, and whispered, 'If you haven't had this before, drink little, but make it look as if you're enjoying it. Strong stuff. I think it's a great little drink, but it's not everyone's cup of tea'.

Madi could barely control herself from breaking out into a bold laugh. It's certainly no tea party, she thought. 'So what else are you doing out here?'

'I'm studying the potential of plants used by these Amerindian people. To use the jargon of the times, it's interactive discipline—my institute can learn from them, and hopefully we pass something back to them.'

Pieter began speaking with confidence and ease. 'Xavier and I agree that it's no longer acceptable for international pharmaceutical companies to come into the rainforests of the world and take away plants and reap the economic benefits when the indigenous people have been using them for centuries. The notion of intellectual property rights suggests the wealth should be shared with the indigenous people.'

It wasn't quite how Madi expected the day to develop. A deep discussion on economic revolution in a

Third World country was certainly a surprising follow-up to a scorpion wound.

Pieter continued. 'Unless countries like Guyana are involved in extracting these medicines from plants up to the point of patenting them, they won't see a cent.'

Madi questioned him. 'So once you have a patent you have the right to license your medical knowledge to a big company that can develop and test it. If they come up with something—at their expense—Guyana should get a hefty royalty.'

'That would be the ideal way,' endorsed Pieter.

The men discussed how best to approach the public meeting at the village, which gave Madi the chance to nurture an idea that was running around her head.

At the first lull in the men's conversation she spoke up.

'I can see an opening here,' she said.

The Amerindians who sat stoically around them stared with concealed amazement at the young white woman speaking her mind to the two great men.

'I want to set up a meeting between Xavier, Pieter and Connor Bain. He's a friend of mine in Georgetown, a representative of the International Funding Organisation. They assist in funding Third World projects and he's out here working with Guyminco and another mine. This is exactly the sort of thing the IFO should be considering for investment.'

Xavier looked keenly at Madi who for a moment was a little embarrassed, feeling as if her speech had been interpreted as unrealistic. Xavier gave her a warm smile so Madi wouldn't feel he had dismissed her suggestion. 'Thank you very much, Miss Wright. It could be very productive. We'll talk about it later, perhaps in Georgetown.' He rose and some Amerindian elders were quickly at his side. 'You must excuse me, I have to talk with the local leaders.'

Lester and Madi rose too, resuming their walk around the village. Madi was quite excited, keen to think through strategies to consolidate her idea for supporting and expanding the plant project. With a little shock she realised she had lapsed into what she always called her 'marketing mode' and it hardly seemed appropriate in this remote and rather primitive village. But that didn't deter her. She only came down to earth when she tripped over a rope leash tied to a piglet which bolted between her legs as she absently walked into its patch.

'Yo gone blind?' joked Lester as he helped her up from the dirt.

Madi dusted herself down. 'No, not blind, Lester. Perhaps just a little passionate about something.'

'Ah,' exclaimed Lester approvingly. 'Dat what I say last night. Yo' gotta have passion in life.'

As twilight quickly faded, fires and lanterns were lit around the meeting area and in the flickering light the men settled in communal groups on the ground in front of a few chairs on which sat Xavier and some of the tribal leaders. The women were in the background, cuddling sleepy children. The men had painted their faces and chests in red and black dye and many, including the women, wore traditional armbands, necklaces and ornaments. 'All dressed up for the occasion,' observed Pieter, good-humouredly.

Once all were settled, the shaman—'He's de magic man and keeper of de knowledge,' whispered Lester— and the piaiman, the medicine man, made short speeches. Then Xavier rose to speak in Carib, the communal language of the Amerindian tribes.

Pieter and Lester both knew enough of the dialect to

follow what Xavier was saying. But the passion in his voice was enough to carry Madi along. Glancing around at the copper-skinned men and women, their faces lit by the glow from the fires, she felt that she was witness to an important event. As Xavier spoke, there were occasional nods and murmurings of agreement and understanding and frequently, Madi sensed a wave of anger roll over the audience.

'They seem impressed with what he's saying,' she said quietly to Pieter.

'They know the time has come to unite and deal with these issues,' Pieter whispered. 'They are generally not materially minded, but they know if they don't act soon, they are doomed.'

When Xavier finished, several local leaders fervently endorsed the need for some direct action to make the government take notice that the Amerindians, and all ordinary people of Guyana, wanted a better deal.

Soon the Amerindians began chanting, accompanied by drums and rattles—small gourds filled with pebbles. This was followed by dancing and singing which soon swept Madi along and she clapped and swayed with the others watching the foot-stamping dance.

'Dis be de trad stuff, later come de rock 'n' roll and guitars,' said Lester with a grin.

A pottery calabash like a small bowl was handed to Madi and she took a sip of the paiwarri but found the cassava beer acrid and unpleasant. She gagged, then wiped her mouth. 'It's not a threat to Fosters,' she joked to herself, and passed the bowl to Lester who took a long and satisfying swig.

Xavier, who had been dancing, joined them and sat beside Madi.

He gave her a friendly smile and studied her closely. 'Did you learn much today?'

'I guess so,' said Madi. 'I mean, to be honest I'm here by accident. Not just here tonight, but I'm in this country by a sort of whim. But I am learning. A lot in fact.'

'And what will you do with what you learn from us?' asked Xavier gently.

Madi was aware that Xavier, Lester and Pieter were watching her intently, awaiting her answer. She swung her cotton shoulder bag around and reached into it.

'I am learning that if we don't heed the signs, and care for the small things of our world—like the little singing frogs of Kaieteur—then we will all be in danger.' She opened her hand to show the small carved wooden frog in her palm.

Xavier gave a broad smile and touched the carving. 'This is good. You're listening to the singing. These small messengers could sing the last songs on the Earth if the world destroys itself.'

'Then we must make sure the singing doesn't stop,' said Madi in a quick reply.

Xavier reached out and gripped Madison's hand. 'You are welcome among us anytime, Miss Wright,' he said warmly.

Madi caught Lester's satisfied half smile and wink of approval. She winked back.

Long into the night the men discussed plans to form a political alliance between the nine Amerindian tribes of Guyana. Madi wondered how these people, so scattered, so protected in their forest passivity, would adapt to being politically active and aware. She thought back to the murder and drugs at New Spirit, the wheeling and dealing of the powerbrokers and the bureaucratic and political intrigues of the mysterious El Dorado company.

She looked at the Amerindian men sitting with Xavier. There was a politeness and gentleness about them that hid what they were truly thinking and feeling. She wondered if outsiders could ever really know these people.

Xavier was speaking of organising a rally, of bringing as many Amerindian men and women as possible from all over the country to Georgetown to demonstrate.

'What will they demand?' she asked.

'Demand is an ugly word. We will simply ask for our rights so that our people can determine more of our future.'

'We have similar discussions at home over land rights for the Aborigines, mining and tourism in Aboriginal territories, and who owns what is in the ground. The bureaucrats and politicians are still grappling with it all,' said Madi.

'You are involved with these issues in Australia?' asked Xavier.

Madi was silent for a moment. 'To be honest, no. Since being here and exposed to well, different people, culture . . . I suppose it's opened my eyes.'

'And your mind,' said Xavier softly.

After the singing, the dancing and drinking, the village settled for the night. Two women came to Madi and showed her a hut with several hammocks strung in it, indicating she would share this space. Madi noticed they gave her the biggest and newest of the hammocks and was touched at their warmth and hospitality at being treated as an honoured guest. A girl suckling a baby in the shadowy corner of the dirt floor gave her a smile and pointed to the tiny string baby hammock. The interior of the dark hut was messy, food preparations were scattered about with the paraphernalia of community living. Madi was given a soft woven cover to wrap around herself in the hammock. It was another revealing and stimulating experience, to be so much part of the ordinary life of these people, so different from her own. But she felt totally at ease and comfortable. In the dark she heard soft voices, murmurs or the occasional cry of the baby. Then they all seemed to fall asleep together, as if a gentle coverlet had been dropped over the village.

FOURTEEN

Madi sat outside a hut with a half-formed clay pot between her knees. Rolls of cylindrical lengths of clay she'd made earlier were piled beside her. Dia, Madi's teacher, sat opposite her watching Madi's slow progress with the 'buck pot'. Dia was slightly built but her arms and hands were strong. Madi thought she had a beautiful face with its wide jaw, high cheekbones, flared nostrils and curved lips. Her young baby was slung across her chest in a soft sling tied around her neck. Babies were carried close to the mother all the time, reaching for a breast as they wanted. As they got older the sling was sometimes worn across the forehead with the toddler sitting in it leaning against the mother's back. In halting English, Dia explained the baby stayed close to the mother or father till they were about two or three then joined the rest of the family group as a new sibling took its place. She was younger than Madi and, giggling, she'd pointed out her husband Uman, who was too shy to join them.

Concentrating, Madi blended the last clay coil on top, using a piece of calabash shell to smooth the edge. It was a wide round bowl, a pleasing shape if not exactly as perfect as it might be on a potter's wheel. Dia explained they made all the pottery by hand and, using a well-worn pebble, she polished the outside and said the pot would be left in the sun to dry then decorated and baked over a fire. The bowl would be used for cooking and storing food. Dia handed Madi a sharp stick and asked her to write her name on the bowl.

Madi was pleased with her efforts and wished she could take it with her.

'So what do you think?' demanded Madi as Lester eyed her bowl.

'It be good. Man yo is sure goin' native,' he chuckled.

Madi patted Lester's arm. They rarely exchanged any physical contact, though Madi had noticed how affectionate the Guyanese were with each other. While not subservient, Lester had kept a respectful distance between them. But he smiled warmly at Madi's touch. 'Lester, I can't thank you enough for making this possible. I've loved every minute.'

'Even de scorpion?'

'It was just a scratch and you know what *really* fixed me?' she said. As he shook his head, Madi took her frog from her pocket and rubbed it along her leg. 'This did the trick.'

*

Pieter called out to them as he strode past the hut where Lester and Madi were sitting.

'I'm going for a walk, want to come, Madison?'

'You bet! Lester, you coming?'

'No, I pack up de tings, we go back to camp later, okay?'

'Sure, back to work!'

Madi followed Pieter into the jungle around the settlement. He walked briskly. Madi, with Matthew's hat scrunched over her long braids, hastened to keep up with Pieter's large strides.

'How do you normally travel "in the field"?' asked Madi.

'Walk, canoe, drive if I can, carry everything I need. I camp, hunt—not that I'm very good. I carry specimens, my plant box and notebook. Sometimes it's difficult to reach plants in the tops of trees or inaccessible places, but I generally find a couple of Amerindian teenagers to act as helpers.'

Pieter, affable, affectionate, a man who tramped bear-like through the jungle yet had eyes to spot a tiny hidden bud and feet that stepped over small shoots and delicate plants, paused. He drew his knife from his belt and made a slanted slash in the tree and watched the white balata bleed into a small cup he held against the trunk. 'Wild rubber. The local people use it.'

'Pieter, what do you really think . . . I mean about the rainforests . . . everywhere. Do you really believe they hold answers? Like you said, so many of our drugs come from these plants.' Madi stared up at the tops of the trees and the shadowy greenness surrounding them.

Pieter glanced around the forest, the small plants, the furry leaves, clinging vines, lichens and moss and flowers that sprouted from tree trunks. 'Yes, I do believe the answers are here. But not just in the rainforest. I believe nature, and that means insects and animals as well as plants, holds the key to our health and future.'

Madi was beginning to view the environment through new eyes, seeing a pharmacopoeia of possible cures. 'No wonder the big pharmaceutical companies want access.'

Pieter gave a slight smile. 'So many factors come into it. Like how do they do the research, are the specimens fresh, what are the screening procedures? The answers are here . . . But the process needs to involve the people who own, nurture and understand their place in this world.'

Madi stared at the ethnobotanist.

'Pieter, isn't that what we all want? To find our place in this world?' Madi was silent for a moment then added softly, 'I wish I could do something to help. I feel that my life has been so aimless and . . . shallow. Since coming here it's like my eyes have been opened'.

'You've grown up, you mean,' he answered gently. 'Tell me about yourself, Madison.'

'I grew up with a loving family. I had a safe and fun life and married young.'

'You made a bad choice, eh?'

'As it turned out. I did think I loved him. But looking back now, it seems like every time I wanted to unfold my wings as it were, he held me back. I never grew or learned or experimented or flowered, I suppose.'

'You were the one that allowed that to happen.' Pieter chided with a smile to soften his words.

'You're right. And it's made me hesitant about future relationships. I wish I'd taken control of my life earlier.'

'You can only do that when you're ready. It must have been a big step to come to Guyana, and while you came to the safety net of your brother, you have now stepped outside that. And you must follow this path that has opened up to you.'

His words hit home with Madi. She saw she had turned towards a new path, but whether she should plunge down it, not knowing where it might lead, was another matter. She pushed the thought to one side.

'What about you, Pieter. Are you married?'

'I have a lovely lady, she's fair and pretty, like you. And fortunately for me, she shares this passion of mine.' Pieter leaned towards Madi. 'It is important that the person you love shares the same interests. I bet you and that husband of yours didn't have something special in common, eh?'

'No. Nothing. Just two lives that overlapped domestically in the end.' The realisation troubled Madi. Thoughts of Connor flashed into her head. What did they have in common? At the moment only Guyana.

Two hours later they returned to the settlement. Lester and Xavier hailed her. 'So has our jungle gatherer persuaded you to save the rainforest?' laughed Xavier. Despite his flippant tone Madi knew the question was a serious one.

'I've always been a bit of a greenie. I just never knew about the broader issues. I've certainly learned a lot, from all of you.'

'So now yo have to tell de bruddah and de boyfriend 'bout all of dis, eh?' said Lester.

'They're going to tell me I've become a tree hugger,' laughed Madi. Still, she intended to talk to them and try to share what she'd learned.

She turned to Xavier. 'Seriously, I think you should meet Connor. I'll suggest it so you can put the case for funding assistance. And why can't we approach the foreign mining companies to make donations to plant research as a way of making some restitution to the people for what they're taking out of the country, apart from paying government royalties? It would be a good public relations gesture.' Glancing at their dubious looks she added, 'Hey, I'm a marketing whiz, you know'.

Pieter nodded. 'I can see that. Actually I'm already getting some funding from a local outfit. A machinery spare parts company funnily enough. It's run by a Colombian, Antonio Destra. Do you know him? He's indicated there could be more investment down the track.'

'I've met Antonio,' said Madi evasively. 'He's a businessman. I can't help wondering what he would expect from such an investment.'

'He made a completely unsolicited offer. Maybe there are more companies willing to be so generous,' mused Pieter.

'I'll set up a meeting with Connor,' she said firmly. Then giving Lester, Xavier and Pieter a big smile, added, 'Anyway, count me in. I'm with you guys!'

Lester nodded sagely, quite believing her. 'Well now yo spent time with de village, we go back to work, eh?'

Two days later, Madi was settled back into her routine at Lester's camp. They worked independently, sometimes not speaking for hours, then as one would make a small find, they'd stop, examine it and discuss it in detail, then return to their panning, sluicing and digging. The sounds of the forest were familiar to Madi now. She knew when certain birds would appear, had seen a small agouti, rather like a large Australian bandicoot, and seen Lester stung by an electric eel when reaching into a crevice between rocks in the creek to test for gravel. It was a mild shock which soon wore off but Madi paid more attention to where she moved about the deeper patches of the tributary.

At sunset she cooled off in the natural pool they used as a waterhole before putting on a clean shirt of Matthew's which covered her arms because in the evening all manner of insects came to bite and cause itchy rashes.

One morning while she was bathing in the waterhole she heard a motorboat come up their creek from the main river. Curious, she dressed, tied back her wet hair and walked back to the camp. Lester was down at the landing talking to two men. As they headed up the track, Madi shouted with delight when she realised it was Connor, with Sammy the storeman.

Madi called out and seeing her, he rushed to sweep her up, swinging her in the air.

'How did you find us? You didn't say you were going to come up!'

'I've missed you.' He kissed her. 'If Lester hadn't left contact details about the store, I wouldn't have got here. Thanks to Sammy, here I am.'

'Dis be great. Come, come to de camp,' said Lester.

While Lester brewed coffee and talked to Sammy, Madi showed Connor the camp. 'Well, it's certainly rustic,' he said.

She demonstrated her panning technique and explained the procedure of digging up the gravel, washing it through the tom box then through the pans.

'And do you do this all day?' he asked. 'It's hard

work.' He tried not to sound as surprised as he felt. He listened to the enthusiasm in Madi's voice and her excitement as she produced their finds to date. Connor stared at the tiny glittering stones. 'I guess it must be a thrill to find one . . . even a tiny one.'

'You want to try panning? We've got spare battels,' she said.

'Yeah, well, I guess so. As I'm here.' Madi gave him a penetrating look. 'Just why did you come, Connor? I can't believe you made this trek, took off from work and all, just because you missed me!'

Connor staggered, clutching his heart. 'Oh, you wound me, madam! Of course I missed you. In fact it shocked me a bit that I did miss you so much.' He gave an embarrassed grin.

'You haven't come on some mission from Matt to drag me back to civilisation?' she said suspiciously.

'You don't want to come back yet? It's been nearly two weeks, Madi.'

'No, I don't, Connor. It's not just the experience of being here, which is wonderful, or the fun of slogging away to find a stone or two—and I pull my weight,' she added. 'But I'm learning so much. I've just spent two days in an Amerindian village . . . it was fantastic, even if it was because I was stung by a scorpion . . . '

'What! Are you all right?'

'Of course . . . but listen, Connor . . . I met Pieter again. Remember he was at the falls. I want you to talk to him.'

'What about?' asked Connor who didn't particularly want to troop around meeting some fellow Madi had befriended in the jungle. He was weary after the trip upriver or more specially the night spent at Sammy's shop and the amount of rum they'd consumed.

'Pieter's an ethnobotanist . . . '

'The Dutchman, the plant gentleman. I know him,' said Sammy who knew all the business of the river and around the settlements.

'He's looking at investment into the uses of forest plants for medicines and indeed the whole future of where the Amerindians are going with development of rainforest products.'

'Sounds interesting,' said Connor, sounding not the least bit interested.

Madi realised this was not the time to get Connor on side. 'When we go back to Georgetown we'll have to look up Pieter and Xavier.'

A flicker of interest showed on Connor's face for a moment. 'He's in cahoots with the Amerindian leader? I suppose that makes sense.'

They finished morning tea and Sammy headed back down the river. Connor rubbed his head. 'Gawd, that man can drink and talk and eat. So, what's the plan? Let's go for a swim so I can clear my head.'

Connor followed Madi to her tent. 'I must say, Madi, you seem to have been leading a pretty social life up here.'

She laughed. 'You go for days in the quiet routine then you have a bit of madness. Breaks the monotony.'

'And you haven't been bored?' Connor threw his rucksack down and reached for her.

'Bored? No way. I'm having the time of my life!'

'Didn't you miss me . . . just a little bit?' He held her to him and licked her ears and kissed her long and hard.

They drew apart and Madi grinned. 'Well . . . I s'pose I did . . . ' she teased. She sat on the mattress hugging her knees as Connor pulled off his T-shirt and shorts and began rummaging in his pack for a swimsuit.

'Connor, the times I missed you most . . . were those moments when I stopped and thought, God this is so beautiful . . . I'm so lucky to be here . . . this is so fascinating . . . and wished you and Matt could share it.'

'Weren't there times when you had the absolute hots for my body?'

'Oh, Connor!' she laughed and threw her pillow at him. 'Yes, I did think that on occasion! Come on, let's cool off . . . you need it!'

Lester left them to themselves as they wallowed in the swimming hole. 'So how have you and Lester got on? He hasn't made a pass, argued with you or got fed up with you yet?'

Madi glared at him. 'No, to all of that. And I don't appreciate you saying such things. Lester has been fantastic. He's a good friend.'

'I apologise. Out of line. It's just that I've been going crazy down there. I don't know what you've done to me, Madi. I've felt like the missus left behind while the boss goes off to war and adventure.'

Madi laughed but it struck her once again that he seemed to have missed her far more than she had him. He had been the one left behind while she was having all the fun and she had been so swept up in this incredible experience she hadn't actually missed him. 'I was looking forward to getting back and seeing you and telling you all about it. I thought you'd be so wrapped up in your job and all the intrigues that you'd barely think of me. But I am glad you're here. Really glad.'

The day passed as Lester and Madi fell into their routine and taught Connor how to pan. At first he found the sieve, half-filled with gravel, heavy to swish round and round so the weightiest bits settled in the centre. But Madi showed him how to do it in the water so the river took the weight of the pan until it was nearly empty and then came the final hopeful search for gems or gold left behind. As he crouched at the water's edge, arms aching, eyes glued to the residue in the pan, he had to admit Madi was tenacious. He wouldn't have thought many women would stick at this sort of work all day, day after day.

They stopped for a simple lunch, cassava bread brought back from the village wrapped up like a tortilla and stuffed with tinned meat and pickled vegetables, then Lester announced it was siesta time.

He retreated to his hammock discreetly hung some distance from Madi's tent where Connor headed with Madi.

'If we're going to "nap" in there we'd better get a couple of buckets of water from the creek,' advised Madi.

'What are you planning to do with them, cool my ardour?'

'No,' she laughed. 'Pour them over the outside of the canvas so it runs down the sides but doesn't soak through. The breeze blows across the dampness and cools us off.'

'Just like our Coolgardie safe. Don't forget I'm a West Australian,' laughed Connor.

They made love under the canvas in a steamy tangle of wet bodies and passionate energy, then lay back exhausted.

'Connor, I'm going outside to my hammock under the tree.' Madi wrapped a sarong about her and quickly fell asleep in her soft shaded cradle, while Connor tossed about on the mattress in the tent feeling mildly put out that she hadn't wanted to stay and cuddle him.

*

But during the afternoon as the three of them worked at the river, Connor turned to Madi and remarked, 'You know, I can see how this would get you in. Every minute you think you're going to hit the jackpot,' he grinned.

'And suddenly you find several years have passed,' said Madi. 'It's the pork-knocker's disease.'

The only sounds were those of the shovel grating on gravel in the pit, the rattle of the stones in the box, the trickle of water, the scratching shake of the grit in the pans, the call of a bird echoing across the river. It seemed to Madi it must have been just the same in Gwen's day. Gwen had moved all over the Mazaruni River, shifting to various camps with Major Blake and their team. Madi glanced at Connor crouched doggedly over the pan at the water's edge, wearing one of Lester's old hats. He looked a far cry from the elegant city banker image he would have projected in London, New York or Sydney.

She chuckled to herself and turned back to lift the bucket of gravel and tip it into the sluice box when Connor suddenly straightened up giving a shout. 'I've found one!' He rushed towards Madi, a huge grin splitting his face. 'I've found one!'

Madi and Lester both hoped it wasn't a false alarm, they hadn't explained the crystals and quartz that were found here as well.

His eyes were glued to the pan as he ran and Madi called out in alarm, 'Connor, look where you're going, don't trip, for God's sake!'

The three of them came together and peered into the pan. There at the bottom along with bits of gravel, there was no mistaking the shimmering, glittering sparkle of a diamond.

'It be a clear one . . . not opaque, dat good!'

329

Madi lifted it out of the pan and put it in her palm. 'Look at the colour . . . it's pale pink . . . a rose pink . . . Oh, Connor,' she smiled at him. 'It's a beauty.'

Connor seemed to be in shock and couldn't lift his eyes away from the stone that appeared as brilliant as a laser light.

'Man dat be over de carat,' declared Lester. 'Where yo dig him from?'

'I just decided to stick the shovel in the edge under that tree,' said Connor talking fast and excitedly. 'There were roots but I got under them to the gravel like you said. My God . . . I can't believe it.'

'Yo is a lucky man . . . on de first day. Dis be a good omen. Dis one make a beeyootiful ring,' sang Lester.

'Oh, I mean, what's the protocol here. Who owns this?' asked Connor. 'It's your claim.'

Lester shrugged. 'Finders be keepers. Yo is supposed to pay a commission . . . so de drinks be on yo!'

Madi thought of Lester's little boy. She'd speak to Connor later, but she didn't want to spoil his elation.

'Drinks! That's right, I lugged two bottles of champagne all the way from Georgetown. Tonight we can really celebrate!'

Lester and Madi continued to dig around where Connor had found the stone and Lester found two smaller diamonds of great clarity and coloured a pale canary yellow. 'Dese be good,' he said with satisfaction. 'But de rose one . . . dey be scarce.'

At sunset as they freshened up in the swimming hole, Madi explained to Connor the reason Lester was here was to try to make money to send his boy to a good school.

'But Madi, I want that stone to go in a ring . . . for you,' he said, disappointment in his voice.

'That's sweet of you, Connor. Tell you what, why don't you sell the diamond and give the money to Lester and you can get me something else. Just something small, a token of Guyana.'

'You're right, I guess,' he said. 'About Lester needing the money. But I wanted to give you something special.'

Connor realised with a pang that Madi hadn't even considered the fact that a diamond ring was the first step towards a lifelong commitment between two people.

'It can be special . . . do you know what I'd love? I don't know if they make them, if they don't they should . . . it'd be a fantastic souvenir,' she said.

'What? You know there's nothing to buy here except gaudy gold Indian necklaces, slave bangles or little gold maps of Guyana as pendants. I looked for a present for you,' he admitted.

'A gold frog,' said Madi. 'A little gold frog like a brooch, or a pendant. That would be special.'

'Indeed it would. That's a great idea. Okay, my darling . . . consider it done. Have you still got your other frog, that wooden thing?'

'That wooden thing as you call it, is always with me. It's my lucky charm.'

By the third day Connor was part of their routine and enjoying himself immensely. He and Lester had gone out hunting as the early morning mist wreathed through the trees which Lester described as 'de secret fires o' de forest spirits'. They'd shot a bush hog after a wild and energetic chase, which they'd carried back to camp lashed to a pole. Connor described the event with such elation that

Lester winked at Madi. 'Yo gonna give up dat city job and be a pork-knocker, eh?' asked Lester. 'Yo got de lucky touch, dat for sure.'

'This is satisfying work,' admitted Connor. 'You work physically hard and you've got something to show for it even if you haven't found anything. At the end of the day, you've moved a great pile of dirt,' he grinned.

'You feel you've earned a tot of rum at sunset, eh,' added Madi.

'So when yo gonna go back to dat other job den?' asked Lester, voicing what Madi had also been wondering.

Connor didn't look at Madi. 'Actually, I've taken leave. Haven't had a decent break for over a year. I'm on holidays.'

Madi straightened up and stared at him in amazement. 'So what are you going to do, fly off to Barbados . . . go back to Australia . . . ?'

He stopped and stared at her with a small smile. 'I thought I'd hang out with you for a bit.'

Madi was pleased and touched but she was slightly hesitant about the idea. She hoped he wasn't reading anything more into their relationship than what they currently shared . . . that of friends and lovers. 'It isn't exactly sitting under a palm tree sort of holiday,' she said.

'Well, heck man. Yo know what yo two should do?' said Lester beaming at them. 'Tomorrow yo should go up to Ladies' Hair Falls. Take de boat up de river, den it maybe a two-hour hike . . . but really pretty and den you come to a cliff and de falls.'

'A picnic . . . a day off, that sounds great,' said Madi.

'I'll go along with that,' agreed Connor.

*

By mid-morning the next day Madi and Connor had entered a world of their own. Sitting in Lester's little aluminium dinghy, they weaved up the glassy river. Lester had told them only a few holdings had been worked up here and it seemed to be a remote area. The thicket of forest leaned over the river and at the sound of their motor, soft grey and white herons and pink-tipped cranes lifted off from the tops of trees, and little spotted sandpipers trilled a piping alarm while the rich blue-black flash of kingfishers broke the surface of the water as they lunged for dragonflies.

The solid curtain of green jungle was splashed with blossoms and vines of golden russet, scarlet and white. The air felt clean and clear, a breeze kept the humidity at bay. Occasionally a monkey screeched, alerting the creatures of the deep forest that strangers approached.

'I wonder how long since anyone has been up here. I feel like we're the first explorers,' said Connor softly. 'It's quite beautiful.'

Madi nodded and smiled, glad Connor was discovering what had captivated her so strongly.

'Now you understand why I like it here so much.'

'I guess so. But you have to go back some time, Madi.'

She lifted a hand to halt him. 'Let's enjoy today and not think past that.'

They found the landmarks described by Lester and pulled into a natural clearing on a small stretch of clear shallow water. They secured the boat and hoisted on their backpacks and, following the needle of Lester's small compass, headed through the lightly timbered landscape.

'I suppose there're snakes around here,' said Connor.

'Bound to be. I've yet to see the deadly bushmaster. I'm assuming they'll hear us coming and go away,' said Madi cheerfully.

But as they stopped to admire a delicate cluster of orchids on a tree trunk, Madi stiffened and nudged Connor, pointing to a low branch. Sunning itself there was a long slender snake. 'Look, you manifested that, talking about snakes,' whispered Madi, not taking her eyes off the beautiful creature. It was the bright green of fresh shoots and along its sides were stripes of deepest blue. It had china blue eyes and, as it lifted its head, showed a creamy underbelly. 'What a beauty,' said Connor.

'Poisonous, though. You can tell by its arrow-shaped head.'

'Did Lester tell you that?'

'No, I read it in Gwen's book.'

They moved cautiously away. 'That Gwen has a lot to answer for,' grinned Connor. 'I feel I'm in competition with her all the time.'

Madi laughed. 'She has been something of a catalyst in my life. I so wish I knew more about her. I wonder if she ever came back here again, or settled in England or went back to Ballarat, keeping her time in Guyana as her sole Great Adventure,' mused Madi.

'Is that what this is for you?'

'Oh, I'm never going back,' teased Madi. 'I'm going to become queen of the jungle.'

Connor pulled down a length of vine studded with small starry white flowers, twisted it into a circlet and put it on Madi's head.

'Your tiara, your highness.'

She danced ahead of him. Despite her walking shoes and thick socks, long shorts and cotton singlet, her hat tied to her backpack and her crown of flowers tilted to one side over her flying blonde braids, she reminded Connor of a carefree bush sprite. Again came the niggling thoughts about where he and Madi were headed. He knew he had fallen in love with her but her elusiveness disturbed him. He'd never felt like this about any woman before and was perturbed that his love didn't seem to be reciprocated.

When they came to the cliff, they walked along the creek gully to the base of the small falls that splayed down the rock face like white hair against a smooth naked back. A large clear pool twinkled as the water splashed into it, and behind the shimmering veil they could see a small cave where swifts and bats nested. Amongst the trees, palms and bushes, growing at the edge in the refreshing mist, burst wildflowers and orchids.

Madi clapped her hands. 'It's a movie set!'

Flushed and hot from the long walk they stripped off and waded into the cool pool, splashing and singing in delight.

They sat under the falls and let the needles of water tingle on their heads, they held their breath and swam along the sandy bottom to pop up in the foaming bubbles where the waterfall hit the pool. They floated and drifted, not thinking, just being. Two children at play.

They lay naked in the dappled sun to dry. Connor picked an armful of flowers and scattered them around and over Madi's lean firm body, placing orchids over her nipples and belly button.

They crushed the flowers as they made love on the carpet of blooms, a rich earthy smell of nectar and petals rubbing into their skin.

They ate their lunch and, after one more swim, reluctantly packed up. 'Let's explore a little way at the back of the falls before we head back,' suggested Madi.

So they climbed up the side of the falls and in fifteen minutes had a wonderful view from the top, looking down to the gully, to the distant strip of river where they'd left the boat.

They wandered through open country that had tall straight trees where no canopy closed over them while natural trails wandered through clearings and low undergrowth.

They were about to turn back when Connor touched Madi's arm and put his finger to his lips. 'Ssh, what's that?'

'What?' Madi had been humming with her thoughts far away.

Then she too heard the distant buzz. 'That's no insect, that's a damned chainsaw,' she said.

'Now who would be working up here, do you suppose?' said Connor.

'I'll tell you who. Illegal loggers,' said Madi. 'They do terrible damage in so many ways. The big companies obey the rules and appear to do the right thing in their allocated areas, yet they've made it known they'll buy illegal logs at the back door. These people destroy so much, felling trees improperly, dragging them out haphazardly, they pollute the rivers, cause erosion. They're pirates, Connor.'

He blinked at her vehement outburst. 'How do you know all this stuff?'

'That's what happens with these fly-by-nighters, although some of them make a full-time living from raiding the forest. Pieter is concerned at the species of trees they take and how they break up eco systems and destroy plants.'

'Ah, your plant friend.'

'Listen, I think we should see what's going on and get

Lester to send word back to the Amerindians. They report them to the authorities as well as sending out their own little vigilante groups.'

Connor looked dubious. 'Sounds a bit risky. We can only give them a rough idea of the location.'

'Connor, it won't hurt to get closer, that's got to be less than two kilometres away. Let's see what they've been up to without them seeing us.' Madi started out towards the sound of the distant saw.

'You want to play cowboys . . . but we're not getting close to them,' warned Connor.

They walked for an hour, picking their way through the jungle, and then came across a recently used track. While the sound of the chainsaw was still distant, they realised they were approaching some sort of camp. They crossed a large clearing and then caught sight of a tent and a hammock.

'Stay in the trees and we'll circle round,' whispered Connor.

'I don't think there's anyone there,' said Madi.

'Well then, let's go back.'

'What for, we haven't seen anything yet. If we're this close we might as well see what's going on,' hissed Madi.

'If you don't think there's anyone there, why are you whispering?'

They kept to the scrubby growth between the scattered trees and then, before they realised how close they were, they were facing a clearing and a camp area. Madi and Connor stopped beside trees that screened them from sight.

There were several crude huts, a cooking area and a pile of logs. There was a small loader with chains attached to it that was used for dragging up the logs. Connor peered at the logs. 'They look hollow,' he whispered.

'Rubbish, what would be the point. Okay, I've seen enough, let's go.'

'Wait. I hear voices.' Connor motioned her to be still and silent.

A group of men came into the clearing and went to one of the huts and unlocked a padlock. Connor and Madi exchanged a glance of surprise. Why would anyone need a padlock out here?

A man who looked to be Indian emerged a few minutes later carrying white plastic bags. He tossed them to another two men who squatted by one of the logs and began stuffing the packages into the log, using a pole to push them into the centre. It became clear it was a hiding place as a plug of wood was rammed into the opening, disguising the hollow log.

Madi turned to Connor and raised an eyebrow, a nervous twitch starting in her belly. He mouthed one word at her. 'Drugs.'

They were afraid to move, fearful of attracting attention. They stood there, motionless, barely breathing, in the speckled light of half shade, hoping the men would move away.

The men filled three logs in the same manner, one standing back and checking that the wooden plug looked in place. When they'd finished, they talked together and turned around to go back into the forest on the far side where the sawing had just stopped.

In the brief silence that followed there was the unmistakable low groan and creak of a tree beginning the slow motion fall to its death.

Connor nodded to Madi and took her hand. 'Let's get out of here.'

They turned and took four or five hurried, tiptoeing steps, when a man stepped out in front of them. He held a gun which he levelled at them and spoke calmly. 'Stop right there, please.'

He was solid, round and muscular and the first impression that leapt to Connor's mind was that a fight was out of the question because this man was built like a brick wall. He was a pale-skinned man whose dark bushy eyebrows joined above his nose, a beard bristled like wire around his jaw and he had tombstone teeth with gaps between them. He would have been intimidating enough without the revolver.

Madi gave a start and caught her breath, tightening her grip on Connor's hand.

'What the hell are you doing?' demanded Connor. 'Don't wave that thing at us, we're just bushwalking.'

The man gave a short laugh. 'Yes? What bad luck. You have just bushwalked into trouble.'

He lifted the gun into the air and fired a shot before swiftly pointing the gun at Madi. Connor tried to weigh his chances of grabbing the gun or distracting the man. If he got Madi to run and he leapt at the man . . . but he quickly pushed the idea away as he realised the risk to Madi. And by now the other men were running towards them.

'Walk.' The man with the gun motioned them to move. Connor put his arm around Madi as they headed towards the huts, followed by the man with the gun still aimed at their backs.

'Don't worry, Madi,' was all Connor managed to say.

Madi bit her lip and the knot in her stomach rolled over. 'I'm scared, Connor. I can't help it.'

There was shouting and questions as the men reached them and Connor realised that he too was scared. He was frantically trying to think, his stomach knotted in fear and urgency. How was he to protect Madi in this situation? The odds were totally stacked against them. They had stumbled across and seen a drug operation in action by undoubtedly one of the infamous South American drug cartels. He knew their lives would be worthless in these circumstances. Such men wouldn't be interested in ransom either.

Two of them grabbed Connor. The man with the gun grasped Madi's elbow and she squealed in fright. 'Let us go, you stupid bastards,' shouted Connor, 'we're only on a picnic. We don't care what you're doing.'

'Oh, and what are we doing, sir?'

Connor gaped at the man. 'I don't know, cutting down trees, who cares?' Connor's flippancy had a desperate air.

The men conferred and several gave a cynical laugh. Then two men took a grip on Connor and Madi and pushed them towards one of the huts.

'What are you doing! Let go of me,' shrieked Madi, trying to twist her arm from the man's iron grip. Frantically she looked at Connor.

'Don't panic, Madi, just wait. It'll be all right.' Connor tried to sound calm but was feeling utterly helpless. Madi threw him a wild look as she was shoved into the hut followed by Connor.

The door slammed shut, the bolt scraped and the padlock clicked.

After bright light, the gloom was disorienting. Madi rattled the door, shaking it as hard as she could. A sob rose in her throat.

Connor gently moved her away from the door. 'Don't waste your energy, Madi. Come here.'

He wrapped his arms about her and she fell against his chest, breaking into frightened sobs. Connor smoothed her hair, muttering words he hoped would sound comforting and help camouflage the helplessness and fear that threatened to overwhelm him. They clung together in the stuffy dim hut, the happy bright day of adventuring lost to them.

FIFTEEN

Time slowed, seemed to stop, and in the lull between reality and the dream-like state Madi had sunk into, all she could do was hang on to Connor as they sat on the dirt floor of the little hut.

Chinks of light crept through the old boards and the air seemed to drop onto their skin like a foul damp blanket.

'What time is it now?'

'Five minutes since you last asked,' said Connor.

'What do you suppose is going to happen?'

'Let's just hope they go away and leave us, thinking no one will find us.'

'They won't.' Madi's voice was flat and dispirited.

'Lester knows we came to the falls, he'll start looking

for us. Listen, let's see if we have anything to eat.' Trying to distract her, Connor groped for the small backpacks they'd been wearing when pushed into the hut. 'A few dry biscuits seem to be all that's left,' he said ruefully.

Madi suddenly fumbled for the clasp of her pack and felt inside, pulling out her small wooden frog. She pushed it into her bra next to her heart and leaned against Connor wondering if the frog really was a lucky talisman.

'Do you suppose they're part of a big drug ring or just loggers smuggling as a sideline,' wondered Madi.

Connor spoke softly. 'By the look of those bags of stuff, that's a big haul. I would say this is a pretty massive operation.'

'That looks bad for us then.'

'This place doesn't look very permanent, maybe they use different locations which means if they leave us here we won't be a problem. Don't worry, Madi, it will be all right.'

'I can't believe this is happening. God, you read about tourists being captured in border disputes or whatever in Third World countries . . . ' her words trailed off. The horror stories she'd read in Sydney newspapers had seemed so far away, and she'd often wondered what those tourists were doing in remote and dangerous areas of places like Burma and Cambodia. She could imagine how this story might read, splashed over the pages of the *Australian*.

Connor was having similar thoughts. He doubted they would ever run into these people again and be able to identify them. They were bush couriers, not the Mister Bigs likely to turn up in the city. But he knew drug dealers didn't take chances. He recalled the weekend conversation with Ann and John da Silva at New Spirit where they'd talked of the growing concern over drug trafficking.

'The drugs they had at New Spirit, do you suppose they came from people like this?' asked Madi, appearing to read his thoughts.

'Maybe at the end of the line. There's sure to be outlets and dealers in Georgetown who cater to people like them.'

Slowly an awful possibility dawned on Madi. 'It might be tied up with what happened to Ernesto . . . Oh my God, Connor. Maybe they'll try to kill us too!'

'Calm down, sweetheart, that's a bit far-fetched. No, the drugs might have been part of it. I think Ernesto St Kitt got too close to unmasking the El Dorado outfit.'

Suddenly they heard the sound of a helicopter.

'This is either good news or bad,' said Connor.

'Who would bring a chopper up here? The police? Maybe it's the police looking for people like this,' said Madi, hope rising in her voice.

'Seems a long shot. But let's keep our fingers crossed.'

'Connor, we have to attract their attention. How can we do that? Set fire to something?'

'And cook ourselves and save them the trouble?'

Madi held Connor's hand and, with her other, pressed the little frog against her skin.

The chopper landed with a thwack, the bleat of its blades slowly whirring to a stop. They could hear voices and their hearts sank. This was no raid, but an expected arrival. Greetings were swiftly exchanged and then a deep voice asked, 'Where are they?'

Connor and Madi sat in silence. The droplets of light outside had faded to mellow and a frightening night faced them.

But before the sunset they heard the bolt being opened and Connor and Madi scrambled to their feet.

Two of the men came in while another stood guard at the door. In silence they swiftly bound blindfolds around the prisoner's heads, tied their wrists behind their backs and shoved them back against the wall.

Then they were aware of another man entering. Connor felt he was studying them. Then the man began speaking slowly.

'This is most unfortunate. You had no business here.' He spoke with an educated accent.

'Please, just let us go, we won't say anything to anyone,' pleaded Madi.

'I wish I could believe that, my dear. But it's a risk I can't afford to take.'

'I give you my word. Look, we'll just leave the country. No one need know anything. We have no idea what's going on,' said Connor.

'I can't believe you could be so naive.' The man sounded amused, then spoke to one of the men. 'Search the bags.' Their backpacks were snatched and taken outside.

The man sighed heavily. 'I have been called away from very important matters to deal with these two very foolish foreigners. It is all very unfortunate.'

'What are you going to do with us?' whispered Madi.

'Calm yourself, dear girl, we are not going to do anything with you.' Madi's heart leapt then twisted in fright as he went on. 'You will be victims of a tragic accident. So sad, so very sad.'

'Now wait a minute, we're foreign nationals, you can't treat us like this, I work for a major international banking organisation, maybe we can come to some arrangement . . .' Connor clutched at straws.

The man chuckled and took several steps close to Madi. She could smell hair oil and was aware he was right in front of her and she decided to fall to her knees.

'Please, I beg you, just leave us be. We can't hurt you, we won't talk.'

'My dear girl,' he leaned down and seemed about to help Madi to her feet. Madi raised her head and started to cry, then discovered that she could just see beneath the bottom of her blindfold. Only a tiny slit of vision opened to her, but in the last rays of the sun she could see the man's hands clasped before him. The skin was dark but Madi was silenced by what she saw. He wore a gold ring. Above his gold watch was a tattoo. The ring and tattoo were both in the shape of a frog.

The man flexed his hands and the knuckles cracked. Madi lowered her head. The sight burned into her brain. The man turned and left without another word. Their backpacks were thrown in and the door slammed and bolted. Then they heard their fate delivered in a bored matter-of-fact voice.

'They know too much. Get rid of them. Take them down to the falls or the river, strip them, leave their clothes and bags. Make it look like a drowning accident.'

'Both of them?'

'Of course, idiot. And cover your tracks well. I'll leave at first light. Get rid of them as soon as I've gone then get the truck up here and move the stuff as quickly as possible.'

'Connor . . .' Madi stumbled towards him. 'They're going to kill us.'

'Turn around back to back, see if we can get these ties off.'

It only took a few fumbling minutes and they had freed their hands and pulled off their blindfolds.

Connor wrapped his arms around her. 'Lester will come looking for us if we're not back by dark.'

'He won't come until morning and we have the boat! It'll be too late.' She began to cry and Connor rocked her in his arms as she called out for her brother Matthew. He kissed her wet face, fear in his own heart. 'I love you, Madi. I would lay down my life for you, God I wish . . .' He kicked at the wooden wall in anger at the frightening realisation facing them. He turned back to Madi reaching for her in the darkness and found her tightly clenched fist. Prising open her fingers he felt the wooden frog. 'Hang on to this, Madi. Don't give up, we won't make it easy for them. We'll get out of this, I know we will.'

'Why would he wear a frog?' asked Madi as she rocked to and fro holding the small carving to her cheek.

'What do you mean?'

She lowered her voice. 'I saw his hands under the blindfold. He was wearing a gold frog ring and he had a tattoo of a little gold frog.'

'I don't know, Madi,' Connor said wearily, wondering if they would ever escape.

Lying on the dirt they held each other through the long night, dozing then awakening as nightmares crowded in. Just before dawn the helicopter engine whirred into life and it took off.

A little later they heard several men talking and could smell a fire and food cooking.

Connor rubbed his head. 'We have to work out a plan. They don't know we've untied ourselves, we can grab one of them when they come in, use him as a shield . . .'

'And then what? Connor we're outnumbered and

they have guns. They could save a lot of effort by shooting and burying us.'

Eventually the padlock rattled, the door was pushed open and four men rushed in, two grabbing Connor, the other two moving towards Madi. They gave each other a look. So much for any plans to escape.

They were shoved, stumbling, outside. There was a short discussion among the men which neither of them could follow, then one of the men tied Madi and Connor's arms behind them once more. Exhausted and numb, Madi said nothing, feeling as if she was in a trance. Connor whispered out of the corner of his mouth. 'We'll try and make a break when we get a chance . . . do something . . . just watch me, okay?'

Madi stared at him uncomprehendingly. All fight had gone, replaced by a paralysing acceptance of their dreadful fate.

The man with the gun called to one of the others and each held onto Connor and Madi and began walking them across the clearing.

They were approaching the trees when Madi heard the call of an eagle, followed immediately by another on the other side. Something made her glance back over her shoulder and the tableaux she saw became fixed in her mind forever.

Standing a few feet away from the edge of the trees stood two Amerindians. Faces painted and wearing only small aprons, they were aiming long wooden blowpipes. Madi swivelled her head back to the front and couldn't believe her eyes. Two more Amerindians holding bows and arrows stepped from the trees in front of them. At the sound of another eagle's call, there was a soft whishing as arrows and blow darts tipped with poison silently hit their targets. The man with the gun died instantly with an arrow through the temple. The other men, hit by poison darts, buckled, fell and writhed in agony before gasping and lying deathly still.

The Amerindians melted into the trees except one who trotted forward with an almost casual loping barefooted gait. Madi gasped as he drew a knife and slit the ropes around the wrists.

'Uman!' she said, recognising the husband of Dia, her pottery teacher. 'How did you get here?'

'Yesterday, we were hunting and we heard a gunshot. We saw what happened. We waited for the right time to get you.'

'My God, how can we thank you . . . ' Connor shook his hand then glanced around at the bodies. 'What are we going to do about this?'

'These are bad men. They steal our trees, sell drugs. Now they hurt you. We have ways of sending a message to these people they are not welcome in our lands.' He paused and looked each of them in the eye. 'You must never speak of this. You do not know what tribe or where we come from. Yes?'

'Of course, we understand,' said Madi.

'You go back same way.'

'Did you see the helicopter, see anyone else?' asked Connor.

'City man in helicopter, fat one. No markings on the helicopter.'

Madi took Connor's hand. 'Let's get out of here. Thank you, Uman. We won't speak of your part in this.'

The Amerindian gave a quick smile and trotted back

into the trees. Connor and Madi picked up their packs and began running.

They were halfway down the river, the little outboard motor going as fast as possible when they saw a small woodskin canoe sliding along the water close to the bank in the shadow of the trees. Cut from one piece of bark, the little one-man craft skimmed along paddled by the unmistakable figure of Lester. He waved the paddle at Connor and Madi and they stopped the engine. Lester scrambled into the aluminium dinghy and tied the wood-skin to the stern.

'I was gettin' worried bout yo' lovebirds, reckon I'd better check.'

As they headed back to Lester's camp they told him the story. He shook his head in disbelief. 'Man, yo in a heap of trouble. Better keep dis one under de hat. Yo spose dat chopper man comin' back soon. And what about de drugs in de logs? Dey won't leave dat sittin' in de forest.'

'They don't know where we are or who we are. And they're not going to broadcast the fact they're involved in drug smuggling. We'll report what happened to the police. Of course we won't be able to offer anything at all in the way of information. We were blindfolded, had no idea of who saved our lives. We are innocent victims.' Connor drew a breath. 'That's our story and we're sticking to it. All I care about now is a decent feed and a sleep.'

Lester looked worried. 'I don' know 'bout dat. Talking to de police. Fo sure dat drug boss be somebody important and he be knowed in de town.'

'He's right, Connor. You know the sort of people who are into drugs. If any of them find out what happened to us, they could drop the word to the frog man. He's already tried to kill us once.'

Connor tried to calm Madi whose voice had risen until she seemed on the edge of hysteria. 'Let's just head back to Georgetown as soon as we can.'

'Sammy can fix dat.' Seeing Madi's set and stubborn face, Lester spoke gently to her. 'It be best ting fo now, Madison. I be back down soon fo de rally and see ma boy.'

Despite her brief recovery at Lester's camp, Madi was still locked into a feeling of hollow numbness, operating on some form of remote control, as they headed into Georgetown in a rattling truck driven by a friend of Sammy.

As the truck shivered over the potholes, she leaned against the door, not listening to the chat between Connor and the driver. She stared out at the passing sugarcane country. The fields were filled with neat, straight soldiers of cane in regimented rows, plumed heads erect, while narrow canals of dark snaky water dissected the green army.

The driver pointed to a small house. 'That be de house of Joe Solomon. Man, he threw down de last Australia wicket in de tied test match at Melbourne back in de sixties. He was a famous son round dese parts.'

Connor nodded. 'I guess so. I think I've seen that replayed on TV.'

They rattled past small townships of field workers whose wooden houses squatted astride fat pillars with steps leading to small verandahs where families watched the passing parade of other families. These were Hindustani towns and faded cloth pennants flapped on leaning bamboo poles beside small shrines in the front yards. Amid the squalor of faded paint and scrawny dogs sniffing through litter, little girls in bright dresses and coloured hair ribbons shone like flowers on a bleak vine. The truck passed patches of activity—streetside restaurants exuding the smell of curry and spices, Indian music blaring tinnily through loudspeakers, peeling flapping posters of Bombay films.

Madi found herself physically aching for the solitude and beauty of the river. These shantytowns seemed so temporary, so depressing. On a river she felt she was journeying into the past, was part of the essence that created the landscape. The vastness, the emptiness, the aloneness of the riverscape and interior touched a nerve in her soul.

Her appreciation of the import of nature had grown in these past weeks, and with it had come an awareness that people evolved within nature and that man's destruction of the unique beauty of the natural world was like a bite into the human soul.

It was only the bare facts of what had happened that they related to Matthew once they were back in the safety of his house.

But Matthew was aghast and even more so, as they related their experiences in detail over drinks at sunset in the garden. 'How did you get into such a situation? It's unbelievable! You're just supposed to be on holiday, Madi, not landing in the middle of some drug ring and nearly getting killed! I never did like the idea of you going bush with that fellow.'

Connor tried to placate Matthew. 'It's another world out there, mate, and not all as it appears.'

'So what's new?' retorted Matthew trying to control his rising concern. 'We all know that this part of the world is a real hot bed of drugs and corruption.'

His sister came to the rescue. 'Matty, don't blame Connor. It's all my fault. If I hadn't wanted to be out there with Lester and we hadn't gone exploring, he would have been spending his holidays in Barbados with a pina colada and a bevy of beauties.'

Connor gave a small grin. 'Those days are over. Anyway, the bottom line is, we were saved by a stroke of luck . . . the next question is how safe are we back here?'

'I think you should clear out and go on to London, sis, just as soon as I can get you on a flight. Just to be on the safe side,' said Matthew calmly.

Madi and Connor exchanged a quick glance. 'Why me leave? Connor's in just as much danger. I'm not ready to leave, Matt . . . for lots of reasons. I've decided, and it's not likely that we're going to run into that horrible man again. What would he say? Hi, remember how we met when I was smuggling drugs across the border? They should be more nervous of us.'

'That's the point, Madi. If he's so ruthless and if he's feeling nervous when he learns what has happened there's no knowing what he might do. When are you going to report this to the police?'

'First thing tomorrow morning,' said Connor. 'We'll ring early and make an appointment with Inspector Palmer, since we've had some business with him before.'

Matthew shook his head with concern. 'Cops like Palmer make me uneasy. They're either very good, or very corrupt. Either way, he's sure going to raise an eyebrow when he hears your story, Madi. It seems that every time you take a nature walk you end up with a body or two.'

They were greeted effusively by Inspector Palmer who politely ushered them into his office and heard their story without saying a word, leaning back most of the time fiddling with a ballpoint pen and not taking his eyes off them. Something in his eyes, his manner and his attitude, disturbed Madi. She hadn't liked him during the interview at New Spirit after Ernesto's death and her gut instinct told her to tread warily now.

At the end of their story Palmer offered them tea. 'It must have been a terrifying ordeal for you both. Most unfortunate. The deaths don't surprise me too much. The natives that far into the jungle still prefer their own laws in preference to those of the state. I'll have my staff take statements from you both,' then he added with slight emphasis, 'separately'.

'We understand,' said Connor with firmness and assurance.

'It's a shame, Inspector,' said Madi with equal firmness, 'that such a beautiful country with so much potential is being invaded by drug cartels.'

He gave a small smile. 'My dear Miss Wright, it is good to hear you speak so fondly of our country but it occurs to me you have been quite out of your depth. You are not really equipped to deal with the subtleties of the local scene. And you seem to have a . . . shall we say, a knack, for finding yourself in awkward situations. Frankly, I would advise you to move on to somewhere a little more suited to your interests. I believe you were on your way to . . . London, was it?'

'You're telling me to leave the country?'

'Of course not. You must make such a decision yourself. But frankly we cannot guarantee your safety. Need I say more?'

Connor was furious. 'Was there really any need to say that? Miss Wright has been through a great deal, there is no need to alarm her unduly. Anyway, I think she is handling the stress of all this amazingly well.'

'And my interests are here,' said Madi firmly, then added 'for a little while at least.'

'And those are?' queried the inspector, leaning forward with increased interest.

Although taken slightly aback at the inspector's interest, Madi saw no problem with telling him. 'I'm fascinated by the Amerindians, the wilderness, the country as a whole. It has huge potential, beyond digging holes for minerals. I'd like to see more of this country, perhaps get involved in a way I can help its people.'

Palmer leaned back in his chair, smiling with understanding. 'Ah, a new age woman! Well, I'm sure we'll be grateful for your input, Miss Wright.' He pressed a buzzer on his desk and a policewoman came in at once. 'Constable, would you please arrange for teams to interview Miss Wright and Mr Bain and take statements. I'll brief the officers first.' He rose and escorted them to the door. 'I'll probably be back in touch after I've read the statements. By the way, I don't expect to find any bodies.'

Connor and Madi stopped in their tracks. 'Whatever are you inferring, Inspector?' snapped Connor.

'Because you have taken more than a day to inform us of these deaths the bodies almost certainly will have been removed by the time our men get there, even by helicopter. The trail will be very cold unfortunately. The drug

bosses cover their tracks very well indeed.' He shrugged.
'It will be hard to follow up on your reports.'

Later, over lunch, they compared stories of their inter-
views and were relieved to find that they were consistent
in vital detail. Both found the interviewing officers polite
and efficient, but Madi was still annoyed at the attitude
of Inspector Palmer. 'Conceited, condescending bastard,
isn't he? I don't like him one bit.'

Connor raised an eyebrow. 'That's a pretty tough
assessment of the man. You're more upset because he
suggested you run off to London.'

'It was a sexist suggestion,' said Madi. 'He didn't suggest you run off to somewhere, did he?'

Connor smiled and leaned towards her in a gesture of
affection. 'That's one of the reasons why I love you,
Madi. You're strong and straight up.'

Madi smiled back, responding to a surge of inner
delight. 'You know, Connor, I think that is the nicest
thing that anyone has said to me for a very long time.'

A few days later Lester arrived in town. Madi decided to
have a small dinner to welcome him back and say thank
you for his hospitality up the river. 'Just you, me, Connor
and Kevin if he wants to come,' she told Matthew.

'Good idea. Count Kevin out though. He's up at the
mine and when he is here he seems to spend all his time
over at Viti's house.' He gave a broad smile.

'How serious is he?' asked Madi, who felt she'd been
out of touch with Matthew and Kevin's social life since
leaving Georgetown for the interior.

'As serious as these things ever get,' said Matthew.

'That's how it is for blokes like us. Moving around, being in a place for a limited time, there's no point in thinking in terms of permanent relationships. But it's nice to have female company, local or expat, and then we all move on. The diplomat's dance they call it.'

'Like you and Sharee. And Connor, is he a dancer too?'

Matthew became serious. 'He has been, Madi. Very much so from what I've gathered from him and people who've known him. I don't doubt he is incredibly fond of you, but be careful, sis. I'd hate to see you let down, or hurt again.'

'No chance of that, Matt,' she retorted. 'He's been doing the chasing that's for sure, but I'm not about to step into anything serious . . . I'm not ready. I'm playing and dancing—like you guys. Guyana is just a lovely interlude,' she gave him a cheeky wink. 'Well I'd better go and consult with Hyacinth on the menu for dinner.'

Matthew watched Madi head for the kitchen feeling somewhat deflated. He'd never seen Madi quite so self-assured before.

But in the kitchen Madi's light-hearted attitude evaporated. As she opened cupboards and stared at the pantry shelves she was wondering just how truthful Connor had been with her. Was his slightly confused, vulnerable and besotted attitude just part and parcel of his game plan? How real were those protestations of love? He'd certainly been passionate and seemingly genuine, but she asked herself, 'Will he still love me in the morning?' Was she being too careful in case she was just another dancing partner to him? Or were her doubts still a reaction to all those years of low self-esteem caused by her disastrous marriage?

'Is you lookin' for someting special or just inspecting

de cupboards?' sniffed Hyacinth coming in the back door with a bucket as Madi stood, unseeing, before the open food shelves.

'Oh,' she blinked, 'just thinking, Hyacinth. We're having a friend to dinner tonight, what do you think we should have?'

Hyacinth, ever immaculate, tied a full apron over her orange and black flowered dress and pointed to the bucket with glee. A large fishtail poked out the top. 'I jist buy fish from de fish man. Man, I fix him today. He come to de gate and sell fish with his scales an' I jist know he tricking me. So today I take down de scales and weigh myself. He no cheat me today, so we got one big fish,' she said.

'Good. Baked fish, and what about one of the curried rice and vegetable dishes you do, and a baked custard with some fruit?'

'I do some of dose savoury meatballs for de drinks. Better make de ice too.'

She lifted the pot of boiled water off the stove where it had been cooling, and using a dipper began filling ice cube trays with the safe drinking water. 'So who de guest be?'

'My friend Lester. He's back from his holding upriver. Said he found some good diamonds.'

Hyacinth glanced at Madi. 'You keep different company to de rest of de expat ladies, dat's fo sure.'

'You don't have to stay back and serve, Hyacinth, we'll manage.' Madi had been made aware that some servants didn't like waiting on other Guyanese. The status amongst the various ethnic groups was complicated by economic, racial and social factors.

Madi recalled a campfire conversation with Lester where he'd talked of the effect of slavery. 'We had plenty bad tings go on, so now we just want to be left to do our ting. Some people tink dey is better dan 'nother person. Dat be okay. But we is all Guyanese, dat be de main ting.'

Following dinner they sat in Berbice chairs, like Australian settler's chairs, with their legs casually draped over the extended arms. A relaxed and mellow foursome, sipping good brandy. Lester was pleased with the price his haul had fetched and attributed his good fortune to having Madi and her frog talisman in the camp. He reported that more Amerindians than originally expected were planning to descend on Georgetown for Xavier's rally.

Matthew was sceptical. 'There are rumblings around the traps, bits in the paper saying the Amerindians are going to make huge demands, that there are activists down at the hostel stirring things up and so on. Rumour has it there could be trouble between certain factions. Doesn't it all sound very much like the Aborigines back home with their tent embassies and faction fighting?'

Lester saw it differently and politely, but fervently gave Matthew and Connor another perspective on the political rumblings. He pointed out that the Guyanese of all races were tired of the poverty and waste and corruption that seemed endemic in their society. Aware of the links his dinner companions had with international companies, Lester was a little reserved. But he made it clear that at the street level, the Guyanese people were increasingly questioning just how much long-term good was coming out of the rapidly expanding foreign control of key sectors of the economy.

His thick Creole patois belied the depth of his understanding of the economic trends. He cited the recently developed Columbus goldmine and asked why there was no Guyanese equity in it? Why there were so many expatriate employees in key positions and so little training of local personnel? And, for good measure, he questioned the environmental standards of the company.

'Why is it,' he asked, 'dat we said to be a mighty rich country when everyone so poor?'

It was quite a speech, thought Madi, who had learned upriver that there was a lot more to Lester than met the eye, and she turned to Connor to see his reaction.

He ignored Lester's view of the big picture. 'What's worrying you about the environmental standards at the goldmine? I was up there only two days ago and everything seemed fine—big tonnage turning over.'

'Yo' not heard 'bout de dead fish?'

'No.'

'Well, 'cordin' to de Amerindians near dere, de river at de goldmine got lot of dead fish. Even dead pigs floatin'. An' mine bosses running about here and dere very angry. Xavier been dere to look.'

Matthew and Connor exchanged knowing and concerned glances.

'Sounds like cyanide—a tailings dam leak,' said Matthew.

'I didn't hear a whisper of it, or see anything untoward,' said Connor defensively.

'Ah, but you never left the air-conditioned offices, did you?' said Madi. 'There's only one way to find out what's really going on in this place and that's to get a bit dirty, get down with the workers, Connor.'

'Xavier stir tings up, yo see,' said Lester.

Connor thought for a moment. 'The sooner I meet this famous Xavier the better, I think. He's not going to be a popular man . . . taking on the government over land rights, development partnerships, and now mining issues,' said Connor. 'I have to meet this man. He sounds quite a force.'

'I told you that,' said Madi.

'We make it happen, we get yo and he together,' said Lester.

'Between you and Madi I don't stand a chance. But I can't make any promises. All I can do is listen. It's not the sort of area I normally get involved in. However, I agree, I owe the Amerindian people a big favour,' added Connor, seeing Madi's expression.

But Connor was worried. Trouble, particularly political trouble, could jeopardise the sale of the bauxite mine. And a scandal over any environmental problems at the goldmine would really inflame what was obviously a fast developing difficult political situation. The IFO's investment in rehabilitating Guyminco could be jeopardised, and future investment from abroad for other projects, lost. He had to get detailed information on what was happening and fax his head office in New York.

Matthew made a mental note to write a short briefing paper on the Columbus goldmine for his boss. Stewart Johns liked to be across the local political gossip so that he could trade information over drinks at the Georgetown Club with his contacts from the American and British diplomatic corps. It was all part of the essential networking in such situations and Johns had impressed on all his senior staff the importance of keeping him informed of anything interesting they heard.

The following night Connor took Madi to dinner at the Embassy Club. 'Used to be the Russian Embassy. When they got strapped for cash they made an entrepreneurial move to open up for business.'

They found the club amusing with its old world pomp and obsequiousness mixed with the everybodies who were somebodies and the nouveau riche. 'Interesting how these people claim to be so egalitarian and the minute they get in a place like this they start to play their little games . . . best table, who's in to be seen with and so on,' remarked Connor.

'Well, it's not as stuffy as the Georgetown Club.'

'Want to go dancing at some sleazy great music joint later?'

'Maybe. Let's linger over dinner for a bit,' smiled Madi.

'Tablecloths and linen serviettes make a bit of a change.'

'Ah, they do,' agreed Madi, 'but you've got to agree there's something special about a bush stew on an enamel plate by a campfire in the jungle. Mind you, Gwen and her friend, Major Blake, did it in style when they went bush looking for diamonds. They had meals served by staff at a fold-up table in a mess tent. Sounds unreal, doesn't it? Wouldn't be surprised if they had linen napkins as well. Very much Gwen's style.'

After dinner, Madi and Connor went to a club—a dark room partly lit by coloured neons, smoky, with a steel reggae band whose music made the thin walls shake. Madi danced with abandon, often finding herself part-nered by strangers as the crowd moved around the floor. The Guyanese men were limber, sexy dancers who taught her how to move her hips, keeping her shoulders still while keeping the calypso beat. 'Man, don't dey have slow dances?' drawled Madi as Connor pressed his hips against hers in an attempt at a calypso rumba.

'I think it's time we went home,' he whispered in her ear. 'I've missed making love to you.'

In the car Connor hesitated before starting the engine. 'Madi, there's something I want to ask you . . . I've never asked any girl this before but . . . '

Madi stared at him, a feeling of despair creeping over her. 'Connor . . . don't . . . '

'Madi, I do love you, you know. And I can't believe how much I missed you when you went away. So . . . I want you to move in with me.'

Madi had to stifle the laugh that rose in her throat. 'Connor . . . oh, never mind.' She glanced at him as he sat in the darkness, hands resting on the steering wheel. 'You mean, you've never asked a girl to move in with you . . . even during your dancing days?'

'My what?'

'I understand you fancy-free, travelling men regard each country as a moveable feast. There are always women to play with, so to speak, then your job finishes and you move on . . . it's called the diplomatic dance. You must have left a string of broken hearts around the world. So am I the Guyanese distraction?'

'Madi! I don't deny I've played around in my time. But lately I've felt different. I realise I've been looking for something . . . someone special. I'm now in my thirties, I don't understand what you've done to me, why I feel so different about you. Maybe it's time to . . . '

'Connor!' She cut him off. 'Look, I love being with you, we're great together. But I must say it bothered me a bit when I realised how you, Matthew, Kevin, all of you, lead such selfish lives . . . no commitments, not prepared to settle, always in hardship locations, the perfect excuse to move on. And then I thought, wait, this is what I've been missing. To be free, to pick the flowers and move on . . . '

Connor gave a wry grin. 'You mean I'm *your* Guyanese distraction?'

'Yeah. I guess you could say that.'

'Madi! I'm shocked,' laughed Connor, starting the engine.

'What's sauce for the goose . . . '

'Is sauce for the gander . . . all right, you've made your point. There's just one problem, my darling . . . ' He put the car in gear and moved away from the club. 'And that is, that I love you. And I've never loved anyone before. So there.'

Madi was silent. Something in his voice rang true and touched a sensitive spot deep inside her.

But she was determined to hold back her feelings. She had promised herself she'd be careful.

'Let's not get into that, not now. Let's just go back to your place and spend the rest of the night together.'

'Just tonight?'

'I'll think about it.' She reached out and touched his leg. 'And thanks for asking.'

Late as it was, Madi rang Matthew to tell him she was staying at Connor's knowing that he would worry if she wasn't at home in the morning. 'Matthew is concerned about me,' she told Connor. 'Do you think I should take his advice and go on to London?'

'That's not a fair question. I don't want anything to happen to you but, selfishly, I don't want you to go. I can't get over how much I missed you.' Connor looked rather bewildered and it struck Madi again that he seemed to be genuinely confused at these new feelings.

They made love and, lying beside him as he slept, his breathing slow and deep, his hand linked trustingly in

364

hers, Madi was overcome with tender feelings towards this gentle man. And she had to admit, if she weren't careful, she could fall deeply in love.

They were awakened by the phone shrilling in the living room and it took a while to reach it as Connor had to unlock the metal grille door across the hall to the bedrooms. After a break-in and 'teefing' while he was away, Connor, like many expat residents, had locked away the liquor, stereo, camera and personal valuables behind metal grillework as well as a safety door to that section of the house.

He glanced at his watch, it was barely 7 am, and when he heard Matthew's voice he hurriedly began to assure him Madi was safe and there with him.

'I got that message, that's not why I'm ringing. Johns has just called. Seems there's been a massive accident at the goldmine, all hell is breaking loose, although we don't have much information yet. But I thought you'd want to know.'

'What sort of accident?'

'At first we heard it was a really big leak from the tailings dam, then that the whole thing was about to collapse.'

'Is this what Lester was talking about?'

'No. Much worse, from all accounts. Christ, it could be a disaster of massive proportions. An environmental nightmare.'

'Not to mention economic, political, you name it,' Connor said.

'Anyway, you'd better meet us at the Pessaro to hear what's going on,' added Matthew. 'AusGeo has already sent a team up from Guyminco, led by Kevin, to help.'

'That's good. There's got to be first-class damage control on this one in every way possible.'

Madi sleepily appeared at the door. 'What's going on?'

'Matthew, see you in half an hour.' Connor hung up and told Madi the news.

'Dear God! It's what Lester just warned us about. It will be terrible for the villages downstream.'

'Saving the mine will be the first priority, that's a third of the country's GNP,' snapped Connor, grabbing some clothes and heading for the shower.

'Connor! Think of the people who live along the river! And what it will do to the environment,' said Madi.

'If they don't patch up the mine things will get worse. Now we don't know how bad it is. I'm off to the Pessaro, there's a briefing happening there.'

'I'm coming with you.'

The gathering in the small private dining room included heads of mining companies, government ministers, US embassy officials, Stewart Johns and Matthew. To Madi's surprise, Antonio Destra bustled in, as she was politely escorted out by her brother to 'have a cup of coffee while we get this little meeting out of the way. I'll fill you in over bacon and eggs'.

'God, they're blaming everyone and everything. Even sabotage by the Amerindians,' said Connor.

The briefing by inspectors from the mines department was brief and focused. They confirmed the spill, it was massive, the dam was indeed in danger of total collapse, and sabotage was not ruled out. The minister pleaded for a joint effort by all in the mining industry to tackle the problem and pledged as much support as the government could give. He did not rule out the possible need for international assistance. Eventually someone asked the question that they'd been silently asking themselves. 'If sabotage is suspected, who is behind it?'

'Off the record, of course, and I hope you will all respect the confidentiality of this meeting, we have solid reports of Amerindian activity around the tailings dam area recently. Add this to the fact that their leaders have been stirring up the tribes for a big protest rally in Georgetown, seeking more rights and that sort of thing. You can come to your own conclusions.'

'That's ridiculous!' Madi leaned over the breakfast table as Connor whispered the details of the meeting to her. It came out louder than she'd intended and several diners turned to look at her. She dropped her voice. 'He wouldn't do something like that. Never. If they're trying to blame Xavier then it's a set-up, that's my opinion.'

Connor repeated the briefing details. 'Millions of litres of the stuff has already flowed into the river from the leak. If the whole wall goes the impact will be unimaginable.'

'What are they going to do?' asked Madi, shocked.

'Emergency repair crews are already on the scene. Matthew has dashed off back to Guyminco to run things at that end, and today everyone along the river will be warned not to drink the water, and not to bathe or fish in it either.'

'The international press will have a field day with this one,' said Madi.

They were on their coffee when Antonio Destra strode in and, without waiting to be asked, pulled out a chair and plopped down with them. 'Not the industry's greatest day by any stretch of the imagination. It certainly puts the Amerindian uprising centre stage and makes the miners look like a bunch of cowboys. What's your feeling, Connor?'

Madi gave him no chance to reply. 'It's not an uprising, Antonio,' she spoke sharply. 'It's a movement for a greater say in the running of this country and the use of its wealth. I think it's disgusting that the Amerindians are being so readily blamed for this disaster before there's even been an investigation.'

Destra smiled indulgently. 'Of course, perhaps we are jumping to conclusions. Anyway, the word is about that Xavier Rodrigues is holding a press conference mid-morning at the hostel. I'm popping over with Olivera.'

There was a small crowd gathered in the dining area of the hostel, and Madi and Connor were immediately greeted by Lester. 'Good, I try to phone yo, and tell yo to come here. Bad news, eh?'

Xavier walked into the room to a lectern and a photographer's flash went off as he lifted his hands for silence.

He spoke passionately, denying there had been any Amerindian involvement in sabotaging the mine. 'No matter how strong our objections to excessive mining in sensitive areas, no Amerindian would be foolish enough to protest in a way that would harm our country, our people.' Claiming it to be an accident, he launched a blistering attack on what he described as the corner-cutting, makeshift and shoddy construction of the dam. 'There have been signs for some time of small leaks. All efforts by us to consult with the goldmine owners have been ignored. This is the result—a tragedy that will shock the world.' He then demanded the mine be closed and the government adopt a policy of consultation with the people.

He answered questions, his black eyes blazing, occasionally running his hands through his long hair that fell softly about his shoulders. He wore an open-necked blue shirt, khaki cotton pants and jungle boots. Around one wrist hung a woven bracelet.

'He's certainly charismatic,' said Connor to Madi. 'He's got that special quality that marks out the real leaders in this day and age. They'll love him on TV.'

When the conference broke up, Xavier came over to them and Madi introduced him to Connor. 'This is a sad day for Guyana, a sad day for my people, but in one way maybe fate has stepped in to aid our cause.'

'Pretty drastic way to get attention for your case,' said Connor.

'One has to utilise opportunities where one can in order to achieve the end,' Xavier commented, then smiled at Madi. 'I'm glad to see you are safely back in Georgetown.' And glancing at Connor added, 'I'm sorry your wilderness experience had such a serious downside'.

'Yes, my visit was cut a bit short.'

They made no other reference to their rescue but obviously Xavier was aware of the whole story. 'Madison has told me a lot about you, and I would very much like to discuss some ideas with you. Perhaps we can get together shortly.'

'Well, somewhere a little quieter certainly would be in order,' said Connor.

'I am busy with all this, but let's stay in touch. And you, Miss Wright, what are your plans?' Xavier asked.

'I'm supposed to put a proposal together for the casino complex. Amazonia, you know about it?'

'Indeed I do. It is not a project I favour.'

'Everyone is doing it you know. Casinos are the flavour of the nineties it seems,' said Madi with resignation. 'Back in Australia, Sydney has just got one. It's created lots of jobs.'

'Ah yes, but at what cost?' queried Xavier. 'We must question whether it should be high on the agenda of a country like ours when there is so much to be done in other areas. And you can be almost certain that foreign interests will be involved, and that in itself is questionable, wouldn't you agree, Mr Bain?'

Connor was evasive. 'Depends on what else is around to attract free enterprise capital really. Progress can happen on many fronts at the same time.'

Xavier smiled. 'Ah yes, of course. You almost sound like a politician rather than a banker.'

Connor responded. 'Perhaps it's inevitable that bankers have to be political as well, given that aid financing is so closely related to politics.'

Xavier nodded in agreement. 'Perhaps you might find it diverting and profitable to look at some other aspects of our country that don't have a high profile at this stage. You too, Miss Wright. I can recommend a visit to the Rupununi plains in the south of our country. You would be welcome to stay with my friend Kate McGrath. A most unusual woman. She is known by my people as the otter lady. She has a rather interesting place called Caraboo not far from where your casino is planned.'

He reached into his shirt pocket and produced a small notebook. 'I'll write down the details of how to get there and how to make arrangements. Please give it some thought. Now will you excuse me, this little battle has a long way to run.'

Xavier shook hands with them and followed by a trail of Amerindian supporters left the dining room.

'Well, what do you make of that?' asked Madi, somewhat taken aback by the obvious planned approach.

'It's an invitation too good to refuse, I'd say.' Connor pecked Madi on the cheek. 'It's going to be hard to hang on to my holidays, given this bloody mine disaster, but I'll work out something. By the way, wherever did this guy get his education?'

'London School of Economics, according to Lester,' said Madi.

'Oh, well that explains it. Very smart as well. That man is as tough a wheeler-dealer as you're likely to come across. Don't be fooled by the casual gear and backwoods associations. He knows exactly what he's after.'

Madi glanced at the notepaper in her hand. 'What, do you suppose, is an otter lady?'

SIXTEEN

The Columbus goldmine disaster put Guyana on the front pages of papers all over the world. Newspapers ran graphic accounts of the polluted rivers and TV pictures of dead animals beside Amerindian villages were wired around the globe. Foreign correspondents and environment writers were soon pounding out stories of potential disaster on a massive scale.

As it turned out, the damage control plan implemented by the miners and the government worked well and, at an undisclosed cost, the leaks were being plugged and the tailings dam wall strengthened. Water from the dam had been pumped temporarily into open cut pits to facilitate the work and ease pressure. All production at the goldmine had been suspended. Troubleshooting engineers from the United States were flown in and, using equipment hired from Antonio Destra, led a repair operation to bring the spill to manageable proportions.

Connor Bain was closely involved in monitoring the whole operation for his organisation, which was keen to see the country's mining industry reputation propped up as much as possible. Later in the year, it could have a major influence on the final price obtained from the sale of Guyminco.

For more than a week Connor saw little of Madi, spending most of his time at the goldmine. But as soon as the crisis was under control he telephoned head office in New York and got the green light to resume his holiday for a few more days. Anxious to spend more time with Madi, he proposed they take up Xavier's suggestion to visit the mysterious otter woman.

Lester drove Connor and Madi to Ogle airport outside Georgetown to catch one of the light aircraft that serviced the Rupununi region of south-west Guyana. Matthew had sent them off with a light-hearted plea to make it a danger-free excursion for a change. 'I think that one more dead body, Madi, will be enough for the immigration department to deport you as an undesirable influence. If Inspector Palmer doesn't get you first on suspicion of being a serial killer.'

'Ha, ha. Very funny, Matt,' said Madi.

Lester, who seemed to know practically everything about Xavier's activities, briefed them on the destination. The owner of Caraboo ranch, Katherine McGrath, was 'one swell lady', he said. In his opinion, she was 'a legend'. The Rupununi comprised extensive grasslands, cattle country and attractive waterways including the legendary El Dorado lake. But in Lester's opinion it was not in the same class as his jungle hideaway. But then, he admitted, perhaps diamonds made him biased.

Ogle airport, used mainly by light aircraft, was basic in a quaint sort of way. The set of scales for weighing passengers looked like a bathroom reject. The plane, in Madi's eyes, looked like a flying cane toad. A small ramp dropped from its rear behind the high stubby wing. Passengers and freight were loaded together. A man in navy shorts and white shirt with gold-coloured wings over one pocket, licked the end of his pencil and added Madi's weight, including her baggage, to a list of figures, toted it up and drew a line. 'No more,' he called to the freight handlers. 'We be over.' Madi eyed Connor nervously.

They climbed up the ramp to find the interior was very open plan, a single row of seats on either side, freight stowed wherever there was space and the pilot and co-pilot perched up front. Madi found her seat belt broken, so draped it across her lap and leaned back in her seat—which promptly collapsed.

'You could sleep all the way,' shouted Connor jovially above the engine noise and helped her secure the seat upright.

They were headed for Letham, the administrative centre of the Rupununi district, and close to the Brazilian border. In little over an hour they landed with a bounce and bumped along the dirt, engines screaming as the plane raced towards a rusted chain-link fence at the end of the runway. A thud and a shudder went through the aircraft as it slewed and the pilot seemed to momentarily lose control, then the aircraft steadied, slowed, did a U-turn and headed towards a few small buildings.

After quickly looking out of his window, Connor turned to Madi. 'Well, that's what the bang was.'

'What, did a propeller drop off or something?'
'No, but it must be bent. We just decapitated a goat.'

It looked as if they had stepped into a wild west frontier town. On the perimeter of the red dirt airstrip was a ramshackle building with a bell tower that leaned precariously. Faded and peeling paint proclaimed 'Airways Office'. Nearby was a rum shop, a general store, a hotel, a scatter of houses and cattle yards. Goats and dogs snuffled in the litter and broken bottles. Yet beyond this there was a sense of space as the open grassy savannahs stretched to low hazy hills in the distance. Both Madi and Connor found it a refreshing relief from the coastal humidity and bustle.

A stocky, smiling man came forward to greet them. 'You must be Madison . . . the only blonde in this part of Guyana. You're easy to spot. I'm Joseph. I'm taking you to Caraboo,' he said with a natural informality.

'That's very kind of you, this is Connor Bain.'

'I hope we're not taking you out of your way,' said Connor, shaking his hand.

'No. I was going to take some supplies out to Caraboo anyway. So when Xavier contacted me I said no problem. You're welcome.'

Joseph supervised sides of beef wrapped in wet sacks and plastic being loaded in the main cabin of the plane alongside passengers for the return flight.

'Yours?' queried Connor.

'Some of it. It's all been sold. Chilled prime beef for the hotels.'

Amongst the casually dressed passengers flying back to Georgetown, two men in suits with loud ties and sunglasses looked incongruous as they walked out to the plane carrying small but expensive cases, securely locked. Connor looked at Madi and raised a questioning eyebrow. Joseph caught the look and grinned. 'Brazilians. Probably carrying gold and illegal cash down to unload in Georgetown.'

'So Brazil is just over there somewhere?'

'Boa Vista is about an hour's drive. It's a big city over the border in Brazil. My wife likes it for shopping. Lots of action over there. Here it's sleepy, except when we have the big rodeo at Easter. Now *that's* something to see.'

The plane lumbered out onto the strip for take-off.

'Come and have a cold drink,' Joseph grinned. 'And take in some of the local colour.'

Settled on stools covered in cowhide in the wire-meshed annex to the general store, they met Joseph's wife, Christine, and a local identity who described himself as a 'businessman'. Looking at his old shorts, grubby T-shirt, leather sandals repaired with twine, Madi dismissed him as a barfly passing the time of day. It was only later she learned the pudgy scruffy fellow at the bar was one of the richest beef barons in the south-west.

After spending the night as guests of Joseph and Christine, they waved goodbye to their hostess and were on the road an hour after dawn. Joseph drove them through magnificent beef country, dotted with occasional outstation huts, some livestock yards and scattered herds of grazing cattle.

There was something about it that made Madi think of the Australian bush. Strange, she thought, that a herd of cattle should trigger a twinge of homesickness. But a glance at the man riding behind the cattle made the picture of home fall apart. The horse was short-legged and squat, the rider wore leather chaps. The saddle was high backed and ornamental—silver glinting in the sunlight—as the rider sat back, his legs far forward, a straw hat rolled up at the sides at a rakish angle.

'The vaqueros . . . cowboys, they're good horsemen,' said Joseph. 'But I've seen Kate outride most of them during round-up.'

'Tell us about her.'

'Kate's grandfather started Caraboo. He was an English prospector who took up ranching. His wife hated it and went back to England leaving her baby son, so the old man took an Amerindian mistress. He established an extended family and they all worked for him and their descendants are still there. The stories about Kate's grandfather are legendary. Her daddy married an Englishwoman and they lived at Caraboo although they spent a lot of time in the UK. Kate also went to a good school and lived over there. Apparently she mixed in high society. She never married and came back when her parents died.'

'So why would she come back here?'

'Ask her. No one else was going to keep it going, I guess.'

'What's she like . . . as a person?' asked Madi.

'She's in her sixties but strong as an ox. She still rides with the vaqueros, and a few months back when her car broke down she had to walk twenty-four kilometres in the dark, some of it across a flooded plain. It took hours before anyone came across her. Everyone has a Kate story.'

'She sounds formidable,' said Connor.

'She's tough like rawhide, but has a gentle soul. A very smart lady. I don't always know what she's talking about, the poetry and stuff.'

'We're looking forward to meeting her,' said Connor, then added for Madi's benefit, 'Lester was right, it seems. She is a living legend.'

They drove in silence for a while, Madi enjoying the scenery while Connor dozed fitfully in the back seat of the Land Rover. The spacious scrubby grasslands stretched to a long line of low hills in every direction. They bounced on log bridges over creeks, passed stands of unusual trees that Joseph said had leaves just like sandpaper. They glimpsed a distant glint of water. 'That's the famous Lake Parima. You heard about Sir Walter Raleigh's El Dorado?'

'Yep.'

'That's supposed to be the lake where the gilded man appears.' Joseph drove on without another glance.

'And do you think it's true, the story about a secret golden city?' asked Madi, trying to imagine a casino and hotel out here by the lake, a modern El Dorado of gambling for the high rollers.

Joseph grinned and took his hands off the wheel briefly in a gesture of uncertainty.

'Who knows? Guyana still holds many secrets. Many places probably never explored. But it's a good story for the visitors, eh . . . the lost Golden City of Guyana.'

'Joseph, have you ever heard of a plan for a place called Amazonia, a casino to be built near that lake?'

Joseph gave her a curious glance. 'I heard a rumour over the border in Boa Vista, but you hear a lot of wild stories down there. What do you know?'

'Nothing, just a rumour too, I guess,' said Madi realising if she said more she'd breach the confidence she'd promised Sasha St Herve when he had asked her to work on the project.

'A casino that would recreate the city of gold, eh?' mused Joseph. 'Sounds like someone's pie in the sky dream that one.'

Two hours later the countryside changed. They drove into a jungle thicket and the rough road became little more than a trail. It was slow going but finally they drove into open country again. 'This is the start of Caraboo,' said Joseph.

'Looks like pretty good grazing land,' said Connor, but soon they were driving into something between a swamp and a flood plain. There were pools of water everywhere, including over most of the track, which Joseph happily splashed through as comfortably as if he were driving down a superhighway.

Connor leaned forward and curled his hand at the nape of Madi's neck, smoothing a tendril of her hair as he peered out of the muddy windscreen. 'We'll never be found,' he whispered.

'You won't be if you keep making cracks like that. It's a wonderful adventure. Beats playing banker, surely?'

A short distance ahead was a small hut on a slight rise where an Amerindian stood waiting for them. As they splashed towards him, something rose out of the long grass, leaping from behind a tree. For a moment, from a glimpse at the edge of her peripheral vision, Madi had the impression of a gazelle, a deer, some long and graceful creature. She turned to see, and there, running through the watery scrub, was a tall lanky woman, laughing and waving her arms in great sweeps as she came closer.

Joseph grinned. 'That's Kate. God knows what she's been doing.' He stopped by the thatched shed and greeted the Amerindian warmly. Connor and Madi leapt out to watch Kate McGrath lope out of the scrub. 'Madi,' said Connor as he took in the spectacle, 'I think I'm really going to like this. Have you ever seen anyone like her?'

She was nearly two metres tall and thin as a reed, brown-skinned with khaki trousers rolled to her knees, a fawn shirt tucked into a wide leather belt and stout leather sandals. Her hair was tied on top of her head with a bright red bandanna. Her laughter echoed as she splashed through the watery grass.

'Welcome to Caraboo.' She held out long fingers and shook hands with a strong clasp. Her voice was deep and throaty, her speech beautifully enunciated, but Madi was mesmerised by her face, which her mind immediately classified as magnificent. A wide square jaw, impossibly high cheekbones, and hazel eyes set wide apart. She had a broad smile and white, even teeth. There seemed to be no spare flesh on her and the tautness of her fine-boned face stretched away any wrinkles or sagging skin. Squint lines under her eyes and between her eyebrows and two furrows on either side of her nose to her mouth, hinted at her mature years. She wore no make-up and Connor thought what a beauty she must have been, and still was.

'I'm so glad you are here, and you've brought mail! Good news indeed—well, one hopes it is.' She chuckled, and, as Joseph began pulling bags from the back, she gestured to the stoic-looking Amerindian man who hadn't moved. 'Dali, come. Help with these bags.' Turning to Madi and Connor, she gave a wide smile. 'We are flooded in, so you are lucky. While it's a longer way in, the boat trip is the scenic route.' She waved to a wooden longboat

380

pulled into the bank with an old outboard motor on the stern.

With their bags stowed, Kate dragged out some kapok-filled life vests in faded orange canvas. 'Regulations. Now settle yourselves. Joseph, you can steer; Dali, you sit in the bow and be lookout.' Then in an aside to the visitors added, 'He's the only one who knows the way.' She stepped gingerly into the longboat which could have held a dozen or more people.

Connor and Madi sat beside each other and faced Kate who began delving into a cooler as they set off along the marshy waterway. Out came a rum bottle filled with punch. She passed them plastic cups of a powerful fruit and rum concoction. 'Have you had lunch?'

'I had a chocolate bar,' said Madi.

'I slept,' said Connor. Kate reached for a plastic container. 'Some biscuits to go on with. We'll have a nice dinner.' She lifted her cup. 'A toast—welcome to Caraboo, may you leave enriched.'

Madi and Connor touched plastic cups and exchanged soft smiles. Kate beamed and passed a cup of punch to Joseph, and the tin of biscuits to Dali who squatted in the bow, his eyes scanning the way ahead. Silently he took a handful without looking back.

They carefully navigated across the flooded landscape of channels and small lakes into a creek that soon became a river. Madi could see how it had overflowed and simply made the land around part of it.

Connor was enchanted by the off-beat way in which the trip was developing, much to Madi's delight. 'I think I feel a bit like old Sir Walter, plunging into the unexplored depths of the continent.' He turned to Kate. 'Is all this yours? How do you cope with the isolation and the work?'

Kate threw back her head and laughed. 'I am not alone, I live in a community of fifteen people!' She explained that most of the Amerindians on the property had been born at Caraboo, it was as much their home as hers. 'But life for them is harder than it's been for a long time. The hunting isn't like it used to be and even the fish are becoming harder to find. Too many people overfish the rivers for the big market in Brazil. The balance has gone. The future is uncertain for the Amerindians. Those on our place are okay for the time being, but for thousands of others, it's tough. It's no good trying to leave them as subsistence farmers, quaint and colourful though it may look for the occasional tourist.'

'There isn't work in the towns or cities?'

'These are simple people, mainly poorly educated. They are not city people. Certainly the young people get lured to the bright lights, but it is more difficult there for them without the support of the family and village. Or else they leave to work as domestics or in the goldmines or on farms here and in Brazil. Then it's hard to resist consumer goods and little, if any, money goes back to the villages.'

'It's the story of indigenous minorities all over the world,' said Connor sympathetically. 'You sound like a disciple of Xavier's.'

Kate smiled. 'The Amerindian political evangelist, eh! The emerging conscience of the country.' She paused to take a sip of her drink and to shout briefly in Carib to Dali. 'He's the right man at the right time in this part of the world, in my opinion. Guyana is at the crossroads and someone of greater integrity and wisdom than our current crop of politicians has to speak up for the ordinary people . . . to help them get a real stake in this country.'

'You really think he's going to become meaningful for the other races too?'

Kate thought for a moment. 'I'm no politician, can't abide the big city power games that people play but I've seen this country put on some ridiculous political acts over the years. I can't see why an Amerindian can't emerge as a unifying national leader for all races, one who is going to stand up against foreign exploitation.'

Connor gave Madi a nudge. 'It seems there's a visionary or a revolutionary behind every tree.'

Madi took his hand. 'Perhaps you ought to listen carefully to what they're saying. Then you might be able to write off the trip as work and feel great about not wasting time.'

He squeezed her hand. 'Don't be nasty, it doesn't suit you.'

They took in the scenery for a while, the craft being carefully guided by the bowman signalling to the helmsman.

'Have they started farming native animals down your way?' shouted Kate, above a temporary acceleration of the engine. 'You know, kangaroos and that sort of thing.'

Madi shrugged. 'You can get 'roo steaks in supermarkets now.'

'Aborigines have some big emu farms in the west, I think,' added Connor. 'And crocodile farming is big in the Northern Territory. I once had a croc burger in Darwin. Tasted okay, bit fishy. Why do you ask?'

'Well, it's an idea I have for Caraboo, get the Amerindians farming wildlife. It's becoming pretty scarce in some areas. There's something neat about the idea of farming wildlife to preserve it, and at the same time give people who need it an economic boost. We've got crocs we could farm . . . the black cayman.'

'Couldn't this go hand in hand with tourism?' asked Madi, and Kate nodded in agreement. 'Good idea, but getting the money and support won't be easy. Still, that's hardly a reason for not dreaming, is it?' She passed the punch again, causing Connor to raise an eyebrow in resignation and refill his mug while Madi declined. She wanted a clear head to develop fresh ideas for the policy paper on tourism in Guyana that she was determined to prepare for Xavier. Kate's little dream fitted neatly into Madi's embryonic plan.

The boat skimmed up a small tributary and turned to a landing from which a wide track wound through a stand of flowering trees. A young Amerindian girl hurried down to help carry the bags as the party trailed up to the compound.

The wooded pathway opened onto a cleared area of white sandy soil dotted with mango trees burdened with over-ripe, fat yellow fruit under glossy green leaves. In between them were frangipani trees, blossoms scattered like a cream and gold carpet. By the clearing were four small Amerindian-style thatched guest bungalows with a small palm-leaf awning shading a hammock at each entrance.

The main house was large and almost completely open-sided. Inside the low mud brick walls were hammocks strung between poles supporting the heavy, thatched roof. This looked to be the main rest area, a sort of verandah where hammocks replaced sofas and chairs.

Kate led them inside. 'Not your five-star hotel layout, but it works well enough,' she said, more in assurance than apology. In the open plan area behind the hammocks was a long wooden dining table and chairs of solid English oak. Several internal walls of mud brick sectioned off rooms but went up little more than a couple of metres towards the high-peaked thatched roof that capped the building. A cool breeze circulated through the whole living area.

'A very practical design,' observed Connor, keeping a straight face. 'Totally air-conditioned.'

Amerindian women and girls seemed to be everywhere and one of them carried out a tray of cool drinks from the kitchen and put it on the table. 'Help yourselves, and relax,' said Kate. 'I'll join you later . . . have a few urgent matters to attend to.' She disappeared out the back and they could hear a firm discussion ensue about the state of the generator.

'I'm not getting in a hammock or I won't get out,' said Connor. 'That trip was exhausting.'

Joseph grinned. 'Don't go to sleep, you'll miss the afternoon swim.'

'That sounds good,' said Madi, who was browsing through a massive bookcase. The spines of nearly all the books were missing and wonderful old editions of English literature faced the world in tatters. She gently drew out a volume of Dickens. 'Oh dear, what a shame. Did the humidity get to them?'

Joseph came over with a cool drink for her. 'No, it was Oscar. Oscar the Wild, she calls him. A billy goat. Big fellow. I wouldn't argue with him. Came in and ate the lot. Just the backs, though. I think he liked the glue.'

'How very Guyanese, fact or fiction,' mused Connor as he randomly reached for a book.

They were still chuckling over the quaintness of some of the titles when an Amerindian woman came in and introduced herself as Amelia. She seemed to be the housekeeper in charge. 'Come, I take you to your hut.'

Their bags were on a plain wooden bench and the large room was furnished with a cane-framed bed, a mosquito net swinging above it, a small wooden cupboard, a chest of drawers that smelled of mothballs, and a rickety desk. The bathroom had a stone floor, a modern septic toilet and a shower that worked by gravity from a large drum of water sitting outside on a mini tower. 'Sun keep him warm and we fill every day,' Amelia smiled.

Opening a cabinet above the sink she showed them that Kate had provided every amenity from toothbrush and toothpaste to soap, deodorant and shaving cream.

'Five stars,' quipped Connor.

'Careful, mate. At the slightest suggestion of sarcasm you'll end up sleeping next door with Joseph,' retorted Madi. 'It's different, that's all. And I like it.'

The ceiling of the hut was high, and loose dried palm leaves rustled lightly in the breeze. Both rooms had electric lights but Amelia showed them the candles and matches. 'Generator sometimes sick,' she said with a big smile and left, closing the woven palm leaf door behind her.

Connor flung himself on the bed. 'What bliss.'

'I'll say. A real shower in the interior is a novelty,' grinned Madi.

'No. I mean being here with you. Come here,' he opened his arms.

Madi lay down beside him and he wrapped himself around her, kissing her face and neck and hair before finding her mouth, nibbling her lips and plunging his tongue between them. She kissed him back, then realising the extent of his passion, pulled away. 'Let me get in the shower, I feel so yucky.'

Connor licked her ear. 'You smell like the forest and you feel wonderful. No, stay . . . we'll shower later . . .'

They peeled away their clothes and made love beneath the arched, leafed roof where, unnoticed, geckos and other tiny creatures scurried between the papery brown thatch.

They were sound asleep when Amelia called outside their shutters. 'Madam says to come, she bathing with the water dogs in the creek now.'

They joined Joseph and Kate at the big house as the sun began to sink low to the horizon. Kate was wrapped in a sarong over a black one-piece swimsuit and they followed her as she walked outside calling in a high pitched but affectionate voice. 'My darlings . . . my loves . . . my own dear ones . . . come along . . . come along.'

Madi and Connor exchanged a glance, unsure just who she was referring to as no one else was in sight. Then around the corner of the house waddled several huge otters.

'Good lord,' exclaimed Connor.

The otters, each as long as Madi was tall, were being herded by Amelia and several boys with sticks. They were followed by several smaller otters.

'Oh, they're absolutely gorgeous,' said Madi excitedly. They were giant otters, some bigger than seals, with solid heads too large for their cumbersome flippered bodies, protruding eyes that held a ferocious glint, and snouts that sprouted large spiky whiskers. Despite their awkward swaying gait they moved with determined speed.

The darlings, sighting their mistress, rushed forward and one of the young boys ran protectively in front of Madi and Connor who stood mesmerised by the herd of screeching and grunting animals complaining in querulous old-man tones.

'Do stand back,' commanded Kate, 'they are very protective of me. Don't try to pat them.'

'I wouldn't dream of it. They could take a hand off,' muttered Connor. Madi was fascinated at the cooing and loving phrases that Kate poured out to the wild creatures as they rushed to her, nudging and rubbing against her, leaping up on their tails to push their front flippers against her body. She picked up a small one, the size of a large dog, cradled it in her arms and marched down the trail towards the stream, her throaty, cultured voice floating back as Madi, Connor and Joseph followed at a distance. 'My beauties, my dear ones . . . have you missed me . . . what joys you are.'

They soon reached the creek and at a tail-dragging, running stagger, the otters dived into the water and Kate waded in beside them.

'She's tamed them and bred them up. She knows more about them than anyone in South America, I think,' explained Joseph to the incredulous visitors. 'I come here a lot to pick up her beef and it always amazes me.'

'It's safe to come in now,' called Kate. Madi and Connor gingerly edged into the creek while a gaggle of local children came plunging out of the shrubbery, squealing with delight, to dive into the water. Joseph squatted on the bank, puffing a cigarette, amused by all the activity. The children swam around with the otters who dived and leapt and swam underwater, continually returning to Kate as she called them by name.

'This is Madison and Connor, they are guests and friends, be nice to them,' admonished Kate. Madi was suddenly confronted by a face surfacing in front of her, alert eyes, dripping whiskers and a barking mouthful of teeth. As she stood waist deep, her knees were hit by a powerful rocketing furry body and she lost her balance, falling under the brown water that churned with the energy and activity.

Gradually they joined in the play as they were accepted, but the giant otters only allowed Kate the game where they would leap in her arms and dive over her shoulders.

Madi and Connor joined Joseph on the bank as Amelia produced a bucket of fish. Kate waded out to get the bucket and the brood waddled from the water to receive, one by one, a large fish from their mistress. 'They have a pecking order, and once they have come to the table showing their manners, then it's a free for all,' laughed Kate, tossing the rest of the fish into the creek where all the otters raced for them.

'They're amazing,' declared Connor. 'I had no idea they got so big. What will happen to them?'

'This is their home, they're free to go any time. But why should they? They have a good life here. It was an experiment and it seems to have worked quite well. The younger ones could not defend themselves alone in the wild, I suspect. Sometimes the wild creatures go back and join their friends, other times they entice their friends to join them. I hope to do this with other creatures.'

'She's got others,' warned Joseph.

'They're only babies, Joseph. Now, let us go back and change for drinks before dinner.'

Amelia served cold beers and rum punch and Connor presented a delighted Kate with several bottles of wine they'd brought from Georgetown. 'Oh, such a treat. Thank you. Now it's drinks all round for everyone.' And she produced a box and lifted from it what Madi thought at first were tiny ring-tailed possums.

'They're coatimundis,' said Joseph.

The size of kittens, they were a brindle brown, their long tails banded in black and dark brown coiled around Kate's arm. She lifted one and handed it to Madi. 'What a dear little face,' exclaimed Madi as the baby nuzzled its long pointed snout with a rubbery nose into her neck. It squeaked and mewed until a doll-sized feeding bottle of milk mixture was produced and it sucked contentedly in Madi's arms.

It was only later when the sleeping coati was returned to its box that Madi discovered the warmth on her chest where it had nestled also came from a large pee stain.

They showered again and dressed for dinner, which was heralded by a call from Amelia and launched by Kate ringing a small dinner bell beside her plate. Amelia, accompanied by a shy barefoot daughter, shuffled in and set the baked dinner on the table. Kate served and passed the assorted plates, some plain glass, others fine bone china, with a poise and graciousness as much suited to a stately home in England as this thatch and mud brick home in the lonely vastness of the South American savannahs.

Kate proposed a toast. 'Welcome to the Rupununi, my paradise. Thank you for sharing it. I hope you carry away pleasant memories.'

As the meal progressed, with Amelia being summoned by the bell twice to remedy a lacking implement and condiment, Kate talked of her childhood in this place. She told them of the great snake that lived in her parents' bedroom and each night had to be shooed from beneath the covers of their bed before they retired, and of the numerous adventurers who passed through.

'Tell them the diamond bird story,' suggested Joseph.

Kate chuckled. 'Ah, that was my grandfather. He was

a prospector and a diamond buyer. He had a pet toucan and a visitor arrived to find him sitting at the kitchen table with his pet toucan chained to the table. You know those magnificently coloured birds with the huge beak, I think it was the red-billed variety. Anyway, it was his pet and used to roam free around the house, but on this day it had swallowed a parcel of diamonds he'd just bought. So he fed it castor oil and was sitting there with forceps, a dish of water and a diamond scale, waiting for nature to take its course so he could retrieve his diamonds!'

Amid the laughter, Kate shook her head. 'Ah, such dreams and schemes he had. I remember my grandfather every time I recite one of my favourite lines of poetry . . . from Thomas Hardy: '*He does not die who does bequeath some influence to the land he loves*'.

'And you, Kate, what are your dreams for Caraboo? Did you see yourself settling here when you were living the high life in London all those years?' asked Madi.

'In my heart I always knew this was my home. I've been back here seventeen years. I haven't been back to the UK for nearly nine years.'

'Don't you miss the culture, theatre and concerts?'

'I have my father's gramophone, my grandfather's books—sans spines—and I listen to the BBC world service on my radio.'

The dinner plates were cleared away and a bowl of sliced mangoes, melons and bananas smothered in custard served for dessert.

'Have you thought of having paying guests here? You're certainly set up for it,' said Connor. He sensed finances must be difficult for this proud woman.

'I intended to do that. But my timing was wrong. I worked out an itinerary for people to come for long weekends. The bank manager asked, why wouldn't I have people here all the time? And I said, what an appalling idea! I like my own time and space, too.' She gave a throaty laugh. 'I did not get the loan I asked for and I was sent packing with the words, you go into business to make money, not to enjoy yourself.'

'Sounds just like a bank manager,' said Madi with a glance at Connor, who responded with an exaggerated mock smile.

'It was also the time of Forbes Burnham's era. A political disaster. Thanks to the bank I discovered Burnham was serious when he said he didn't want tourism turning the country into a nation of lackeys. At least the place has been preserved.'

'Now is the time, perhaps,' said Madi, glancing again at Connor.

Kate rang the bell for Amelia to bring the coffee. Then she unfolded her long lean frame, stood, and smiled at them. 'We shall see what the fates have decreed. I don't drink coffee at night, so I'll leave you to enjoy it, together. Tomorrow, I shall show you my country. Goodnight. Sleep well.'

Later, snuggled under the cloud of mosquito netting, Madi talked to Connor about Kate and Caraboo. 'Connor, this is what everyone should see, share this sort of experience . . . '

'She's got more stuff planned tomorrow . . . ' sleepily he began kissing and nuzzling Madi.

'But don't you think this could be made into a proper tourism project . . . '

'Madi . . . stop talking, and just kiss me. I'm on holidays.'

'Exactly!' She nudged him in the ribs. 'And look

where you are! This should be available to everyone. Think how it would help Kate, help the local people, start a small industry that could grow and—' He stopped her words with a kiss. Madi's mind was buzzing, but then she began to switch her attention to Connor, responding to his lovemaking . . . and putting other thoughts on hold . . . temporarily.

SEVENTEEN

The next morning Madi sat on the little verandah outside their bungalow eating a mango and Connor swung in the hammock, both enjoying the mild temperature and low humidity before breakfast. The day would hot up soon enough and they could expect a tiring day out in the savannah, for Kate had hinted that she had an interesting program of activity lined up. They already realised that keeping pace with Kate would require effort.

Connor was still tired. 'This is so relaxing. I just love being with you. Why don't we put it off and just hang about and . . .'

He didn't get to finish the sentence. As Madi tossed the mango seed into the bushes she spoke over him. 'That's for evenings, Connor,' she said with a cheeky grin. 'We're going to make the most of every minute of the daylight seeing the wonders of this neck of the woods. I rather think you're very much out of condition.'

'Exactly the point I was trying to make. I'm sex starved. Need the exercise.'

'Rubbish. Come on, shower time. That's about as good as you'll get at this hour. I've just got to get this sticky mango stuff off my hands.'

He followed her into the bathroom and leaned against the door as she washed her hands. 'You're really enthusiastic about this part of the country, aren't you? Most people take in a few sights and lapse into a state of cynicism bordering on despair. A tropical boredom sets in. But not you. Everything is wonderful and exciting, and full of tourism potential.'

Madi turned and dried her hands. 'So?'

Connor shrugged. 'Well, sure it's a bit of fun, but surely you don't seriously believe that places like this really have the potential to turn over big bickies, or are the stuff this country needs to get on its economic feet, a sort of grassroots alternative to industrial development.'

Madi thought it was the most absurd bathroom discussion she had ever heard and had trouble keeping a straight face. 'Connor, we are about to strip and jump in the shower together and you want to raise the question of economic feasibility of tourism. You've lost a shingle.' She pulled off the shirt she wore as a nightdress. 'I want to say two things. Firstly, it probably will help this country more than you think. Secondly, get your gear off and into the shower or miss out on the fun.'

After breakfast they boarded a large canoe, called a corial, made from a hollowed-out log with a painted ornamental bow and a wide stern where Dali sat by the outboard motor.

'He made this one,' explained Kate. 'Absolutely ideal for a small party exploring the backwaters.' After a short run, Dali cut the motor and using the paddle, propelled them slowly around the bend of a creek into a small lake. The surface was covered in giant green Victoria Regina lilies with burnished undersides to their great, round bowl-shaped leaves, which Kate said could hold an infant. Between the lily pads rose majestic pink flowers. Kate reached out and pulled one up and handed it to Madi. 'Beautiful,' exclaimed Madi, 'absolutely beautiful.'

Connor took off his sunglasses to appreciate more fully the colourful magnificence of the scene. 'You're right. It's like a scene out of a fairy story.'

They paddled on and heard the birds before they saw them, though their nursery had been heralded by occasional swoops of warning adults gliding above them.

'Oh, just look,' sighed Madi.

The trees that fringed the waterways were festooned with scores of large twig nests precariously balanced on thin exposed branches. Hundreds of white egrets and grey herons preening feathery tails and wing feathers sat on the nests or flew idly around the area calling to each other. In some nests, babies' beaks jutted out as they cried for food. Kate handed each of them binoculars so that as they drifted they were able to study the birds more closely.

They paddled to another area where they heard woodpeckers hammering at tree trunks while kingfishers darted at the water and the air rang with the call of the aggressive, yellow-breasted kiskadee . . . 'kis-ka-dee . . . kis-kis-kiss-ka-dee . . .'

Madi suddenly spotted a strange bird and pointed it

out to Kate, who studied it through her father's old field glasses.

'Red-fan parrot, see the red and blue ruff standing up around its head, and the round tail? It's giving out "intruder beware" signals.'

'The dark bit round the eyes makes it look as if it's wearing sunnies,' chuckled Madi.

'Every part of Guyana has its own special bird life attractions,' said Kate. 'In the Pomeroon in the north, the scarlet ibis are magnificent. Thousands of them coming in to roost at sunset completely change the landscape into a rose-toned world. The same when they fly out at sunrise.'

Once they were past the natural bird sanctuary, Dali restarted the motor and they headed out into the river. The marshy, thick mangroves and bush gave way to open grassland on either side.

'There they are,' said Kate, pointing ahead to a small group waiting with several horses.

'My gosh, do we have to ride horses?' Madi sounded nervous.

'Ah, ha! Something to daunt the adventurer at last!'

Madi turned to Connor. 'Can you ride?'

'You bet. Spent holidays out on my uncle's sheep farm. And once rode with the hounds in Oxford.'

Kate quickly sized up the situation. 'If you want, you can be a Land Rover vaquero, Madison. We're only trotting about the savannah to check on the cattle and cull a steer for meat.'

'Sounds fun,' said Connor enthusiastically.

'Now you're doing boy's own stuff you're enjoying yourself, eh,' grinned Madi.

He kissed her cheek as Dali steered the corial into the bank. 'I'm glad I met you. I could have spent this entire job in Georgetown and never got to play cowboys and Indians,' he whispered. 'You're fun to be with.'

Madi felt she was on horseback even in the front seat of the Land Rover. It bounced and lurched as Dominic, the Amerindian driver, raced through the grass that brushed the car at window height. Ahead of them and to one side, the four riders galloped—Connor, Kate and two vaqueros. The driver, clearly enjoying the bolt across the country as much as the riders, never stopped grinning as he furiously twisted the steering wheel, letting out occasional loud whoops of delight. He spun the wheel from side to side as the vehicle lurched and slithered through the grass and bucked over hidden obstacles.

The sun was high and hot but it was a dry and not unpleasant heat. The exhilaration of the ride, the sight of the horses streaming away in the distance and the thought of what Connor was experiencing, made Madi's spirits soar. The plains stretched ahead to the hazy line of mountains where great rocky outcrops rose like lunar hills. Then above the grass they saw the horns of steers, then a fence and a thatched shelter. One of the vaqueros signalled to Connor to help him cut out a large steer as Kate and the other rider guided the rest towards the corral.

Racing around the herd, Dominic pulled up the Land Rover beside the corral and indicated to Madi that she should sit on top of the wooden railing. 'You count.' They were his first words of the day to her.

She shaded her eyes, watching the athletic turns of the horses as they streamlined the cattle into formation. The two riders on the outside—one she recognised as Kate by her red bandanna—prevented any breaks and finally the lead steer led the herd into the corral. Dominic shuffled the two gates in the pens, separating the calves from the herd.

Madi had to concentrate on the counting and called her numbers to Dominic who rammed the gate shut and nodded. Obviously her figures tallied with his.

Meanwhile out on the savannah, Connor and the vaquero raced after the lone steer, driving it towards a tree which stood with its leafless dead branches akimbo in the waving grass. The vaquero lifted a rifle to his shoulder, a shot rang out, and the running steer dropped into the long grass. The men dismounted and within minutes, the steer was swung by a rope around its back legs into the lower branches of the tree, ready to be butchered and collected later by the Land Rover.

Back at the corral Kate rode up, spoke briefly to Dominic, then turned to Madi.

'There's a new calf missing. Very new. I saw it. Come, Madi, let's look. Hop on that horse, he'll go softly.'

Madi hesitated, so Kate dismounted, boosted her into the saddle of the vaquero's horse and swiftly shortened the stirrups. She folded the reins neatly and placed them in Madi's hands. 'Feel his mouth, don't yank or pull or panic. Let him lead you. Relax. Just follow me.'

Madi nodded, her confidence raised by Kate's own confidence in her. She let the horse walk out and sat back in the saddle determined to enjoy this new experience.

Within minutes, Madi's body responded to the gait of the walking horse, she dropped her hands to the saddle, keeping a gentle connection with the animal, her spine beginning to meld to the rhythm as a feeling of elation swept over her.

The view around her looked different, she felt now as though she were part of it all and, as she followed Kate who glanced back and gave her a rewarding smile, Madi experienced a new sense of exhilaration. Had anyone else, even Connor, told her to get on a horse and ride, she would have found reasons to refuse. But Kate instilled a sense of well-being and fun along with an empowering belief—*you can do it*. Instinctively Madi gave a little nudge with her heels and obediently her horse moved up beside Kate.

'What do you think happened to the calf?'

'Lost its mother in the long grass. We might be lucky and find it.'

They rode on in silence, Madi enjoying herself enormously, wishing her former colleagues back at the hotel in Sydney could see her now.

The daydream was shattered with frightening suddenness as a great shadow swooped in above her and for a mad moment Madi thought a plane was crashing on them. There had been no warning of danger except the rush of air and a shout from Kate who kicked her horse and galloped forward. Madi's horse followed suit, plunging forward while Madi gripped the reins for dear life, her knees hugging the saddle, trying to stay put as the horse surged after Kate's.

In front of Kate, a huge bird swooped low, turned and dived and for a moment looked as if it was going to knock Kate from her horse.

The bird was an eagle, its wingspan stretched over two metres and its extended feet showed talons the size of a grizzly bear's. To Madi's amazement Kate rode at full gallop straight at the bird, standing in the stirrups to wave her arms and shout at the eagle. The bird veered away, gaining height in seconds to circle above, screeching. Kate pulled up and Madi's horse also stopped and she slid around its neck, losing her balance, her feet coming out of the stirrups, but she stayed in the saddle.

'Harpy eagle. What a beauty.' Kate shaded her eyes as the cream and brown bird of prey drifted on an updraught, its wings motionless.

'I thought it was going to attack you. I've never seen a bird so huge.'

'Largest eagle in the world. On the endangered list too. Means that calf is around here somewhere.' Kate dismounted and helped Madi down. 'Let's lead the horses for a bit, see if we can find any signs or hear anything.'

They walked in the shoulder-high grass and Kate pointed to a small trail of broken stalks. They followed it and Madi touched Kate's shirt. 'I heard something.'

Kate nodded. 'It's over there.'

It was a low gurgle, a kind of bleat, and there, lying in the grass in a small dip, was a new-born calf, one leg ripped and bleeding. Stricken brown eyes pleaded at the two women. 'Hold the horses.' Kate handed Madi both sets of reins and scrambled down the slope.

She was quite near the animal when the eagle struck, landing on the calf's neck, its talons encircling and piercing it. Blood gushed and the calf struggled. Kate rushed forward, as Madi screamed 'No!'. The horses reared, Madi tried to hold them steady, and the eagle lifted in the air. With a furious pounding of wings, it sought to gain the freedom of the sky with its limp burden of dangling Bambi-like legs and twisted neck. It struggled low and slowly for a hundred metres, then the calf fell from its grasp. The eagle circled, then swept in and crashed down on the fallen prey hidden in the grass. It didn't rise again and Madi knew that its hooked beak was now ripping the tiny carcass to pieces.

Kate turned and calmed the horses.

'A shame. I hope it died quickly. Law of nature, eh?' They rode back in silence.

Leaving the vaqueros to do their work with the cattle, Kate, Madi and Connor rode for an hour along a trail that took them into a low range of hills to a gorge with a sparkling pool. A waterfall that ran over rocks of jasper and sandstone fed the pool which was fringed with spindly palms. Madi and Connor stripped down to their swimsuits and dived in, welcoming its refreshing coolness with enthusiastic shouts and a splashing waterfight.

Kate puffed at a hand-rolled cigarette and grinned. Eventually Madi and Connor joined her on the shady bank. 'It's a little paradise,' enthused Madi, leaning back on her elbows, and taking in the beauty of the spectacular gorge.

She tried to imagine a casino and hotel filled with thousands of tourists here, but it didn't make any sense at all. 'Have you heard about the casino project being talked about for these parts?' she asked casually, deciding the need for more information was critical to her decision to take the casino job.

Kate responded with a hint of disdain in her voice. 'Yes. I heard the rumours. An El Dorado company project, I believe. Sir Walter would turn in his grave. Possibly it's more serious than just talk. As you can see, what this spot really needs is a casino. Quite uncivilised without one, wouldn't you say?' She gave Madi a smile and stubbed out her cigarette on a rock.

Connor reacted with intense interest. 'Kate, what do you mean a company called El Dorado?' he asked.

Kate nodded. 'That's what the rumours say.'

'Did you know El Dorado was involved in this casino, Madi?'

'Sasha St Herve refused to name the backer,' Madi said. 'He didn't give me much detail at all. I'm to get that later if I decide to prepare a promotion concept for him. Apparently, they plan to fly the gamblers in from North America, Europe and Asia. Be something exclusive, I suppose, a casino in the beautiful wilds of Guyana.'

'Well, it could provide a lot of jobs. Bring money into the area,' Connor said. 'What do you think, Kate?'

'The money would go into the pockets of the rich, as usual, and not to my people. They'd be in service as they've always been.'

'Kate, a big casino can become a catalyst for development and bring other businesses and opportunities into the area. Casinos are popping up all over the world, and making a big economic impact. Surely a deal will be made to put something back into the local community. I mean, who owns the land?' asked Connor.

'Most of the Rupununi is state owned. It's leased in allotments of five, twenty-five, and ninety-nine year leases mostly.'

'So there, it's easy. The government can insist that a percentage of profits must be ploughed back into civic amenities or develop some other industry to support the casino. Where would their fresh food come from, for example? Couldn't local villages supply that?'

'That's all very well but it's tokenism in the big scheme of things,' retorted Kate. 'And given the history of this place there'll be corruption at the top and very little money will find its way down the economic ladder.'

'If it did get the go ahead, what would you do?' asked Madi.

Kate stiffened slightly. 'Fight. I'd fight. If I had to, I'd fight alongside Xavier and our people to prevent such a monstrosity erupting on our doorstep. The perceived benefits would not be worth the epidemic of social problems that it would bring.' Kate stood, a gesture that signalled an end to discussion of such a distasteful subject. 'We should get back to the river. It will be difficult returning in darkness.'

Night closed in swiftly on the water and kabouri flies descended in swarms to bite and suck blood from exposed skin. Kate produced a torch and began picking out the innovative navigational aids—a series of tin cans tied to trees along the waterways.

Back in their hut after dinner that night, Madi sat cross-legged on the bed beside Connor as he tucked the mosquito net in around them. 'El Dorado—dream or nightmare,' said Madi.

Connor was relaxed about it. 'As Matthew said, untangling who is really behind this El Dorado group is another matter. Not that we should be so concerned with that, I suppose. El Dorado only affects us obliquely. Matthew says progress at the bauxite mine is going smoothly. Gordon Ash is a hard worker and has rallied the troops. Stewart Johns says there is light at the end of the tunnel now. Whatever happened with funds being siphoned from the old mine company to El Dorado is yesterday's news. However, I always have to be alert to possibly corrupt machinations behind the scenes in any deals I set up here for IFO funding.'

'What about poor Ernesto?' demanded Madi. 'If El Dorado owns the casino, then his murder could also be connected to that.'

'He obviously started to do some unravelling in

government departments. We'll probably never know who was involved with his death or what level this corruption reaches.'

'Well, this certainly influences my attitude to the whole casino proposal. I'm not getting involved with anything that's got shonky backing and furthermore—'

'Madi, you don't know that it's shonky or illegal or underhand or whatever. Business is done in many ways. A consortium forming a shelf company is common business practice for tax or privacy purposes.'

'Secret purposes, you mean,' exploded Madi. 'Connor, you're missing the most important point. Who wants a huge complex like the Amazonia casino out here? Though I have to admit, initially I thought it sounded sort of fabulous. But not now.'

'It'd be good business, provided it was all above board. I admit it's a ripe opportunity for shady practices, but you don't know that it isn't a completely legit concept. St Herve seems a straight operator.'

'Connor!' Madi's frustration got the better of her. 'Think where we've been today. What we saw. Do you want that spoilt?'

'Who says it would be spoilt? It should be shared, more people should be given the opportunity to experience this sort of thing, but on a more businesslike scale, of course.'

'No! That's where you're wrong. By businesslike you mean commercial, up-market, big deal operations. Complexes, for God's sake. That's wrong.' Connor drew back at her vehemence and Madi took a breath, trying to talk calmly. 'Look, ever since Kaieteur, since I've been up the river with Lester, since being here at Caraboo, it's been gnawing away at me and I can see exactly what should be done in this country. And the way to go is with eco tourism. Small, special, unique experiences. This place doesn't have the infrastructure to carry tourism on the sort of scale you're thinking of. And it's not environmentally sound tourism. You'd destroy the very environment people want most. Don't you see anything wrong with a huge great casino out here?' she demanded.

Connor tried again, speaking quietly to counter Madi's growing anger. 'It would be like an island on its own and, if sensitively done, it would benefit the people, and—'

'Connor, I didn't believe we could be on such different wavelengths.' She pushed open the door and climbed into the hammock on the verandah. Connor sighed and fell back on his pillow. He was too tired to deal with this now. He'd get up shortly and give her a cuddle. But in two minutes he had fallen asleep.

Madi wrapped her arms about her as she swung in the hammock, then hearing Connor's steady breathing, she tiptoed back in and pulled on a long-sleeved shirt and a sarong, picked up her pillow and went back outside.

As she rocked gently in the string cradle she looked out at the mango trees and the white sandy soil gleaming in the moonlight. The argument with Connor had disturbed her deeply. Not because they'd disagreed, but the fact they held such different views. She couldn't believe that Connor wasn't as swept up and influenced by the magic and unspoilt beauty of this country as she was. This was a fundamental divergence of attitude between them which meant they had different outlooks on life.

What had Pieter Van Horen said to her about two people needing to share the same passion? Connor was a pragmatic and practical banker, who looked at life from a nuts and bolts and figures perspective. And then she realised, Matthew would probably agree with Connor.

Was it a male attitude? A western businessman's outlook? Stewart Johns and Kevin Blanchard would agree with Connor too.

On the other side, there was Pieter, Kate, Xavier and Lester who would not want the casino. Would Connor agree to a casino at Ayers Rock? Or another uranium mine in Kakadu? Madi sleepily rubbed her eyes, it was all too hard and dispiriting to think about. She pulled the folds of the hammock over her and fell asleep.

At some point in the night, she stirred, shifting her weight to one side and glanced across the moonlit ground. Standing between two trees beyond the hut was a shadowy animal that she thought was a dog, but seeing the way it moved its long tail, she came wide awake. It was a jaguar, beautifully marked with dark spots, its compact head lifted as it paused, before stalking slowly and regally away across the compound. She closed her eyes again, totally calm and accepting. Nothing she saw in Guyana came as any surprise any more. Smiling to herself she drifted back to sleep.

Connor kissed her awake. 'Don't be mad at me, Madi,' he whispered. 'Come back to bed and cuddle me.' He looked so contrite Madi kissed him back. 'Connor, you can't solve everything with a cuddle.'

'But it's better than arguing.' He nuzzled her and tried to lift her out of the hammock and instead she almost landed on the floor. Laughing, she pushed him playfully in the chest. 'You're impossible. By the way, we had a visit from a jaguar last night. I bet we can see its paw marks out there.'

Connor rolled his eyes as Madi ran out to check. Sighing, he had a sudden longing to be in New York, Washington or Sydney. Fascinating as all this was, there was a lot to be said for First World comforts. He wondered if Madi would soon get over this obsession with the charm of primitive Third World experiences. Hovering in his mind drifted the big question . . . and then what? He had been thinking this through for some time. There had been many women pass through his arms for brief periods of time, some longer than the two and a half months he'd known Madi. And then inevitably had come the day when—often conveniently—he'd had to move on.

He cherished many of the relationships and realised he'd probably broken a few hearts. But Madi was different somehow. She frustrated him when she held back the love he knew was there, the love he snatched and shared when she let the barriers fall. For the first time he felt that someone else held power over him, simply by not wielding any power, playing any games or making any claims.

Like Matthew he had been slightly taken aback by her transformation from innocent abroad to a very self-possessed young woman discovering the intoxication of passion for a cause that went beyond herself. But in discussing her, both men had decided Madi's passion for Guyana and the need to address its social inequities would pass once she left the country and picked up the threads of her life again. Now Connor wondered if he and Matthew were underestimating Madi and he felt even more confused. A swim might clear his head.

Madi showered and strolled down the sandy track beneath flowering trees to the creek where Connor was floating on his back. She sat on the log where he'd dropped his towel and shorts and watched him slowly backstroke. She smiled to herself. Despite their difference of the night before, she was very attracted to him. She was so glad they were together, sharing this time.

Connor splashed out of the creek and sat beside her, towelling his hair. She picked up a corner of the towel and began drying his back and impulsively leaned over and kissed his shoulder. He turned and returned her kiss, and between them suddenly flooded feelings of warmth, affection and a sense of bonding. Each felt it and knew the other did too.

'Madi . . . this isn't how I planned it, but . . . seems as good a time as any,' said Connor softly, with a hint of a smile.

'What?'

He reached for his shorts and dug into his pocket for something, telling Madi to close her eyes. She did, then felt his hand taking hers and placing something metallic in her palm. 'You can open your eyes now.'

Madi stared at the exquisite ring sparkling in the morning sunlight.

'Oh Connor . . . oh my. It's the pink diamond you found!' She held it up to the sun and rosy splinters of light seemed to crackle from within the now beautifully faceted stone. 'The setting is from Guyanese gold too. I did a deal with Lester,' he hastily added, 'to help his son.'

'You're giving this to me?' Madi stared at him and began shaking her head. 'Connor, I can't accept this.'

'Madi . . . my darling. I'm giving it to you for a reason . . .' Connor lifted her left hand and slipped it on her engagement finger. 'I want you to marry me.'

Madi was silent, utterly overwhelmed. She hadn't expected this.

'Connor, it's beautiful . . . but it's so soon . . .'

'Madi, I love you. I know you love me too. I also know we are meant to be together. It doesn't matter about time, how long we've known each other. When you know, you know. And I just know that you're it. I can't imagine not having you in my life.'

'I think I do love you, Connor . . . but you know I'm cautious. You've never been married, and when you've made a mistake, you can't help . . . being fearful.' Madi was close to tears and desperately wishing she didn't have to deal with this right now. She felt she was being rushed and he'd taken one step too many and was close to spoiling the relatively uncomplicated relationship they'd shared up to now.

Sensing her hesitation Connor went on with faint desperation. 'I'm not putting any pressure on you. We can stay engaged as long as you like. Madi, I just had to make a commitment, I love you and I want you to know I am serious about this. I've never felt this way before and I realise now, I've just been paddling around waiting until you showed up.'

'You're sure it's not the fact you feel time is marching on and you should settle down?' She gave a small grin, then looked back admiringly at the ring, twisting it a little on her finger.

'Hell, Madi, it's not like I'm some middle-aged Romeo grabbing a young bimbo to boost his ego.' Connor sounded agitated. This wasn't the reaction he'd anticipated, but as they sat in silence for a moment, Connor had to admit to himself that this was just what he should have expected from Madi and why he'd felt the need to pin her down.

'Madi, I don't want to lose you. And that's the truth. I thought if I gave you the ring . . .' he paused, a little lost for the right words, then went off on a tangent to cover his embarrassment. 'I want you to have it anyway . . . Lester and I both agreed it should be yours, no matter what.'

Tears sprang to Madi's eyes at the tremble in Connor's voice and the unashamed honesty with which he spoke.

'Connor, I'll wear the ring, but on my other hand. And I'm very flattered.'

'Don't say that . . . it sounds like a speech . . .' Connor wrapped his arms about her. 'Just love me, Madi, then you'll see how things will fall into place. It's easy . . .' He kissed her long and hard as if willing her to love him back as passionately.

Madi's mind was whirling. It would be easy to just love Connor and let events take the course he obviously envisaged. For all his worldly sophistication and romantic experiences, Madi suddenly saw him as a simple boy who wanted something and had made the appropriate claim and expected success to follow. It was how he'd led his life, she had no doubt. But the underlying assumption that she would go along with his wishes, even when she did love him—and she had to admit that she did—bothered her.

They drew apart and holding hands walked back to the compound. 'Connor, it's not you . . . and it's not that I don't love you . . . I still need a little time . . . for me . . .'

He squeezed her hand. 'I'll wait. I understand.' However, in his heart Connor didn't truly understand, but he was prepared to go along with Madi's wishes and hope that somehow everything would work out just as he wanted it to.

Madi was thankful there seemed to be some diversion

at the compound. Several horses were tied under a tree and a vaquero was talking to Amelia. They were hailed by Kate. 'We have a visitor! A friend of yours, Madison.'

Pieter Van Horen, smiling broadly, stepped out of the house and waved, his yellow beard glinting in the sunlight, and his fair hair shining like a silver halo.

'Pieter! How lovely to see you!' Madi ran forward to give him a hug. 'This is wonderful, now you can meet Connor.'

The two men shook hands and Connor was struck by the charisma of the older man. He'd imagined some academic wimp, not this tall, powerfully built and striking Dutchman.

'Breakfast is ready,' announced Kate, 'so let's talk over the eggs and toast.' They joined Joseph already at the table with hot pepper sauce lined up in front of his plate, waiting for Amelia's eggs.

'So how come you're here?' asked Madi, smiling with delight at meeting up with Pieter again.

'I've been collecting, talking to the captains of the villages down here, investigating this and that.'

'Putting in a good word for Xavier here and there no doubt,' she added.

'I don't need to do that. He has put in a good word for me. Everyone is most co-operative,' he said, then turned his attention to Connor. 'And you, Mr Bain, do you find Guyana as enthralling as Madison does? Or is it just another insignificant Third World country?'

Connor knew immediately that the craggy ethno-botanist could read people as well as he could read plants. He was spared the need to reply immediately when Amelia and her daughter arrived at the table with platters of scrambled eggs, slabs of beef and toast.

'Well, yes, it is just another Third World country from

my banker's perspective, but thanks to Madison's enthusiasm, I'm finding it more interesting almost by the day. By the way, Pieter, call me Connor. Aussies don't have much time for the formal mode of address.'

'And, Connor, what aspects do you find interesting beyond the bottom line of the project you're working on, important though that is?'

He's a bloody straight shooter this one, thought Connor. He got a little kick from Madi, as if she read his thoughts.

'Well, I've seen a bit of this country and its people in a way that bankers seldom do, thanks to Madison and friends like Lester and Kate here. Yes, it's really got a lot going for it beyond the mines, lovely country to enjoy, lovely people.' Connor dived into his eggs, hoping the conversation would move on without him.

Pieter too attacked the eggs and, as if in synchronisation with Connor, picked up where he left off as their eyes met over empty forks. 'These lovely people, it seems to me, aren't getting much interest on their stake in this country. Would you agree, Connor?'

'Look. There's no turning back the clock. Mines are here to stay. So are a lot of other industries that don't sit too prettily on the landscape. If the people are going to share in this wealth the industries create, the industries first must be efficient and profitable. And if the people want stronger environmental safeguards, and that's the trend almost everywhere these days, then they must be satisfied with lower profits. Guyana is damned lucky to have so much wealth in natural resources.'

Pieter leaned forward, waving his fork. 'I agree with you, Connor. The question we must surely address at this point in time, is how to give the people real power in determining the development process? Shall we take our coffee in the garden?'

Connor gave Madi a big raised eyebrow as they passed the coffee pot along the table. Madi smiled reassuringly and gave him a peck on the cheek.

They sat on rustic bush-crafted chairs under a frangipani tree of great size and age. Kate saw them settled then left with Joseph to discuss a beef shipment.

'Lovely coffee,' said Pieter. 'Nice to have a break in the routine of work, isn't it?'

Connor was delighted to agree on something. 'Yes, we've had a great time here. Gives one a chance to recharge the batteries.'

'Oddly enough,' said Pieter, 'I never really get tired when doing my work.'

'Just what exactly are you doing?' Connor wanted to bite his tongue the moment he spoke, recognising where Pieter had cleverly led him. 'Madi seems to think the plant business has enormous potential,' he added.

Pieter knew his subject well. He presented a briefing of such focus, fact, and depth that it left Connor with few questions.

'I told you Pieter was an expert,' said Madi smugly. 'Impressed?'

'Yes, I can't deny it. Amazing that the drug companies really do spend tens, even hundreds of millions of dollars investigating these natural medicines and in ninety-five per cent of cases it is money straight down the drain. Yet, they keep coming back for more.'

'Because the profits, when they come up with a commercially successful new drug, are enormous,' said Madi. 'Don't you agree the people who inherited the knowledge, should share in the profits?'

414

'Well,' said Connor hesitatingly, 'it's not up to me. It's decided by government policy.'

'Maybe an alternative would be to fund research on behalf of the people, and give them ownership of the patented drugs,' suggested Pieter, almost as if he had just thought of the idea.

'But it would take millions just to get started,' protested Connor.

'So?'

'I don't know of a precedent for something like this.'

'So?' repeated Pieter.

'IFO wouldn't put money into something like that.'

'But you haven't asked them yet, have you?'

Connor realised he had very little room left to manoeuvre and his faltering resistance crumbled when he saw the loving, expectant look on Madi's face. 'Okay. Who has the project paper and who has the political connections?'

Pieter smiled. 'Xavier and the other Amerindian leaders have put together a proposal. A meeting in Georgetown can be set up at short notice. The briefing paper is very detailed. You realise, of course, that all this has political implications, so your discretion would be appreciated.'

'Of course.'

It was then that Madi sat back in her chair, slightly stunned. Not at Connor's capitulation, but at the realisation that this had been a carefully-planned power game played by Xavier, Pieter and Kate. For a moment she felt guilty that she too had unwittingly been a party to getting Connor in this situation.

Then, almost as if on cue, a group of Amerindians led by Kate came up the path, some of them carrying bags of plants. Kate settled them in a semicircle on the edge of the compound clearing and Amelia appeared with a tray of refreshments for them. Kate called to Pieter, 'Your specimens have arrived, Doctor. Time for real work.'

'Perhaps you would like to see a little of my work?' he said to Connor. 'I believe some of the plants they've gathered have most interesting properties.'

'Naturally,' he replied, and they both laughed at the unintended pun as they strolled across the compound.

EIGHTEEN

Antonio Destra parked in the compound of the Amerindian hostel in Georgetown, and allowed himself the leisure of a cigarette as he ambled around watching some craft workers weaving and painting in preparation for their weekend market of artefacts. That he was a little late for his appointment with Xavier worried him not at all. Making the Amerindian sweat wouldn't hurt a bit.

He stubbed out the cigarette with his shoe then went inside and was immediately taken to Xavier's office. A secretary with a note pad left on a nod from Xavier.

'Good morning, Xavier,' he said jovially. 'Checking on arrangements for your rally? Must say, I'm a little surprised at the amount of support you've managed to drum up among your indigenous community. But it's good to see this revolt against marginalisation of minority peoples. Very nineties stuff, got a lot of politicians worried.'

'It's a rather healthy sign when politicians get worried, don't you think,' said Xavier, relaxed, but on guard because he regarded Destra as a man not to be trusted. At an earlier meeting at the hostel, he'd formed the impression Antonio Destra was sympathetic to the Amerindian cause for some unrevealed advantage to himself.

'Right on, hombre. Right on. I reckon some of the guys down at the prime minister's office must be puzzled as to what you're really aiming for, Xavier, trying to figure out what's in it for you?'

'Our people are simply asking for their rights, their dignity. If the times dictate that we must be confrontational to achieve those ends, then so be it. There are many other minority groups in Guyana who are looking to us for a lead.'

Destra opened his briefcase, took out a large brown envelope and plonked it on the desk in front of Xavier. There was nothing intimidating about the way he did it, but Xavier knew by instinct that it carried bad news. He made no effort to open it.

'So sad about the goldmine leak,' remarked Destra, suddenly changing the subject and ignoring the envelope. 'It serves as a warning to all mining operators in the country, wouldn't you say?'

'Yes, it's very unfortunate. The damage to my people's environment and lifestyle will go on for some time. It serves, as you say, as a warning. Reckless exploitation of our land cannot continue like this.'

Destra kept a straight face. 'A bit of a God-sent incident for anyone campaigning against the multinational mining companies.'

Xavier wondered just what Destra was setting up. He knew the dam spill at the goldmine had been a political gift, but he would not admit that to Destra. 'We would have preferred that the incident had never happened. We have a good case without such disasters.'

'True. True indeed. And that's why I think you should have a look at some material that has come into my hands.' He leaned forward, tapped the envelope with an index finger and looked Xavier firmly in the eye.

Xavier opened the envelope and took out a sheaf of photographs and thumbed through them slowly, not letting his face show any reaction. When he had looked at them all, he put them back and pushed the envelope to Destra. He said nothing.

Destra said nothing either. It was a battle of wills. The Colombian cracked first.

'Bejesus, Xavier, they're dynamite,' he exclaimed. Annoyed at the Amerindian's lack of expression, he emptied the photographs out of the envelope and spread them over the table. 'Look at them, man. Every shot shows you acting damned oddly around the spill area of the Columbus mine—just before the dam collapsed.'

Xavier had immediately realised the photos taken on a telephoto lens had made him look suspicious. They'd been taken when Xavier had surreptitiously visited the goldmine after reports from the villagers that something was poisoning the fish.

'Who took these?' he asked calmly, covering the anger he felt inside. He knew that in the wrong hands they would be political dynamite.

'Obviously, I cannot reveal my source, and there is always the chance other copies are circulating.' Destra paused briefly. 'As you know I have been very supportive of the Amerindian cause and your own career.' Xavier nodded in agreement. 'I'm willing to use my connections to quietly purchase the negatives and have all copies suppressed. The owner is threatening to sell them to the newspapers. I have made him a better offer.'

Xavier drew a deep breath. 'Thank you, Antonio. You have been very good to our cause and I am sure that one day we will find a way of repaying you.'

'Of course. I'm sure you will.' Then he adopted a less serious tone. 'Well, I'll be off. Glad to have been of assistance. It pays for friends to stick together, don't you think? Particularly in these complicated times.'

Xavier was silent for a moment. 'Yes, you're probably right. By the way, Antonio, do you do business with the Columbus goldmine?'

Destra smiled. 'Indeed yes. I supplied them pumps and other equipment to repair the damage. They're excellent customers. They know when and how to make a deal.'

Their eyes locked for a few seconds and they both nodded knowingly to each other. Destra gathered up the photographs and slipped them back in the envelope. They shook hands and Destra walked out of the office with a cheerful little wave at the door.

Back in Georgetown, Madi went through her 'culture shock' of settling back into city life. She tried to explain to Matthew the beauty and impact of the Rupununi, the wonderful wildlife, the fascinating people and Kate McGrath. He smiled at her as he poured a welcome home drink. 'And did Connor enjoy it too?'

'I think so. But he comes at things from a different perspective to me. It's a bit unsettling at times.'

'What do you mean?' Matthew stretched out and put his feet up on the sofa.

'Money men are hard nuts to crack.'

'Personally or professionally?' Matthew raised a quizzical eyebrow.

'Professionally. Pieter turned up down at Caraboo, at the behest of Xavier, as it turned out. They took up my suggestion to approach Connor and the IFO to set up a pharmaceutical program to be run for the Amerindian people.'

'Is that viable? It sounds long term and risky.'

'Not if it's done properly.'

'It's not my bag. I have my hands full dealing with the day-to-day dramas at one small bauxite mine.'

'But Matt, I'm interested. I want to be part of seeing something constructive happen.' Her eyes sparkled and she spoke with a new passion in her voice.

'Jesus, Madi, since when? You've only ever been a token greenie, where do your new credentials come from? A subscription to *Greenpeace* magazine? Back home, how often did you get out and demonstrate, or do anything to help environment and conservation groups? You've been a couch potato greenie, swallowing whatever line the radicals were pushing. Have you ever looked at the changes in corporate attitudes? Environmental impact studies are part of ground floor thinking for any mining or engineering enterprise these days. Eco-efficiency or eco-competitiveness is fundamental to big business now.'

'I know all about that,' said Madi, 'don't be patronising. And the truth is business is only recognising environmental issues in order to get up projects and make money.'

'What's wrong with that? If they don't abide by the environmental laws and have an environmental policy— they don't get the money! It's already happening, Madi.

Don't paint business corporations as the bad blokes. They can bring about change for the better because of their clout.'

'They can abuse it too!'

'So can governments and individuals and shonky companies, that's human nature. Get real and stop being such an idealist, Madi.'

'And what's wrong with that? The world needs idealists to have vision.'

'Crap.'

'And DO something about it. I can be instrumental here. I'm not going to be a part of this casino project, but I can see a whole eco tourism industry could be established in Guyana. And I'd like to be part of it. If you'd been at Caraboo you'd see what I mean.'

'Are you crazy? For God's sake, Madi, you can't jump on some appealing hobby horse on the other side of the world from home. You won't save this tinpot country. You're way out of your depth. Go back to Sydney, go to London but get out of here before you get caught up in God knows what. You know first hand the sort of people you're up against.'

'Stop it, Matt. This time I'm sticking to my principles and beliefs and I'm *not* backing down. I know I'm right. Maybe I was a token greenie at home but now I have the chance to prove myself. And that's exactly what I intend to do, Matthew.'

Matthew called Connor and met him at the Tower Hotel for dinner.

They carried their drinks to an outdoor table. 'We might as well sit out here before the band starts and conversation is impossible.' Connor glanced quickly at the menu and pushed it to one side. 'Chicken in the rough?'

'Yeah. That's fine, seems to be their speciality.'

'It's everyone's speciality, hadn't you noticed?'

'Yeah. So what do you make of Madi's outburst?'

'You're both right you know. Having been out there, to the interior, I can see what's appealing to her. It is bloody magnificent. I can see both sides of the argument.'

Matthew looked sullen. 'I hadn't expected this reaction from you. I thought you were more pragmatic.'

'I am. But I can recognise a business opportunity when it's put to me. The big question is about Madi's involvement.'

'She's on some hobbyhorse about being instrumental in getting this up. I know she's got good marketing skills, but this . . . who would have thought this would happen when she arrived here?' Matthew shook his head.

'She has blossomed somewhat,' said Connor with a wry grin.

'That's an understatement. Jeez, I wish she'd move on to London. Once she's there, she'll love the buzz of those great old hotels. Surely she'd get work.'

'Don't encourage her too hard to leave,' said Connor quietly.

'Why the hell not? I mean . . .' Matthew glanced at Connor and paused before asking, 'So what exactly is the deal with you two? She is my sister and I don't want to see her hurt. I figured from your point of view, you could both enjoy a bit of a romantic interlude, so to speak. I warned her not to get too involved.'

'Oh, did you? Thanks a lot.' Connor looked miffed.

'Do you blame me?' asked Matthew mildly.

'No, mate. No I don't. But this time things are different. Did she show you the ring?'

'Ring?' Matthew shook his head. 'We got stuck into that bloody row . . . what ring?'

'I gave her the rose diamond I found up at Lester's. I asked her to marry me.'

Matthew stared at Connor, trying to absorb this bombshell.

'You haven't known each other very long.'

He gave a small smile. 'They say when you know, you know. I do love her, Matt. I found I missed her terribly when she wasn't around, and the more I thought about her, the more I realised how powerful were my feelings. I have to admit it's taken me a bit by surprise too. When I picked her up at the airport, I thought, well, here could be an agreeable lady to share some time with. Now I'm just . . . passionate . . . is the only word I can find.' He stopped. He was upset Madi hadn't shown her ring to Matthew. Here was another example of Madi's casual attitude to their relationship, and it disturbed him.

'Well . . . this presents something of a dilemma . . . I mean, where do you both see the future? Is she going to marry you?' Matthew asked suddenly.

'She said she wanted more time . . . she didn't say no.' Connor gave a rueful grin. 'I asked her to move in with me.'

'And?'

'I don't know the answer to that either. She wanted to talk to you.'

'Well, I blew that. She's probably packing as we speak.'

'I'm sorry, Matt.'

'Not your fault. It'll settle down. I'd feel better knowing she was under your wing. Maybe you could get her to rethink some of these wild ideas.'

Connor twisted his glass in his hands. 'They're not totally out of left field. I just don't want to see her get too swept up in it all.'

'I'll drink to that. So, have you talked about the future at all with her?'

'No. She says she needs time, still feels a bit leery about going into another marriage so soon . . . I'm happy to go along with delaying the actual event, so long as I know she's willing to make the commitment—at some stage.'

Matthew was thoughtful. 'I have to say if I had to pick a bloke for my little sister, you'd be number one. But I can't interfere . . . she's a woman with her own mind these days.'

'That's for sure. Well, it's nice to know I have your backing. Let's just see how things work out. If she does move in, it might settle a decision in her mind one way or another. She did say we might fight like cats and dogs over our differing views . . . but that's a risk I have to take,' grinned Connor.

Madi was packed and she announced coolly to Matthew at breakfast, she was moving over to Connor's place.

'Lester will be here in a little while. I'll let you explain the situation to Hyacinth.'

'Gee thanks. Now listen, Madi, are you sure you're moving because you want to be with Connor and not because you're mad at me?' Matthew moved to her and put his arms around her. 'I love you too, sis. And all I want is for you to be happy.'

Madi choked up and didn't speak for a minute. Her brother had always been there for her and she knew no matter what differences they had or what either did, they would be first to the other's side.

'Thanks, Matty,' she said in a muffled voice, using their pet childhood name. 'I love you too, and I know you only want what's best. And frankly, I don't know how I feel about Connor—long term. He's gorgeous and fun and sexy and a responsible adult—unlike Geoffrey. In my previous life, this would have been an easy decision. What's really getting in the way is this passion I feel to be involved in something worthwhile.'

'Can't you do this at home? Australia has similar problems.'

'Maybe. Who knows? I do sense my life is taking on a new direction. But I have the opportunity to be involved here and such opportunities might not present themselves so easily at home.'

'And what about Connor? Getting married, having babies? You always wanted that too. A career was only for the interim, you said. You can't turn your back on those things because you made one mistake. We all make mistakes.'

'I've learned that and I'm going forward with my life and I feel stronger because of it. Anyway, I might ask the same of you, Matt. When are you going to "settle down"?'

'Okay, I'm like Kevin and how Connor used to be . . . playing the field and moving on. It's a good life. I'll wait till someone really special comes along. Connor tells me when you know, you know.'

'Well, I'm glad he's so sure. I'm just taking it day by day.' Lester's car tooted at the gate and they heard Singh drag it open and exchange morning greetings as they loaded her bags into the cab. 'I'm only fifteen minutes away. We'll see just as much of each other.' She kissed his cheek and hurried down the stairs. Matthew went out to the balcony and watched Madi walk through the garden

426

and shake Singh's hand. Lester held the cab door open but before she stepped in she looked up and, seeing Matthew, blew him a kiss.

Matthew looked at the slim girl, her blonde hair sparkling in the sunlight, and was overcome with a feeling that his sister was moving on to a new life, and while he would always be there, he knew she was more in control of it. In one way he was glad, in another he couldn't get rid of the worry that Madi was plunging into risky waters.

The first evening she and Connor shared together, Madi cooked dinner, lit candles and filled the house with flowers. 'Hey, I like this domesticity,' he declared, producing a bottle of champagne.

'Don't get used to it. I'm just trying to make a good impression,' she teased.

They talked at length and laughed and reminisced about their time in the interior. 'You seem more relaxed about this idea. How did Matt take it?'

'He just wants me to be happy.'

'Me too. You make me happy, Madi, I pray I can do the same for you.' He reached over and squeezed her fingers, noting the ring was still on her right hand.

They finished the champagne and Connor insisted they leave the dishes. 'So what are your plans for tomorrow? If you want to buy anything, change the house around, feel free.'

'I'm meeting Sasha St Herve. I'm going to tell him I don't want anything to do with the Amazonia casino project and furthermore I'll tell him that I think it's totally inappropriate. I won't mention the story Kate heard that it's linked to El Dorado. Why invite trouble?'

Connor threw up his hands. 'Okay, go for it, Madi. Just be careful what you say and to whom. I still worry there's a price on our heads for stumbling on that drug cache.'

'Rubbish. That was an isolated thing. We were damned lucky, thanks to our Amerindian friends . . . we owe them, Connor Bain.'

'All right, I read you loud and clear. I'll talk seriously to Pieter and Xavier about their plans and if they're sound, I'll put them to the IFO for backing.'

'Good.' She leaned over and kissed him. 'Let's go to bed.'

Lester waited while she met with Sasha St Herve. Madi emerged wearing dark glasses and looking subdued. 'Want to go for a mate's coffee, Lester?'

'Sure ting. So, what he say bout yo thoughts on de casino, eh?'

'He wasn't too impressed. He thinks Amazonia is a fantastic concept and sees it as part of his future direction. We kind of left it up in the air. He says I should meet some of the "senior management" behind the casino and see if I change my mind. But he said he'd rather not name them until I agree to meet them. I tried to talk to him about smaller, eco tourism-style developments but he is definite it has to be a casino . . . that's the appeal, he says.'

'Just fo high rollers, eh?'

'You got it. Makes me sick now I've seen places like Caraboo and Kaieteur Falls.'

'Man, yo 'bout to see dis place called Georgetown like yo never see it. It be Carnivale time. Man, dat Carnivale be sometin' yo an't goin' believe.'

'So I hear . . . Where's the best place to watch Carnivale?'

'Anywhere yo can get a place along the route! The VIPs have a special grandstand set up on Main Street. It be de parade to end all parades man . . . de best bands and dancers come from all over de Caribbean.' Lester did a small calypso jiggle with his hips, clicking his fingers and 'jivin', making Madi laugh.

'Lady Annabel is giving a big bash at the haunted house, a few days before the parade.'

'Yo watch out fo Uncle Eric.'

Matthew, Sharee, Kevin, Viti, Connor and Madi arrived together at Lady Annabel's pre-Carnivale party. Despite the lights, the cars, the music, people about the grounds and on the verandah, the house still loomed melancholy and strange in Madi's mind. She took Connor's hand as they went upstairs to be welcomed by Lady Annabel, resplendent in a gold lamé turban and a flowing caftan that was hand-painted with Amerindian symbols. Waiters weaved through the crush with trays of drinks and hors d'oeuvres, the steel band in the garden played non stop, guests had dressed as requested—'with a carnival flair'—and Lady Annabel, waving a cigarette holder and glass of champagne, looked in her element.

'You've gone overboard, haven't you, Lady A?' remarked Matthew.

'I'm not footing the bill, just playing mistress of ceremonies. Or genie with the lamp. Did you have a particular wish?' She kissed Madi. 'My dear girl. Did you enjoy your sojourn in the interior?'

'I loved it. We both did.' She smiled at Connor.

Lady Annabel glanced at them both. 'It seems to have put a sparkle in your eye. Madison, there are several people I'd like you to meet. Connor, may I steal her for a while?'

He waved a hand. 'Of course. Have fun. I'll find Matthew.'

Lady Annabel linked her arm through Madi's. 'So, my dear girl. What's really going on?'

'What do you mean?'

'With you and Connor, with your involvement in local affairs, your interest in Xavier Rodrigues and his plans . . .'

'You seem to be keeping tabs.'

'I hear things, Madison. And may I say to you—as I am very fond of you—don't make any rash decisions.'

'About what, Lady Annabel? My love life or my "other interests"?' Madi spoke lightly but her eyes were brittle. She was trying to fathom what underlying message Annabel was trying to send.

'About anything, Madison . . . projects and people aren't always what they seem in Guyana.'

Several guests descended on Lady Annabel. Madi turned, looking for someone she knew, and was immediately confronted by Antonio Destra.

'The woman of the bush returns. You're looking very glamorous, Miss Wright.' He kissed her hand. 'What have you been up to?'

'Just playing tourist. More to the point, what have you been up to?'

He gave a shrug. 'Hard to do anything but concentrate on the spill at the Columbus mine these past weeks. They sure needed a mighty lot of gear up there. Great for my business, but bad news for the country, don't you agree?'

Madi was really puzzled by Antonio Destra. He seemed to be everywhere that mattered when it mattered. He always said the right things, and was respected among the mining fraternity. She knew too, that he had helped the Amerindians over the years. But there was something about him that made her feel a little uncomfortable. It was hard, she found, always to believe what he was saying. Insincerity, that was it, she concluded. He was definitely suss in the sincerity department.

'You're right there, it sure is bad for the country,' Madi said. 'The issue is, what will be done to ensure such things don't happen again? Maybe the goldmine accident will be a catalyst for changing the political and economic agenda in this country.'

Destra almost choked on his whisky and water. Well, he thought, the little mouse I met at the airport, when she arrived in Guyana, is turning into a roaring lion. She's starting to sound like Xavier when he's on his soapbox in the bush. God knows what she will get up to next. But before he could resume the conversation in depth, Madi sighted Sasha St Herve talking to Colonel Bede Olivera, and returned his wave with her glass. 'Sorry, Antonio, but I must talk to Sasha. Business.'

'Never one to stand in the way of a little business,' he quipped. 'See you later in the evening perhaps.'

Sasha gave Madi a charming smile. The colonel was effusive in his greeting. 'I hear you have been exploring the interior. Excellent, excellent. I hope you are suitably impressed with our country,' smiled Olivera.

'How could I not be . . . the Rupunini, Kaieteur, the Essequibo River.'

Sasha St Herve stepped in quickly. 'I've been trying to persuade Madison to work for us, to put together a proposal to market and promote the Amazonia casino.'

'Ah, yes, that's right, you are a hotel marketing lady. Can't we persuade you? It would be a unique and high profile project to work on,' smiled Colonel Olivera.

A small alarm bell rang in Madi's head. 'We? Are you involved in Amazonia?'

'Indeed he is. I told you we have a most impressive group of individuals backing the casino. Come, you must meet the chairman of the Amazonia committee.' St Herve took her arm, and Madi mumbled parting words to the colonel.

'Madison, please meet Mr Rashid Bacchus, a banker from Brazil and the head of our Amazonia project. This is Miss Wright, visiting us from Australia.'

Bacchus was an older man, his plumpness straining at the tightly buttoned Nehru jacket he wore buttoned all the way to his neck, the folds of dark skin dropping over the high collar. His face was damp with perspiration, but he gave Madison a jovial smile. As they reached out to shake hands, they made eye contact, and she saw his eyes were hard and cold.

'How do you do,' she smiled hesitantly. And then, as she released his hand, her eyes flashed down to what she'd felt—a ring. Shaped like a gold frog. Again she lifted her eyes to his face, and this time tried to read his bland expression.

Drink in hand, Sasha St Herve began gushing to Bacchus about Madi's marketing credentials. 'However, since being in the interior, she has become a fan of eco tourism ideas,' he laughed lightly.

Bacchus was instantly dismissive. 'I do not think that a viable concept at all. As a banker, I couldn't endorse such risky small-time operations. Something like a casino is guaranteed to succeed. Look at what casinos have done for your cities like Melbourne, Cairns, Perth and Sydney. So, did you enjoy your time in the wilds of our beautiful country?'

He looked at her over the lip of his glass as he sipped a mineral water. The gold frog blazed at Madi. More tellingly the frog tattoo was as clear inside Bacchus' wrist as when she'd first glimpsed it beneath her blind-fold. His hand and the glass partially covered his expression, but his eyes were penetrating hers, hard and threatening.

'I wasn't exactly in the wilds. I was staying with friends at their ranch in the Rupununi district,' she said hoping her voice didn't tremble too much.

The moment she had feared had happened, when she had least expected it, and when she was beginning to think the drug episode was just a bad dream. Here was the man who had ordered their deaths, standing right before her.

She simply couldn't tell if Bacchus recognised her, but he must have. She had to keep calm. As far as he knew, she'd never seen him because she and Connor had been blindfolded. And his voice was not exceptional in any other way.

Concealing her agitation as best she could, Madi listened to Sasha St Herve chattering on, and was relieved to see Lady Annabel bearing down on them. 'Madison, my dear girl, there's someone I would like you to meet. Gentlemen, you can't monopolise the pretty girls for too long, excuse us.' Madi smiled and shrugged as she was scooped up by Lady Annabel.

'Who am I meeting now?' asked Madi in a tight voice.

'No one. You looked like you needed rescuing.' Lady Annabel gave her a shrewd look but said nothing else. 'Go find your lovely man.'

Gratefully Madi fled to where Connor was standing with Matthew. Both of them saw immediately that she was upset.

'What's up, sis?' asked Matthew in a low voice.

'Don't look now. But he's here, Connor. The Indian man who ordered those drug men to kill us. He's here.'

'Oh God. Are you sure, Madi?'

'The ring, I saw his frog ring.'

'Who, which one?' Matthew spoke urgently.

'Don't draw attention to us. I don't think he knows that I recognised him,' Madi said. 'It's the fat Indian man, in the Nehru jacket. Don't turn around, Connor.'

'I've got him in my sights,' said Matthew who was facing Madi and Connor and could see across the room behind them. 'He's talking to Olivera.'

'He's in it too,' she hissed.

'In what, Madi?'

'They're all part of the casino consortium. They're the men behind the mysterious El Dorado company which is the financial backer of the casino.'

'Christ. Time to leave, I think,' said Matthew. 'You two go first, I'll follow in a little while. Go straight back to Connor's. I'll meet you there in an hour and we'll see if we can make sense of this.'

They sat in silence as Connor drove them back to the house. Once inside, Madi flung herself into Connor's arms. 'Oh God, that was horrible. I kept trying so hard not to show that I recognised him. Do you think he suspects? Lady Annabel said I looked like I needed rescuing.'

'Don't panic yet. That could mean you just looked bored, anything. Sit down and have a drink.'

Matthew arrived, and a short time later another car drew up and Stewart Johns joined them. Matthew quickly filled him in on the meeting with Bacchus. Connor handed around fresh drinks and the group began to

434

weigh up the links between El Dorado, Guyminco, Ernesto St Kitt's death, the drug scene and the casino.

'The casino is the key to it all. The perfect way to launder money. And if Bacchus is also head of a bank, is also running a drug racket, it's obvious where the money to fund the casino is coming from,' said Johns.

'But what's the connection with El Dorado and Guyminco?'

'Blackmail, or so-called economic pressure, call it what you will. Guyminco—and who knows how many other companies—must have had the hard word put on them to cough up protection money, otherwise contracts and other things didn't happen for them.'

'Like what?' asked Madi.

'Like parts and supplies not getting through, approvals and permissions, you name it. Bankers, government officials and political lobbyists can be very persuasive,' said Connor.

'So how exactly does the Amazonia casino and resort fit in?' Madi persisted, trying to get the full picture.

'What better way to move money around and make money at the same time? Under cover of a legitimate business that is going to provide jobs and boost the economy,' said Matthew.

'Can't we tell the police . . . or someone?' asked Madi.

Johns spoke up. 'Now, this is where we're going to have to be very careful. For a start I would recommend Madison leave the country and Connor you keep a low profile.'

'I'm not going. Sorry, Mr Johns, I can't leave. Can't something be done to prove what's going on?' said Madi in frustration.

'Like what? When there are government officials, the head of a South American bank, and probably the police, all in it,' said Matthew.

Madi thought back to Police Inspector Palmer and his handling of her original complaint about the attempt on their lives by the drug runners. And she had to agree Matthew was probably right.

Johns finished his drink then spoke calmly and decisively. 'Not everyone in the government is corrupt. There are good guys—like poor Ernesto St Kitt. It's around the middle area of the bureaucracy where the mud starts sticking. I could take this issue up very discreetly with the relevant ministers and go right to the top.'

'We have no proof,' said Matthew.

Johns rose. 'Let's wait till after this Carnivale shindig is over and everyone's back at work, we'll deal with it then. Good night. And you keep your head down, Madison. And you too, Connor. Bacchus will recognise you, as well.'

'Thank you, we will,' Connor replied for both of them.

Matthew walked with his boss down to the car.

'I suppose he's apologising for the uproar that's gone on since you arrived in this country,' grinned Connor.

Madi glared at him. 'You sound as though I'm responsible!'

'Well, you have landed in some amazing situations and you are certainly making it clear where your eco political allegiances are . . . and that can't make people like Sasha St Herve, Olivera and Bacchus too happy. You have rather stirred the possum, although I admit I've been there with you.'

'Listen, Connor, you know very well how strongly I feel about this country and its people. I'm not making a stand or getting involved for selfish reasons. I feel motivated to fight for them . . .'

'At the cost of possibly your life! Get real, Madi,

436

you're way out of your depth in this one. This is a complex political game with heavy players . . . you can't sail in and push your green barrow here and think everyone will go along with you. You'll get shot down in more ways than one.'

'Don't be so condescending,' she said in frustration and, she had to admit, fear. She knew their lives were in danger and the knowledge made her head spin.

Connor rushed to Madi and wrapped his arms about her. 'We're tired, it's been a dreadful experience seeing Bacchus and bringing up all that stuff again . . . it's scary. Don't worry, my darling. Matthew and I are going to keep you safe.'

'You're in danger too, Connor,' she said in a muffled voice.

In the morning, Madi felt no brighter. Connor showed her how to lock the security grilles and kissed her goodbye as he headed to his office in town. 'Have a quiet day. Stay low and read a good book,' he grinned.

She nodded and half an hour later picked up the phone. 'Come and get me please, Lester.'

NINETEEN

Lester parked the taxi, locked it and tossed a coin to the boy hovering at the roadside who swiftly pocketed the money, calling, 'Yas sir, yas master, dere be four wheels on yo car when yo come back. Ah does watch him good fo yo!'

'Dere better be four wheels on him boy, ah don' own dis one. Yo watch him very good.'

Lester and Madi headed for The Pepperpot, their favourite small cafe. On the drive to the area, Madi had told Lester of the shock meeting at the cocktail party the night before. As they walked along the crowded street, rarely finding room on the sidewalk, Lester gave his grass-roots appraisal of the banker Rashid Bacchus. 'He be a powerful man, mighty powerful. Dat banker like an octopus man, he got tentacles everywhere. His name get mentioned in certain deals, but never de mud stick. He one slippery customer, I tink. Dangerous too. An' he very, very rich.'

'Where's his money come from?'

'He say India family. I say, we poor people. De bank all de time throw de poor people out of de houses and de land, dey do some money trick, legal trick, and de poor people always be de ones payin.'

'I think a big chunk of it's coming from drug running. You know, Lester, when I look at some of those huge houses going up in the suburbs, the mansions, now where are those people getting the money when they're not employed by foreign companies?'

'Yo' right dere! Friends of mine, dey be drivers and maids and gatemen, and dey tell me 'bout cars late at night, trips away, strange tings dat go on. It all smell bad, but everyone too scared to say nuttin'. Everyone hopin' some of de profit come dere way.' Lester shook his head as he stepped in front of Madi as they walked single file along the roadside. 'It be no way to run a country, man.'

They were forced to the edge of the road by the crowds, the parked cars and overflowing vendors, people, bicycles and milling people.

Behind Madi, there was a roar of a motor as an old American model V8 car suddenly accelerated, swerved and would have collected her if, for some reason, Madi hadn't stepped sideways behind a man wheeling a small cart laden with crates of beer. The speeding car clipped the cart sending bottles of beer flying everywhere. But it didn't stop and, with its horn blowing loudly, ploughed a path through the confusion of traffic.

Madi's heart was beating fast and she felt slightly

faint, then realised she was clutching her wooden frog tucked into the pocket of her white slacks.

'Man, dat was close. Yo be lucky. How come yo stepped away? Yo hear him coming?' Lester took her arm.

Madi was dazed. 'It was like I was pulled to one side, I can't explain it.' They looked at each other. 'Do you think he was deliberately trying to hit me?'

'We sure need dat coffee. Let's get out of here.' Lester led her into the coffee shop as the chaos on the street continued to escalate.

They sat away from the door, facing the street. Madi was shaken by the experience because she knew that the swerving car had been no accident, but a deliberate attempt on her life.

'I guess we don't have to figure out who was trying to hurt me,' she said weakly.

'I tink you—and Connor—better git out of town for a bit. Wait and see if yo brudder's boss can do some good wit de government. Who he talkin' to?'

'I don't know, Lester.' Madi rubbed her eyes. 'Seems to me it's impossible to know who's honest.'

'Den I tink you go away . . . another little holiday, eh?'

'I don't want to miss the Carnivale.'

'Yo talk to your brudder . . . maybe yo could go to stay at de guesthouse at yo brudder's mine. It not be so far and yo all be looked after up dere,' he suggested.

'Lester, that's a great idea. I'll suggest that. I'm sure Matthew can always find some reason to go to the mine. And Connor too.'

Lester looked relieved to once again see a smile on Madi's face. But her effusiveness disappeared as the reality that someone had seriously tried to injure or even kill her, continued to dominate her thinking, no matter how hard she tried to suppress it. God, what had she gotten herself into?

Matthew and Connor swiftly agreed to a few days at Guyminco. Both had been appalled at the story she'd related of the hit and run attack. Matthew spoke to his boss and the following day he drove Connor and Madi up to the mine.

Sitting on the enclosed verandah of Wanika House and looking out at the calm gardens and smooth expanse of the Demerara River, Madi felt a sense of tranquillity she hadn't felt since being in the interior.

While Connor spoke with Gordon Ash about the future of privatisation and the sale of Guyminco, Matthew did the rounds of all the administrative departments and came away impressed with the steadily improving attitude and positive approach to their work by staff at all levels. The prospects for the sale of the mine as a going concern were looking far better than when they'd first arrived.

Madi set herself up at a table in the downstairs sitting room and resumed writing her proposal for Xavier on the establishment and marketing of eco tourism as a practical and viable industry.

The housekeeper, Shanti, was thrilled to have the three of them in residence. The plump and happy woman was a delight and exuded a sense of wisdom and earthiness. Madi remembered Matthew's letter describing how Shanti had taken him to the obeah man after the bat had attacked him soon after he arrived in Guyana.

While the men spent their time at the bauxite mine, Madi was waited on with biscuits and coffee as she worked on the upper verandah with her notebook. Shanti asked Madi what she was writing and Madi described her idea of developing small holiday places where visitors could experience the 'real Guyana'.

'Not all the real Guyana be beautiful places like Kaieteur and Rupununi, Miss Madi. Dere be poor places and scary places, too.'

'But that's in the cities and shantytowns. And Guyana isn't unique in having an ugly side. Even rich countries like America and Australia have poor people. Shameful, but there it is, I'm afraid.'

'You know what make dese problems? Greedy people. De government say we let in foreigners to dig de gold and minerals and make Guyana rich. But ah don't see no riches dropping in ma front door.' Shanti gave a wide smile. 'But you would be welcome in my home. You come visit one day. My family live just down there.' She pointed through some coconut palms.

'The nicest thing about Guyana is the people. So friendly, so hospitable . . . that's a big attraction for visitors,' said Madi, smiling at the dark-skinned, motherly woman.

'Trouble is we don' believe we have same culture or past. We Indians come as workers like the African slaves, even the Amerindians fought each other in early days. Then we get ruled by all different people from Europe. It's like we haven't decided who we be as just Guyanese people.'

'That's a pretty good place to start, Shanti, just being Guyanese people.'

'But we still have de old powers if you know where to go. Sometimes de old ways work good.' There was a shout from the cook below, and Shanti turned away.

She clattered down the stairs and Madi was left pondering over her last remark. She turned back to her proposal and continued writing.

That afternoon Madi wandered along a canal where a coconut grove lined the banks. Piles of coconuts and husks were heaped beneath the feathery-topped trees. A nanny goat, pink udder bulging, snuffled amongst the debris.

As Madi stood there, a sense of foreboding crept up on her. Suddenly the shadowy grove looked sinister, and she had the overwhelming sensation she was in danger. Panic suddenly took over and she darted through the trees, across the lawn and into the back door of Wanika House's kitchen, startling Shanti, who was seated at the table in the spacious kitchen.

Shanti looked at Madi's ashen face. 'What be wrong?'

'I just had a feeling someone was . . . after me,' she finished lamely. It sounded so stupid when she had not actually seen anyone.

Shanti led Madi into the empty dining room and sat her down. 'What trouble you be in, girl?'

'Oh Shanti, I'm scared. Such strange things have happened these past few weeks. I think someone is trying to hurt me . . . kill me. I know something I shouldn't . . . that's why I'm up here, keeping out of the way. But I think they know. This means Connor could be in trouble too . . . and Matthew.'

'That brother of yours be safe. He be protected. Obeah man fix him up. Now, what be de story, Miss Madison?'

Briefly, in short sentences, without giving names, Madi explained why she believed someone was trying to harm her.

Shanti folded her arms. 'This be a bad story. They be serious 'bout harmin' you, eh?'

'It certainly looks like it. Matthew's boss is getting the official people to look into it.'

Shanti sniffed. 'Official people not be the right people, just now. They be slow. While they think and shuffle papers, you be in trouble.'

Madi nodded and looked at Shanti with stricken eyes. 'So what do I do?'

She spoke slowly. 'I told you de old ways sometimes be de best ways. You want to try de old way? It work for your brother. We can get help to stop dat feller following you.'

'You can . . . how?' asked Madi dubiously.

'You come to my house. We got to do it soon, before he go away.'

'You mean, you think there is someone around?' Madi's fears returned.

'I always trust de instinct. When feelings come on you like that, they be telling you, look out girl.' Shanti stood and patted Madi's shoulder. 'Now, you wait till I finish up here and send a message to de magic man. We tell the houseboy to tell your brother and Connor we be back later.'

Madi sat in the front room of Shanti's little house. The garden was overgrown, but a row of pot plants were neatly tended along the small verandah. There were lace doilies beneath cut glass vases of plastic flowers, orna- ments, a wooden clock, a doll in a glittery dress. Framed photographs and pictures cut from magazines were pinned to the walls, coloured crochet throws draped on a sofa. In the next room she saw an old nut-brown lady

444

holding a young girl on her lap. Madi was left in the best room with a glass of warm, fizzy orange drink. She gave the little girl a small wave and the child giggled and hid her face in her grandmother's chest.

Shanti returned, having changed into a simple dress, a straw hat on her head. 'Come, we go now.'

'Shanti, I'm not sure about this. Will it be all right?' Madi was apprehensive.

'You believe and it will be so,' was all she said. 'You say you trust the Amerindian ways, this be the old Carib shaman way. I tell him we is comin' and he be ready.'

'Who and what is this magic man?'

Madi followed Shanti out of the house as she explained. 'De shaman be like de doctor, de priest and de magician in one. He heal de body with herbs, and talk to de spirits to find out what to do. It take special training, he has to learn de traditions and de ceremonies. And he got to have de gift for it. He be a big man in de village. Very important. Only de shaman can send away de kanaima—de evil spirit man.'

Shanti loaned Madi a bicycle and they set off along the pitted dirt road that wound through the small township. Madi hadn't been on a bicycle for some years and the rusty machine she rode was no Malvern Star. She wobbled around dogs, chickens, children playing cricket, mounds of dirt and scattered cans and bottles. The chasm of the mine was behind them, the drone of the dragline endlessly gouging the rich sandy earth into containers faded in the distance, and soon they were riding on a quiet path into trees.

Dusk was some time away, but it began to look like rain, and clouds, punched and bruised blue-black, loomed oppressively above the last streaks of pale gold light. Beneath the trees it was gloomier, birds called an alert, and the only person they saw was a stooped woman carrying a massive pile of twigs and sticks on her head.

They reached a small shack built, it seemed, from left-over planks, doors and windows from abandoned dwellings. Shanti wheeled to a stop with a flourish and lowered her bike to the ground. Madi dismounted, leaned her bike against a tree and nervously followed Shanti round the side of the house into the backyard where an open fire sent a plume of smoke trailing into the deepening sky.

Although they were only metres away from the village track, the place felt quite isolated. As they walked towards the fire, Madi jumped and clutched at Shanti. 'What's that?' For a moment in the firelight a strange creature appeared in the half light. It was a tree, but carved into the folds and creases of its trunk was the face of a man. Grotesquely leering, the wild-eyed creature had his mouth agape and tongue protruding. Above his frighteningly expressive face, which appeared half human half animal, wild tresses of hair formed by the twists of some serpentine limbs and creepers, curled and rose upwards to blend with the foliage of the tree.

'That be the green man. Half man half tree, he look after de nature spirits,' said Shanti, taking her towards the fire.

Tending the fire was an old Indian man, wizened, black and shiny as though dried and glazed. Madi expected his skin to crackle as he moved. But he simply sat cross-legged, throwing small sticks onto the fire, and watched them approach through sultana eyes. He wore an old red sweater and dark pants. He nodded to Shanti who gestured to Madi. 'This be de lady with de trouble.'

He motioned Madi to sit, and she sat on the other side of the small fire and glanced questioningly at Shanti.

'It be all right now. I will help you with the questions. His English not so good.' She sat beside the old man so they were both facing Madi. The old man began taking slow deep breaths first through one nostril and then the other and then such long breaths that Madi wondered if he'd stopped breathing. He closed his eyes and appeared to be in a form of trance. Slowly he began to speak with Shanti translating. Shanti's voice changed slightly, becoming deeper and slower, each word carefully formed.

'*Did you bring your zemi?*'

'What's that?' whispered Madi.

'*Your idol, your totem.*'

She drew out the wooden frog and leaned over and placed it in the old man's hands. He turned it over and began a soft chanting, then threw some leaves into the fire.

Madi found herself mesmerised by the increasing smoke which almost obscured those on the other side of the fire and she felt as if she was dreaming, for suddenly, like seeing pictures in clouds, she imagined she could see wraith-like figures of babies and young children rising in the smoke.

'*First come de bush babies, he say they be immortal child of dreams . . .*'

A flick of the hand and the smoke changed again to deep impenetrable black.

'*We enter the land of unknown . . .*'

He breathed and flung powder once more and the smoke billowed densely pure white.

'*And comes the dawn of awakening . . .*'

And then in a final burst of some sort of ephemeral

447

energy, the smoke and flames seared into the colours of a peacock, which made Madi gasp at the sheer beauty and force of the dazzling light and colour. Did she imagine a strange flute-like music?

The colours waned and, as if inhaling, the fire swallowed its glorious tongue and returned once more to a small glowing centre. Madi saw the old man was playing a strange little bone flute. Without explanation, she knew that this was the bone of a past enemy.

The last note faded and the old man lowered his head, and seemed to nod to sleep. Shanti handed Madi back her frog and said simply, 'You are protected'. Rising to her feet, Shanti indicated they should leave. They quietly went to the front of the house and walked with their bicycles back through the trees.

'Can you explain that to me in any way I can understand?' asked Madi.

'Don't ask for explanations. Just accept the gift. In the old days, the missionaries say such men are possessed by evil spirits. We choose to believe what we wish, eh?'

She remounted her bicycle and, in the near darkness, Madi silently followed the little red plastic glow on the back of Shanti's bike.

By the time they reached the grounds of the guesthouse, spats of rain, flat and heavy, were slapping at them. 'Shanti . . . thank you. How do I repay the old man . . . and you?' Madi looked at the woman who seemed such a paradox, so practical and yet so accepting of a tradition that was beyond Madi's intellectual capacity.

'You will find a way to repay us.' She headed for the kitchen and Madi went upstairs to the verandah where she could hear Matthew, Connor and Kevin chatting over drinks. Lightning and rain streaked the Demerara River.

'Cook said you went out with Shanti . . . have fun?' asked Matthew cheerfully.

Madi didn't think she could adequately begin to describe the events she'd just experienced. She sat down and stared out at the rain before answering. 'Fun isn't the word. I went out with Shanti . . . I got a bit freaked this afternoon. I felt that whoever is after me, us, is here.'

'Why? What happened?' The two men looked anxious.

'Nothing at all. It was just a feeling, an instinct. So I told Shanti,' she paused and her brother gave her a penetrating look. 'Did she take you to the Indian magic man?' he asked softly.

Madi nodded and Connor looked from one to the other. 'The bat doctor?'

Madi shook her head. 'Someone different. He cast a spell . . . Shanti says now I'm protected . . .'

Matthew drew a small pouch on a long strip of leather from inside his shirt. 'This is supposed to keep me safe.'

'Well, that's great for you blokes, what about me?' demanded Connor with a grin.

'Speak to Shanti,' smiled Madi, feeling relieved. 'I'd love a drink, by the way.'

'Do you want to tell us about it?' asked Matthew.

'Not right now, but I will.'

Matthew leaned over and kissed her cheek as Connor handed her a drink. She gave them both a big grin. 'Maybe this is something I won't write home about!'

Matthew pulled the leather thong holding the little bag over his head and handed it to Connor. 'Here, mate, keep this in your pocket for a bit.'

Connor flushed slightly. 'No . . . I'll be right, that's yours.'

'I have a feeling it will work for someone I like . . . and I don't think I'm quite the target that you and Madi possibly are.'

Matthew spoke lightly and turned to the bar to freshen his drink. Connor looked deeply touched and he put the small bag the obeah man had given Matthew into his pocket.

Madi went and gave her brother a kiss. 'Thanks, bro.'

Matthew sat back down. 'If a tree falls on my head, I want it back. Now pull up a chair and let's watch the fireworks.'

They watched the dancing lightning illuminate the pockmarks where rain met river until cook rang the bell for dinner.

By the time they'd finished eating, the rain had stopped and the watery moonlight shone feebly across the wet landscape.

'Want to go for a walk?' Connor took her hand. 'We can't stay cooped up in here all the time.'

They headed down to the water's edge where the lawns stopped and a small path, dotted with palm trees, shrubs and an occasional stone bench, wound beside the river.

'I wanted to get you on my own for a bit.' Connor kissed her. 'It's been one of those go go days, all meetings and talk.'

'Go on, you're in your element,' teased Madi. They linked arms and she felt contented and calm. Despite the eerie light, provocative shadows and rustling palm fronds, her fears had been put to rest by the visit to the old shaman.

They sat on the bench and Connor kissed her again and she leant her head against his shoulder.

'How's your tourism proposal coming along?' asked Connor.

'Well. The more I think about it, the more ideas I have and the more sense it makes. It's getting all the infrastructure to happen that's difficult ... transport, things like that. The places to visit aren't a problem.' She sighed. 'We've seen some marvellous sights out here, haven't we?'

'It's one of the blessings of my job. I sometimes whinge about the gypsy life but I've been in some fascinating places ... fascinating awful and fascinating good. But this has been the best,' he answered. 'Because I found you ... Madi ... have you thought any more ...' he reached for her hand, feeling the ring. 'You don't want to put this on the other hand?'

'Don't rush me, Connor. We went through this. We're still going through the getting to know each other stage.'

'I haven't found any faults with you yet,' he grinned. 'You wake up smiling, you're fun to be with, I even love arguing with you.'

'Now don't make me cross. That sounds like you don't take my arguments seriously.'

'I do, I do! Wanna fight?' He held up his hands in a mock boxing stance.

'No. I want to get off this wet seat and go to bed. It's been a big day for me too. Come on.'

She pulled him up and holding hands they began walking back, Connor leading her on a short cut across the lawns. He stepped ahead of Madi to lift a dripping arc of bougainvillea to one side, and kissed her lightly as she brushed past him. 'I love you, Madi.'

She didn't answer but squeezed his hand, and together they walked up the wide stairs towards the open front door. Suddenly there was a deafening crack and a window beside them shattered, glass splinters flying in all directions.

'What the hell . . .' Connor pushed Madi ahead of him. He kicked the door shut and in one fluid movement he switched off the light and pulled Madi to the floor, crouching beside her.

Madi was shaking, 'What was that?'

'A shot . . . a bullet. Someone was having a go at us.'

'Oh my God,' gasped Madi and flattened herself on the floor. 'Get down, Connor. Get down.'

He put an arm about her shoulders. 'Stay calm Madi. Don't panic. I think we're safe now.'

Matthew appeared at the top of the stairs. 'What the hell is going on down there?'

'Put out the light up there, Matt. Someone took a shot at us.'

'You're joking.'

'Not bloody likely, mate. It was a shot, all right.'

'Christ. I'll phone mine security right away,' snapped Matthew and ran to the telephone in the upstairs hall.

Madi's voice was still trembling. 'What do we do now?'

'Stay inside and give him time to get away. He's not going to hang around now the alarm has been raised.'

They crept up the stairs and joined Matthew taking a cautious look out of darkened windows at the grounds around the building. Soon two mine vehicles arrived at speed, one of them with a siren howling, and their armed drivers began searching the grounds, flashing powerful torches into the surrounding bush.

Matthew took his sister in his arms. 'You all right?'

She sniffed a little, then forced a smile. 'Yes. I've got over the heart attack. Why Matt? Who?'

'Someone very powerful is getting very nervous.'

'So what do we do now?' Madi asked.

'Go back to Georgetown and report the incident. But don't expect anything to come of it. You two are going to have to be very, very careful from now on.'

By mid-morning the group were packed up and heading back to Georgetown, discussing whether Madi and Connor should risk going to the Carnivale celebrations. It was decided that there would be safety in numbers in a public place.

The group was subdued and even in the safety of the car travelling with three men in broad daylight, Madi couldn't quash her growing feelings of fear. She was in danger and she had no control over it, other than to run from this country which so held her under its spell.

As the car carrying the Australians drove towards Georgetown, a group of women living in one of the villages downstream from the mine began gathering branches blown down by the night's storm.

Arms filled with firewood, they gossiped as they headed along the muddy track. A teenage girl walking ahead of the others suddenly gave a start and dropped the bundle of sticks she had balanced on her head.

The body of a large black man, dressed in city clothes, lay to one side of the path. Beside him was a Colt .45. But what caused the women to chatter in shock and fright as they peered into the bushes, was the sight of his body entangled in the brilliant coils of a rainbow camoodi, the giant land snake of Guyana, a close relative of the river anaconda. Such a fate was regarded as a reprisal death, caused by magic, a punishment for some unjust deed carried out by the man. As they hurried away to fetch the shaman, they surmised the storm had been sent and justice had been done.

No identity papers were found on the man. His body was quietly removed and the incident was never reported in Georgetown.

Next day was a holiday and by sunset crowds were already lining the route of the parade, while thousands more were flowing in colourful, festive waves towards the city. Arches strung with lights and bright paper streamers and balloons straddled the streets. Banners, painted with *Carnivale—Go Yo, Go We,* fluttered from light poles and buildings. Houses along the route overflowed with partygoers and radios and TV sets were tuned in to the festivities with preview stories of the bands, singers and dancers due to appear in the next few hours.

Connor, Madi and Matthew had decided to get into the spirit of the event and forget their past worries as best they could. Joined by Kevin, Viti and Sharee they clapped their hands and jigged in their seats as the car radio blared a calypso ditty. As they nosed through the jammin', dancin', singin' throngs, Connor felt the fears of the previous two days being pushed aside.

'It's like everyone is on holiday or on stage,' cried Madi.

'Great atmosphere ... and the whole thing hasn't even started yet,' said Matthew.

'I'm so glad we can all share this together,' said Madi, hugging Sharee and Viti beside her. 'But I'm sorry Ann and John couldn't be here. We got a postcard from them in London saying they were having a great time and to be sure we didn't miss the Carnivale parade.'

'The parade happens after the speeches, then it's party time till dawn. The Pessaro is doing a breakfast cookout in the carpark and there's a street market along the sea-wall,' said Kevin.

'The parade is the main thing,' said Connor. 'The people work on the floats all year.'

'When is Xavier having his big rally?' Matt asked.

'In two days' time. He wants the madness of tonight to settle down first. Lester says there will be a big group of Amerindians in the parade,' said Madi, 'and they'll stay in town to hear Xavier speak.'

'There's the VIP grandstand, we're next to that,' said Connor.

'Where the heck are we going to park?' Matthew asked.

Darkness began to creep in and the crowds were shoulder to shoulder. 'There's Lester. Cooee Lester!' shouted Madi. Lester, with his son Denzil on his shoulders, was pushing through the crowd. He heard the Aussie cooee, which Madi had taught him up the river, and lifted his arms in salute, doing a little dance step as his laughing son clutched his father's hair to keep balance.

Lester and Denzil were swiftly swallowed up in the crowd as Madi and the others pushed their way into the roped off section beside the grandstand. They showed their passes and ducked under the rope to join Stewart Johns and Gordon Ash. 'Should have brought those shooting-stick seats you take to the polo,' said Sharee. Their section was a raised wooden platform, while in the grandstand beside them were politicians, diplomats and their wives, government officials and some heads of large businesses.

Glancing over at them, Madi went cold and nudged Connor. 'He's there. Third row from the front.'

Matthew and Connor surreptitiously studied the row of VIPs and saw Rashid Bacchus, with a large woman in a sari wearing elaborate gold jewellery, seated prominently next to a senior politician.

'What are we going to do?' whispered Madi.

'We do nothing. We're in a group in a public place. It must be the safest place in town. What's he going to do, for God's sake. Just don't even look his way,' advised Matthew.

'Have you had that chat to your discreet friends?' Connor asked Johns.

Johns nodded. 'Matters are being looked into. Naturally they have to move with discretion and care.'

'Will anything come of it?' Madi asked bluntly.

'Let's wait and see, and in the meantime enjoy the parade, eh?' smiled Johns.

There was a burst of fireworks and a distant cheer. As the parade swept past them, the beat of the music was intoxicating as band after band in splendid outfits swayed and played on the back of elaborately decorated flatbed trucks. Each steel band had its own distinct sound and the musicians, dressed in wild and crazy costumes, swayed and jigged as the sticks hit the pans.

The humour of many of the floats sparked cheers and laughter as none of the nation's celebrities or well-known organisations escaped the barbed wit of the calypso singers and dancers, their banners and signs.

There were dancing men on stilts, men dressed as toy soldiers in long striped satin pants or crinolines and pantaloons that covered high wooden poles.

The women dancers were dressed in barely covered sexy spangles, over-the-top enormous ball gowns and frilled rumba dresses that showed their legs, and all had tall and outlandish headdresses.

'It's a bit of a cross between what I imagine the carnival in Rio to be, crossed with the Sydney Gay and Lesbian Mardi Gras, but the music is better,' shouted Matthew to Madi.

Agile limbo dancers contorted their bodies beneath impossibly low poles, their limbs splayed as they arched under, heads just above the ground.

'They look like spiders,' declared Madi and Sharee nodded.

'They say limbo came out of the slave ships when the men had to twist and contort their bodies into such small spaces. There are also spider fables connected with limbo theatre.'

'Nothing here is ever what it seems on the surface,' grinned Madi.

Inhibition was tossed aside and those watching swayed and gyrated to the rowdy band rhythms, while others danced on the spot or joined in the parade.

Most of the parade performers wore masks which were garishly painted, outlandish creations of myth and fantasy.

A different kind of music heralded the next section. Drums and wind pipes sounded through the cheering as a contingent of Amerindians led by Xavier Rodrigues approached carrying a new flag decorated with Amerindian symbols which linked the nine tribes under the outline of a tree.

The people of the forest made a striking contrast to the glittery extravagance of the calypso dancers. Their faces were painted blue, white, red and yellow, some wore tall feathered headdresses, and both men and women were bare chested, wearing their traditional aprons and simple bone and plaited jewellery. The women held baskets, pottery bowls or matapee tubes. The men carried their traditional spears, bows and arrows and blowpipes. They moved in unison, in a slower snake-like rhythm, sure footed, their muscular legs and arms displaying their strength and agility. Grinning broadly, the men would occasionally lift an arrow or point a blowpipe or spear at the crowd, causing shrieks of good natured alarm. Kevin stood with his video camera trained on the spectacle.

No one could recall the actual moment it happened ... no one could clearly identify who might have been responsible ... but the incident turned the grandstand into a blur of colour and chaos.

From the centre of one group of Amerindian dancers, a blowpipe had been lifted and in a fraction of a second, a deadly dart dispatched. No accidental shot, it hit straight and true into the neck of Rashid Bacchus, who clutched his throat and fell sideways, fatally hit.

Once the screams and panic in the grandstand had been identified as terror, attention shifted from the parade. But the dancers continued to shuffle forward, still in unison, unaware of the incident.

Connor grabbed Madi's hand as police whistles blew and there was a scramble around the fallen banker. Matthew nudged Kevin, who continued to shoot video-tape of the grandstand, panning around swiftly to capture the street scene, then back to the now chaotic crowd gathering around the body. Johns and Ash quickly led their group from the scene, their place eagerly taken by curious onlookers.

By the time they got to their cars, they heard the

police and ambulance sirens, but with Kevin driving, and directed by Viti and Sharee, they sped through a string of deserted back streets to his house. Singh and Hyacinth had the day off, so Kevin jumped from the car and opened the gates. Johns' car with Gordon Ash in the passenger seat was right behind him.

In less than half an hour after the dart had struck its mark, they were seated on Matthew's balcony with drinks, each of them feeling stunned and overwhelmed by the murder.

They discussed over and over the sequence of events, debating whether the killer had been a plant, or whether the Amerindians and Xavier knew about it.

Johns leaned back and rubbed his eyes. 'If the Amerindian contingent knew what was going to happen they sure as hell didn't show it. It's most certainly the work of a loner, but who was he working for? That, as the Americans say, is the sixty-four thousand dollar question.'

'It might be a question worth a helluva lot more than that,' said Ash. 'There's no denying whoever organised it has done this country a community service.'

'Surely Xavier won't be held responsible for this,' said Madi in a worried voice.

Everyone turned to Johns. 'His people will be prime suspects, but you can bet your life not one of them saw anything, or knows anything. The police will get nowhere in that direction, but it won't do Xavier's image any good. Maybe Mr Bacchus had become an embarrassment to the powerbrokers above him. Maybe they felt he had gone too far by linking his drugs racket to big business in Guyana. Particularly as he had been fingered by Madi and Connor running drugs up the river.'

'But hardly anyone knew that,' protested Madi.

'Once we mentioned it in government circles, it would have circulated at the speed of light,' said Johns. 'Maybe Bacchus had become an embarrassment to his political cronies. A great many people could have had a reason to want him dead.'

'It will sure put a dent in some of the deals he was involved in,' said Connor.

'Oh good,' added Madi. 'Perhaps that will be the end of the casino.'

No one followed up on Madi's hopes that the casino project would finish with the killing. Then Connor suggested another angle. 'Just suppose Bacchus had information, political and business names for example, of others involved in this drug scene. Blackmailing them would make him a prime target, don't you think? And how convenient for everyone to blame it on the Amerindians.'

Madi was aghast at the possible extent of the corruption, but at the same time she was convinced that the real threat to her life, and Connor's, was now removed. Bacchus must have been behind the attacks on them. Now that danger was gone. That at least was a relief, but even so she needed another stiff drink and helped herself at the bar.

'One thing we can be sure of,' said Johns with the assurance that comes from a lot of experience in Third World countries like Guyana, 'there will be some interesting ripple effects from tonight's little episode. Very interesting ripples.'

There was a jangle from the buzzer at the gate and Matthew leant over the balcony and looked down. 'It's Lester and Xavier,' he shouted over his shoulder.

*

Everyone settled themselves in the living room as Kevin played the video he'd shot of the Amerindian dancers parading past the VIP grandstand. Xavier leaned forward at the point where one of the dancers was lifting a blowpipe to his mouth. It was a relatively close shot and it lasted only a few seconds before Kevin had panned left and caught Bacchus clutching his throat. The camera had then panned back to the parade. Kevin rolled the tape back and froze the picture on the man with the blowpipe. Xavier shook his head. 'I have no idea who that is. He's not one of our people, he looks the part but his face painting is not quite traditional. Who do you suppose is behind this?'

'You mean you honestly don't know?' asked Connor.

Xavier shook his head. 'So many people could have a motive to kill Bacchus, particularly after he was identified as the man who ordered the execution of Madi and Connor.'

'That's what I said,' added Johns.

'I'm cancelling the rally,' announced Xavier calmly. 'Naturally, the police and media are going to make a lot out of this. We must be careful that racial inferences don't aggravate an already delicate situation. Our political enemies could gain much from blaming me for what has happened.'

'Hey, look at this,' shouted Kevin, who had been forwarding through the video. He rewound a segment and stopped the tape. 'Look who's standing at the side of the parade.'

'Antonio Destra! Now what do you suppose he was doing there?' exclaimed Madi.

'Possibly watching from the sidelines, like everyone else?' said Stewart Johns.

'Damned odd,' observed Gordon Ash. 'Who is this guy, apart from being a dealer in mining machinery?'

'A wheeler-dealer of the old school. He's mixed up in everything, knows everyone, and, by local standards, squeaky clean from what I gather,' said Johns. 'You know him, Xavier?'

'Destra, as you say, knows everyone. He has given money to help Pieter Van Horen's research in the medicinal plants project. No one solicited him, he just came forward a few months ago and said he would quietly like to help. He wrote a cheque on the spot.'

There was a stony silence, everyone trying to understand how Antonio Destra could fit into the already complicated puzzle. More drinks were passed around.

'He was up at New Spirit when Ernesto St Kitt was killed,' said Matthew in a low, neutral voice.

Madi's heart missed a beat. 'I thought he was one of the crowd doing the hard drugs at New Spirit. But I figured I must have been mistaken. He seemed such a good family man.'

Everyone looked again at Xavier, expecting some illumination, but Xavier merely shrugged and raised his hands slightly in a gesture of despair.

While the men discussed the situation a while longer, Madi made coffee and tried to sort out her confused feelings. She went back to the balcony and sat in a cane chair looking up into the tropical night sky as if the answers might be written in the stars.

There was a sense of relief that a serious threat to the future of Guyana had been removed. But tempering this relief was a disturbing feeling that if she decided to fight for what she believed was right here, there would be new enemies and new threats to her life.

Lester wandered out with a beer and squatted beside her. 'Yo not lookin' too happy, Miz Madison. Should be, yo is safe now. Tings is lookin' good.'

Madi looked at him affectionately. 'Do you really believe that, Lester, truly?'

'We wait an see, eh? See what de day bring tomorrow, or next day,' advised Lester.

Inside the house Johns poured himself another whisky, then he walked out onto the balcony, nodded to Madi and Lester, and strolled to the far end. He stood looking at the sky, as if he too were seeking answers. But he already had one.

Can't figure why it took me so long to tumble to it, thought Johns as he sipped the drink. Must be getting old, mind slowing down. Bloody CIA, that's who Destra's working for. Bloody CIA. Has to be. It's a perfect front for an in-country agent. Still, no need to broadcast it around. The final act of this little drama hasn't yet been played, that's for sure. What's more, I'm bloody sure Xavier knows it too. Whose side is Destra on, or is he playing the field? Interesting, he mused, very interesting. Gives life a bit of an edge to get mixed up with that lot, always interesting in these sorts of countries.

TWENTY

The funeral of the banker Rashid Bacchus attracted a huge number of Georgetown's Indian population. However, outside his vast network of family, his business associations attracted more than enough people to give his passing the dignity a man of his position and wealth would normally command. But many of those professing great sorrow did so with little genuine regret. It was important to be seen at the funeral, it was important to say the right things, it was important not to do anything that might fracture the flimsy facade of decency.

After all, when someone like Bacchus went down, there was no saying what the repercussions might be.

Inspector Palmer of the Georgetown police attended the Bacchus funeral, partly in the line of duty, partly out of personal obligation. He would never admit it, but he was relieved at the demise of this man. While Bacchus' death had generated a search for the killer, it also removed the need for an investigation into claims that were certain to upset a lot of powerful people connected to the banker.

Odd, he thought as he nodded to acknowledge greetings from other mourners, that the Australian woman, Madison Wright, was linked to yet another dead man. Bacchus was dead so there would be no point in interviewing her now about her allegations that he was connected with drug trafficking—a story that had been discreetly circulating in high quarters. He amused himself by contemplating whether many Australian women had this penchant for being associated with bodies and violence, and the possible reason for such an unfortunate trait.

The object of Inspector Palmer's thoughts was at that moment being ushered into the office of Xavier Rodrigues at the Amerindian hostel.

Seated with Xavier was Pieter Van Horen and both rose to greet her enthusiastically.

Pieter gave her a big hug, Xavier grasped her hand with both of his, shaking it warmly.

'It's so good to see you again, Miss Wright, this time in more positive circumstances,' said Xavier. 'I was amazed that you had completed your tourism proposal so rapidly. Ah, if only the Guyanese had such a work ethic, what a place it would be. Don't you agree, Pieter?'

'There is room for a little improvement,' replied Pieter with deliberate understatement, 'but there first has to be an opportunity for change.'

465

'True. That's what we're working towards, and making some unexpected progress, I might add,' responded Xavier, but he didn't elaborate. 'You have the eco tourism paper for us to look at?'

Madi reached into a briefcase and pulled out half a dozen printed and bound copies of her proposal, along with a presentation folder of relevant photographs, and advertising and promotional concepts in draft form.

'My brother, Matthew, was kind enough to let me pay the mine office printers to work overtime to help put it all together for you.'

Xavier flashed her a smile of appreciation and thumbed speedily through the text folder, pausing here and there to take in some of the facts and figures.

Then he cleared a space on his desk and spread the photographs and promotional material for each of them to examine.

'These concepts are for a later stage, of course,' explained Madi. 'First stage to be addressed is the targeting of specific locations and the setting up of the infrastructure needed. It would require co-ordination with the airlines, an improved communications system, better accommodation and development of local cultural features. Where possible, I've included two to fourteen day package suggestions, using four-wheel drives, boats and hiking to give a full experience. It's very much aimed to appeal to the more adventurous holidaymaker. If you can entice tourists over from the Caribbean and from the United States for a more exciting nature-lovers' vacation in an unspoiled and unique corner of the world, then the Guyanese ecotourism industry should prosper.'

'Most impressive. Very fine work,' said Xavier, looking at the supporting papers with a keen eye.

She ran through the specifics dealing with each tourist

location separately, and then sat back. Pieter held out his great paw of a hand. 'Congratulations. It's exactly what should be done here.'

Xavier nodded. 'I agree. This is a first-class concept. But there remain a few other parties to be convinced and funds to be found—and there are always more pressing needs. And it will be some time, because of the small number of tourists involved, before it makes significant money.'

'You're sounding like a politician,' said Madi with a tight smile, a little deflated by his reservations, practical though they might be.

Xavier hastened to be reassuring. 'The politicians are the people we have to convince. With your permission, I will present it at a forum of government officials and our people which is being planned to take place at New Spirit.'

Madi shrugged. 'It's yours. My gift to Guyana. I hope next time I come back, I can book into one of these successfully operating eco tours.'

'You're leaving?'

'I'm not sure what I'm doing at the moment. The experience I had upriver with Connor was most distressing, and the murder of Bacchus hasn't made the situation any less alarming.'

Xavier began collecting the papers on his desk to put back in the folders. 'Such events impact on all of us more than you think, Madison, devastating as they were for you. They are all an essential part of the emerging big picture of changing Guyana. Drug running represents part of the contemporary power play. Distasteful as it is, we have to determine how deep crime and corruption is embedded here, and work out what to do about it. No one willingly wants to abdicate positions of power. The fight to hold onto it can become very tough, very dirty. Those of us who hold other values must be ready to adapt our tactics as the situation changes.'

Madi was puzzled. She had never heard Xavier talk like this. He had seemed the perfect example of a new age indigenous politician. But here he was hinting at what?

Xavier stood and moved from his desk to stand beside her.

'Whatever happens, Madison, remember this. You know what is special about the ground beneath me? I am allowed to stand here because I choose to be here. No person, no government can say to me: You are not allowed to be in this place, you cannot live here, you have no right to be here. This is our country, we are not slaves, it is our land and we are fighting for the right to be part of the decision-making process that determines how we live *our* lives in *our* country. Whether we be Amerindian or descendants of slaves or accidents of colonial rape. I want our Guyanese children to have the right to live in a harmonious, sustainable and beautiful country. That's what I'm fighting for, and I'll use whatever means I have to achieve it.'

Madi was greatly moved by Xavier's words. All her doubts about him disappeared and she once again felt a surging confidence that this man might one day lead his people, perhaps the nation, to a better future. 'I'm sure your dreams will come true, Xavier.'

'We must always hang on to our dreams, even if sometimes they become a little nightmarish.' He gave a laugh. 'Enough of this. Thanks again for your paper. I will study it closely and will keep in touch. You won't leave without letting me know, will you?'

'Of course not.'

Pieter walked Madi to Lester's cab. 'By the way,

thanks for putting in such a good word with Connor about our work. He called me this morning to say his company's head office was interested in principle about doing something—whatever that means—to help us. But it sounds promising.'

Madi was delighted. 'That's great news, Pieter. I'll give him an extra kiss when I see him tonight.'

She was about to get in the taxi when someone loudly called her name from across the compound. It was Lady Annabel, pottering around the doorway of the Amerindian artefacts shop. Madi gave Pieter a quick kiss on his bushy cheek. 'See you later, no doubt. Have to join Lady Annabel over at the shop.'

Pieter watched as she strode across the compound to embrace Lady Annabel. He slowly shook his head as he turned to walk back inside to resume talks with Xavier about strategies for the important meeting coming up at New Spirit. He was feeling a little sad for he knew that before long the idealistic young woman he admired so much was going to have some of that idealism sorely tested.

Lady Annabel linked her arm through Madi's. 'Dear girl, come and help me choose. Colonel Bede wants a painting and there are several just in, wonderful work from interior artists. They're not all traditional Amerindian style but they capture the place, don't you think?'

Madi walked slowly past the poorly framed paintings hung on the shop wall. Memories came flooding back as she looked at the paintings of savannah country, Kaieteur Falls, Amerindian village scenes and primitive-style Amerindian symbols and animals.

Lady Annabel chose a large painting of Kaieteur Falls.

'With a better frame, something large and gold, it will suit Bede's office, don't you think? Lester, would you mind lifting it down.'

Lester carried the picture to the counter as Madi remarked, 'I didn't think the colonel ever went to his office at the old house?'

'He says he has high expectations of being more involved now he's been asked to host some conference of national consequence. Can't imagine how. He talks about the country going straight, once the dust has settled over the demise of the unfortunate Mr Bacchus.' She gave a hearty laugh. 'Well, straighter.'

A painting at the far end of the gallery, half hidden by a stand of postcards, caught Madi's eye. She went closer and smiled when she was able to take in the detail of the work. It was a pretty little oil of a lush green plant touched by sunrays which glistened on drops of water. And if you looked closely, you could see the tiny gold frog crouched between the long waxy fronds. Without a word Madi reached up and lifted it from the wall and turned to find a smiling Lester. 'Ah reckon dat artist must have had yo in mind when he do dat one.'

She held the picture at arm's length and looked at it again. 'Ah reckon dey sure did, Lester. Ah reckon dat right, man.'

Lester drove them back to Lady Annabel's flat where he waited while the two women had what they promised would be 'a quick coffee'. It was hot enough for him to decide to stretch out on the back seat for a midday snooze.

'What did you make of the death of Mr Bacchus?' asked Madi, without displaying any emotional connection with the event. 'We were quite close to the stand when it happened.'

'Make of it? Goodness, my dear, one could make a great deal of it, if one had real evidence and not just coffee shop gossip and rumour. He was a big player with a finger in this country's honey pot. I've always thought that the ideal way to operate in Guyana would be to have a bank behind you. All that money, even if it's not yours, says one thing—power. And that means you can get things done, get more power. Oh, it's a ruthless game, Madison, and getting more so every day. Everywhere in the world. It was all far more dignified—no more honest, I daresay—but more dignified in our day on the diplomatic circuit.'

Coffee was poured and, after the maid had left, Madi raised the subject that had been puzzling her ever since the Bacchus murder. 'You know Antonio Destra, of course?'

'Oh yes,' she laughed. 'The puppetmaster.'

'The what?'

'The puppetmaster, my dear. One who pulls the strings behind the scenes, and watches everyone jump around to his command.'

'I'm sorry, but I don't understand what you're suggesting.'

Lady Annabel looked at her in mock dismay. 'Really, Madison, where have you been all your life? The Agency, girl, the Agency.'

Madi looked blank.

'Goodness, do I have to spell it out . . . C-I-A. Now do you understand?'

For a moment, Madi was speechless. 'How do you know?' She spoke almost in a whisper as if there might be a spy behind the curtains.

'Well, one doesn't, does one? You have to put two and two together and get five to figure out how the CIA operates in countries like this. But, my dear Madison, I'll

471

wager London Bridge that I'm right. He has fingers and eyes everywhere, always doing favours, and no doubt calling them in when he needs the leverage.' She sipped her coffee. 'Now, Madi, tell me all about your trip to the Rupunini. Swimming with otters was all the vogue I hear.'

Madi could hardly wait for Connor to get home for dinner. She stood on the verandah with drinks ready, quickly adding the ice when his car arrived at the gate.

Her welcome home kiss was more passionate than usual, which made Connor cock his head to one side and ask, 'Well, what did I do to deserve that bonus?'

'It's a little thank you for so promptly putting together a submission to the IFO on the plant medicine project. I saw Pieter today and he told me that you phoned him.' She kissed him again lightly on the cheek. 'But guess what I've heard?' He shook his head. 'Antonio Destra works for the CIA.'

Connor's jaw dropped slightly. 'Who told you that?'

'Lady Annabel.'

'Could she prove it? I mean he doesn't exactly have it on his business card.'

'She can't prove it,' replied Madi, a little miffed at Connor's doubt. 'It's her conclusion, based on the way he is always around in the right places with the right people.'

Connor took time to sip his drink, then sat down on a cane chair and twiddled his glass thoughtfully. 'If she's right, what's at the top of his agenda? He's put up some money to help sponsor this national think-tank forum up at New Spirit in a couple of weeks.'

Madi was curious. 'What will the think-tank think about? Who's going?'

'I got an invitation to represent the IFO today. Pieter and Xavier will be there. I'm surprised they didn't mention it to you.'

'They did say they were tabling my eco tourism paper at a meeting, but it went right over my head at the time. Who issued the invitation?'

'Colonel Olivera. He's chairing the show. Sort of a neutral chair. Reps of all the big companies, government departments, and leaders of the major ethnic groups in Guyana will be there. It's to work out directions and make recommendations to the government on ways to tackle the current crisis of confidence in the country. Nut out some compromises, get new projects launched and, as is the way in Guyana, swing some deals behind closed doors.'

The news stunned Madi. Suddenly the whole picture became clear and she recognised the message that Xavier was signalling to her earlier that day. It was a realisation almost beyond belief. Xavier was prepared to accept compromise, and perhaps even co-operate with the very people who were now running Guyana into the ground.

'What sort of recommendations do you expect to emerge?'

'There's talk of setting up a vast forest reserve as a national park, with Amerindian involvement. The trade-off, I guess, will be more licences for forest harvesting. There'll be statements about greater environmental controls on loggers and miners—the international bankers with their new enviro-policies will be demanding that, as well as Xavier's mob. There's talk of greater representation of the views of the minority groups too.'

Madi was incensed. 'It's a sell-out, a damned sell-out,' she said rigidly, feeling the rage surge in her chest. 'I can't

473

believe it. And you seem so relaxed about going along with it. It even looks like the whole thing has been organised on the quiet by the CIA.'

'That's over the top, Madi. Pressure for change has been building up here for a long time.'

Madi rounded on Connor, seething with anger. 'You're talking as if it's all wonderful.'

'Madi,' pleaded Connor, 'please calm down.' He stood up to go to her, but she put out her hand in a traffic-stopping gesture.

'Don't touch me, Connor. I'm so mad I could throw something. Can you understand how wrong it is that the future is being worked out by spooks and corrupt officials, sitting around a table with other powerbrokers. The whole thing made to look as if it's respectable and worthy. It makes me sick.'

Connor tried to be soothing. 'You have to be part of the system to change it, Madi. It's the way of the world, darling. Even if you're idealistic, like Xavier, you have to divert the current in your direction. Bend like the bamboo, but stay strong.'

'But it's a betrayal of the Amerindians.'

'That may be how it looks to you. But later, they may see he has made great gains for them. It's a matter of perception.'

Madi slumped back in her chair and buried her face in her hands.

Connor reached out and touched her lightly on the shoulder.

She looked up, and gave a weak smile in acknowledgment of his gesture. 'It's hard to stomach really. It was just that I saw Xavier as a saviour of this country. Why couldn't he be strong and stand alone?'

'Because, sweet love, he couldn't win by standing

alone. That's why. The system is stacked against those who stand alone.'

Madi took a deep breath. 'When is this conference going to be made public?'

'Tomorrow, I understand. There'll be a joint statement by Olivera, Xavier, and the Prime Minister. At the Pessaro.'

'At the Pessaro,' she repeated with resignation. 'That's the final irony. Now I know why Xavier called off the rally. It wasn't because of the Bacchus death. The conference deal had already been set up.'

'Madi, don't be so angry. All these people coming together at New Spirit realise as individuals they can try to influence matters. So each person will push his own agenda and it will be a consensus at the end of the day. Give a little, take a little. It's how the world works, Madi.'

'I don't agree with it. That's why there are still good, honest idealists who will fight on to make the world a better, safer, cleaner place. The sort of people who care about little gold frogs at the top of a waterfall.' Her voice was starting to rise.

As much as it hurt, Madi now understood more clearly why Xavier had ended up this way. In a revealing flash she saw that she too had been making a journey, but hers had been without compromise.

'I need some time to myself. I'm going out for awhile. I'll probably call in and see Matt. Don't wait up.' She spoke in a resigned calm voice and went to get her handbag and picked up Connor's car keys.

'I won't stop you, Madi. I understand this isn't the happy ending you envisaged. But then nothing in life is predictable in any way. Circumstances change and we have to adjust to them.' He sounded tired.

*

Madi drove down to the seawall. She parked the car and walked over to the low stone barrier that held back the Atlantic Ocean. Further down, a courting couple leaned against the wall, arms wrapped about each other. The breeze was fresh but it still carried the special tang of mud, salt and rotting vegetation. The tide was in and slapped gently below in the darkness.

Madi peered over but could see little. She'd always meant to come down at low tide with Lester, who liked to dig for antique bottles that had been kept intact in the inky mud since colonial days. Lester sold the odd-shaped heavy blue, green, black and clear bottles to the gift shop in the Pessaro. Now she'd have to buy one before she left, not as much fun as digging up your own.

As she stood there in the faint moonlight it dawned on Madi that she had subconsciously begun to think of final things to do. As if she was leaving soon. And she realised she had made the decision without being fully aware of it. Madi thought back to a passage in Gwen's book that she'd written before leaving Guyana. It had touched Madi because it was just how she felt.

I am glad there are still secret remote places on this overcrowded earth where the fairies and spirits take refuge, where the boulders move mysteriously, the forests are enchanted, the trees sing to each other, and the rivers flow living gold. I am thankful that I shall never see that dreadful day when science has solved all mysteries and the scar of civilisation has defaced every acre of wilderness.

Madi looked up as a dark-coloured family sedan pulled in at the end of the seawall. To her surprise Antonio Destra climbed out of the driver's seat, gave a slight wave and walked towards her. He was grinning and she was reminded of the cheery and helpful companion

476

she'd first met at the airport while waiting for the painfully slow immigration officer to process their papers.

His introduction to his wife, his offer for her to stay the night with them rather than face the risks of Georgetown alone, had immediately put her at ease. She'd liked his friendly manner and her instinct had been to trust him.

Then she remembered how his behaviour in the following weeks had confused her—like the time she'd seen him at the Amerindian hostel, then he'd later denied being there. Could Lady Annabel be right? Could he really be working for the CIA?

'I followed you from Bain's house,' Destra said, leaning in his relaxed way against the seawall beside Madi as if it were perfectly natural for the two of them to be together in this isolated spot at night.

Destra lit a cigarette. 'It's time you and I had a little talk about life, and particularly life in good ole Guyana.'

'Good ole Guyana, as you call it, does not appear too conducive to a good ole long life,' Madi said. 'Since I've been here, I've witnessed too many killings and almost been killed myself. I don't know what your role in this country is really all about, Antonio, but I do know you've been mixed up in these killings. In fact, I don't know why I'm standing here talking to you.'

Destra gave a casual shrug. 'Madi, I'm not here to harm you. I'm here to give you an explanation that I really should not be giving you at all. But it involves you. You're an intelligent woman and I'm hoping that when you hear what I have to say, you'll decide to leave Guyana for awhile. At least until life here can get back to normal, or what passes as normal in Guyana.'

'Is that a friend's advice or a threat?'

'I'm your friend, Madison.'

She looked silently across the water, then turned back to Destra, her eyes reflecting her irritation.

'Then tell me why Ernesto St Kitt had to die. You were with those people using drugs at New Spirit that night.'

'I was. And if I'd not allowed myself to be distracted by that, St Kitt might be alive today. But I was keen to see which government officials were part of that particular little group. St Kitt had been invited but he'd flatly refused to join in. He was disgusted and he stalked off in the direction of the path by the river. It gave Bacchus' hitman the perfect opportunity he'd been waiting for—to remove Ernesto completely.'

'But why?'

'St Kitt was determined to dig out the past performances of the El Dorado company which had been ripping money out of organisations in Guyana for years. Your brother's mine, Guyminco, was only one of many companies paying Bacchus bribes to break through government red tape.'

Now Destra had Madi's full attention. 'All that had to change when El Dorado decided to go for the biggest prize of all, the licence for the Amazonia Casino. To own the casino licence, Bacchus and his company had to be lily white, pure as angels.'

Destra paused to light another cigarette then continued. 'Bacchus had his front as a respectable banker, but too many government files and officials were witness to the company's strange dealings in the past. All that had to be dealt with. And it was . . . until St Kitt started nosing around.'

'So that's why he was murdered and that's why the official line was that he had overdosed on drugs?'

'El Dorado's problems would have been solved then,

except you and your friend Bain stumbled on Mr Rashid Bacchus' logging operations in the forest. A very foolish move if you don't mind me saying so . . . You were very lucky to escape.'

'We may have escaped that but there have been two attempts on my life and one on Connor's since then.'

'Because the information you have on Bacchus could still have stopped him from getting the casino licence. He couldn't afford to let you live.'

'But why did you kill him? I know you were involved. You had that man made up to look like an Amerindian in the Carnivale parade. And you were there to make sure he got away.'

'You amaze me, Madi. You always seem to have more information than you should have. But yes, we decided he should dress as an Amerindian because the facepaint and the headdress would make an effective disguise.'

'But why did you kill Bacchus?'

Destra looked at Madi and a tiny smile formed around his mouth. He shrugged his shoulders. 'Madi, my dear, you still don't understand, do you?'

'You mean because of me? Bacchus died because of me?'

'It is certainly not my duty to act as the white knight to save beautiful damsels in distress. But Madi, it was him or you. And wherever you went you would still have been in danger. Bacchus could not afford to lose that licence. And the slightest whiff of scandal associated with any company running a casino is enough these days to scare off the big gamblers. They want a fair chance and they avoid casinos run by crooked operators. 'And,' said Destra quietly, 'I will admit it served my purposes to have Bacchus out of the way. He was getting sloppy. That drug-packing operation in the forest so close to an

Amerindian village was just plain stupid. And those attempts on your life later were signs of a man panicking. Can you imagine how the world spotlight would have fallen on Guyana if a beautiful blonde European woman had been murdered here?'

Madi shivered at the thought. Then she realised there could be another advantage gained from the death of the corrupt banker. 'So now the casino won't go ahead?' she asked.

Destra flicked his cigarette butt over the seawall. 'Olivera who works with me has already taken over as head of El Dorado and he'll get the licence up with no problems. Amazonia *is* going to happen, Madi. The hefty tax from gambling revenue will help keep this government in business.'

Madi shook her head in resignation. 'I really think it's wrong.' She glanced at Destra. 'Why are you involved?'

'Because my job is to make sure Guyana keeps surviving under a democratic government, to make sure the socialists, and their Cuban allies, never get into power again.'

'So you do work for the CIA?'

'Let's just say my brief is to watch that emerging countries like Guyana keep moving in the right direction.' He turned back to face the sea. 'As you have already learnt, nothing is ever what it seems on the surface. I wanted you to know the facts before you decide what you will do next.'

'I've already made my decision, Antonio.'

A silence settled between them and Madison had difficulty controlling her turmoil of emotions. When she finally spoke there was a tremor in her voice. 'And what about the dreamers, Antonio? The dreamers of a better world?'

She didn't expect a reply. She threw him a look that said

she'd heard enough, then turned towards her car. She'd taken only a few steps when Antonio called after her.

'Madison'.

She stopped and swung around to look at him.

'Madison, I read once, that in a corrupt society, the dreamers of a better world—like you and Xavier—are potentially the most powerful of people. Perhaps your dreams for Guyana will come true one day. Good luck, Madison.'

He gave a brief wave and strode along the seawall to his car. He didn't look back.

She opened the car door and glanced back at the old seawall, painted with crude advertisements and slogans. The lights from the Pessaro Hotel, the small light atop the Georgetown communications tower, and the glow from the old lighthouse dimly illuminated the soupy brown sea.

Madi knew one day she would stand on a sunny golden Sydney beach beside the clear blue and white surf of the Pacific Ocean and feel deep nostalgia for this murky milky waterfront, and this peculiar city, in this wonderful country.

A sleepy Singh opened the gate with a broad smile. 'It be very good to see you, Miss Madison. How you be?'

'Adeh,' said Madi, realising how familiar the servant's language had become to her. 'And you?'

'Good. I be good. Mr Matthew is upstairs.' Singh opened the front door and turned on the light for her.

'That you, sis?' called Matthew. 'Connor rang and said you were on your way. Where've you been?' He kissed her warmly. 'Cuppa or a rum?'

'Oh, what the heck. A rum. Make it the ten-year-old.'

When they were settled he gave her a shrewd glance. 'Been doing some thinking, hey? Connor told me you were a bit upset.'

'Not upset so much as disillusioned, toughened, resigned, but determined. Cheers.' She downed a mouthful of the velvety aromatic rum.

'What about? Everything is working out very well. Connor and I were discussing Xavier's ideas. You know what we reckon? That he'll eventually end up forming a new political party and leading the country.'

'So he's used this whole push to further his own political ambitions? I can't believe that.'

'It probably didn't start out that way, but how else is he going to make life better for the people?' When Madi didn't answer he added, 'Anyway it's a long way off and we'll all be out of here by then. Change happens slowly in a place like this. Speaking of which, I'll let you in on a little secret. We have a potential buyer for Guyminco.'

Madi looked pleased. 'Hey, Matt, that's great. You AusGeo boys have pulled it off. And ahead of schedule.'

'Keep it quiet. There are problems that will hopefully get ironed out at the conference at New Spirit.'

'Ah yes, the great gambling table where all the warring factions deal the cards and place their bets.'

'You don't have to sound so cynical. It's not gambling, it's deal making.'

'So who's the mysterious buyer? Do they know what sort of place this country is?'

'Of course, they're already here.' He gave a grin. 'It's the Columbus goldmine company. The US is keen to up its role in this country and Columbus is already in the game, so they know what's what.'

Madi wondered if the night could possibly yield any

more surprises. She recalled the first party she'd attended in Guyana and the declaration by the US Ambassador that America was keen to lift its commercial presence.

'Columbus mines, after what has happened?' she said almost in disbelief.

'It's a straight-out commercial deal. The price is right, as they say in television.'

Madi gave a little laugh. In a way, it was all like something out of a television show, one of those biting British political dramas about the almost obscene use and abuse of power. 'I guess it's time to move on, Matt,' she said with sadness and resignation.

He gave a small smile. 'You've really blossomed, Madi. Hard to think of you any more as my little sis. I'm very proud of how you've embraced this country, these people, how you've tried to help them. You're quite a gal! Infuriating at times. But I know no one will ever walk over you again. Guyana has changed you forever.'

Madi reached out and hugged him. 'Oh, Matty, I'll always be your little sis . . . I now realise how special and important you are. Thanks for putting up with me.'

'You'll never lose your sweetness, I hope.'

It suddenly occurred to Matthew how special she was. If she married Connor then Bain would be a lucky man. And, Matthew wondered, would he ever find a girl like Madi?

Madi sat hugging her knees and staring into the large pond filled with the old Victoria Regina waterlilies. The tall pink lotus blooms waved their regal heads. The more Madi looked at them, the more they seemed like people chatting to each other at a frightfully elegant cocktail party, one head slightly bowed, one nodding, another thrown back in laughter. The thought amused her. But then the glassy surface of the water was disrupted as a big black hulk slowly surfaced between the giant green leaves. Madi leaned forward and watched the dugong swim slowly across to the far bank before sinking below the surface to look for fresh grass and roots.

Madi leaned back against a gnarled tree where orchids and bromeliads clung, trailing roots and flowers. The scene before her looked so tranquil. Yet not far away crowds were swarming over hoardings around the cricket ground. Perched in trees that overlooked the oval and jamming the stands, they roared and cheered the Guyanese against Barbados. As another wicket fell, Madi got to her feet and walked through the deserted gardens to where she'd parked Connor's car.

Her private tour of Georgetown was over. She had circled the town, re-living special memories so many landmarks conjured up for her. The Blue Toucan coffee shop, the Amerindian shop, the Bourda Markets, the big Stabroek marketplace, Guyana Stores, the Universal Bookshop, the Pepperpot coffee house, the Pessaro Hotel, the Georgetown Club and Embassy Club, Lady Annabel's father's house, the little bridges over the littered drains choked with lotus flowers, the simple temples and houses, the grand old homes, the distant sugarcane fields.

So much had happened to her in such a brief time. Was it so significant just because it was different? Or had this tiny pocket of a country, plonked onto the edge of the great lamb chop of South America, become a defining milestone in her life. If she'd gone to visit Matthew in say, Greece or Bahrain, would the effect on her have been the same?

She thought of the rivers, the rainforests, the savannahs, the magnificent waterfalls, the gentle forest people, her warm, laughter-loving coastlander friends, and knew this place was special. She touched the little frog at her throat and thought of the tiny gold frogs in their sparkling green home at the lip of Kaieteur. They symbolised this country . . . beautiful, rare, endangered. For as long as the frogs kept singing in their clean air and sunshine, all would be right with the world.

Despite the dangers she had experienced, she had only happy memories of Guyana. She'd discovered her own strengths and had come to like herself. She knew that whatever the world threw at her from now on, she was better equipped to deal with it.

She'd developed a new relationship with her brother. He now saw her as a woman of intelligence and independence. He respected, as well as loved her.

And in this country she'd met Connor. Would she have fallen in love with him in a less romantic place? Shared adventures and adversity had helped their bonding. She had yet to decide her feelings for Connor. That could only be done away from here, away from him.

Connor had been offered the choice of two jobs . . . in China or in Papua New Guinea. He'd asked her to go with him and asked which place she'd prefer. 'Both will be rugged, but you seem to like adventuring,' he said with a grin. Then added more seriously, 'I can't imagine being anywhere without you now, Madi'.

Again, she'd told him she wasn't ready to make a decision. She hadn't raised the other issue that disturbed her. In both these places IFO money was backing new mine developments.

*

She drove back to Connor's house and let herself inside. Connor was over at Matthew's discussing the next day's forum at New Spirit. Madi didn't want to know about their deal-making. The disillusionment still unsettled her. She would drive to Matthew's later for a farewell supper party with their friends before going to the airport for her 11 pm flight to London.

Her suitcase stood inside the door. The frog painting and an Amerindian fish trap Matthew had given her were safely wrapped inside the bulky roll of her hammock.

There remained one last thing to do. She changed for the flight, putting on her R.M. Williams jodhpurs and boots, and a soft blue cotton shirt. She put her bags in the car.

Lester had given her directions to his house. She parked just down from the brightly floodlit US embassy and walked between two houses to where he lived with his mother and son.

He was sitting on the darkened verandah, Denzil perched on the top step waiting for her.

'Hi, Denzil,' called Madi and the little boy jumped up, gave a shy wave and ran to Lester.

'Yo find us okay den.'

'Here I am,' smiled Madi as she reached the small front verandah.

'Come in and meet Mumma. She very shy 'bout yo coming here, but happy to meet yo at last.'

Lester's mother gave Madi a warm embrace and fussed about, settling her on the sofa and bringing them soft drinks and a plate of sweet biscuits.

'Just the three of you live here?' asked Madi.

'My sister lives with us but she be workin' at de hospital. She be a nurse's aide,' said Lester proudly. 'So now. What yo plans, Madison? London den what?'

'I honestly don't know, Lester. I don't know where I'll go or even if I'll stay in London. The hospitality industry doesn't interest me in the same way it did before. I'd like to try the eco tourism side of things back in Australia perhaps.'

'Maybe yo work with yo people, yo native people, eh? And what about Mr Connor? Now he be de big question.' He gave her a quizzical look and she couldn't help laughing.

'Oh Lester. I don't know . . . just yet anyway.'

Lester rolled his eyes. 'Ooh, dat poor feller.'

His mother clicked her tongue as she listened while handing around more of her homemade biscuits. 'Don' yo rush in where yo not sure what waiting for yo. Marrying be a long time to have a headache. Yo be sure.'

'Now, Mumma, dis be none o' yo business,' admonished Lester gently.

His mother stood and placed one hand on her hip, the other still proffering the plate of biscuits. 'Maybe. But yo can't say I don' speak from de knowing. Lookit you and young Denzil . . . dat woman you take up with . . . she never tink 'bout tings . . . just rush in cause yo is too soft, boy. And look where it got you. It be smart to go slow, be sure . . .' she shook a finger at Madi. 'Don' you let dat moonbeam set in yo head girl.'

'I won't. I've learnt a lot about myself since I've been here.'

'Dat be good.' She bobbed her head in satisfaction as Lester looked acutely embarrassed.

Madi gave him a grin. 'Don't yo feel bad, boy, we gals still give yo 'nother chance.'

'Well ahmen,' he mimicked her accent.

Madi reached into her handbag. 'Lester . . . I have a little present for you.' She handed him the small package which he opened to find a framed photograph of them both standing knee deep in water, looking up from the gold pan with laughing faces.

'Hey, Connor take dat when we find de nugget! Now dat be good, I put it here.' Lester carried the picture to the shelf crowded with knick-knacks and photos and made a space in the centre front. 'Now I can say hello to my friend every day,' he said softly.

Madi was touched. 'There's something else. I'll give it to you . . . but it's really for Denzil. I'd kind of like to be considered what we call a godmother. So every month I'll send him something that he might find useful . . . just fun things,' she added. Madi felt offering money would have offended Lester, so she hit upon the idea of sending his young boy practical items, clothing, toys, school things, once a month.

'Yo don't have to do dis, Miz Madi . . . yo gonna get back dere . . . and we gonna be someting just happen one time in yo life.'

'Lester . . . I know it's easy to think that . . . I'm going to another world, but I promise you, I want to keep some link. And I thought the most practical way would be to help Denzil a little bit.'

Madi rose and put her plate and glass on the little carved coffee table. 'I must get on.'

'Okay, I take yo to yo car . . . I wish I could take yo to de airport. But dat be a job fo de bruddah and de lover, eh?'

'Lester, next time I come back I'll let you know and I expect you to be there to meet me.'

'Yo got it, boss.'

Madi hugged little Denzil, shook hands with his grandmother, and followed Lester onto the verandah. 'So. Dis be goodbye to ma Guyana sister. I never thought I be such a friend with a lady like yo.'

'Lester, I can't begin to thank you. I feel so lucky to have met you. I've always thought you gave me the keys to Guyana. If I hadn't met you . . .' Tears suddenly welled in Madi's eyes and her voice broke '. . . I would have just milled around the party circuit in Georgetown. I wouldn't have known and learned all that I have.'

In the darkness she couldn't make out Lester's expression but his voice trembled as he struggled to maintain a light manner. 'Yo mean yo wouldn't have had dem people shootin' at yo, lockin yo up, making yo out to be a threat to de society . . .' They both chuckled. 'Madison, I got a small present for yo too.' He reached out to a cane table for a package wrapped in brown paper and handed it to her. She felt its shape and looked at him. 'It's a book . . . Is it about Guyana?'

'It be yo lady's book. Gwen, de Aussie lady.'

'Lester! How? Oh thank you!' Madi gave him an excited hug. 'I didn't think I'd ever find one, where did you get it?' She had always figured an obscure book such as this would be like finding a needle in a haystack.

Lester shrugged. 'Well, after we take de book back, me and de lady at de library came to a kind of arrangement,' he said with a hint of amusement.

'I see. I won't ask any more about it then. I'm just thrilled to have it. You know how much it means to me.'

'Good, dat be good.' Lester sounded pleased. 'Dere also be a tape in dere of my favourite steel band, de Silvertails, de boys made it fo yo.'

'Oh Lester. Every time I play it I'll be right back here.' Lester played the tape constantly in his taxi.

He took her arm and walked her down the steps and back to her car.

'I hate goodbyes, Lester.'

'Den we jest say, we be seein' yo round.'

He opened the car door. Madi gave him a quick kiss on the cheek and got in behind the wheel as he gently closed the door.

'Dat frog be watchin out fo yo. Remember dat.'

'I will, Lester. Be seeing you round then.' She started the car and brushed away a tear as she pulled out into Duke Street.

'I never forget yo, Miz Madi.'

It seemed all the people she'd become friends with were crammed into the living room at Matthew's. Hyacinth and Primrose passed platters of snacks and Singh in a white shirt and long pants, but bare feet, was waiter. How she would miss these people. She had made such good friends and enjoyed their hospitality and generosity.

When it came time to leave, Madi waved from the car as the party guests spilled into the garden to send her off. Singh held open the gate and gave a salute.

It was a long drive to Timehri airport and Matthew kept up a stream of inconsequential chatter about the party to cover the silence between Madi and Connor. In the back, Connor rubbed Madi's neck, occasionally leaning forward to kiss behind her ear.

At the airport it was chaos as emotional relatives farewelled families who were emigrating to the meccas of Canada, the UK and the USA.

'I hope this changes,' said Madi quietly. 'Families should stay here and have a good future, not want to get out.'

'That's what Xavier is working towards. Wouldn't surprise me if he's running the country in the future,' said Matthew.

Once they'd fought their way through the check-in

Matthew went looking for coffees, leaving Connor and Madi alone at a small plastic table.

He took her hands. 'So?'

She looked into his face, seeing the love and pain and confusion in his eyes. Madi bit her lip and gently pulled her hands away.

'I do love you, Connor. But I'm just not ready. Please, keep this for now.' She pulled the ring from her finger and put it in his hand, curling his fingers over it.

'No. No. Keep it, Madi. A souvenir or something . . . please don't do this.' There was a desperate note in his voice. 'As long as you have the diamond, I know there'll be a chance for me . . . this seems so final.'

'A ring, beautiful as it is, can't bind me to you, Connor, my darling. I have to make the decision myself, with no strings attached.'

Connor looked down, biting his lip, not trusting himself to speak.

'Don't be hurt, or upset. I'm not throwing you over. I just want more time. Breathing space of my own, away from this mad, crazy, wonderful hothouse of a country. Everything has been so intense the whole time. It's like living in technicolour while the rest of the world is black and white,' said Madi gently.

'You're not going to write me a Dear John letter . . . promise me that. Madi, just make me one promise. If your eventual answer is to be no, if you decide you don't ever want to marry me, live with me, be with me, then tell me to my face. Wherever I am. Please. Promise me that.' He spoke urgently and Madi understood how much this meant. He was not going to give up on her, he believed he'd always be able to try to change her mind. And it dawned on her how much he loved her. She nodded. 'I promise.'

Matthew returned with a tray of coffees which they didn't finish before the flight to London was called over a crackling loudspeaker, interrupting the reggae music.

Matthew hugged her tightly. 'God speed, sis. I'll miss you.' He kissed her cheek and whispered in her ear. 'I hope you found what you came for.'

Tears were running unchecked down her face. 'I did, Matty, more than you know.'

He stepped back and Connor took her in his arms and kissed her. And once again the passion that he aroused in her swept over her, and with his strong and loving arms about her she thought how easy it would be to simply say yes, and be his wife and have his children and be swept along in a life that would be good and exactly what she wanted . . . travel, a man who idolised her, someone she respected, liked and loved. It was everything she thought she didn't want when she had set out on a career path.

Now she had discovered she wanted all those things, and she'd never find anyone better than Connor. But there was still a part of her that had just bloomed and this fragile flower needed its time in the sun.

She pulled away from his kiss. 'I do love you, Connor. Be patient. If you can't, I understand.'

'I'll always be waiting for you, Madi.'

She was pushed through with the crush of boarding passengers and had time for only a glance over her shoulder for a final smile at the two Australians watching her leave.

They waited till the flight rose into the night sky. Connor looked at Matthew and gave a rueful smile. 'Well, I guess this is where I came in.'

Matthew nodded. 'Yeah, well that's life, mate. Let's see if Singh and the mob have left any rum.'

Connor didn't move. 'I can't help wondering about the effect of all this on Madi.'

'She needs time, Connor.'

Connor turned and walked beside Matthew as they made their way back through the crushing crowd. It would take time for Madi to come to terms with the complexity of the power plays, her disillusionment and, finally, her future. And Connor couldn't help wondering whether, as she recognised the harsh reality of life brought home to her by the events here, would she keep her faith and idealism intact?

Madi closed her eyes. She could see nothing from her window other than the reflection of her tear-stained face. She knew down below the two men she loved so dearly were driving back to the city along a potholed road. And further inland stretched the vast interior of a land she'd come to love. And in one part of it, beside the top of a magnificent waterfall, a handful of golden frogs were singing their chorus into the night.

EPILOGUE

Sydney, Australia, September 1996

D ear Lester,
Please find enclosed some Aussie togs for Denzil, a book about Blinky Bill and my favourite, *The Magic Pudding*. Some good news. I just got back from Ballarat where I found some clues about Gwen from the archivist at Clarendon Ladies College where Gwen and her sister Cecily, went to school. Their brother Lawrence attended nearby Ballarat College. It seems Gwen left Guyana to go to New York to sing opera on the stage! She was apparently a friend of the famous actress Ellen Terry. Maybe that was the reason she had to rush away from the Mazaruni to go to New York!

And after all that . . . you know how she ended up? As the wife of Major Blake. There's a reference in the school's newspaper *The Touchstone* in December 1930 that '*Mrs Blake (Gwen Richardson) author of* On The Diamond Trail in British Guiana *is revisiting with her husband, Major Blake, British Guiana and is planning to travel far inland in search of diamonds and gold*'.

How I long to know more about her and her family. Still this is a start.

Like Gwen, I have come home . . . I caught up with Ann and John da Silva in England and had a great three months working for the British Eco Tourism Task Force. I hope to be able to put my experience and expertise to work back here in Australia.

Enough! I'll get off my soapbox.

Connor is coming home from China in a few months so we'll see where we stand with each other then. He's taking up a new appointment in Australia.

I have decided I would like to have children. Yes, I know there are too many people on the planet and I respect my friends who have chosen not to have kids.

But I think about you and your Denzil often and the closeness you share. I hope he can grow up in safety and plenty and get a good education in Guyana. And I'd like my kids to be able to do the same here and have a mother and father who contribute to making this world a better place.

As always, talking to you, my good friend, seems to clarify things in my mind.

Let me know the minute you strike the big one.

Good luck,

Love, Madison.

LIST OF ILLUSTRATIONS

Map of Guyana in South America

Area:	214 970 square kilometres
Population:	740 000
Religions:	Christian 50%, Hindu 33%, Muslim 9%, other 8%
Languages:	English, Guyanese Creole, Indian dialects
Ethnic Groups:	East Indian origin 51%, African origin 30%, mixed 15%, Indian 4%
Agriculture:	Sugar, rice
Natural Resources:	Gold, bauxite, diamonds, timber, prawns, fish

Di Morrissey
Heart of the Dreaming

Di Morrissey's first novel quickly established her as
Australia's favourite female novelist.

This is the story of Queenie Hanlon. A story of
belonging, of a woman's fight to hold onto everything
she has ever loved — her ancestral home in the
outback and her spirit's Dreaming place. It's a fight
against tragedy, a brother's treachery and the fates
that conspire against her ever finding happiness with
TR Hamilton, the quintessential Australian bushman.
Queenie — independent, courageous and
determined — so captivated readers they demanded
a sequel.

Follow the Morning Star continues the story of
Queenie and TR. Set during the wool crisis of the
early 1990s, the story swings from the desolate
outback to the Gold Coast, and captures the drama,
romance and conflicts of an Australian family.
Characters such as the Aboriginal elder Snowy,
beloved housekeeper Millie, the mysterious Tango
and free-spirited Saskia have made these two books
Aussie favourites.

Di Morrissey
The Last Rose of Summer

A novel that enfolds the reader in the secrets of a
magnificent Edwardian mansion on the banks of
Sydney's Parramatta River.

Odette, an ambitious TV journalist finds her life
dominated by another young woman. . . Kate, the
strong-willed heiress who defied convention in the
early days of the twentieth century to establish the
legendary estate.

From turn-of-the-century India to contemporary
Sydney, *The Last Rose of Summer* is a spellbinding
story of struggle and jealousy, possession and
intrigue. . . and of two women connected across the
decades by the men who loved them. . . and the
magic of the house called Zanana.

Di Morrissey
The Last Mile Home

From one of Australia's finest storytellers comes a
classic tale of family love that will remain in your
heart forever. . .

It is 1953 in a small country town in Australia, a time
of post-war prosperity and hope, a time when class
and religious faith ruled society.

It is the story of two families from vastly differing
backgrounds. The Holtens are wealthy, austere
graziers who have lived on their land for generations.
The McBrides are a large and loving shearer's family
who have moved to town for the shearing season.

When the eldest McBride daughter falls in love with
the Holtens' only son and heir, the barriers to their
marriage seem overwhelming. But in the end love
triumphs over tragedy, and hope and joy are their
enduring legacy.

The Last Mile Home is an unforgettable story to
touch the heart of every Australian.

Di Morrissey
Tears of the Moon

Broome, Australia 1893
In the wild and passionate heyday of Australia's
pearling industry, a young English bride, Olivia
Hennessy, becomes the business partner of pearling
master, Captain John Tyndall. As she adapts to life
on the rugged West Australian coast, their fates are
linked by the power of the world's finest pearls.

Sydney 1996
Following the death of her mother, Lily Barton
embarks on a search for her family tree which leads
her to Broome. But her quest for identity reveals
more than she could ever have imagined. . .

Tears of the Moon is an evocative, thoroughly
researched novel that also explores what it means to
be an Australian.